"Tonight you will sing for me, little nightingale,"

Raile whispered, his mouth only inches from hers.

He gazed into green eyes that were so innocent and yet so alive. It was as if she were taunting him, and when he pressed his lips to hers, he wanted to tear away the remaining clothes that came between them.

He pulled her against him, while his body trembled against her satin skin. He closed his eyes, relishing the feel of her.

"If you knew anything about nightingales, Raile," Kassidy said, "you would know that it is only the male that sings."

"Then," he answered, "you will make me sing tonight, little nightingale."

Also by Constance O'Banyon

Forever My Love
Highland Love Song

Available from HarperPaperbacks

Harper Monogram

Song of the Nightingale

CONSTANCE O'BANYON

HarperPaperbacks
A Division of HarperCollinsPublishers

Special edition printing: February 1994

This is a work of fiction. The characters, incidents, and
dialogues are products of the author's imagination and are
not to be construed as real. Any resemblance to actual events
or persons, living or dead, is entirely coincidental.

HarperPaperbacks   *A Division of* HarperCollins*Publishers*
10 East 53rd Street, New York, N.Y. 10022

A trade paperback edition of this book was published in
1992 by HarperPaperbacks.

Cover illustration by Pino Daeni

First HarperPaperbacks printing: February 1993

Printed in the United States of America

HarperPaperbacks, HarperMonogram, and colophon are
trademarks of HarperCollins*Publishers*

❖ 10 9 8 7 6 5 4 3 2 1

This one's for you, Bobbi Smith Walton. If wealth can be measured in the loyalty of a friend, I am rich indeed.

To my husband, Jim, and my children, Pam, Rick, Kim, and Jason, who allow Mom to go into metamorphosis when I near a deadline, and still love me when it's over. To you, Sharon, wonderful daughter-in-law, who so often comes to my rescue.

My special thanks to a lovely little girl, Kassidy Sullivan, who allowed me to borrow her beautiful Scottish name.

SONG OF THE NIGHTINGALE

On the breath of summer winds, if you listen well, you may hear the song of the nightingale.

On the eve of true love's awakening, he serenades with a passionate tale. So heed, ye lovers, the enchantment of the nightingale.

Driven by melancholy, he sings with intensive longing, to hold back the night and winter's impending dawning.

—CONSTANCE O'BANYON

1

London, 1810
A House On Percy Street

Raile DeWinter ascended the steps of the fashionable town house, wondering why his uncle, the duke of Ravenworth, had summoned him so urgently. His uncle had been ill for over three years, and now Raile feared he was dying.

He handed his hat to the butler, who greeted him with a stiff smile.

"Do you have any notion why my uncle wants to see me, Larkin?" Raile asked, knowing the butler was aware of everything that occurred in his uncle's house.

The old retainer's eyes did not flicker. "His grace does not confide in me."

"Does he wish to see me now?"

"I was told to show you up the moment you arrived. The doctor, Lord John . . . and your stepmother are already with his grace."

Raile's eyes clouded. "So, but for my brother, Hugh, the clan has gathered."

"Your half brother is not expected," the butler stated, as he turned toward the stairs and climbed briskly upward, expecting Raile to follow.

When they reached his uncle's bedroom, Raile forestalled Larkin. "Why don't you go about your duties. I'll announce myself."

The butler looked disapproving for a moment, but obediently turned and moved stiffly away while Raile opened the door and slipped inside.

The duke had an aversion to sunlight, so Raile was not surprised to find the bedroom in darkness. The only light came from a lamp on the bedside table which illuminated the bed but left the rest of the room in shadows. Even though it was a warm day, a fire smoldered in the black marble fireplace, making the room unbearably hot and oppressive and intensifying the sickroom smell.

Since no one had noticed Raile's entrance, he stood in the shadows so he could observe them.

His grace, William DeWinter, the duke of Ravenworth, lay in a massive bed, his gouty leg propped on several pillows, and a twisted scowl marring his heavily lined face.

Dr. Worthington, after giving the duke a nervous glance, moved to the foot of the bed and began adjusting the bandages that were wrapped about his leg, then dodged the old man's cane when he touched a sensitive place.

Raile's lips twitched. The duke was not near death as he had feared, and he was relieved, for he was truly fond of that bitter old man.

Raile glanced at the others gathered in the room. His cousin John, heir to the title, had been Raile's friend since boyhood. John stood near the bed, talking to his father in encouraging tones.

Raile's gaze moved reluctantly to his stepmother, Lavinia, who stood apart, seemingly detached from the proceedings, her eyes unreadable. He had never felt close to the woman his father had married after the death of his own mother. Of course, he had never lived with them, so he'd had little opportunity to know Lavinia. His father had died only a year after Raile's half brother, Hugh, had been born, and Lavinia and her son had continued to reside in London, while Raile remained in the country, on his uncle's estate.

Raile tried to think of Lavinia objectively. He could see why his father had been attracted to her. Her dark hair was clustered about her face in ringlets, and her figure was as slender as a young girl's. She had an arresting face, and in her youth she must have been beautiful, for she was still an attractive woman. Of course, he found something distasteful in the hardness of her eyes and the pout to her lips.

Raile pitied Hugh. Lavinia so dominated her son that he had become a weakling, clinging to her every word as if he had no mind of his own. Raile did not admire either of them, but he tolerated them because they were his family.

Suddenly the duke uttered an obscenity and hurled a glass through the air. It missed Dr. Worthington's head by inches, but some of the water splattered on him. The poor doctor dabbed at his face with the cuff of his shirt.

"Your grace, how can I treat your gout when you criticize my methods? When I would have relieved some of your pain, you admonished me not to use any of my 'new scientific treatments' on you. Then when I suggested wrapping your legs in tight bandages, you accused me of practicing antiquated medicine. I ask you, your grace, what am I to do?"

"Get out, man—get out!" the duke roared with such force the veins in his neck stood out. "Take your witch doctoring out of here and torture some other wretched fool."

The doctor brushed past Raile, tore open the door, and made a hasty exit.

"Good morning, Uncle," Raile drawled, stepping into the light. "I see you are still terrorizing Doctor Worthington. It's a marvel he keeps coming back."

The duke's eyes snapped with anger. "I sent for you over three hours ago. You sure took your time getting here," he said sourly.

"I came as soon as I received your message, Uncle. I can see my concern for your health was unfounded if you can still torment poor Doctor Worthington and keep him under your domination."

For a moment the old man's expression held respect. "You're the only one I could never control, Raile," he said grudgingly.

Their eyes met in understanding. A faint smile tugged at Raile's lips. "That's not entirely so, Uncle. Like Doctor Worthington, do I not come when you summon me?"

The duke eased himself to a sitting position, his eyes suddenly hard, his temper barely controlled. "I have little liking for the circumstances that made me send for you this day, Raile," he snapped.

"Why is that?" Rail asked, mystified. "Are you disturbed about something?"

"I treated you like a son, took you into my home when my brother remarried and raised you with my own son, John, did I not?"

Raile looked quizzically at John before answering. "You did, Uncle," he agreed at last. "I have always been grateful to you for that."

"And when you reached your twenty-first birthday, did I not allow you to leave Ravenworth Castle and seek your own life—answer me that!"

Raile moved closer to his uncle. "That is so. You did all those things."

"And you repay my generosity by bringing dishonor to the very old and distinguished DeWinter name," the duke accused, his face reddening as he shook his fist at Raile. "I tell you, I won't have it!"

Raile stared at his uncle for a long moment. "I know of no instance when I brought shame on our name," he said in a controlled voice, his own anger tapped. "If I have been charged with something, let my accuser step forward."

"Have you or have you not been seen in the company of Lady Harriet Pinsworthy?" the duke demanded.

Raile looked quickly at his stepmother. At the moment Lavinia appeared to be inspecting the hem of her gown, but Raile noticed she was smiling smugly. Lavinia knew it had been Hugh who had taken up with Lady Harriet—all of London knew it, but apparently she was not going to admit it to his uncle.

Wordlessly, he turned back to the duke.

The old man continued raving: "It's my understanding that you not only flaunted that shameful alliance, but you also shot the woman's husband in a duel of honor."

The duke's face turned ashen with anger, and his gnarled hands trembled as he squeezed them into fists. His voice rose. "A duel of honor, where by your cowardly action, Raile, you shot the man while his back was turned! It's a mercy that Lord Pinsworthy lives. Did you think just because the disgrace occurred in an obscure little village that it would escape my notice? Did you think I would allow this family's name to be linked with cowardice?"

Raile's expression showed none of the turmoil that churned inside him. A bolt of pain stabbed at his heart that his uncle could believe such a villainous deed of him. His eyes were cold, his voice even. "May I inquire how you came by this information?"

His uncle's face paled even more, and he lay back, closing his eyes. "You may well ask, but I don't feel inclined to answer."

Raile looked at John, who nodded slightly in Lavinia's direction. He swung around to face his stepmother, who stared at him with unmasked triumph in her cold blue eyes. It was as if she had told this lie deliberately—he could not think why.

Raile's voice was controlled, but his eyes emitted sparks of anger. "You told my uncle this, Lavinia?"

She moved forward hastily to stand beside the duke, putting the bed between her and Raile. "I didn't want to tell, Raile, but to allow your actions to go unchecked, would be the ruination of us all," she said in a tremulous voice.

At last Raile understood that Lavinia must have lied about him to discredit him and to keep Hugh in their uncle's good graces.

"What of my brother, Lavinia?" he asked grimly. "Why is he not present when I face my accusers?"

"I'm not accusing you, Raile," John spoke up with rare defiance against his father.

"No one asked your opinion, John," the duke roared. "Just keep quiet while I deal with your cousin."

For a moment it looked as if John would say more, but his gaze fell away from his father's, and he stepped back several paces.

Raile knew he would get no support from John. He was in this alone. Could he untangle the wall of lies Lavinia had woven? "You didn't answer me, Lavinia. Where is my brother?" he pressed.

"My son is at school. As one would expect of him, he is applying himself to his studies." Lavinia tossed her head and met Raile's contemptuous gaze defiantly. "I told your uncle you would deny this, Raile."

Pride struggled with pain. "No," he said at last. "If my uncle believes this of me on your word alone, Lavinia, I will not deny it."

The duke eased himself up on his elbow. "Of course,

I believe her. Unlike my brother's first wife, Lavinia is from an old and respected family. I told your father nothing good would come from marrying a tradesman's daughter. But he would not heed my warning. I'm only glad he didn't live to see the shame the tradeswoman's son has brought down on this family."

Enraged, Raile took a step toward his uncle, who shrank back against his pillows. "Say what you like about me, but I won't hear another word against my mother. My father was a broken man when she died. It was his first marriage that brought him love and wealth, and you know that as well as I."

The duke's face turned livid, and his hand shook. "What I know, Raile DeWinter, is you can't buy respectability. Oh, I realize that you have been paying my expenses these last five years. But I never asked you to, and don't expect me to be grateful to you, because I'm not."

"Does it gall you, Uncle, to know it's my mother's money that keeps the DeWinter family from living in a less magnificent manner?"

His uncle glared at him. "Keep your money and be damned, Raile!"

"Why would I, Uncle? I want you to remember, every time you put a morsel of food in your mouth, or pay your butler to attend you, that it's money, earned in trade by my mother's father, that makes it possible."

"You are a discredit to us all," the duke raged. "Leave this house and do not come back in my lifetime. If my son foolishly allows you back after my death, he will suffer for your scandalous conduct."

With fury choking him, Raile turned to leave, wishing there was someone or something he could strike out against.

His uncle's angry voice followed him out the door and down the stairs. "Take yourself out of the country and never come back to England."

He descended the stairs angrily and was at the front door before John caught up with him.

"Wait, Raile, I must talk to you."

Raile shook off John's hand and shoved the startled butler out of the way, ripping the front door open. He knew that John was following him, but he didn't want to talk to anyone at the moment.

John insisted on being heard. He took Raile's arm and swung him around. "We both know Hugh is the one who fought the duel with Lord Pinsworthy."

Raile glanced upward, trying to cool his temper. "Everyone in London knows Hugh was responsible for the duel. I can't believe your father wouldn't have heard the rumors. Worst of all, I can't imagine why he would think so little of my character."

"He hears only what Lavinia wants him to hear. You know how she has always set out to charm him," John responded bitterly, "and Father is easily duped by her."

"I would have thought Hugh would come forward with the truth."

John's face became stony. "Damn it, Raile, when will you understand that Hugh will do whatever Lavinia says?"

Raile was disbelieving. "But if Hugh had been there today, he would have admitted his guilt. My brother would never have allowed me to take the blame."

"I don't think so, Raile. Remember the time when that girl in Ravenworth village gave birth to a bastard child? It was Hugh's baby, but he told everyone that you had fathered the child. You took the blame for him then, just as you did today. When will you admit Hugh is not worthy of your loyalty?"

"Not until he proves it to me himself, John."

"Hugh's a bastard, Raile. He always has been, he always will be."

"I'm sure he knows nothing of Lavinia's lies." Raile drew in a deep breath, wanting to believe in his brother.

"No matter, I'm off to find myself a regiment."

"You don't mean that you are taking my father at his word? You aren't leaving England?"

"I have been thinking for some time about acquiring a commission in the army. This incident merely helped me decide."

John poked his hands in his pockets. "I know you well enough to realize if you have made up your mind, nothing I say will deter you. I only wish—"

"It's over, John. Let it go. Just take care of yourself and my uncle, for I cannot find it within myself to wish him ill. And if either of you needs anything, just contact my solicitor, and he will see that you get it."

John looked ashamed. "I'm glad it came out at last that you are paying the expenses of this family."

"I had hoped my uncle would never have to know. How did he find out?"

"I was in the solicitor's office one afternoon last summer, and the man warned me that my father needed to curtail his spending. After much coaxing, he admitted that it was you who was taking care of the family's expenses, and had been for years. I told my father. I thought he should know what you have done for us." John shook his head. "We owe you so much and have offered you so little."

Raile was impatient to leave. "You owe me nothing. It is I who owe you and your father, John. He gave me a home for many years."

"Why didn't you tell my father the truth about Hugh?"

Raile stared for a moment at the clear sky before looking into John's earnest blue eyes. "Why didn't you tell him, John?"

Without another word, Raile turned and walked away.

2

Six Months Later
Another House On Percy Street

Thirteen-year-old Kassidy Maragon dashed down the steps of her aunt's fashionable town house, with the impression of her brother's slap still visible on her cheek. She dodged several carriages and ran quickly to the park across the street.

Henry had not been in the least understanding with his daughter, Trudy, when she discovered her favorite doll had been broken by a careless playmate. The child sobbed brokenheartedly, while her father admonished her for not taking care of her possessions and restricted her from playing for one month.

Kassidy was not sorry that she had comforted the crying child against Henry's command. She had called her brother an unfeeling monster, and he had slapped her.

Kassidy drew in a deep breath and brushed the tears from her eyes. After tomorrow she would never again have to be under Henry's harsh domination.

Her parents had been in India for one long year, and at last they were coming home.

Henry had grudgingly complied with their parents' request that he bring his sisters to London to meet them. This was Kassidy's first time in London, and she refused to allow her brother to spoil it for her. She forgot all about him when she saw a colorfully dressed vendor sing out his song as he hawked his wares.

Hearing her name called, Kassidy glanced across the street to find her older sister, Abigail, waving to her. She motioned for Abigail to join her in the park.

They were as different as sisters could be. Abigail had blond hair and beautiful features. Her manners were refined, and her actions were always correct. Kassidy had never liked her own blond hair, and she considered herself anything but a lady.

The three years that divided the sisters had never seemed to matter; they were the best of friends. Kassidy attributed their closeness to Abigail's loving nature. She saw her sister as sweet and patient, while she was hot-tempered, and had very little time for fools.

"Are you hurt, dearest?" Abigail asked with a worried frown on her pretty face.

"No, he couldn't hurt me. I'm too happy today."

"Henry *is* the monster you called him, and I shall tell Mother and Father how he has mistreated you." Abigail drew Kassidy's head against her shoulder. "I'll never allow him to strike you again. He's only fortunate Aunt Mary didn't witness the incident. She would have given him a proper dressing-down."

"Aunt Mary probably would have struck him back, and you know it."

Both girls giggled.

"Look," Kassidy said, already forgetting her brother's harshness with her, "there's a squirrel in that tree."

"We have to get back, Kassidy," Abigail reminded

her. "You know Aunt Mary is expecting guests for tea."

"What do I care about that? It's just Henry's old mother-in-law and her darling daughters, who are so full of their own worth, I can hardly bear to be in the same room with them."

"That may be so, but we wouldn't want to disappoint Aunt Mary. She's gone to a great deal of trouble on Henry's behalf."

"Look." Kassidy pointed above them. "The squirrel's gone into that hole in the tree. Do you suppose it lives there all year 'round?"

Abigail, at sixteen, fancied herself above such childish matters. "I'm sure I don't know. I have no interest in the habits of a rodent."

"I wonder what a squirrel would find to eat in London?"

Abigail smiled at Kassidy's great enthusiasm for life. "I'm sure Uncle George could tell you."

"Do you suppose Mother and Father will take us to Drury Lane?" Kassidy asked, reaching above her head and snapping off a small branch. "I want to see the flower girls selling lavender in the streets and buy lemonade from a street vendor."

"I was hoping to see the palace. Uncle George has already promised I can visit Parliament," Abigail said, placing a dainty foot on the walkway. "I want so desperately to sail down the Thames River on a covered boat."

"I would like to go to Ascot and see the fine horses that race there," Kassidy said thoughtfully. "Do you suppose Father and Mother will want to return to the country immediately?"

"It doesn't really matter what we do as long as we're together," Abigail admitted. "I have missed them so dreadfully."

"And just think, Abigail, Henry won't ever be able to tell us what to do again. A year is a long time to live by his stern dictates."

Abigail nodded in agreement. "Henry cannot be a happy man. He never smiles and resents it when others do. I feel such pity for our nieces. Why do you suppose he's the way he is?"

"I don't know. He doesn't take after Mother or Father," Kassidy said reflectively. Then she smiled impishly. "Perhaps the Gypsies left him."

"I suppose we should feel pity for him," Abigail said seriously. "After all, Patricia doesn't treat him very well."

"Sometimes you're just too good, Abigail," Kassidy said scornfully. "I don't care about Henry *or* his wife. I want to have fun, and they're no fun at all. Henry thinks London was built by the devil for the devil. He deserves to be miserable."

Kassidy and Abigail exchanged glances. "But we don't!" they said in unison, then shared a laugh at their brother's expense.

"We had best get back to the house, Kassidy." Abigail glanced up at the sun. "You'll ruin your complexion if you stay out much longer."

"You go on. I want to stay for a while. I promise to return before tea."

Abigail looked doubtful for a moment, thinking it wouldn't be proper to leave Kassidy alone in the park. But when she saw several nannies with their charges nearby, she relented. "Don't soil your new gown. You'll want to look your best when we meet Mother and Father."

Kassidy watched Abigail cross the street and disappear inside the house. She dropped down on a marble bench and intently studied a goldfish that darted in and out among the lily pads. Of course, she loved the country most of all, but in London every day was like a new adventure.

She was so lost in thought that she didn't see the two boys who came up behind her until one of them stepped between her and the pond.

"What we got here, Elmer? Do you think this's one

of the fancy girls from across the street? Mayhaps she's too fancy for the likes of us."

Kassidy blinked her eyes and stared at the bold boys who carried brooms and brushes on a harness across their shoulders. Their clothing was covered with soot and their faces were blackened. It was obvious that they were chimney sweeps.

She turned her back on them. They had no right to be so familiar with her.

"See how she's too grand to speak to the likes of us," one of them taunted.

"I'll not talk to you. Be gone," she said airily.

"Come on, Hank," the second boy said. "Why don't you leave her be. She ain't done nothing to you."

The one called Hank smirked. "I wonder if she'd be so haughty if I landed her in that fish pond?"

Kassidy quickly turned to face the boy, her green eyes sparkling and fearless. "You wouldn't dare!"

Hank moved forward while his companion hung back. He grabbed her arm and pulled her toward the pond. "We'll just see, miss—we'll just see."

Kassidy kicked at him and connected with his knee. She then wrenched her arm free and at the same time drove her fist into the boy's midsection. He howled in pain while his companion looked on gleefully.

"You got what you deserves. Now leave her be. Pa will be expecting us." Without another word, Elmer walked away.

When Hank caught his breath, he lunged at Kassidy with anger boiling in his eyes. But poor Hank never reached her because he was jerked off his feet and dangled in the air by an officer in His Majesty's army, who wore the insignia of a colonel.

"Well there, young lad, it appears you have nothing better to do than torment helpless little girls. Surely it would be no great feat for you to push her in the pond."

The officer glanced at Kassidy. "And she's such a small girl. You are at least twice her size."

Hank tried to wriggle free. "She's anything but helpless. She's a demon!"

Raile looked at the little girl who faced her tormentor defiantly, her fists doubled, her eyes flashing like green fire. "I see what you mean." Raile released the boy. "If you want to fight, join the army and fight the French."

The boy looked shamefaced. "I'm sorry, sir." He looked quickly at Kassidy. "And I'm sorry to you, too, miss." He lost no time in picking up his brooms and scampering away.

"Did he hurt you?"

Kassidy looked up at her rescuer. He was the handsomest man she had ever seen. If only Abigail had remained a little longer, she would have been there to meet him. He would surely have been smitten by her beauty and fallen in love.

"I'm not hurt a bit, thank you, sir."

He smiled as he knelt before her. "Perhaps you aren't hurt, but you soiled your pretty white gown."

She looked at the dark smudges on the sleeve and shook her head in dismay. "Aunt Mary bought this gown and I wasn't supposed to get it dirty. I was to wear it again tomorrow to meet my mother and father."

He removed a handkerchief from his pocket, dipped it in the fish pond, and dabbed at her sleeve. "Perhaps I can help." He gently rubbed the smudge while Kassidy watched hopefully.

She was overcome with relief when the stain disappeared. She wanted to throw her arms around her savior, but of course she dared not. Surely he was the most compassionate man she had ever met.

"There," Raile DeWinter said, standing to his full height. "If you don't tell her, Aunt Mary will never know about your trouble."

He handed her his handkerchief. "There is a black

smudge on your forehead, but I'll let you attend to that."

She rubbed at the spot until he nodded in approval. When she would have given him back his handkerchief, he closed his hand around hers. "Keep it as a token." He laughed. "And who knows when you may need it again."

"Thank you." She watched the wind ripple through his dark hair. "I have to go now," she said, backing toward the walkway. "But I won't forget your kindness."

"Yes, hurry along."

She took several steps and turned back to him. "Will I ever see you again?"

His eyes suddenly darkened with sadness. "I'm afraid not. You see, I'm leaving tomorrow."

"Will you be fighting against the French?"

"Yes."

"I will think of you and know that I am safe because you stand between Napoleon and me," she said with feeling.

He smiled at her exaggeration. This green-eyed minx was a real charmer. "I will do my best to keep you safe."

"I will think of you as my champion," she said sincerely.

He bowed formally to her, trying to keep a serious expression on his face. "I am honored to be your champion. I assure you I shall not shirk in my duty toward you. Now I must bid you good day."

Kassidy made her way quickly across the street. When she turned back, he was gone.

Glancing down at the handkerchief, she saw it had an initial embroidered in black. She traced the bold outline of the letter R, wishing she had asked him his name.

Kassidy tucked her treasure into her pocket and raced up the steps.

Wait until she told Abigail about the handsome officer who had rescued her from a spill in the pond. Wouldn't she be jealous?

Kassidy sat beside her Aunt Mary at dinner, as far away from Henry as was possible. In defiance of Henry's wishes, Aunt Mary had insisted that Kassidy dine with the adults rather than the children.

Kassidy dipped her spoon in the lemon ice and raised it to her mouth, while returning her Uncle George's smile. She adored him. Although her uncle wasn't titled, he sat in the House Of Commons and was a most important and distinguished presence in Parliament, she had been told. But to her he was just Uncle George, and she had always found him to be warm and humorous.

She watched the affectionate glance her uncle and aunt exchanged. Aunt Mary was her mother's sister. She had always insisted that Kassidy was like her, but Kassidy doubted she would ever grow into the beauty her aunt was. Both of them did have blond hair, though, and they always had an understanding between them.

Dipping once more into her lemon ice, Kassidy stole a glance at her brother, Henry, and his wife, Patricia. Henry was in his thirties, tall and lean, and although he resembled their father, he was as disagreeable as their father was amiable.

"I don't approve of children eating with the grown-ups," Henry said pompously, his eyes hard when he looked at Kassidy. "It spoils them and makes them unmanageable."

Patricia, with her pale skin and darting gray eyes, agreed with her husband by vigorously nodding her head.

"Rubbish," Aunt Mary said, smiling down at her favorite niece. "Kassidy is on the threshold of becoming a lovely young lady. While she's in my house, she will not sup with the children and be sent to bed at sundown."

Kassidy met Abigail's eyes, and her sister smiled, enjoying Henry's discomfort. Their brother would never dare to oppose Aunt Mary.

The butler caught Kassidy's attention when he entered the room and approached her uncle, handing him a letter. "I'm sorry, sir, but this was marked urgent."

George read the note. His eyes widened, and he glanced at his wife. "Let's retire to the study," he said.

Everyone rose immediately and began to leave the room. George grasped his wife's hand, detaining her. "Your aunt and I will join you in a moment."

Kassidy and Abigail sat down on the wide leather sofa, clutching each other's hands. "I'll bet Mother and Father were delayed," Abigail said worriedly.

"Most probably," Henry grumbled. "I hope their delay isn't a lengthy one. I tire of London."

When their aunt and uncle entered the study a short time later, it was apparent Aunt Mary had been crying.

"Is the letter from Father and Mother, Uncle George?" Kassidy asked anxiously. "Will they be arriving later than we expected?"

His eyes softened when he looked at her. "I'm afraid they won't be arriving at all," he said sadly. "You see, Kassidy, their ship went down at sea. It falls to me to tell you that there were no survivors."

Kassidy shook her head in disbelief. Tears ran down her cheeks, and she was sure she could not bear the grief.

"No!" she cried, and Abigail reached out to comfort her. "It cannot be—not Father and Mother!"

Aunt Mary came to the two girls, sliding her arms around them. "Oh, my dearest ones, what can we say?"

Kassidy clutched Abigail to her, and they sobbed brokenheartedly.

The day that had started out so hopeful had turned to tragedy. To Kassidy it seemed life was over. She would never see her beloved mother and father again. A feeling of unreality took hold of her.

Abigail was crying uncontrollably. In that moment, Kassidy pushed her grief aside and became strong for Abigail. "There, there, dearest, we have each other, and we will get through this," Kassidy assured her. "Cling to me and I'll lend you my strength."

Henry came to his feet and said in a voice that broke: "Well, it seems I am head of the family now. I'll try and carry on as Father would have expected."

Abigail and Kassidy exchanged hopeless glances. Knowing they were now under the guidance of a cold, unloving man made their grief tenfold.

It was raining the day the coach left London. Kassidy was seated beside Abigail, clutching her hand. Henry and Patricia were across from them, while the children followed in the second coach with their nurse.

Henry had indeed assumed his place as head of the family. He had inherited his father's title of viscount and was taking his responsibilities seriously.

Aunt Mary had beseeched him to allow Kassidy and Abigail to remain with her, but he had stubbornly refused, insisting that girls of their age needed a firm hand and someone to watch their every move.

Abigail leaned her head on Kassidy's shoulder and whispered, "I don't know how I can bear the pain."

"You will always have me, Abigail. I will never leave you."

"I don't think I would make it without you, Kassidy. I have come to depend on your courage."

Kassidy closed her eyes, feeling as if she had left childhood behind. Abigail was fragile, so she would have to be strong for them both.

3

Belgium—June 17, 1815
Waterloo

Night fell early as ominous storm clouds shrouded the sun. Flashes of light from the electrical storm cut through the inky blackness, illuminating the countryside, while thunder reverberated across the sky like the sound of cannon fire.

Bone-weary and battle-fatigued British regiments were huddled beneath makeshift tents, hoping to find protection against the rain that would surely come. In the distance the sound of sporadic gunfire cut through the night as snipers from both sides exchanged volleys.

A jagged streak of lightning danced tumultuously across the sky, and a strange hush intruded upon the land. The first drops of rain fell heavily earthward, soaking into the fertile farmland.

Col. Raile DeWinter pulled his greatcoat about him and headed toward the bivouac fires. He had ridden for two days to join his troops, and had been in two skirmishes along the way.

As he walked along, his silver spurs jingled, because had been too exhausted to remove them.

He nodded to a group of soldiers who scurried to their feet to salute.

"At ease, men. Save your strength for the battle tomorrow," Raile instructed them.

He paused at the entrance of his tent to gaze across the encampment and beyond to the woods. The outriders had reported that Napoleon and his forces were in hot pursuit of Wellington. In the morning they would undoubtedly clash with the enemy. Many of the soldiers camped there tonight would be dead by this time tomorrow.

Victory would belong to the strongest, and Raile, like most of the British, would place his faith in Wellington.

"We'll give them frogs hell tomorrow, Colonel!" one of the soldiers, who was intent on polishing the brass buttons on his tattered uniform, cried out with enthusiasm.

Raile studied the man carefully. He was young, hardly old enough to shave. His clothes were wet, and he must be cold and miserable, but there was an eagerness reflected in his eyes that Raile envied.

"That we will, Private. If we didn't believe that, we wouldn't be here."

The 34th Regiment of the Light Dragoons had been under Raile's command since the Portuguese Campaign, and he had every reason to be satisfied by the performance of his men, for they had covered themselves with honors. Even though their uniforms were tattered and muddy and their faces were etched with fatigue, something in their eyes told Raile they would give their all in the battle ahead.

"Will it be over tomorrow, sir?" the young private asked, wanting reassurance from his commander. "Can we stop Bonaparte this time?"

"I believe, as General Wellington does, that we shall deal a stunning blow to Napoleon. If the Prussians arrive, we shall most certainly be victorious," Raile replied matter-of-factly.

He moved into his tent and nodded to his valet, Oliver Stewart.

There was a hint of reproof in Oliver's greeting. "I expected you earlier, Colonel."

"I would have been here by noon but for the pockets of resistance we encountered along the way," Raile said wearily. He unbuttoned his red tunic. "The woods are crawling with the enemy."

"Here," Oliver said, rushing forward and removing Raile's coat. "I'll do that for you, sir. You're soaked to the bone. You'll surely catch your death."

"You fuss too much," Raile stated, dropping down on the edge of his cot while Oliver removed his muddy boots.

"Have you eaten, Colonel?"

"I don't want anything," he said, suddenly overcome with exhaustion. "I just need to rest."

Oliver saw the tired lines under Raile's eyes and nodded in agreement. "Your boots will be needing a shine, Colonel. You'll want to look your best tomorrow."

Raile struggled out of his tunic and fell back. "Get some sleep yourself, Oliver. Tomorrow will test the fortitude of us all."

The devoted servant, with the muddy boots dangling from his fingers and the discarded clothing under his arm, extinguished the lantern and withdrew.

Raile closed his eyes, wishing sleep would come. If only he could turn his thoughts off, but for some reason, persistent memories from the past plodded through his mind, denying him rest. He drew in a deep breath and tried to concentrate on the impending battle. The French would throw all their forces at them tomorrow—they had to—this was their last hope.

He was weary of war, and ready to return to England. When the fighting was over, he would go home and face his past.

He had not thought of England in months—at least not consciously. Why had painful memories now come unbidden to him? He supposed it was because it finally mattered to him that he might die before he could vindicate himself with his uncle.

His lips twisted with rancor. There was much he had to settle when he got back to England. His honor had been questioned, and he swore to clear his name before he died.

He thought of how insignificant his life had been before he fought under Wellington and faced death at each battle. In London his nights had been spent in the arms of beautiful women, and his days had been spent gaming and drinking with the Prince of Wales and his favorites.

How unimportant that life seemed to him now—and how far away. With rain heavily pounding against the leather tent, Raile finally nodded off from exhaustion, his anguished mind soothed by a dreamless sleep.

Sunday, June 18

It was almost the noon hour when the first shots echoed through the valley.

Raile raised his spyglass to observe the enemy position across the open field. The plowed ground was muddy from the previous night's storm, and the allies were having trouble moving the heavy equipment. Cannons were bogged down in mud up to their axles, making it difficult for the soldiers to turn them toward the oncoming enemy. After a long struggle, the heavy guns were aimed, spiked, and ready to fire.

Each time a cannon spoke, fire bellowed across the valley. The biting, acrid smell of gunpowder permeated the air. Spiraling smoke seemed suspended above the landscape and was slow to dissipate. As the battle heated up, clouds of sulfur mingled with the ever-present mist like a ghostly omen predicting hellish devastation. The countryside was quickly becoming littered with the dead and dying.

Raile's eyes darkened with irony as he looked at the battlefield where crops of barley and potatoes flourished—a bit of reality in an otherwise illusory world that was being trampled beneath the boots of advancing armies.

He watched the French forces mass to charge across the open spaces. Did they actually believe they could win today? He had been in enough battles to know that death honored no allegiance, favored no nation, respected no cause. Surely the valiant fools realized that in the end it would be the strongest who would prevail. And only God knew who was the strongest. Had it all come down to Napoleon's strategy against Wellington's cunning?

For long hours fierce battles raged, with neither side giving ground. Napoleon was sending out massive columns that struck hammer blows at the British front positions.

It was late afternoon when Raile's attention was drawn to the advancing French infantrymen who marched in double-time toward Wellington's right.

A fierce battle ensued, and Wellington was being driven back.

Raile and his men met the French Lancers with sabers ready. The clash of swords rang out even as the cannons echoed across the valley. Raile heard someone shout that the Prussians had arrived. God let it be true, he prayed as an enemy lance hit him in the shoulder and propelled him from his horse.

Searing pain stunned him for the moment. Shaking his head to clear it, he jumped to his feet, noticing that several hundred Prussians had dug in on his right. But something was wrong. Apparently their commander had been killed and chaos had broken out among the ranks. The Prussians were abandoning their positions and scurrying toward the safety of the woods.

Raile quickly assessed the situation and realized that if the panic-stricken Prussians didn't hold their ground, the enemy would penetrate the lines and come up on Wellington's right, his weakest point. Pushing his booted foot into the stirrups, he bounded back into the saddle. Amid a punishing cannonade, he turned his horse in the direction where the enemy was advancing on the fleeing Prussians.

Raile's maneuver had been observed by his own men, who, inspired by his heroic action rallied behind him, their horses thundering across the field.

The sun reflected off drawn sabers as a daring charge ensued.

With his mount running full out, Raile reached down and scooped up the fallen Prussian flag attached to a lance. Without breaking his horse's stride, he met a wall of French cavalry. One Frenchman, whose sword was already bloodstained, charged toward Raile. Without thinking, Raile plunged the lance into the enemy, driving it into his heart.

There was a surprised look on the Frenchman's face as he fell forward and slid from his horse, the bloodstained Prussian flag waving above his prone body like a banner of victory.

The spectacle of seeing their flag flying atop a slain enemy caused pride to surge through the fleeing Prussians. They turned back, rushing down the hill to meet the French with renewed fervor.

It soon became a struggle for supremacy, a hand-to-hand combat with Raile in the middle, spurring loyalty in the breasts of Englishmen and Prussians alike.

At one point, Raile's horse was shot out from under him, so he continued his fight on foot. Sweat and blood stung his eyes, and he didn't know if he was tasting his own blood or that of the enemy, not that it mattered. Raile swung his sword, connecting with flesh and bone. He felt a sting of pain and glanced down to see blood spurting from an open gash on his leg. Ignoring the pain, he wielded his blade and met the enemy with a clash of steel.

Time had no meaning—the only thing that mattered was to kill or be killed.

Suddenly a cannonball exploded nearby, and Raile reeled from a stunning blow to his head. He staggered and fell to his knees, only to rise again. All at once, the ground tilted, and he felt himself falling into a black void.

He was unaware that his men circled him like a protective shield, fighting to keep the enemy at bay. He did not hear the ghostly bugles that sounded the French retreat. He was unaware of the bedlam that broke out among the enemy ranks, or that the battle had turned and the French forces were being pursued by Wellington.

Raile regained consciousness just as several men lifted and carried him toward the hospital tent behind the lines. Through a haze of pain he observed a land that had been turned into an inferno that would bear the scars of this war for many years to come. He thought for a moment that he was in hell.

For the French, hope had turned to despair, and with despair came the knowledge that their mighty emperor had been thoroughly defeated. Raile watched as abandoned French flags were trampled beneath retreating boots.

Oliver appeared beside Raile and spoke encouragingly, trying to hide his distress.

"You'll be all right, sir. Just a little nick, I suspect."

In truth, Raile's face was a bloody mass, and the wounds on his leg and shoulder were bleeding profusely.

Raile tried to rise, but the pain was so great he fell back weakly. "My command?"

"Seven dead and twenty wounded. They did you proud today, sir," Oliver assured him. "You mustn't talk. The surgeons will expect you to lie quietly until they can tend your wounds—you'll be up and about in no time, sir."

Raile drew in a ragged breath. Both he and Oliver knew he was gravely wounded.

"Did we win today?" he insisted on knowing.

"That we did, Colonel. Even though I'm told there are yet pockets of Napoleon's crack regiment, the Old Guard, who stayed at their posts, determined to remain until the end to protect their emperor's withdrawal. But they can't hold out for long."

"Praiseworthy in battle, praiseworthy in defeat," Raile murmured, still gripping the handle of his saber. His eyes moved to Oliver, and he said with considerable effort: "Today we are witnessing the Corsican's demise, Oliver. He will not recover from this last folly."

Raile glanced at the battlefield that was littered with dead bodies of men and horses—comrades and enemies alike. "So many dead—it all seems so senseless—"

He was placed in a cart with other wounded to be transported to the nearby field hospital. Oliver sat beside him and cushioned his head as the rig jostled over rutted roads. The pain became too great and Raile was again enveloped in darkness.

In the early hours of the morning, the surgeon's knife removed the musket fragment from Raile's leg, but the head wound was another matter. The surgeon cleansed it and bandaged it before turning to a worried Oliver.

"I've done all I can for him," he said, wiping his bloody hands on his apron. "The rest is up to God."

"He's strong, he'll make it," Oliver said with conviction.

"If I were a betting man, and I'm not, I'd say he

won't. His head wound is deep, and there was a fragment I dared not remove, fearing it pressed too close to the brain. Even if by some miracle he does live, he may be mindless or even blind."

Oliver grasped the doctor by the arm. "You have to save him. He is a man like no other—brave and courageous—a hero."

The doctor flexed his aching muscles and glanced at the rows of cots filled with the wounded and dying. "Every man you see here is a hero, but most of them will die, as I'm sure will this man."

Throughout the long hours of the day and into the night, Oliver kept his vigil, while outside the hospital tent the victorious soldiers of the 34th Regiment of the Light Dragoons waited in the rain to hear if their commanding officer would live or die.

At sunrise the next day it was still dark as dense clouds covered the sun. By midmorning a feeling of gloom hung over the men of the 34th Regiment when they were ordered to move out with the other troops, leaving their commanding officer behind without knowing his fate.

Oliver sat beside Raile, watching the rain pound against the window as his comrades departed.

It was late afternoon when a British officer appeared at Raile's bedside. The valet quickly came to attention, buttoning his tunic and trying to smooth down his disheveled hair.

"Stand easy, soldier," the man said, staring down at Raile. At last he turned his attention to the valet. "I am General Greenleigh of General Wellington's staff. He has sent me to inquire about Colonel DeWinter's condition."

"The doctor holds out little hope that he will survive, sir."

"Your colonel covered himself with glory in the battle yesterday."

"Yes, sir, that he did," Oliver agreed with pride. "He was an inspiration to us all."

"General Wellington knows of his heroism and will see that he is duly commended."

Oliver met the general's sympathetic gaze. "Little good the glory will do him if he's dead, sir."

General Greenleigh stared at the tip of his own shiny boots. "I was ordered by Wellington himself to see that Colonel DeWinter is transferred to Brussels, where he will receive the best medical care."

"I'm not certain he could survive such a journey, sir."

"General Wellington has placed at your disposal one of his own coaches, which you will find well sprung. The fact that Colonel DeWinter is unconscious could prove a blessing. He will not feel the discomfort of the journey."

Oliver nodded grimly, wondering if the colonel would live long enough to reach the hospital.

The doctor appeared beside General Greenleigh and sadly shook his head. "He'll be gone within the hour, General."

"Oh, well," the officer said absently, his thoughts already on other matters. "I shall write the necessary letters to his family. Damned shame. He was a good man."

Oliver glanced down at Raile, who was pale and pain-racked, his breathing deep and labored.

"You'll fool them all," the valet said, feeling resentment toward the two men who had so readily abandoned Raile. "They don't know about your fighting spirit. They have never seen you come through against impossible circumstances. You're going to come out of this, Colonel. I know you will. You have faced harder."

4

Kassidy was in the garden when she heard the church bells in the village begin pealing the joyous news. England was celebrating her victory. At last the war was over and Napoleon had been defeated!

She smiled as she remembered the officer she had met as a young girl at the park across from Aunt Mary's house. She had once childishly called him her champion, but she had come to think of him as just that. Even though she had forgotten what he looked like, it had become her habit to say a prayer for his safety each night—she only hoped he had come through the war alive. It was a pity that she would never know for certain if her champion had survived.

She went into the bedroom she shared with Abigail, moved to the mirror, and stared at her image as she removed her bonnet. Without vanity, she could see that she was pretty. Gone were the freckles; her skin was now creamy and flawless. Her hair hung across her shoulders in spiraling curls and was a burnished blond in color. She was slender and delicate. Her fighting spirit was not gone, but was often tempered with reserve. A child no longer, she was a young lady.

She had become accustomed to seeing admiration in gentlemen's eyes. At church, she could feel them watching her. But none of the men of the village was considered suitable by Henry. And none would dare approach her because they feared her brother.

Abigail and Kassidy had never been alone with a gentleman, and if Henry had his way, they never would. He ruled his house as if he were king, and his sisters were little better than unpaid servants. Even Aunt Mary's pleas to allow the girls to have a London Season at her expense went unheeded.

Kassidy knew there would be dancing and merrymaking in the streets of the village, and the celebration would go on well into the night. She sighed regretfully. She would not be joining in the festivities. Henry would never allow it.

Kassidy threw open a window and listened to the sound of cheering. After lighting a candle, she moved back to the window, pulled aside the curtains, and looked at the dying rays of the sun. She anxiously searched for her sister. She was worried because Abigail had not yet returned. Perhaps she was among the merrymakers in the village.

Henry, God-fearing man that he was, was permitting Abigail to help tend the vicar's children until his sickly wife gave birth to their fifth child. When Kassidy had seen the vicar at the market today, he had inquired about Abigail and had implied that he had not seen her since last Sunday. If Abigail wasn't going to the vicarage when she left the house, then where was she spending her days?

Kassidy heard steps in the hallway, and she moved quickly to the door to find Abigail, face flushed as if she'd been running.

"Where have you been?" Kassidy asked in a whisper, dragging her sister into the room and closing the door behind them. "Henry wanted to know where you were. He was in a temper."

"Little I care about Henry's temper."

Kassidy looked at Abigail closely. "You had better care. I saw the vicar today."

Abigail avoided looking into Kassidy's eyes. "Oh." She untied her bonnet and allowed it to dangle from her fingers. "I suppose he told you I haven't been to the vicarage all week."

"Abigail, we've never kept secrets from each other. Why are you doing so now? Are you in trouble?"

"Oh, Kassidy, I can no longer keep it to myself. I'm in love!" Abigail laughed and hugged her sister. "He is more wonderful than you can imagine. I'm happy just being with him."

Kassidy was astounded. "When did you have a chance to meet anyone? I know every gentleman of your acquaintance, and not one of them would I consider wonderful."

Abigail's blue eyes took on a glow. "I met him at Lady Broadwick's Christmas party last December. Remember how you refused to go because you find her parties tedious? I went because it's the only social gathering Henry will allow us to attend."

"I remember."

"He . . . we were attracted to each other right away. All the ladies flirted with him outrageously, but he saw only me. Lady Broadwick's nose was out of joint because he asked me to dance three times and didn't dance once with her daughter, Emily." She stopped to catch her breath. "It was that night that we made plans to meet the next day. I knew Henry would never allow him to call at the house, so I met him in the graveyard behind the church."

Kassidy felt somehow betrayed. "You never told me about this man."

Abigail looked at her sister apologetically. "Knowing how Henry always singles you out to bear the brunt of his anger, I decided not to confide in you. This way, if he discovers I have been deceiving him, he will punish only me. You can't be blamed for what you don't know."

"But, Abigail, you must stop seeing this man at once. If Henry does find out, I don't know what he would do to you."

"It's too late for that, dearest." Abigail's face brightened. "Be happy for me, Kassidy—I'm going to be married."

Kassidy felt conflicting emotions. If Abigail were to be married, she would escape a life of drudgery under Henry's control. But how dreadfully she would miss Abigail, and how alone she would be without her.

"What if this man isn't worthy of you, Abigail? You know so little of the world, and even less of men. You see only good in everyone. How can you judge a man when your heart is involved?"

Abigail pulled Kassidy down on the bed beside her. "If you only knew who he is, you would be most impressed, for he is a man of great import. Just be happy for me and know that I will be with the man I love."

"Who is he?"

"I can't tell you that, Kassidy, at least not now. But after I'm married and settled in his home, you will come to live with us."

"I'm so confused, Abigail. How can you love a man you hardly know?"

"Since our first meeting we have managed to see each other several times a week. We met on the afternoons I was supposed to be at Mrs. Hardy's to give her daughters singing lessons."

There was reproof in Kassidy's voice. "You should have told me. You know I would have helped you in any way I could."

"I never meant to deceive you. But he and I discussed the matter and decided to tell no one. He made me promise I wouldn't tell even you. You see, his mother has her own notions of who he should marry. He doesn't think she would approve of me. But what can she do if we are already married?"

"I don't like the sound of this, Abigail," Kassidy said suspiciously. "If he is a man of honor, he should at least come to Henry and ask for your hand in a proper manner. What if he's only promising you marriage, so you will go away with him?"

Abigail laughed. "Where you get these notions, I have no idea. I trust him completely, Kassidy." Abigail shook her head. "You know Henry would never give his consent. He would lock me in and never allow me to see my love again."

Kassidy knew Abigail spoke the truth. "I want to meet him then. Someone in this family needs to know the man."

"There's no time, Kassidy. I'm leaving with him tonight."

Kassidy clutched her sister's hand. "Don't do something you may regret."

"I could never regret leaving this house that Henry has made more a prison than a home. My only sadness is in leaving you." She pressed her cheek against Kassidy's. "I promise to get word to you as soon as I'm able. But don't be concerned if you don't hear from me for a time. I have to devise a way to write you so Henry won't find out."

"How can I let you go when I won't know where you are?"

"I will be with a man who loves me and wants only my happiness. You need have no concern for me."

With a heavy heart, Kassidy asked: "What are your plans?"

"I am to meet him at the crossroads at midnight. Before morning, I will be his wife."

Kassidy sighed with resignation. "Then we had better pack your belongings. Come, I will help you."

Abigail's eyes clouded with tears. "I knew you would understand. My hope is that Henry won't make you suffer for what I'm doing."

"Don't worry about me. I can take care of Henry."

"I never understood why he seemed to hate you so much, Kassidy. You were always the one he punished when he was dissatisfied with either of us."

"It's because I'm the one who defies him. Men like Henry want people to cower before them—I don't fear him in the least, and he resents it."

"Please be careful." Abigail pulled a sealed letter from her pocket. "I intend to leave this for him on the hall table. I wrote him about the elopement."

Kassidy opened the wooden chest at the end of Abigail's bed. "It's a pity your wardrobe is so meager. Father left Henry wealthy, but he's so stingy he begrudges every pence."

Abigail pulled a small valise from under her bed. "It doesn't matter. I don't need much. My beloved has promised me a new wardrobe and anything else that I desire."

Again misgiving nagged at Kassidy. "If only I knew more about this man."

"When you learn his identity, you will know that I have married well. He has just come into a fortune and will soon inherit an old and distinguished title."

Kassidy refused to cry as she placed Abigail's scuffed slippers in the valise. She had to think how happy Abigail would be and not think how miserable her own life would be when her sister was gone.

* * *

Henry's face was etched with fury. He tore open the bedroom door and yanked Kassidy up by the arm, waving Abigail's letter in her face.

"Just what's the meaning of this, missy?"

Kassidy had hardly slept during the night, and now as she looked at her brother, she knew the time she'd dreaded had come.

"You know as well as I, that it's a letter from Abigail," she answered, wrenching her arm free of his grasp. "She's gone, and you can't hurt her anymore."

Henry drew back to slap her, but the defiant look in her eyes stayed his hand. "I'll find her, never fear. And, before long, you'll be only too willing to tell me where she is."

Kassidy shook her head. "Even if I knew, I wouldn't tell you. I'm glad she's gone."

He pushed her back with a force that banged her head against the headboard, and still her eyes defied him. "Father and Mother didn't raise you to be to be so cruel. If you had been kinder to Abigail, she would not have been forced to run away."

"Humph," he snorted. "Little either of you know about my life. Even though you and Abigail have never thanked me for it, I have protected you and given you a home. As for Mother and Father, if they weren't off to Egypt or Florence, they were in India, leaving me to look after you two. Well, they died as they lived, pushing their responsibilities onto me."

"You never see life as it is, Henry. Everything revolves around you. Your conversations start with your wants and end with your needs. You see no joy in life, and you see no good in others. Even your own daughters are frightened of you."

His lower lip trembled with rage. "You're the one who has reason to fear me, missy. You have defied me in everything. I blame your rebellious spirit on Aunt

Mary, who has always encouraged it in you."

"I will always oppose you, Henry. Until the day I die, I'll still defy you."

"But in the end you will lose, Kassidy. I'll never give up until your spirit is broken and I have taught you humility."

With jerking motions, he moved to the door, removed the key, and inserted it on the other side. "I think the day will soon come when you will see things my way. Before I let you out of this room, you will tell me what I want to know."

Kassidy glared at him. "I won't tell you anything, Henry."

After he closed the door, she heard the lock click. A tear lingered at the corner of her eye before it rolled down her cheek. She knew Henry was capable of ruthlessness. But no matter what he did, she would not beg and she would not ask him to free her.

She rubbed her head where a knot was forming. "Some day I'll leave," she whispered, sinking down beneath the warm cover and watching the sun rise over a bank of clouds.

5

The square-rigger, Middlesex, rode the choppy waves on her homeward journey across the English Channel. Raile stood on deck, staring at the gathering mist and feeling strangely subdued, his mood pensive. At long last he was going home, but there was no rejoicing in his heart.

It had been many months since his fellow soldiers had returned to the appreciation of a grateful nation and to be welcomed to the bosoms of their families. There would be no one to welcome this returning hero—no one to care that he had survived his wounds.

The brisk wind that rattled the canvases also ruffled Raile's dark hair. He felt a coldness in his heart, and wondered if it was a mistake to return to England.

"You're still weak, Colonel," Oliver said with concern. "Don't you think it's best for you to go below until we make port? You'll want to be strong enough to attend the many celebrations that will no doubt be held in your honor."

"Don't call me colonel, Oliver. You know I resigned my commission."

"I keep forgetting, sir. We were in His Majesty's service for so long, it's hard to think otherwise."

Raile turned his gaze on his valet. The spry little man was as capable as he was optimistic. He had stayed by Raile's side and encouraged him through the months Raile had lain in bed afflicted with pain so sharp he cried out for death to release him. Oliver had been there to assure him he would not die. There were times when Raile had no will to live, but the little man would not have it so. His steadfastness had given Raile the courage to endure the pain.

During the long convalesence that followed, Raile and Oliver had transcended the barrier that separated a common soldier from an officer, a master from a servant. But on the day he realized Raile was going to live, Oliver once again assumed his role as valet.

Raile was not certain at what moment he began to live again. One morning he had awakened to find the birds singing outside his hospital window and the sweet aroma of honeysuckle filling his nostrils.

Two weeks ago, he had been released from the hospital, and now he was going home.

"You really should go below," Oliver urged once more. "You know since you got that head wound, you've been having headaches. The wind can't do you any good."

"Don't coddle me, Oliver. I spent months in that damned hospital in Brussels. All I want to do is breathe air that doesn't smell of medicine."

Oliver knew it would do no good to press, so he moved on to other matters. "Will we be going straight to Ravenworth Castle, sir?"

Raile's eyes narrowed. "Yes. Unless my uncle has changed his habits, this is the only time of year we can find him in residence there."

Oliver's loyal heart burned with resentment against

the DeWinter family, who had so ill-used his master. He knew that even though the colonel's family had turned away from him, Raile had continued to pay their expenses and had left provision for them in his will. In his eyes, Oliver served a man of selflessness and honor.

"If you will pardon me for saying so, sir, I don't understand why you're going to Ravenworth Castle. You have immense wealth and have won fame as a hero. What do you need with those people?"

The swirling fog thinned, and Raile could see the vague outline of other ships that had docked. He watched the angry waves splash against the shore with an endless motion that had sculpted the ever-changing land. He was silent for so long that Oliver thought he would not answer. But with a twist of his lips, Raile said, "They are my family."

Oliver said nothing more. Raile DeWinter would always follow his convictions, and no one could deter him.

Raile's eyes darkened as he wondered what awaited him at Ravenworth Castle. It had never been in his character to harbor bitterness, but five years was a long time to live in self-imposed exile. Like a man in a trance, he watched the shoreline of England materialize out of the disappearing fog. A hero, Oliver had called him. He had met death and slain his enemies with practiced detachment. Now, he would face his uncle, with far more difficulty.

He pulled his greatcoat about him, feeling suddenly cold. He would rather encounter a dozen enemy soldiers than face the duke.

The morning sky was cloud-capped as the coach crested a hill and slackened its pace to enter the village of Ravenworth. Raile glanced out the window. He had always felt a kinship with the village that belonged to the duchy. He loved the cobblestone streets, the thatched-roof cottages built of local stone. With a feeling of homecoming, he looked at the glass-fronted coaching inn and then at the spiraling steeple of St. Matthew's Church. It was good to be home.

On closer inspection, he noticed that some of the houses needed to be painted and repaired. Apparently the village had deteriorated, as had many English villages since their men had gone off to fight the French.

Raile looked upward at the DeWinter ancestral home. It rose out of the valley like an impregnable fortress, which it had been during many invasions throughout the years. The castle had once been a bastion against attack and a haven for the villagers in time of war and unrest. He was sorry to see that the years had not dealt kindly with the castle. Even from a distance, he could tell that the masonry was crumbling.

When Raile and John were growing up, the tower in the west wing had been closed because it was in danger of collapsing. He was angry to see that the windows were still boarded up. Apparently no work had been done on the castle in all the years he had been gone, even though he had authorized payment for repairs.

In his grandfather's time, Ravenworth Castle and its grounds had been well tended, but his Uncle William had not been a reliable custodian for the family trust. He'd had little liking for the country, preferring to live in London, and his neglect was obvious.

The carriage now angled up the steep grade toward the castle. Raile noticed with annoyance that his uncle's flag was not flying above the battlement, which would mean he must still be in London. How could his uncle talk of family pride, yet allow the ancestral home to fall to ruin?

Oliver was seated opposite Raile, and the servant

nodded in satisfaction. "It's good to be in the country again, sir. I have always found the air here invigorating."

"Yes," Raile agreed as the horses slowed to make the last sheer incline. When they reached the courtyard, they clopped along on cobblestone.

The driver pulled up at the front door. Raile drew in a deep breath.

Oliver moved out the door and folded down the coach steps. As Raile descended, he noticed that the butler stood by the door with a look of sheer bewilderment etched on his face.

"Good afternoon, Ambrose," Raile said to the stiff little man who had been at Ravenworth for as far back as he could recall. "You look like you've seen a ghost. Perhaps you heard about my wounds?"

Ambrose's usual calm slipped even further. "Everyone thought . . . that is . . . we were informed that you were . . . dead. But of course, you aren't."

Raile smiled. "As you can see, I am most certainly alive." He adjusted his coat and climbed upward until he was even with Ambrose. "I take it my uncle is not at home."

There was something strange about the way Ambrose gripped the door handle. "No, sir, but you will find your half brother and your stepmother in the salon."

Distaste made Raile's tone biting. "A fitting homecoming to be sure," he muttered, entering the cool hall of the castle. With determined steps, he moved to the salon.

He opened the door and allowed his gaze to run the length of the room. His stepmother was seated near the window, her head turned expectantly in his direction. He watched the color drain from her face, and she caught her throat as if she could not breathe.

"My God, Raile, what are you doing here?" She came

slowly to her feet, her face ghostly white. "They told us you were dead."

He looked past his stepmother to Hugh, who calmly smiled and said flippantly: "I remember, Mother, when I was just a lad and my nurse told me that ghosts of long dead DeWinters roamed the halls of Ravenworth Castle. Perhaps Raile has joined their numbers."

If there was anyone Raile wanted to avoid, it was Hugh and Lavinia. His voice was devoid of feeling as he asked: "What—no 'welcome home, brother' or 'I am glad to see you'?"

Hugh shrugged. "If I said I was glad to see you, we would both know it would be hypocrisy. You and I have never pretended affection, have we, brother?"

Raile glanced about the room with a puzzled expression on his face. "Where is my uncle?"

A strange look passed between Lavinia and her son. "But surely you must know that your uncle has been dead these past six months," Lavinia replied at last.

Raile felt as if a heavy blow had been delivered to his midsection. It had never occurred to him that his uncle might die while he was away—he had just supposed the duke would live forever.

He had thought all affection for his uncle had died that day five years ago. If that were true, why this heavy sadness? There had been too much left unsaid between him and his uncle, and now it would remain unsaid.

"You knew Uncle William was in ill health," Hugh reminded him, yawning behind his hand. "Even so, there were times when I thought that old man would outlive us all."

Raile was still trying to digest the news of his uncle's death. "That would make John the duke of Ravenworth," he said reflectively. "Where is John?"

A strained expression darkened Hugh's eyes. "Poor Raile. I'm afraid we have more tragic news for you. You see, cousin John was rushing to his father's deathbed when he was set upon by footpads and they robbed him of his purse and his life."

His childhood friend dead—how could that be? "My God, no! Not John."

"It was a pity he died so young," Lavinia said. "Of course, John and I never liked each other, so I won't pretend to grieve for him."

This was not the homecoming Raile had expected. His childhood friend and the man who had been a father to him were both dead. But he was not going to allow Hugh and Lavinia to see his grief.

"So," Raile said grimly, "I now understand why I find you two at the castle instead of merrymaking in London. You fancied yourself to be the duke of Ravenworth, Hugh." He swung his gaze around to his stepmother. "And you, Lavinia, fancied yourself as lady of the manor. I can see where my appearance might cause you dismay."

He threw back his head and laughed deeply, at last finding a bit of humor in the tragic situation. "Yes. I can see why I would not be welcomed by you, dear brother. You thought I was dead—but since I still live, *I'm* the duke of Ravenworth!"

Lavinia stared at Raile with loathing in her eyes. "Well, your grace," she drawled insolently, "I suppose you will be wanting me and my son to leave."

Raile unbuttoned his red tunic, suddenly weary. "It matters little to me what you do, Lavinia. But no, I will not cast you out. We are all that remains of the family, and I will take care of you as I always have."

6

Raile had been summoned to Carlton House by the Prince of Wales who, since his father's madness, governed the nation as regent. The letter from the prince had been full of praise for what he called "gallantry against enormous odds."

Raile knew Prinny well enough to realize the King's son would make a public spectacle of the afternoon and he did not relish the event. In fact, at this time he'd had no wish to leave Ravenworth Castle and make the journey to London. But one did not ignore a command from Prinny.

From the torchlit portico, Raile was led forward by a liveried servant. As they made their way through ornate suites of rooms, each seemingly grander than the one preceding, they came at last to the Blue Velvet Room, which was the prince's audience chamber.

Raile remembered the many evenings he had spent here in frivolous amusement. Strange, he thought, how much older he felt than the prince, who must be almost fifty by now.

The room was buzzing with loud conversations and

even louder laughter. Prinny's amusement-seeking disciples, Raile thought in disgust. He had once been among those favored few who hung about the prince, but he could no longer find enjoyment in their trivial pleasures.

Raile's feet sunk into the blue-gray rug as he was announced by the servant who had led him to the prince.

Prinny came forward, wearing a field marshal's uniform. He had a jeweled saber strapped about his bulky waist. It had always been his wish to cover himself with military honors. On his chest, he wore the numerous medals which had been presented to him by allied sovereigns.

Eagerly he greeted Raile, who by contrast, was dressed in black, but for the white lace at his throat.

"It seems we have a genuine hero here," the prince announced as Raile bowed to him. "England is proud of her heroes, Raile—we are very proud of you."

"I thank you, Your Highness," Raile said as his old friends gathered around to add their welcome to the prince's.

The prince was momentarily distracted by a messenger who required his attention, so Raile turned to Lord Justin Callaret, who had served with him in Portugal and had been his friend for many years.

"Raile, we haven't seen much of you in London since your return."

"I find I have little liking for the old life," Raile said in a low voice, so only Lord Justin could hear. "You are better suited to this than I."

Lord Justin glanced about to see if he would be overheard. "Not so much as you might think. After being in battle and knowing I could die at any moment, I find I have changed my opinion on what's important in life."

Prinny now turned his attention back to Raile. He spoke in a voice that held little enthusiasm, as if he had performed this duty many times before. "We made Wellington a duke, Raile, for his services to his country, but since you have already obtained that rank, Parliament has asked that I convey its thanks to you in grants worth one hundred thousand pounds. Likewise, Prussia has recognized your courage and has granted you the equivalent of an additional one hundred thousand pounds."

There was a gasp from one of the women present, and the others applauded to show their acknowledgment of the generosity of the victorious nations to a gallant hero.

Ever the actor, Prinny warmed to his role as benefactor. "In a ceremony tomorrow," he boomed so that all could hear, "you will be given the Order of the Garter, and the Prussian ambassador wishes to bestow on you that country's highest honor."

Again Raile bowed. "You are most gracious, Your Highness."

Prinny waved his hand to an attendant. "Bring wine, this is thirsty business." He smiled at Raile. "I always knew you were a man who would distinguish himself. You have not disappointed me."

"I surprised the hell out of myself, Your Highness," Raile said dryly.

Prinny laughed loudly. "Walk with me in the gallery, Raile. I would like to hear about your famous advance that day at Waterloo."

As they moved away, Raile spoke. "I try not to remember that day, Your Highness. As a matter of fact, much of what happened is a blur."

"I always thought I would have had a brilliant military career, had I been born a common soldier and not been burdened with this irksome responsibility of governing," the prince said regretfully. "Don't you agree?"

He waited expectantly for Raile to give the right response.

Even though the prince had a good mind and had mastered three languages, and introduced poets and artists to the court, he was somehow childlike, needing praise and acceptance.

"Indeed, Your Highness. But I fancy you would have made a better strategist than common soldier."

The prince's eyes brightened. "Yes, I would have. Wellington made many mistakes I would never have committed. He had several opportunities to press the advantage and stop Bonaparte in one blow."

Raile had once found Prinny a humorous companion; he now found him sadly lacking in the qualities that would make a great king. He would always need to be flattered and coddled, and Raile would show him the respect due his rank, but he would no longer be one of his followers.

"Your Highness, it was a brilliant move to place Wellington in command," Raile replied candidly. "The measure of a great man is to surround himself with men of great vision."

Prinny was thoughtful for a moment. "I have missed your wise counsel, Raile. You were always honest with me. I have a mind to install you in my cabinet."

"Not I, Your Highness. I would not take well to court life. I am more for the country."

"You have not always thought so."

"I have changed, Your Highness. I have no stomach for politics."

The prince nodded. "Perhaps not. But I miss having you near, Raile. You spend so little time in London."

"I have found that Ravenworth Castle will need my attention for some time to come."

There was a pout on Prinny's lips. "I suppose you will honor us with an occasional visit."

"Whenever I can, Your Highness."

Prinny's eyes took on a cunning glow. "I was wondering when you would take a wife, Raile. We would not like to see an old and respected title slip into less, shall we say, capable hands. I would not like your half brother to stand in your stead." His eyes suddenly grew cold. "Do I make myself clear, Raile?"

Raile knew the prince had just issued him an order. Damn his interference. He had no wish to clutter his life with a wife at the moment. "Quite clear, Your Highness."

"Next time you appear before us, we will expect to meet your duchess."

Raile bowed. "It will be as you wish, Your Highness," he said, thinking it would be a long time before he returned.

Prinny looked down his imperial nose at Raile. "See that it is."

Raile watched the prince walk away, feeling anger in his heart. Justin came over to him as the prince moved among the crowd, expecting, and receiving, adoration.

"God help England," Justin whispered.

"England has survived much worse," Raile said. "She will survive him as well."

Justin smiled at Raile. "Did the prince ask that you get married?"

"How did you know?"

"He said as much to us before you arrived."

Raile looked at his friend with bitterness. "How is it that he does not condemn you to wedded bliss?"

"I have never been one of his favorites. And I stay just out of his reach. Besides, Raile, I'm not a hero," he said mockingly.

Justin laughed as Raile glared at him. "I will be happy to have you safely married, though."

"I'm not married yet," Raile declared with ill humor. "Nor do I have any prospects. Where does one find a wife?"

"Why don't you ask your ladybird?" Justin said glibly. "Though I doubt if she knows any schoolroom misses. And then when you're married, and setting up your own nursery, I'll see that Gabrielle Candeur is never lonely."

"If you think you can take her from me, Justin, you have my leave to try. Of course, you will have to mend your roguish ways."

"My character is beyond rehabilitation, Raile. And Gabrielle is not for me anyway—I can ill afford the diamonds it takes to keep your actress happy."

Raile pushed his friend aside. "Have your little jest, Justin. I am off for more amiable company."

Justin's laughter followed Raile across the room.

Raile was scowling when he took leave of the prince.

Kassidy dabbed at the perspiration on her forehead with the sleeve of her gown. The heat in the small kitchen was unbearable, and it became worse when she stood over a boiling pot, stirring the redolent liquid.

Her sister-in-law was heavy with her third child. She insisted that only Kassidy could make the oil of rose that she needed to continuously rub on her swollen body.

Kassidy added white beeswax to the bubbling anhydrous lotion. She then measured several drops each of rose water, lavender, eucalyptus, essential oil, and peppermint. She removed the heavy pot from the fire and set it aside to cool while she folded linens.

Her thoughts turned to Abigail as they always did when she was alone. Henry had been unsuccessful in his attempts to locate her, and in a predictably spiteful fashion had forbidden the mere mention of Abigail's name in his house.

Kassidy had only received one letter from her sister, and

that had come through Aunt Mary. Abigail had written how happy she was with her husband. They lived in a small cottage near the banks of the Thames River, and as soon as she was able, she would send for Kassidy.

Kassidy could hear her two nieces' laughter as she folded the linens. She quickly opened the door and caught their attention. "You must play in the garden at the back of the house," she told them, feeling sorry for interrupting their game. "You know your mother has asked you not to make noise when she is trying to rest."

"Can you play with us, Aunt Kassidy?" the elder one asked.

"Yes, please," the younger urged.

"I can't just now. But if you are good and play quietly, I'll have tea with you this afternoon."

The girls readily agreed and went bounding around the side of the house, and Kassidy returned to her chores.

She was about to climb the stairs, her arms piled high with linens, when her sister-in-law called out to her from the sitting room. She placed the laundry on a hall table and went in to Patricia, who was laying on the settee, a damp rag on her forehead.

"Are you ill?" Kassidy wanted to know.

"Of course I'm ill, Kassidy. How would you feel if you were heavy with child and you had to contend with this stifling heat? You could at least keep the children quiet," she criticized. "I shall have to tell Henry that they have misbehaved."

"Don't do that, Patricia. I've sent them to play in the garden. Their noise won't bother you again."

There was a pinched look about her sister-in-law's face. "Don't think I haven't noticed that my daughters prefer to be with you instead of me," she said peevishly.

"That's not true, Patricia. I am just taking more of the responsibility for them until your baby is born."

Patricia sighed. "It's a woman's lot in life to bear children for an ungrateful husband," she said sanctimoniously.

Kassidy was in no mood to hear Patricia's complaints. She removed the cloth, rewet it, and placed it back on her sister-in-law's forehead. "You just rest now. I'll see that the children don't disturb you."

"Bring me a glass of lemonade, but mind that you don't get it too sweet. And bring me a vanilla cake, but scrape the icing off. I've told cook repeatedly I don't tolerate sugar when I'm with child. It makes me ill."

Kassidy moved out of the room and closed the door. It was hard for her to have sympathy for Patricia when all she did was rest while Kassidy took care of the house and children.

She heard an insistent knock on the door, and wondered crossly why the servants had not answered it. With a feeling of impatience, she opened the door to find a man standing there. He was a stranger to her.

"Be you Miss Kassidy Maragon?" he asked, eyeing her speculatively.

"Yes, I am."

"I was told to put this only into your hands, miss." He thrust the letter at her. "I'll wait for you at the crossroads until an hour after dark." He tipped his hat and left abruptly, to climb into a buggy and drive away.

What a strange man, she thought. She stared down at the letter and recognized Abigail's handwriting. She quickly thrust the letter into her apron pocket and hurried to the privacy of her room to read it.

Tearing open the letter, she read:

Dearest Kassidy,
The man who delivers this to you is named Tetch. He and his wife work for us, and he is completely trustworthy. I only hope this letter reaches

you in time. I am going to have a baby any day now, and I need you urgently. Please come at once. I am desperate, dearest—please hurry.

Kassidy quickly rushed to the window, where she could just see the crossroads. Yes, the man was waiting there as he had said. Without considering the consequences, she threw open the carved wooden box her father had given her for her twelfth birthday. There, nestled among her treasures, was the money she had saved over the years. It wasn't much, but she had a feeling she would need it.

If she asked Henry to allow her to go to Abigail, he would only refuse. Besides, he would not be home until later in the evening, and Abigail's letter had said she must hurry.

After scribbling a note for Henry, she placed it on her pillow. She would just slip out of the house before he returned. No one could keep her from Abigail when her sister needed her.

Kassidy hurriedly changed into her Sunday gown and shoes. She folded her only other good gown and placed it in a straw basket with the money and a few other items she thought she might need on her journey. If anyone saw her leave, it would appear that she was only going to the market.

Putting on her bonnet, Kassidy went downstairs. She could hear Patricia calling her, and she realized she had forgotten about the lemonade and cake her sister-in-law had demanded.

Running quickly into the kitchen, she gave the cook Patricia's instructions. She then went into the garden to her nieces. She hugged them both. "Remember I love you," she told them. Her arms tightened about ten-year-old Trudy. "Take care of your little sister."

"I will Aunt Kassidy. But why?"

"Because she isn't strong like you."

Kassidy stood up, knowing she must not make the girls suspicious. In their innocence, they might alert their mother, and she had to be far away before Henry came home.

Kassidy hurried through the garden, her gaze on the distant road. Fear gnawed at her insides. Suppose Henry came back before she could get away?

When she approached the buggy, the man hopped to the ground and assisted her inside. "Miss Maragon, I'm glad you've come. Your sister needs you awful bad."

She felt tension tighten inside her. "Is she ill?"

"I don't know much about women's ailments, miss, but your sister's been feeling poorly. Me and the missus was hired to look after her until her husband returned. But he's been gone these past six months."

He whipped the horses forward. "She'll be better with family about her, miss."

At first Kassidy kept looking over her shoulder, fearing Henry would come after them. But as they left the village behind, her fear lessened.

For two days they traveled, stopping at night in secluded inns, where Kassidy gave a false name, because she knew by now Henry would be searching for her. She watched in apprehension as her savings dwindled. She had no idea travel could be so expensive. It was almost midnight of the third day when Tetch guided the horses into a small stable and nodded at Kassidy.

"Your sister be in the house, miss." He swung her to the ground. "You can go right on in."

Kassidy hurried toward the house, where Mrs. Tetch stood on the steps, a lantern in her hand. "I'm so glad you're here. I fear her labor has started."

"Take me to her at once," Kassidy said.

The servant nodded and led the way upstairs.

Kassidy's mind was filled with questions that she

could not ask Tetch or his wife. Although the house was neat, it was not the home of "a man of great importance," as Abigail had described the man she was to marry.

The housekeeper showed Kassidy into a bedroom and bobbed a curtsy. "If you need anything, miss, I'll be right downstairs."

There was a single candle burning in the room. Slowly, she approached the bed, hardly daring to breathe. "Abigail," she whispered, "are you awake?"

"Kassidy!" Abigail cried, raising her arms. "I knew you would come."

Kassidy dropped down beside her, and they cried in each other's arms. "I'm here, dearest. Everything will be all right now."

"Oh, Kassidy, the baby is coming, and I didn't want to be alone."

Kassidy looked about the sparsely furnished room. "Where is your husband?"

Abigail laced her fingers through her sister's. "He had to go away for a time, but he will return very soon."

"Let me send for him."

"I don't know where he is," Abigail admitted sadly. "I know he would be here if he knew his child was about to be born."

When Abigail saw the anger in Kassidy's eyes, she said softly: "Don't judge him harshly, Kassidy. He didn't know I was going to have a baby."

Kassidy closed her eyes as she held Abigail to her. She would not speak the angry words that choked her. No matter what Abigail said, her husband should be with her.

7

The vine-covered, thatched-roof cottage was nestled in a secluded vale just out of sight of the winding Thames. The noonday sun had reached its zenith, and it was stifling hot within the walls of the cottage.

The stillness was broken by the movements of Mrs. Tetch, who rushed to the well to draw a pail of water, then quickly retraced her steps.

In the upstairs bedroom, Abigail writhed in pain. Her golden hair was damp as it spilled across the pillow; her body was wet with perspiration as she labored in agony to bring forth her child.

Kassidy dampened a cloth and applied it to Abigail's forehead. "Don't worry, dearest, I am here with you."

Abigail licked her dry lips and looked at Kassidy with apprehension in her eyes. "In this you cannot help me. But stay beside me, and I shall borrow your strength, as I always have."

"Be brave, Abigail," Kassidy said, wishing her own heart was not racing with fear. Kassidy didn't know what to do to help her sister. "The midwife will be here soon. She will know how to help you."

"Oh, Kassidy, it hurts so dreadfully." Abigail's voice trembled with fear. She rolled on the bed, her eyes wild with pain. "Help me, Kassidy," she cried over and over, as the pain intensified. "Help me bear the pain."

Kassidy pushed a damp lock of hair from her sister's forehead. "If only I could take your pain upon myself, I would do so, Abigail."

"The baby will soon be born," she gasped. "I am told that when mothers hold their babies, they forget about the suffering."

Abigail gripped Kassidy's hand as intense pain ripped through her body once more.

"Whoever told you that was an idiot," Kassidy muttered. She watched Abigail's eyes close until the pain finally subsided.

"You are so good to me," Abigail murmured. "What would I do without you? I have missed you so much."

"We shan't ever be parted again," Kassidy said fiercely. "Now go to sleep while you can. You are going to need all your strength."

Slowly Abigail's eyes closed, and she fell into an exhausted sleep, while Kassidy tearfully stared down at her.

Abigail had been laboring since before midnight, and it was now almost sundown of the next day.

Kassidy was beginning to fear for her sister's life. She had very little knowledge of childbearing, but surely this was taking an unusually long time? If only the midwife would come. She had sent for her hours ago. What could be keeping her?

She dropped into a chair, but still retained her grip on Abigail's hand. She had sent Tetch to London to fetch Aunt Mary—she would surely know what to do.

Perhaps it was fortunate that Abigail's husband was not here, Kassidy thought. If he was, she would surely make him aware of her anger, and that would only upset Abigail. What kind of man would impregnate his wife and then leave her to have his baby alone?

Kassidy tried not to think of the unborn child; she only thought about Abigail and the pain she must endure.

Abigail groaned in her sleep, and Kassidy went to her side.

A slight breeze stirred the lace curtains, but it brought little relief from the oppressive heat, so Kassidy picked up a lace fan and swept the air. The door opened a crack, and a white-headed woman peered at them. Shoving the door wide, she ambled in. She was stooped and frail, her face was creased with wrinkles, but there was kindness in her faded blue eyes.

"I'm Maude Perkins, the midwife, come to help. I couldn't come sooner, 'cause there's been two other babies I delivered since I got word from you." With a quick assessment of the situation, she nodded. "She's laboring hard. How long's she been this way?"

Kassidy's eyes were pleading. "For seventeen hours. She seems to be resting now." There was a catch in Kassidy's voice. "Please help her."

The wise old eyes blinked. "I know about her situation. Do you want me to allow nature to steer the course, or shall I hurry it along a bit?"

Kassidy swallowed a painful lump in her throat. "I don't know anything about birth. You'll have to do as you think best."

Maude nodded. "There's a Lady Mary below. She asked that I send you down at once. You go ahead on. I'll stay with your sister."

Kassidy was relieved to know that Aunt Mary was there, but she was reluctant to leave Abigail. "I promised to stay with her."

Maude placed her pack on the floor and nodded to the door. "Little good you'll do her if you're done in. Get you down and fortify yourself. If your sister wants you, I'll let you know."

Kassidy lightly touched her sister's cheek. "She's of a delicate nature." Her eyes met the old woman's. "Will she . . . do you think she . . ."

"I've been in this situation many times. I've hardly ever lost the mother."

There was something about Maude Perkins that inspired trust. "Call me if she asks for me."

"Have I not said I would?"

Kassidy tiptoed out of the room and went down the stairs and into the sitting room. She rushed forward to be enfolded in the comforting arms of her Aunt Mary.

"I came as quickly as I could. How's Abigail, dear?"

"I'm frightened for her, Aunt Mary. I never realized the pain involved in giving birth."

"It's nothing to worry about. Women have babies every day, Kassidy. I had a daughter myself."

"And Patricia is having her third child."

Aunt Mary's lip turned up in distaste. "Little wonder you are so concerned. I'm sure Patricia complains all day about her condition. But let's not dwell on her. Let me look at you." She smiled, shaking her head in approval. "You have turned into a beauty, just as I knew you would."

"I'm told I look like you."

"And so you do," Lady Mary said, with a twinkle in her eye.

Lady Mary studied her favorite niece. Kassidy had indeed inherited the wild Scottish beauty of the MacIvor clan. Within her burned the pride and fire of ancient Scottish chieftains. Her aunt recognized the strength of character reflected in those flashing green eyes. Kassidy, she thought with pride, would never bow to anyone's will unless she was forced to do so.

Kassidy's gaze went to the stairs. "I can't seem to think of anything but Abigail. I wish I was lying in that bed instead of Abigail."

Her aunt set a steaming cup of tea before her. "You would never have found yourself in Abigail's circumstances. I'm concerned for her also. But it's time you realize that you can't always protect her. Where is her husband?"

"I don't know. I don't even know who he is, or I'd send for him."

"None of us knows him. I have been to the cottage several times, but he was never here. When I pressed Abigail to tell me his name, she always refused."

"I find this all very strange." Kassidy heard a muffled scream. She was about to rise, when her aunt stopped her.

"Mrs. Tetch told me you have not eaten all day. I insist you do so now," she said, handing Kassidy a plate piled with food. "If we are needed, the midwife will let us know."

"Abigail isn't strong, Aunt Mary."

"She's not strong because you always prop her up and allow her to use your strength. At times I feared she would use you all up, Kassidy."

"But after Mother and Father died, she had no one but me. She needs someone to rely on. I had hoped she found those qualities in her husband—apparently she did not."

"You both lost your parents, and yet you only grew stronger, while she relied on you more and more. I love her as much as you do, but I also worry about you, Kassidy. If I know anything, you have put yourself at odds with Henry and you'll be made to suffer over this."

"It doesn't matter. Henry couldn't have stopped me from coming to Abigail when she needed me. But the one she really needs is her husband. When he does return, I'll deal with him harshly."

Aunt Mary thought Kassidy looked like an avenging angel. But she also looked tired, as if she had fought one battle too many.

Kassidy took a deep breath and pushed the food away. Standing up, she rubbed her aching back and stretched her tired muscles. "I should return to Abigail."

Lady Mary glanced up at the clock. "I am sorry to say that I have to return to London within the hour. I am holding a gala tonight for George's birthday and must not be late since the prince will be in attendance. I'll be back tomorrow afternoon. Unless, of course, you think Abigail needs me before then."

Kassidy did not want her aunt to leave, but the midwife had not been concerned about the birth. "I'll send word to you as soon as the child is born. And give Uncle George my love."

Lady Mary stood up and adjusted her silk bonnet. "Try not to worry, my dear."

Kassidy walked her aunt to her coach and watched until she was out of sight. Then, she slowly climbed the stairs with dread in her heart, and feeling strangely alone.

Kassidy looked from Abigail's swollen stomach to her beautiful face that was distorted with agony. She felt every pain that racked her sister's body in the very depths of her own soul. Tears blinded her as she stood beside Maude.

"The labor's turned bad," Maude informed her grimly. "The baby's turned sideways, and I'll have to try and turn it back. I don't know if I can save either one of them."

"Help her," Kassidy pleaded. "Please help my sister."

Maude looked grim. "Keep your wits about you, 'cause I'm going to need your help."

Kassidy swallowed her fear, knowing she must appear unafraid for Abigail. "Just tell me what to do, and I'll do it."

Three hours passed while Maude worked over Abigail. By now Abigail was too weak to do more than moan.

Kassidy glanced at Maude's bloody hands and shivered. The white bed sheets were stained with blood, and Abigail was colorless.

"The baby is killing her, Maude. I know it is!" Kassidy cried out.

Moments later, a weak, puny cry penetrated the room as Abigail's baby drew its first breath.

"'Tis a daughter," Maude said matter-of-factly, wiping the child off before wrapping her in a white blanket.

Kassidy turned her full attention to her sister, while Maude continued ministering to the child. Dropping down on her knees, she grasped Abigail's limp hand.

Abigail's eyes were closed and her breathing was labored and shallow.

"The pain is over, dearest," Kassidy said, even though she knew Abigail could not hear.

She glanced up at Maude. "She is going to be all right now—isn't she?"

Maude shook her head sadly. "The loss of blood was too great. But the child appears healthy."

Kassidy buried her face against the soft bed and rolled her head from side to side. "I care not for the child. I only want my sister to live."

At that moment, she felt a hand touch her hair and she raised her head. "Poor Kassidy," Abigail whispered in a weak voice. "You cannot hold death at bay for me."

Kassidy licked her dry lips. "Don't say that. I won't let you die."

Abigail sighed. "If it were possible, you would even battle death for me. You have been my strength and I have been your weakness."

"Don't talk—just rest."

"My baby?"

"A girl," Kassidy said woodenly.

"Will she . . . is she . . . ."

Maude held the baby out for Abigail's inspection. "She's small, but hearty."

Abigail sadly placed a kiss on the baby's lips, then her eyes fluttered as she blinked away tears. She knew this would be the only time she would touch her baby. "Look after her, as you have looked after me, Kassidy. She will need your guidance."

Kassidy's mind felt severed from the pain and sadness she was experiencing. She knew Abigail was dying. "Don't talk such nonsense. You will take care of her yourself when you're stronger."

Maude cradled the baby in her arms and discreetly moved to the door. "I'll be below when you need me."

"I feel so weak . . . Kassidy. I don't want to leave you and my baby. And her father . . . will be so proud of his . . . daughter."

Suddenly Kassidy's fear exploded into anger. "Think you he will care?"

"You . . . don't know him, Kassidy. I am sorry that the two of you never met." She stopped to catch her breath. "You would have liked each other."

Kassidy saw the effort it was costing Abigail to talk. "I won't have you upsetting yourself. Just rest for now, and we shall talk about this later."

Abigail tried to rise, but fell back gasping.

"Please . . . listen to me . . . ."

A spasm of grief contracted Kassidy's heart. "If I agree to listen, will you rest afterward?"

Abigail stared at her sister. "I will rest afterward." She closed her eyes for just a moment, and a lone tear trailed down her cheek. "You don't understand. Even . . . with my dying breath I love him."

Kassidy saw anguish in her sister's eyes and it was difficult for her to hide the loathing she felt for Abigail's husband.

"Don't hate him, Kassidy. He didn't know about the baby. He had grave family matters to attend to, so I didn't want him to be burdened with worry about me."

"I care not about his worries or his family. But tell me who he is."

"I hesitate to name him."

"But why?"

Abigail blinked her eyes, trying to clear her vision. "I suppose it doesn't matter now. I will tell you. He is the . . . duke of Ravenworth," she said at last, her eyes begging for understanding. "He loves me, and he will be happy about the baby—you'll see."

Kassidy had never heard of the duke, but it was hard for her to believe a man of such high rank would keep his wife in such straitened circumstances.

Anger burned in her heart for the man who had hidden her sister away. Although the Maragon family had no great wealth, their lineage was a long and honorable one. Abigail was the daughter of a viscount, and the granddaughter of a Scottish laird. Surely she was good enough for the mighty duke of Ravenworth.

Kassidy's eyes fastened on her sister's chest, and she was aware that Abigail's breathing was labored and shallow.

"Take the baby to him, at Ravenworth Castle, Kassidy. I want her to be with her father, but you must see her as often as you can." She blinked back her tears. "She will need you, just as I have always needed you."

Kassidy was unable to answer because of the aching throb in her throat. Tears streamed down her face and fell hotly against her clasped hands.

"Promise me . . . Kassidy."

The words were wrenched out of Kassidy. "I promise."

A calm settled over Abigail's features. "I am . . . contented." And with that, she drew in a long shuddering breath and her body went limp.

An anguished cry tore from Kassidy's lips.

"No, God, please no! Don't take Abigail from me."

Kassidy stayed beside her dead sister throughout the night, crying tears of grief. When the sun came up, she sent Tetch to deliver the tragic news to Aunt Mary.

She refused Maude's offer to prepare her sister for burial. Kassidy insisted on dressing Abigail in her finest gown. She then brushed her golden hair until it shone. She crossed Abigail's hands over her chest, and kissed her cold lips. She was as beautiful in death as she had been in life. Kassidy prayed that her sweet sister had found peace at last.

With a last long look at Abigail, she descended the stairs to find the baby. Without looking on the face of the child, she picked her up and turned to Maude.

"When my aunt arrives, tell her I have taken the baby to her father. She will make all the arrangements for my sister's"—tears brightened her eyes, and she choked them back—"my sister's burial."

Maude nodded, her shrewd eyes seeing past the young girl's hurt. "I overheard you and your sister talking. If you are to take the baby on a journey, you will need help."

"If you heard the conversation, perhaps you can tell me who the duke of Ravenworth is."

"I know only what I've heard, and that is he's the head of the powerful DeWinter family. I had thought him an old man, but I must be mistaken if he fathered your sister's child."

For the first time, Kassidy looked at the baby. Golden curls, so like Abigail's, covered the child's head, and the likeness stabbed Kassidy with renewed grief. Even though she tried, Kassidy could not blame the helpless infant for her sister's death. But she did not want to love this child if she had to give her up.

She held the baby tightly, steeling herself against a second loss.

"You'll need a wet nurse," Maude said, catching her attention again. "I know a trustworthy woman who just might be willing to accompany you on your journey."

"Will you arrange it for me?"

The old woman nodded. "I suppose you'll be using the public coach."

"I have no choice. Tetch has taken the buggy and I am not certain when he will return. I must leave at once."

"You will not stay to see your sister buried?"

Kassidy looked at the floor because she could not look into the midwife's eyes. "I have already said my farewell to my sister."

"Then I'll see that Heloise Gibbins meets you at the coaching inn within the hour."

The midwife moved to the door, slipping her bag over her shoulder.

"Is it far to Ravenworth Castle?" Kassidy wanted to know.

Maude pursed her lips and said in a ponderous voice, "For you, it could turn out to be a journey without end."

"What do you mean?"

The old woman shrugged. "I mean nothing. But have a care. You cannot just walk up to a duke and present him with a child."

Kassidy's eyes blazed with a determined light. "Oh, can I not? We shall just see about that. He may be a man of great wealth and power, but I will make him do right by this child."

8

Kassidy had spent four uncomfortable days in an overcrowded public conveyance. She was angry when she stepped down from the coach in the village of Ravenworth. She had very little money, and it would take most of that to pay the wet nurse and for food and lodging. She only hoped she would have enough for the coach fare home.

With Mrs. Gibbins at her side, Kassidy crossed the street and headed toward the Blue Feather Posting Inn, with the intention of finding a room so she could tidy up before setting off for the castle.

She looked up at the imposing fortress that dominated the small village, and for the first time, she felt fear lurking at the edge of her mind. But she must not give way to that fear, or she could not fulfill Abigail's wish. Her strongest emotion, grief, she would give in to later. She must call on all her strength to get her through the next few hours without weeping for Abigail.

Looking at the steep incline that led to the castle, she considered for the first time that the duke might not be at home. Then her journey would have been in vain.

Her gaze moved to the battlement of the castle, and she saw with relief that his flag was flying, proclaiming he was in residence.

A horrifying thought struck her. Suppose the reason the duke had wanted his identity kept a secret was that he already had a wife. What if he had tricked Abigail into believing he had married her when he really hadn't? Would he even want to acknowledge the baby?

How could she place Abigail's baby in the hands of such a monster?

Raile moved the length of his study, considering how much there was to be done to the castle to make it livable. And there were numerous other responsibilities that went with the dukedom, but had been neglected for many years. At times he wished the title and lands had fallen to Hugh, so he would be free of the burden.

He sat down at the heavy oak desk, his gaze moving along the dusty bookshelves. The neglect had even extended to this room. Old and valuable books would have to be rebound, or they would crumble to dust. It might even be too late to save some of them.

When the rap came at the door, he glanced up at Ambrose with annoyance. He had given instructions that he was not to be disturbed.

"Begging your pardon, your grace," Ambrose said apologetically, "but there is a young woman at the front door demanding to see you. I told her you were not receiving today, but she insists that she will not leave until she speaks with you."

"Did she give her name?"

"No, your grace, she refused."

"Did she give any indication what she wanted?" he asked, irritably.

"No, your grace. She would not say. But she did ask

if you were married or had any children."

"I suppose it's another villager wanting a position," Raile sighed in exasperation. "Have Mrs. Fitzwilliams tend to the woman."

"I would not have brought the matter to your grace's attention, but she seems to be a lady. She's accompanied by a servant, and an infant, I believe."

Raile thought of the paperwork that needed his attention. Since attempting to restore the castle, his days were filled with one crisis after another. If it wasn't the gardener complaining about blight killing the grass, or the housekeeper insisting she did not have enough help, it was Hugh and his mother. And if that wasn't enough, the workmen were awaiting their instructions so they could begin their day.

With resignation, he nodded to Ambrose. "I'll see her. But make it clear that I have very little time to spend with her."

With growing trepidation, Kassidy glanced about the imposing great hall with its high, ornate gesso ceilings. The room was enriched with colored glass and mullioned windows. Arras of gold and silk decorated the oak-paneled walls.

At one time the castle must have been magnificent, but now it seemed to be suffering from neglect. There was a musty smell that pervaded the air. The carvings on the woodwork were chipped, and the once valuable silk tapestries were in tatters. It was a pity such a lovely old castle had been allowed to fall into ruin, she thought.

In her mind the condition of the room represented the man she now hated. He seemed to care neither for people nor possessions.

The butler returned and motioned for Kassidy to

accompany him. "His grace has kindly agreed to see you. But you must understand that he is a busy man."

Kassidy took the baby from the wet nurse and instructed the woman to wait for her. Then she stiffly followed the butler out of the great hall, across a worn Turkish carpet, and down an arched hallway.

What would she say to the duke when she confronted him?

Her footsteps lagged when the butler paused before a thick oak door.

"Go right in. His grace is expecting you."

With the baby clutched to her like a shield, Kassidy advanced with the fervor of a charging warrior.

She stopped short as a burst of sunlight streamed into the room from the floor-to-ceiling windows, blinding her for a moment. When her eyes adjusted to the light, she saw her enemy sitting at a massive oak desk, watching her progress with bored indifference.

Kassidy felt her anger increase with each step that brought her nearer to the man she loathed. She had not expected the duke to be so dark since the baby was so fair. His dark eyes were like needles, boring into her. A cynical twist to his mouth told her he scoffed at life. She was further enraged when he did not show her the courtesy of rising when she entered the room, but merely nodded to the chair in front of his desk.

"Madame, I am told you insisted on seeing me." He glanced at the mantel clock as if to show his impatience. "I have little time, so if you could state your reason for being here, it would be appreciated."

"It's 'miss,' not 'madame.'" Her voice had come out low, and trembled with the conflicting emotions she was feeling. "I am unmarried."

He glanced at the baby. "Excuse my mistake, Miss . . . ?"

"Miss Maragon."

He was reflective for a moment. "Some years ago, I

met Lord Henry Maragon. Is he a relative of yours?"

Kassidy glared at him. Why had he not mentioned that he also knew Abigail Maragon? The devil was even more devious than she had expected. "Yes," she said defiantly. "Henry is my brother."

"I see," Raile answered, still mystified.

"Do you? I doubt it."

He frowned at her biting tone. "Then perhaps you should enlighten me."

Totally bewildered, Raile assessed her carefully. She was young, perhaps seventeen or eighteen. It was difficult to tell much about her because her hair was hidden beneath a wide-brimmed straw bonnet that also hid most of her forehead. She was thin, and her gown was outdated, and he could see it had been mended on the sleeves.

"Don't tell me you don't know who I am," Kassidy challenged.

He looked into her magnificent green eyes, and some vague memory stirred to life. In the recesses of his mind he remembered eyes like hers, but he could not remember when they might have met. There was an air of pride about her, but he also detected defiance. When he looked deeply into those eyes, he sensed an anger that he did not understand.

"You say you are Lord Maragon's sister. How may I be of service to you, Miss Maragon?"

His liquid brown eyes were mesmerizing. Kassidy could see how Abigail had been attracted to this man with his broad shoulders and his dark good looks. But he wasn't going to deceive her as he had Abigail—she knew his true character.

She thrust the baby forward. "Here, your grace, this baby is your responsibility," she blurted out, watching his face for his reaction. She saw only a slight dilation of his dark eyes. Here was a man, she thought furiously, who was schooled in masking his emotions. Most probably he was accustomed to spreading his seed about indiscriminately. Well, he wasn't going to turn his back on Abigail's daughter.

He towered above her. "I don't know what you are about, Miss Maragon—if that is truly your name—but I assure you that you cannot pass off your . . . indiscretions on me. We both know I never fathered a child by you."

She gasped and stepped back a pace. Was he mad? Oh, he was black-hearted.

"I can assure you that I am not duped by your tactics. This child is yours, and I place her in your keeping. You have not even asked about the pain and suffering it took to give her birth."

The duke was shocked. "Miss Maragon, I don't think we should be discussing these matters." He moved around the desk to stand beside her. "Perhaps it would be best if you leave now. Then we shall both forget this has ever happened. Go home to the young gentleman who got you with child and beseech him to make you his wife."

He had spoken softly, but there was a hardness in his voice.

"Oh, you are clever, your grace. I can see that I must force you to accept your responsibility."

In a movement that surprised him, she thrust the child into his arms and rushed toward the door. "I have brought a woman who is willing to stay on as wet nurse until you can find someone to replace her."

Her footsteps were hurried, but she paused at the door, trying to choke back tears. "She . . . is only five days old. I didn't name her because I thought you might want to choose her name. She's . . . a good baby and hardly ever cries. Please take care of her."

Raile was speechless.

He started to go after the woman, but at that moment, the baby let out a loud cry, stopping him in his tracks. He had never held a baby in his arms, and he stared at the child helplessly, fearing he would drop it.

Blinded by tears, Kassidy fled before she gave in to the urge to snatch the baby from the duke's arms. When she reached the great hall, she paused for only a moment before the wet nurse and dropped some coins in her hand. "Please take care of the baby," she said, and turned quickly to the door.

"Leave at once," she told the driver, as she climbed into the hired coach and slammed the door. Her heart was thundering inside her. She was afraid the duke would send someone after her.

As the coach lurched forward with a jerk, Kassidy looked back at the castle. After a while, she lost some of her apprehension. Apparently the duke did not intend to pursue her.

With a loud sob, Kassidy buried her face in her hands. She had never expected it to be so painful to leave the baby. But she had kept her promise, and that was all she could do.

In giving up the child, she felt as if she had severed her last link with her beloved sister.

She lay her head against the seat and sobbed out her misery. She cried for Abigail, she cried for the baby, and she cried for herself.

9

When Ambrose came rushing into the library, he stared at the crying infant in the duke's arms and blurted out: "Your grace, I saw the young lady run out—has she left her baby with you?"

"It appears so, Ambrose," Raile said dryly. "I believe that she is crazed."

"Her coach has already departed. Shall I have Atkins fetch her back, your grace?"

"By the time he saddles a horse, she will have disappeared. She said she brought a wet nurse," Raile said in distress as the baby's howls became louder.

"There is a woman waiting in the great hall, your grace."

Raile thrust the still crying infant into the startled butler's arms. "Give this child to her and bring her to me at once."

While Raile waited for the wet nurse to appear, he moved to the window and pulled the heavy drapery aside. He relived the incident with Miss Maragon, hoping to make some sense of it. Why had she accused him of being her baby's father when they both knew that wasn't so? He could easily prove he had been out of the country when the child was conceived. His eyes darkened. The girl played a dangerous game if she thought to pass off her brat as his.

The door opened, and a tiny birdlike woman moved forward slowly. She held the baby tenderly, and Raile was relieved to see the child had quieted.

He gave the woman a searching glance and motioned for her to be seated. "May I know your name?" he asked, sitting on the edge of his desk, knowing the movement was intimidating. He would have his answers from this woman.

Her eyes darted about the room nervously, and she had a hard time meeting Raile's gaze. "My name's Heloise Gibbins, your grace."

"Tell me what you know of Miss Maragon."

Now the woman did meet his eyes. Heloise was still of an age to appreciate a handsome man. She found herself giddy and lighthearted when the duke looked at her.

"I have just lately become acquainted with Miss Maragon, your grace. I was only employed to look after the baby until you could find someone to replace me."

"Tell me all you know about her," he insisted. "And, I'll know if you are not speaking the truth."

"I truly know little of her, your grace. I was asked by the midwife in our village if I would consider making a journey of some distance with a woman and a newborn infant. Since my sister was willing to stay with my three children until I returned, and I needed the wages, I agreed to come. I must say Miss Maragon hardly spoke, and I often saw tears in her eyes. I didn't know what to think of her."

"Where did you meet her? At the Maragon country estate?"

"No, your grace. I met her in the village of Tibury, when we boarded the coach that brought us to Ravenworth. I can't tell you much more than that."

Raile drew in an impatient breath. "Are you being deliberately vague?"

She shook her head vigorously. "No, no. I know only what the people in the village knew, because the woman kept to herself. That is after her husband deserted her—or we thought he was her husband, but perhaps he wasn't."

"Do you know who the man was?"

"No, your grace. And as to the woman, I only saw her once at a distance, when she was heavy with child. Then I never saw her again until four days ago."

"Are you certain you're telling me everything you know, Mrs. Gibbins?"

"I swear I am, your grace. Except . . . on the journey here, the woman would only hold the baby when I was too weary. It was as though she didn't want to be near the child. Do you not think that odd?"

Raile stood up. "I will allow you and the baby to remain here until such time as the truth is uncovered." He moved to the bell cord. When Ambrose appeared, Raile instructed him to turn the wet nurse and the baby over to Mrs. Fitzwilliams.

An intriguing challenge had opened up before him, and Raile was determined to untangle the mystery of Miss Maragon and her child.

That evening when Raile made his way toward the formal sitting room, his path was momentarily blocked by Lavinia's maid, Meg Dower. The maid was clubfooted and had difficulty walking. She dipped an awkward curtsy when she saw Raile and disappeared in the shadows near the window.

Raile had always found something distasteful about Meg Dower. The woman was devoted to Lavinia and had been with her since before her marriage to Raile's father. Raile did not trust her. Meg never looked directly at anyone, and on occasion, Raile had seen a cunning light in her eyes. It was well known that the maid was Lavinia's ears and eyes and would lurk around corners, spying for her mistress.

Raile entered the sitting room, where he found Hugh and Lavinia waiting for him. He didn't relish spending another evening with his stepmother and half brother. But they were his only family and his cross to bear, he thought.

"Good evening, brother," Hugh said lazily. "I was beginning to think we would have to dine without you tonight."

Hugh's blond hair and blue eyes were a startling contrast to Raile's dark coloring. While Raile wore sober black, Hugh was dressed in the dandy fashion. He was decked out in tight blue pantaloons with a French-cut matching jacket. His cravat was elaborately tied, his hair cut in the Grecian style.

Raile flipped up the tail of his coat and sat down. "Since we have to live together, we should attempt to be amiable," he stated.

Lavinia approached her stepson with a provocative smile on her lips. "Raile," she said in a silky smooth voice, "we don't have to live under the same roof. It's been months since I've been to London because the house your father left me is depressingly small, and in an unfashionable part of town. Why don't you allow me to occupy your London house, so I can enjoy the Season? You know I detest the country."

"I told you, Lavinia, my London house is being renovated. You wouldn't find it pleasant with workmen invading your privacy for the next two months."

"There's the town house on Percy Street that came to you through your uncle," she reminded him.

"Knowing I would never want to live there, I instructed my solicitor to sell Uncle William's London house, Lavinia. I have already pensioned off his servants, and the new owners will take occupancy next week."

Her eyes hardened. "I don't see why you spend money on this musty old castle, when it could be better spent on new carriages and horses. I am mortified to ride around in that old coach that was your grandfather's. And just look at this gown—it's positively ready for the rag heap."

As usual, Lavinia was exaggerating. Raile glanced at the pink satin gown that was adorned with sparkling jewels. Just last week he had paid the bill for several new gowns, including that one.

"You must have patience, Lavinia," he told her. "When the repairs are completed, you shall have your new coach."

"You have money for the coach now," she said in an accusing voice. "Why do you make me wait? I am well aware that your mother left you a considerable fortune. Your father would have expected you to take care of me and your brother."

Raile smiled with irony. "Do you really believe my father would have expected me to furnish you with a new coach and a new wardrobe with money left to me by my mother?"

Lavinia whirled around. "You are just being mean, Raile. Most probably, you resent every morsel of food that passes between my lips. You want to bury me in the country so you can gloat over my misery."

Raile drew in a resigned breath, but did not reply.

"You go to London when it pleases you," Lavinia continued. "Do you think I don't know about your fancy piece and the house you bought her? It's nicer than the one your father left me. And I have been told you buy her gowns and fine jewelry that would put mine to shame."

"Lavinia, I am not prepared to discuss my private life with you. If you find life tedious here, you should feel free to leave."

"Mother," Hugh drawled, "you know Raile's first commitment is restoring this old castle. Your needs will just have to wait." He wrapped his arm about his mother's shoulders, his eyes mocking as they met his brother's. "It rests with Raile to play the family benefactor."

Raile moved away, wishing he could avoid a confrontation just this one night. Perhaps he should send Lavinia and Hugh to London so he wouldn't have to listen to their complaints.

Hugh's voice droned on. "Even if our wants are many, Mother dear, Raile's needs come first." He shrugged. "We, Mother, are reduced to poor relations, living off Raile's charity, thus forced to dwell in virtual seclusion until it pleases him to let us out of this prison."

Cynicism twisted Raile's lips. "As I told you, you are both welcome to strike out on your own if you find living here unbearable. I do not keep you here against your will. I didn't even invite you."

Mother and son exchanged glances. They had agreed not to antagonize Raile—not yet anyway—since they had neither the means nor the inclination to move out on their own. Lavinia had discovered that Raile was not as easily manipulated as his father and uncle had been. There was a strength in him that sometimes frightened her. Until she discovered his weakness, she would have to curb her impatience.

She decided to move on to a safer subject—or so she thought. "I was most curious on hearing from Meg that an infant girl has been placed in your keeping. You know how closemouthed Mrs. Fitzwilliams can be.

When I pressed her for information about the baby, she would tell me nothing. I wonder why you keep that sour old woman around."

Raile smiled. "Fritzy is as much a part of Ravenworth Castle as any one of us—perhaps more than some." He raised a dark eyebrow. "I have always applauded her loyalty."

Hugh dropped down on the green sofa and leaned forward, his eyes dancing with humor. "I have heard that the women are beautiful in France. Can it be, brother, that you have been dallying your way across the continent? Do you have some young French-woman's brat in the family nursery?"

"I am as mystified by the incident as you," Raile said dryly. "Tell me, do either of you know a Miss Maragon?"

Raile was watching Hugh for a reaction, and he noticed that his brother paled.

"Do you know her, Hugh?" Raile pressed.

"I may have been acquainted with her. But I know so many women," Hugh admitted anxiously. He looked at his mother, worried about what her reaction would be if she learned the truth.

Lavinia watched Raile's face with growing concern. "You don't mean some little chit has tried to pass off a bastard child as Hugh's. I will not hear of it!" Her eyes snapped with anger as she rounded on Raile. "You dare not bring a baby into this house and try to foist it off on my son."

Raile ignored Lavinia's outburst and moved to stand over his brother. "She's not some chit, but a young girl from a good family. Tell your mother and me about Miss Maragon, Hugh."

Hugh smiled nervously. "I liked her well enough, as I remember."

Raile pinned his brother with a hard look. "I know

well, Hugh, about your irresponsibilities where women are concerned. Have I not taken the blame for many of your indiscretions? It was the result of your disregard for women that I chose to leave England."

"Whether you believe it or not, Raile, I always regretted that misunderstanding with Uncle William. I hope you will not hold me responsible for the misdeeds of my youth."

Raile looked at Lavinia, who was squirming uncomfortably. She had hoped this conversation would never arise. She should have known Raile would not forget how she had lied about him to his uncle.

"It was not a misunderstanding, Hugh," Raile said in a cold voice. "Your mother can confirm that if there is any doubt in your mind."

"I am not answerable for what my mother does. And it isn't my fault that most women find me irresistible." Hugh's laughter was amused. "And I find them equally irresistible."

Lavinia saw what Hugh had not—she saw the dangerous fire in Raile's eyes, and she decided to save her foolish son before he went too far.

"Raile, I have suffered gravely for causing the rift between you and your uncle. But you are stronger than Hugh, and if your uncle had banished my son, he would not have fared as well as you did. You came home a hero, did you not?"

"You have a convenient little mind, Lavinia," Raile said in warning. "Have a care that you do not push me too far."

The threat hung in the air until Lavinia blurted out: "This conversation grows tedious. Can we not speak of more agreeable matters?"

Raile turned back to his brother, ignoring her. "Tell me, Hugh," he asked, "could that baby in the nursery be yours?"

Lavinia tried to intervene again. "Now see here, Raile DeWinter—"

"I'm going to ask you just one more time," Raile interrupted. "Did you father Miss Maragon's child?"

Hugh toyed with the gold button on the sleeve of his coat. "I have found that I am fertile, so I will not deny it is a possibility that the child is mine. I do recall that the girl was a virgin when we became . . . intimate."

Raile glanced up at Lavinia. "Madame, your son has gone too far this time—he impregnated a woman from an old and respected family. He will now face the consequences."

A feeling of uneasiness moved over Lavinia's heart. She had always turned a blind eye to Hugh's obsession with women because she had never felt threatened by any of them—none had challenged her place with her son. But this might be another matter altogether.

"What do you mean?" she asked.

Raile turned his dark, riveting gaze on Lavinia. "I'm saying, Madame, that if Miss Maragon will have your son, he is going to become her husband."

The room fell silent but for the steady ticking of the mantel clock.

The amused smile had been wiped from Hugh's face, and a look of indignation took its place. "I only admitted the baby *could* be mine."

Raile's voice was even, his tone deep. "Then you will marry her. And you will also recognize the baby as yours."

"I don't think so, Raile."

"You have no say in the matter. You will marry the girl and give the baby your name."

Lavinia became the protective mother and flew across the room to stand before Raile, her chest heaving. "You cannot do this to my son. I will see you dead before you force Hugh to marry some slut with a crying brat."

Raile looked from mother to son. "True, I cannot force you to marry the girl, Hugh. But if you don't, you and your mother will vacate Ravenworth Castle at once. I will not allow you to live on any of my properties, nor will I provide you with living expenses. You will both be on your own."

Lavinia gasped and stepped backward. Raile was asserting his authority over them, and they would have no recourse but to comply. Hatred burned in her heart. Raile had all the power, the money, the means to bend them to his will, and he knew it.

"On the other hand, Hugh," Raile continued, "if you marry Miss Maragon, I will allow the both of you to live in the London house, and I will give you a generous allowance. Will you agree to the marriage?"

"Have I any choice?"

"Only the ones I have pointed out to you."

"What about me?" Lavinia asked.

"You, madame, will remain here at Ravenworth Castle for a time. It is my belief that newlyweds should live alone for the first year of their marriage."

Hugh laughed without humor. "Ah, well, there you have it, Mother. It seems I will be a bridegroom at last. She was a pretty little thing, so it might not be too unpleasant."

"No!" Lavinia screamed, running at Raile and clawing at his face. "You will not do this to us. You are trying to separate me from my son."

Raile caught her hands and held them in a firm grip. "Don't ever try that again, Lavinia."

She jerked free, barely able to control her rage.

"Hugh will decide what to do by Monday next. If by that time, Lavinia, you have given your blessing to the match, I will be generous with you also. On the other hand, if you decide against welcoming Miss Maragon into the family, I will consider my duty to you both discharged."

Without another word, Raile moved out of the room, his long strides taking him down the hall and up the stairs. He no longer wished to be in their company.

His mind went back to his meeting with Miss Maragon. At that time, he had thought she was accusing him of fathering the child—but, no, she had merely been insisting that he was answerable for his brother's actions. And she was right, of course. Someone had to take a firm hand with Hugh, and it would have to be he. Perhaps with guidance, Hugh could be saved from his mother's destructive influence.

The young lady who had faced him today had not been the timid innocent Hugh had described. She had appeared to be more than capable. She had known what she wanted and how to get it.

Raile smiled at her daring. It must have taken enormous courage to face him with her accusations. Her defiant green eyes had been most arresting. It could be that Miss Maragon would be the one to save Hugh from his mother.

Raile somehow envied Hugh the challenge of conquering the hot-tempered miss.

10

Lavinia turned furiously on Hugh. "My God, what have you brought down on our heads? I warned you that your preoccupation with women would be your undoing—but you wouldn't listen. Are you such a slave to that thing between your legs that you would sacrifice your future and mine?"

Hugh shrugged, an annoying habit that was beginning to aggravate his mother.

"It's time you looked around you, Hugh. How long are you willing to live in Raile's shadow? When will you be a man and do something about our plight? We are but dust beneath his feet."

"There is little I can do, Mother. You heard Raile—I am to become a husband and father. I see no way we can avoid the inevitable."

"I'll never allow you to marry beneath you. Don't you know, that with my help, you will one day be duke of Ravenworth, and you must marry well. When the time comes, I'll help you pick a wife worthy of you."

Hugh looked at his mother with a bemused smile. "Haven't you forgotten my brother holds that title? I have my doubts he will relinquish it to me. Besides, it pains me to admit it to you, and I couldn't admit it to Raile, but I already married Abigail Maragon."

"You what!" Lavinia shrieked. "You fool! You will ruin us both."

"It was a moment of weakness. I married her, thinking it was what I wanted at the time. I was sorry later on. I found wedded bliss intolerable." He was quiet for a while. "I must admit that she almost tamed me."

Lavinia stared at Hugh as if he'd lost his mind. Then her eyes narrowed speculatively. "I wonder why she didn't confess that to Raile? Surely it would have been to her advantage to tell him about the marriage."

"I can't guess, Mother. Perhaps she grew weary of waiting for me to return. Or perhaps she has no wish to remain my wife. I did, in her eyes, desert her."

"Fool!"

Hugh did not even hear his mother. "I never knew she was with child." He smiled. "I have a daughter." His eyes gleamed with mischief. "I cannot see you as a grandmother."

"Shut up, Hugh. I'll not tolerate insolence from you. We have a dilemma, and you can only jest about it. You were almost in possession of Raile's title and fortune. How could we have known that Raile still lived and would stand between us and our hearts' desire?"

"What do you mean, Mother?"

She pressed her cheek against his, and said with passion, "I have committed my soul to the devil so you could inherit. I will not stop now."

"I never imagined that I would stand in Raile's place—not even when I thought he was dead. I'm not sure I want to . . . or that I can."

Lavinia wanted to churn the fires of ambition within her son, but first she would have to deal with his admiration for Raile. She would deal with Raile himself when the time came.

"When I married your father, I would never have aspired so high as the dukedom—too many were before you. But when your uncle was dying, and we heard that Raile had died in Belgium, only John was in our way." Her eyes gleamed with sudden hatred. "Now, there's not only Raile to deny you the dukedom, but this damned Maragon chit trying to force her whelp on you."

Hugh was stunned by his mother's malevolence. "I see nothing to do but admit to Raile that I'm not the rogue he believes me to be, and that the baby in the nursery is my legitimate daughter."

"You're crazed if you think I'll let you do that. Now, listen to me. First," she said with a dark expression on her face, "we must deal with the woman. Do you think money would satisfy her?"

"I don't think so. Abigail has honor, which I fear you and I do not, Mother."

She patted his hand. "You just leave that to me. Raile cannot thrust this woman and her brat on you if he can't locate her. If it takes everything your father left me, I'll be rid of her."

Hugh looked worried for a moment. "I wouldn't like it if anything happened to Abigail. I spent six months with her, which is longer than any woman ever held my interest. Since I left her, I have often felt pangs of guilt—don't you think that strange, Mother?" He looked almost apologetic. "Stranger still, I believe I love her."

Lavinia smiled at him with indulgence. "You have loved many women, Hugh. It always passes."

Hugh had left Abigail only when he had received word that Raile and John were dead. Otherwise he might be with her still. Upon reflection, he did not find the notion of returning to her abhorrent—to the contrary, he had missed her quiet gentleness and her soft beauty.

"I would not mind if Raile knew about the marriage. I believe I could be happy with Abigail."

Lavinia's face whitened with repressed rage. "I have spawned a fool for a son. Why are you doing this to me?"

"She is an enchanting creature. I'm sure you would like her."

Lavinia shook her head so violently her hair came loose and fell down her shoulders. "Is she of a wealthy family, Hugh?"

"Her brother is warm in the pocket, but it's my understanding he will not settle anything on Abigail. We lived very simply in a cottage, and only on what money I had."

"Then there you have it—you must marry where it will join two great houses and two great fortunes."

He was suddenly the devoted son. He always gave in to her in the end because she seemed to know what was best for him. "I would do anything to make you happy, Mother. But it is dangerous to defy Raile. You know how determined he can be. And his threat was not an idle one. He could make our lives hell if he so desired."

Lavinia's eyes took on a reflective glow. "My foolish boy—don't overestimate Raile or underestimate me."

Lavinia entered the darkened nursery. The light of the moon illuminated the cradle that had held untold generations of DeWinters.

She moved across the room and stood staring down at the sleeping infant. The sight of the child stirred no feelings of warmth in her.

She refused to be a grandmother. At least not to a girl, and certainly not to this one. A grandson might not be so bad, someone she could mold as she had her son. Lately Hugh had not been so easy to control, and she could feel him pulling away from her. But she knew what had to be done.

How fragile the child was, and how easy it would be to end its life. All she would have to do was cover its face and wait until it stopped breathing. There would be no cries, no marks on the body, and no sign of a struggle. No one would ever know the death had not been natural.

Of course, she would still have to dispose of the mother since Hugh had been such a fool and married her.

She reached into the cradle, and cried out in pain as her wrist was grabbed and pulled behind her back.

"I've been waiting for you, Lavinia."

"What do you mean?" she asked, trying to break his hold on her arm.

"I knew you would come, and I wanted to be here when you did. I didn't have to wait long."

He released her arm, and she spun around to face him with forged indignation. "I hope you aren't implying that I would harm the child."

"I'm just here to see that you don't."

The soft moonlight cast his face half in shadow. Lavinia felt his magnetism. There was something dangerous about him that excited her. She had always felt it, but had never admitted it to herself until now. She wondered what it would feel like to be crushed in Raile's arms when he was aroused by desire.

She saw the disgust in his eyes when he looked at her, and she knew she would have only his contempt. They were bitter enemies—they would be until one of them was dead.

"I have little interest in this child, Raile. I was curious about her, nothing more."

"In there lies the pity, madame. She is of your flesh."

"Don't keep on with this, Raile. You play a precarious game."

"I have been considering your request, Lavinia. You will go to London and remain there until I decide otherwise."

Her eyes burned, and the anger inside her was so deep, she ached to give it voice. "You have control of my life for now, Raile, but the time will come when I will turn the cards in my favor."

"Until that day, Lavinia, pack your belongings and be ready to leave for London by noon tomorrow."

She wanted to scream at him, to run at him and claw his face, but the look in his eyes frightened her. She turned, her back stiff, her breathing tight, and walked out of the room.

Raile looked down at the sleeping infant and stroked her soft skin. He felt a strong kinship with her. He knew what it was like to have no one care. This little girl was not going to suffer as he had as a child.

Adjusting the blanket that covered her, he walked out of the room.

Raile knocked on the door next to the nursery, which was answered by Mrs. Gibbins. "Keep the child with you tonight, and don't leave her for any reason."

If the wet nurse thought his request was a strange one, she did not say so. She watched him move away, and then went to the nursery and gathered the child in her arms.

11

Kassidy stood in the upstairs bedroom of the cottage where Abigail had lived. She avoided looking at the bed where her sister had writhed in pain and finally died in agony.

How sad it was that the man Abigail had loved—the man who had wronged her—denied even knowing her.

Aunt Mary was coming today, and the two of them would be closing up the cottage and packing Abigail's belongings. Afterward, Kassidy would have to return to her brother's house and face his anger.

The future seemed bleak and sad without her sister beside her. Sweet, kindhearted Abigail who was dead because of the hateful man who had seduced her and stolen her innocence, then deserted her in the end.

Kassidy's heart ached for the baby she had left in the duke's keeping. Was the child being properly cared for? What would that little girl's life be like with such a cold, unfeeling man? It had been wrong to leave the baby with him. If Abigail had seen the man's reaction when she had placed his daughter in his arms, surely her sister would expect her to reclaim the child.

Yes, she thought, that was what she would do. If she had the child with her, she could still hold on to a little part of Abigail.

With determined steps, she rushed out of the room and down the stairs. She would go back to Ravenworth Castle and take the child away with her!

Kassidy's mind was racing ahead to what she would say when she again stood before the arrogant duke. He had been so uncaring about her sister, never once inquiring about Abigail. This time, she would let him know it was his fault that Abigail had died.

She glanced at the cloudless sky as she moved down the steps. The sun was shining, and the birds were singing in the nearby oak tree. The Thames ran high to its banks. The pleasant smell of cut grass permeated the air she breathed. It would have been a glorious day if only Abigail had been there to share it with her.

She walked to the back of the house and down a well-worn path that led to the woods. Perhaps Aunt Mary would go with her to Ravenworth Castle so she wouldn't have to face the duke alone.

The brothers, Jack and Gorden Beale, had been born and grew up on Whitechapel Road, a place of poverty and crime.

Jack, the elder, was proficient at his chosen profession. As a lad he'd become a pickpocket—now he would employ any means necessary to line his own pockets.

Gorden Beale was cowardly and not as adept as his brother, but he was easily led by strong-willed Jack.

The two of them had been watching the cottage by the Thames for two days, waiting for a chance to catch Miss Maragon alone.

"What do we know about that woman who hired us,

Jack? I was suspicious of her from the first when she sent word that we was to meet her at the Red Dragon Inn. Even though she tried to stay in the shadows with her face hidden behind that flimsy veil, I knew she was dressed too grand to be 'Mrs. Harper from Billingsgate Street' like she said."

"All you need to know about her is that she has the means to hire us," Jack reminded him, his eyes growing intense with speculation. "I never told you that I followed the woman to find out who she was. I waited until she came out of the inn and followed her coach to Mayfair, where she went into one of them fancy shops where they sell ladies' hats." A smile twisted Jack's thin lips. "The shopkeeper greeted her as Mrs. DeWinter. It appears our mysterious woman is related to the duke of Ravenworth. The shopkeeper thought our woman is the duke's stepma. We have here someone of great importance."

"Did you find out anything else about her? Why does she hate this young girl so?"

"What do we care?

"I don't like this, Jack. This ain't just nobody we're dealing with. The duke is a very powerful man. What if he don't know what his stepma's doing? I didn't shrink from sticking a blade between that fancy toff's ribs, when the woman paid us to do it, and it was easy making it look like footpads done it. But when she wants us to do in a high-born young lady, I don't like it," Gorden said. "I'm glad you decided against killing her."

Jack stared at his brother with piercing, relentless eyes. "So, you're turning squeamish on me, are you? I never thought you'd balk at any means of collecting a fee, be it foul or fair. Besides, if truth be known, what the girl will face might be far worse than death. You leave all the worrying to me. And you don't have to like it, little brother. We get paid by DeWinter and we get paid by Tom Brunson when we turn the Maragon girl over to him."

"What does he want with her?"

"I suspect he'll sell her to a brothel, but what do we care? Where she's going, no one ever leaves. I thought it rather clever of me to get two prices for her," Jack boasted.

"I hope DeWinter don't find out we didn't do what she hired us to do."

"Will you stop grumbling? We'll tell DeWinter the deed is done and she'll believe us."

"You did tell Brunson there must be no record of the girl. No one must know her whereabouts. You did make that known to him, didn't you?"

"I'm not a fool, Gorden. Now shut up, and keep an eye out for the girl."

"I still don't like it. The girl's family's bound to start a hue and cry when they find out she's missing. If they find her, it'll go hard on us."

"You fret like some old woman. I'm beginning to regret I brought you into this with me."

Suddenly Jack saw movement at the edge of the woods, and he pulled Gorden behind a tree.

"Well, I'll be damned. She's coming straight at us."

Kassidy was unaware that hostile eyes followed her movements. She did not see the two men who were crouched low behind the dense thicket along the footpath.

"It can't be this easy," Jack whispered, his gaze fastened on the girl. "Like a sheep being led to the slaughter, she falls into our hands."

Kassidy had not realized she had come so deeply into the woods. She turned, with the intention of returning to the cottage, when a man stepped into her path.

At first she was startled by his sudden appearance, but she decided he must be from the village. There was nothing menacing in his eyes as he smiled at her.

The man removed his cap. "Morning, miss. Nice weather for a stroll," he said respectfully.

She smiled and moved to step around him, but he barred her way.

"You Miss Maragon?" he asked, his manner suddenly changing.

"How did you know my name?" She watched his eyes dart behind her. With sudden fear in her heart, she spun around to see a second man move into the path, blocking her between them.

"What do you want?" Kassidy asked, moving to her left, only to find he moved with her.

The man behind her took her arm and held it in a viselike grip. "You can come with us peaceable, or you can make it hard on yourself."

She stared from one man to the other, fear pounding in her heart. "W . . . what do you want with me?"

The stranger's laughter was so menacing that shivers of fear danced across her spine.

"It ain't so much what we want, miss. It seems there's someone who don't want you around no more. We're just here to oblige 'em."

Kassidy's eyes widened with terror, and she tried to wrench her arm free.

"Now don't struggle, miss. I'm stronger than you, and you'll just make me hurt you."

Kassidy felt a scream building up in her throat, but it was smothered by the rough hand that clamped painfully over her mouth, constricting her breathing.

"I warned you, but you didn't listen," the man hissed in her ear. "You just made it hard on yourself."

Kassidy felt pain explode in her head when the man struck her with a heavy instrument. Blackness enveloped her, and she fell limply to the ground.

"You killed her, Jack," Gorden accused, as he went down on his knees to examine the girl, stroking her long blond hair. "She's such a pretty one. Why would anyone want to harm her?"

Jack felt the girl's strong pulse and lifted her in his arms. "That's not for the likes of us to worry about. We better hurry before she's missed," he added, moving toward the river and the waiting boat they had secured there earlier. Placing Kassidy in the bottom of the boat, they pushed off in the direction of London.

Kassidy regained consciousness in total darkness. Her head ached, and when she tried to move, she found her feet and wrists were bound. Fear screamed through her mind when she remembered the two strangers she had encountered in the woods. Apparently they had made good their threat and were taking her away. But who had hired them to abduct her? And why? She closed her eyes, trying to hold onto her sanity. Her body trembled when she realized she was lying in the bottom of a small boat. Where were they taking her?

As she fought her way out of the thick haze of fear, Kassidy realized the men were talking in quiet whispers. They must think she was still unconscious, she thought.

"Jack," Gorden said, plying the oars to the murky black water, "why do you suppose this DeWinter wants the girl out of the way?"

"How many times do I have to tell you that's no concern of ours?" He sounded angry. "We just do what we're told, and don't ask why."

A sob was building deep inside Kassidy. So the duke of Ravenworth had struck swiftly. She had not even entertained the notion that he might retaliate against her. What kind of monster was he?

"The girl's awake, Jack. I saw her move. What'll we do?"

One of the men laid his oars aside and knelt over her. He was only a vague outline against a pale moon. Kassidy tensed when he pushed her head over the side of the boat until she was almost touching the water.

"Did you hear anything we said?" There was a threat in his voice. "Speak girl—did you?"

She realized it would mean her death if this man knew she had overheard him. "Where am I?" she asked in a small voice, deliberately acting vague. "Why have you done this to me?"

He released her and she fell back, landing hard against the bottom of the boat. Kassidy felt as if she were bruised all over, and her head throbbed painfully. Terror was so strong it pushed every thought except survival out of her mind. "Why are you doing this?" she asked.

"You'll find out soon enough," Jack remarked with a smirk. "Someone wants you to disappear, never to be heard from again." His laughter was evil and had a grating tone. "I have thought of a way so you'll never be trouble to no one again. My brother, he's been wondering what you did to stir up so much hate against you." He laughed. "Never mind the reason. You just angered the wrong person, Miss Maragon."

Kassidy huddled in the corner of the boat, frantically wondering what they were going to do to her. If they had wanted to kill her, surely they would have drowned her while she was unconscious. Where were they taking her?

It seemed like an eternity that they skimmed across the Thames. At one point Kassidy saw bright lights in the distance and knew they were nearing London.

As the docks came within sight, a heavy fog shrouded the city. When the boat bumped against the pier, one of the men gripped her arm and held her fast. When she struggled, he growled in her ear.

"Remember what happened to you before. You don't want me to hurt you again, do you?"

She shook her head, too frightened to speak. Suddenly he shoved a flask at her and urged her to drink. When she shook her head, he grabbed her arm and twisted it behind her.

"Drink—now!"

Too frightened to refuse again, Kassidy took the bitter liquid in her mouth and swallowed it with a painful gulp. Before she could protest, she was lifted in the man's arms and carried ashore.

As he walked along, she felt her head swimming and knew she had either been drugged or poisoned. If it was poison, she hoped it would work fast. At the moment, she prayed for death, as she felt an unspeakable horror awaited her.

She thought of the defenseless baby she had placed in the duke's keeping. She hoped fate would deal more kindly with the child than it had with her or her sister.

Her last conscious thought was hatred toward the duke. Someday he would get what he deserved, and she hoped it could be she who unmasked his evil. She could still see his face, and it was as if he were mocking her—then she was lost in oblivion.

Kassidy had been blindfolded, and the inky darkness was terrifying. She did not know how long she had been unconscious, and even now her mind was still groggy. She could tell she was being carried over one of the men's shoulders, and it was horrifying not to know where they were taking her. She tried to cry out, but because of the drug they had forced on her, her throat was dry and her tongue felt thick.

She heard the grating of an iron door swing open on rusty hinges, and she tried to fight off the heavy weariness that pressed in on her, but her eyes fluttered and closed, and she was lost in a world where fear could not follow.

She was unaware of the money that exchanged hands between her two captors and another man, or that the other man took possession of her limp body.

When Kassidy again regained consciousness, her blindfold had been removed and someone was carrying her down a long dark passageway.

The man set her on her feet, and she felt rough hands on her body and someone forcing her face into the lantern light.

"You're a pretty one," a gruff voice said. "I'll get a good price for you from Madame Ratcliff."

Kassidy looked at her new captor in horror. The loathsome man appeared to be wearing a uniform, but she couldn't be sure because his clothing was filthy and smelled foul. He was tall and muscled. His nose appeared to have been broken at one time, for it lay flat against his cheeks. A long scar ran from his eyebrow down the side of his face to his lip, giving him a menacing appearance.

Kassidy wanted to scream when he ran his filthy hand up her arm, and she did manage to flinch away from his touch.

The man grinned as if he derived some sort of pleasure from her misery, and there was a vicious light in his eyes as she staggered, trying to keep her balance. Finally she stumbled backward and leaned against the cold stone wall for support.

In the distance, she heard groans of despair and cries of pain from others who must also be trapped somewhere in this dark maze of agony.

"Where am I?" Kassidy asked in a haze of pain and bewilderment.

"Some call it Newgate, little lady," the man told her, "but you'll call it hell."

12

Kassidy trembled with fear as she looked at the huge man. He had little black eyes, and there was something evil about the way he leered at her.

"Please help me," she beseeched him.

He didn't seem to hear her words. He ran a hand down her arm, and turned her around, looking her over carefully with a satisfied gleam in his eyes. "You're a beauty, all right. I'll get my price back for you and more."

"What are you going to do with me?"

"Oh, you may ask. I'll take you to a lady I know who'll see that you learn all the ways to please a man. Newgate ain't nothing like the prison you'll find at Madame Ratcliff's."

He ran his hand down her face. "But before I take you to her, it won't damage the goods none if I have a go at you first."

Kassidy backed away from him, a scream rising in her throat. "I'll die before I allow you to touch me."

"No, you won't die." He loomed over her. "You may even like what I do."

She felt revulsion rise up inside her. "I'll scream if you touch me."

His eyes hardened, and he raised up his hand to deliver a stunning blow to her jaw. Kassidy crumpled to the floor and knew nothing after that.

Tom Brunson lifted her limp body and carried her down the long hallway, up a flight of stairs to a cell that was apart from the others. He lay her on the straw mattress on the floor and chained her wrists to the wall.

He stood over Kassidy, taking in her fragile beauty. With a grunt of regret that he must leave and make his rounds, he turned to the door and locked it behind him.

Frantic excitement throbbed through him. After he made his rounds, he had two other girls to deliver to Madame Ratcliff. Then he'd come back to this one. Only when he tired of her would he take her to Leman Street.

Tom Brunson had made the most of his position at Newgate, thanks to Madame Ratcliff's establishment. As head keeper of the cells in solitary, where the troublemakers were confined, he had found wealth in transporting women of looks to Madame Ratcliff's brothel. He had devised a clever way to sneak them out of Newgate, where the poor wretches would make money for him by lying on their backs. Sometimes the women were agreeable, preferring to sell their bodies instead of remaining in solitary—sometimes not.

Even if a woman objected, it mattered but little. After Tom put the fear of the devil in them, they never caused him trouble, and never reported him to the warden. Before a woman's term of confinement was over, he would bring her back without anyone being the wiser.

After making his rounds, he went to a cell and unlocked the door. "Well now, my beauties, it's old Tom, and he's here to free you from this prison."

The two women huddled against the wall. One spoke with anger. "We know where the women go when they leave here."

Tom snorted. "That'll save me the trouble of explaining it to you."

The two women exchanged glances, but made no attempt to resist when he clapped them in chains and led them out into the dark corridor.

"Don't make a sound," he cautioned.

Down the long corridor they went until they came to a side door where the refuse was collected. Tom unlocked the door and pulled the women forward. He lifted them into a waiting garbage wagon, hiding them beneath large baskets.

He bounded into the wagon, picked up the reins and urged the nag forward, as he had done many times before. When the wagon rattled out the gates and they left Newgate behind, Tom laughed at his own daring.

"If you be clever, there's always a way to outsmart others," he said, pleased with his resourcefulness.

After they were safely away, he drove onto a deserted street and halted the horse. Beneath a pale moon, he unlocked the chains on the women's wrists with a warning to them. "If you know what's good for you, you'll not give me no—"

Tom never finished what he had started to say. While one of the women distracted him, the other shoved a knife in his heart and twisted it savagely. He fell forward, twitching and kicking, a baffled look on his face.

"If you be clever," the woman mimicked, "there's always a way to outsmart others."

The women jumped from the wagon and faded into the dark shadows, while Tom drew his last breath in a heap of foul-smelling garbage.

* * *

Back at Newgate, the guards changed shifts, but no one went near the secluded cell where Kassidy lay unconscious. No one even knew she was there.

Kassidy awoke to the sound of water dripping. Frantically groping around in the dark, she felt a damp stone wall. Her head ached and she could not think clearly—why was she so confused?

Slowly she remembered what had happened to her—the abduction, the filthy man who put his hands on her. She remembered the lewd threats he'd made to her.

"No." She sobbed, shivering with revulsion. In her agonized mind she was sure the guard had ravished her while she'd been unconscious. If only she could wash every part of her body that the vile man had touched.

She curled up in a ball and watched the first splinter of light coming through a high window. As the dark corners lightened, and her mind cleared, she looked around the tiny cell. There was a thick iron door with a small opening at the bottom, just large enough to push food and water through. High over her head was a tiny window with iron bars. She was lying on a lumpy mattress that had been placed on the damp stone floor. When she tried to rise, she discovered to her horror that she was chained to the wall.

Finally standing up on shaky legs, she found that the slightest movement rattled the chains at her wrists. She moved along the outer wall, noticing it was damp from water seepage. The floor was foul-smelling and slimy with filth.

"Dear God, what has happened to me?" Kassidy moaned.

She squeezed her eyes shut, hoping when she opened them again she would discover she was having a nightmare. But no, she was cold and began to shiver as deep, wrenching sobs built up within her. This was not a nightmare—it was real!

Kassidy wrapped her arms around herself, trying to keep warm. She wondered if she was going mad. In the distance, strange voices penetrated her consciousness. Some of them cried out with hopelessness, and others were harsh and commanding. Every new sound made her fearful that her tormentor would return. She huddled against the wall, feeling sick in mind and body.

All day Kassidy lay upon her straw mattress, too frightened to move. As the light began to wane and darkness fell, she still shivered from cold and fear. No one came to give her food or water, and she was so hungry and thirsty.

It was as though no one knew she was there, or they had forgotten her.

Finally, hearing heavy footsteps outside the door of her cell, Kassidy thought it would be the guard returning. But the footsteps faded away, and she drew in a relieved breath. Loneliness weighed heavily on her, and she longed for the sight of another human—but not the guard—please, God, not that loathsome man.

As the sun went down, Kassidy watched the corners of the cell fade into shadows and then total darkness encroached.

How long had she been there? There was no way of knowing. She turned her face to the wall, too heartsick to care what happened to her.

She buried her face in her hands as tears of misery rolled down her face. She wept until there were no more tears left. Then she fell asleep, resting her head on the filthy mattress.

Jack Beale watched his brother move up the back steps and enter the kitchen.

Slapping his cap against his thigh, Gorden shook his head. "That woman's made dolts of us, Jack."

"Didn't she give you the money that was owed to us?"

"She told me she didn't have it, but if we'd wait for three more weeks, she'd double the fee. Said she'd be coming into some money."

Jack frowned. "And fool that you are, you believed her?"

It was raining, and Gorden removed his jacket and hung it on a hook next to the cookstove to dry.

"Didn't matter if I believed her or not—she didn't give me the money. What was I to do, wring it out of her?"

Jack stomped across the floor and yanked his brother forward by his shirtfront. "Why'd you come back without our hundred pounds? You should'a stayed with her until she gave you the money." Jack shoved him angrily, and Gorden was slammed against the wall.

Rubbing his sore arm, Gorden tried to explain why he had returned without the money. "I couldn't make her give me what she don't have. We'll have to wait, Jack. She'll have to pay us sooner or later."

Jack shook his head. "No one gets away with cheating me." He rubbed his stubbly chin, and a twisted smile touched his lips. "She don't know that we found out who she is. And I know more about the Maragon girl, too. I can make DeWinter rue the day she went back on Jack Beale."

Gorden looked doubtful. "What are you thinking on doing, Jack?"

"DeWinter wanted the girl to disappear real bad. Suppose the girl was to get free?"

Gorden paled and ran a hand nervously through his thinning hair. "But the girl knows about us. If she talks, we'll be the ones behind the walls of Newgate."

"She knows nothing about us," Jack said with confidence. "She was so scared she couldn't tell anything about that night. She don't even know our names."

"What will you do?"

Jack's eyes narrowed with speculation. "It's just a matter of sending a letter to the right person." His brows met across the bridge of his nose. "And I know just who to send it to."

Lady Mary moved quickly up the steps of Ravenworth Castle. With an impatient breath, she brushed past the startled Ambrose.

"Show me to his grace at once," she ordered. "Tell him Lady Mary Rindhold wishes to see him on a matter of great import."

Ambrose was startled, but he nodded respectfully. "Will you wait in the sitting room, my lady, and I'll tell his grace you are here."

She followed him into the room. Perhaps the letter she had received was a hoax, but she had to know for certain. Until the anonymous letter arrived yesterday, she had despaired of finding Kassidy alive.

Now, unless someone were playing a cruel trick on her, perhaps the duke could help her untangle the mystery surrounding Kassidy's unexplained disappearance.

The man who entered the room was younger than Mary had expected. He approached her with a look of curiosity, but his manner was polite.

"Lady Mary, I have not had the pleasure of meeting you, but I know your husband, George, quite well."

"George has told me that you served under Lord Wellington. He has related to me the details of your daring feat of heroism at Waterloo. He says Parliament was most impressed. I had thought you would be older."

"You are too kind, Lady Mary," he said, offering her

a chair. When she was seated, he sat opposite her. "Ambrose told me you wanted to see me on an important matter."

"Yes," she said doubtfully now that she had met the duke. "I'm at a loss as to how you can help me, though." She handed him a letter. "Perhaps this will explain my reason for being here. Although I confess, I do not understand any of this myself."

Raile hurriedly read the letter:

Dear Madame,
If you wish to know about your missing niece, you might want to begin your search at Ravenworth Castle.

Raile handed the letter back. "I don't understand how I can help you. I don't even know your niece. I can assure you that she is not here."

Lady Mary's face showed her distress.

"I am as much puzzled by the note as you are. You have to understand I am so worried about Kassidy I can't overlook any clue to her whereabouts."

Raile saw tears gathering in her eyes.

"You'll have to forgive me," she said, feeling embarrassed, "but Kassidy is so dear to me, and she has suffered so much since the deaths of her mother and father and now her sister. Since her disappearance, my husband and I have searched everywhere for her. It's as if she vanished into nothingness. Her brother, Henry, has already given her up for dead."

She dabbed at her eyes with a lace handkerchief. "You cannot imagine the grief I have lived through. First losing my elder niece, and now Kassidy. You see, they were the daughters of my dead sister, and I promised her I would look after them if anything happened to her. As you see, I have not fulfilled that promise."

Feeling pity for the woman, but also discomfort, Raile reached for a decanter and poured a glass of sherry, then handed it to her.

"Drink this, Lady Mary, and then tell me how you think I can help."

She took a sip and then pushed the glass away. "Please forgive me, your grace. I don't usually act this way with strangers. It's just that I'm so distressed. Kassidy was so alive—so sweet and kind. I cannot believe she is gone."

"Perhaps you should start from the beginning. When did you last see your niece? And what is her full name?"

"Her name is Kassidy Maragon, and she disappeared about a month ago."

Raile, good at schooling his emotions, did not flinch at the mention of the name "Maragon." "What were the circumstances of her disappearance?" he asked.

Lady Mary wondered how much to confide to the duke. "You see, Abigail died in childbirth. Kassidy was with her at the end. I cannot tell you the guilt I feel for not staying with them until the baby was born. But I thought it was a normal birth."

"I assume Abigail is Kassidy's sister?"

Mary nodded hesitantly. "Yes, your grace, she . . . Abigail . . . died . . . and Kassidy has disappeared."

"Does your niece have flights of fancy?"

"I can assure you she does not. But I can see where you might think my whole family is demented."

"Not at all," Raile said graciously. "I believe I have met your niece, Kassidy, Lady Mary. Although at the time, I thought she was Abigail Maragon." Raile watched Lady Mary's face closely. "She came here to see me. Do you know anything about that?"

Lady Mary was genuinely shocked. "No. Why would Kassidy do such a thing? You weren't acquainted, were you?"

"I never met your niece until she arrived with the baby." Still he watched her face for a reaction. "She left the infant in my care and fled in a curious manner."

Lady Mary shook her head in relief. "Thank God. I have been so worried about the baby. I am relieved to know that she, at least is safe." She looked at him carefully. "She is well, isn't she?"

"I can assure you the baby thrives. She is in the nursery upstairs."

Lady Mary stared at him. "But why would Kassidy leave the baby with you?" She buried her head in her hands. "What trick is this? Why would she bring . . . unless . . . but no you could not be . . . it's too absurd to consider."

"I can assure you I did not father the child, Lady Mary."

She looked at the handsome duke for a long moment. Women by the dozens must fall in love with him. But, of course, he could not be Abigail's elusive husband. He would have been out of the country when Abigail eloped.

"I just don't know what to think. Did my niece tell you why she brought the baby to you?"

"She implied that I was the child's father—or so I thought at the time. I don't want to alarm you, Lady Mary, but she was not rational."

"No," Lady Mary agreed. "She probably wasn't. She loved Abigail and had to watch her die." She stood up. "I won't trouble you any longer. If you will have the baby brought down, I will take her with me. There is no need for you to be involved in this any longer."

"I am involved, Lady Mary, whether or not I want to be. Have you any notion who fathered Abigail Maragon's baby?"

"No — do you?"

"I believe so."

"Then you must tell me at once. Perhaps he can help me find Kassidy."

"He cannot help you. And I would rather not say who he is at this time. But I assure you that I will help you in this."

For some reason, she trusted him. "If you will have the baby brought down, I will leave at once."

"I believe it best that the baby remain here for now. But I will have my housekeeper show you to the nursery so you will know the child is doing well."

Lady Mary stood. "Does the baby want for anything?"

Raile smiled. "She enjoys the attention of all the servants. My housekeeper, Mrs. Fitzwilliams, is accused of neglecting her household duties because she spends most of the day with the child."

He summoned Mrs. Fitzwilliams and instructed her to accompany Lady Mary to the nursery. Raile watched Lady Mary follow the housekeeper, who was delivering glowing reports on the baby's progress.

He turned away, determined to discover what had happened to the high-spirited girl named Kassidy.

13

Like a caged animal, Kassidy paced the cell as far as her chains would allow. She no longer cringed in fear when she heard footsteps outside her cell, for the guard who had locked her in had never returned.

At last, in exhaustion, she leaned against the wall for support. She was getting weaker. She had to have nourishment or she would die.

Twice a day, some nameless, faceless person shoved water and food into the cell—if one could call the watered-down gruel they served in the dirty tin plate, food. As hungry as she was, she could not eat it, but she drank thirstily of the water.

Kassidy dropped down on the filthy mattress, no longer caring that it was bug-infested. She seemed to ache all over, and suddenly felt lightheaded. She was feverish—cold one minute and burning hot the next.

Throughout the day and into the night her fever raged. When the night was its darkest, she began to hallucinate. She could clearly visualize the mocking eyes of the duke and hear him taunting her as clearly as if he were standing in the cell with her. She cried out when she saw the pale lifeless face of her dead sister imploring her to take care of the baby.

Kassidy drew in her breath sharply, as the face of the duke floated before her again, but this time he was not mocking. His eyes were enticing her, pulling at her with a promise of pleasure. His hands touched her arm and slid up to her neck, and she shivered at his gentleness.

"You will not deceive me as you did my sister," she cried. "I will not give in to you."

She used all her strength to drive away the vision. Then she was left with only the harsh reality of her cold, empty cell. This was what he had done to her—cast her down in the depths of despair. She would probably die here, and how he would laugh when he learned of her death.

With stubborn determination, Kassidy decided to overcome her delirium. If she was to survive, she had to help herself, for there was no one else.

Weakly, she dragged herself across the filthy floor to the water jug. When she lifted it to her lips and drank deeply, Kassidy was certain that she was dying because it failed to quench her burning thirst.

Raile looked down at the baby nestled against the housekeeper's ample bosom. "She's enjoying good health, isn't she, Fritzy?"

The housekeeper's brown eyes softened. "That she is, your grace. She's a good baby and has won everyone's heart. Poor little motherless thing. She has no name, so we call her Sweetness."

Raile touched the small hand and was rewarded by the baby curling her tiny hand around his finger. This made him smile. "I never thought much about babies, Fritzy, but this one seems exceptionally beautiful."

"She is indeed," Mrs. Fitzwilliams agreed.

Ambrose appeared at the doorway and cleared his throat to get Raile's attention.

"Begging your pardon, your grace, but there is a 'person' asking to see you. He refuses to give his name, but insists you will want to see him."

Raile extracted his finger from the baby's grasp and turned to the butler. "Doesn't it seem of late, Ambrose, that an uncommon number of people have come here asking to see me, and refuse to give their names?"

The butler's face remained stoic. "It would seem so, your grace."

"I don't suppose this man gave his reason for being here." Raile smiled slightly. "He doesn't have a baby with him, by any chance?"

If Ambrose was amused, it didn't show. "No, your grace. He said only that he wanted to talk to you about a certain young lady."

Raile tensed. "Did he give the lady's name?"

"No, your grace. I assumed you would not want to speak to him, so I took the liberty of leaving him in the grand hall."

Raile startled Ambrose when he pushed past him and moved quickly across the corridor and down the stairs.

Jack Beale turned in a circle, looking at the silken hangings on the walls. He had never seen anything so magnificent. He saw neither the tattered tapestries, nor what years of neglect had wrought. He saw only evidence of riches, and he greedily fancied some of it was coming to him.

When Jack heard footsteps, he turned to see a man coming toward him. The butler had let him understand that he should not expect to be received, but the tall aristocratic man who approached him could be none other than the duke of Ravenworth, himself.

"Come with me," Raile said, indicating that the man should follow him into the library.

Closing the door behind them, Raile faced the man, his eyes searching. "You refused to give the butler your name."

"Let's just say I'm an acquaintance of your mother's, and let it go at that."

"My mother is dead."

"I meant to say, your stepmother, the dowager duchess."

"There is no dowager duchess."

Jack's eyes snapped. "I don't know what game you and your stepma's playing, but she hired me, and I expect to be paid. There are other people besides you DeWinters who would be interested in our little prisoner at Newgate—and I know who they are."

Raile felt sick inside as he realized what the man was telling him. Lavinia had hired him to take Miss Maragon to Newgate. He had known his stepmother was capable of trickery, but until now he had not realized how malicious she could be.

He must allow this man to think he knew about Lavinia's actions so he could learn more. "You placed Miss Maragon in Newgate?"

"I know it wasn't your stepma's instructions to take her there, Your Excellency. I didn't do away with the girl as I was ordered. But she's done away with all the same and no one'll ever hear from her again. I want what's due me, and I'll just take my leave of you."

Raile tried to control the rage that was building inside him. The man should be turned over to the magistrate, but if he did that now, he might never find Miss Maragon.

His voice came out evenly without betraying his anger. "Are you well acquainted with my stepmother?"

Jack nodded. "We have an arrangement. When she

wants someone out of her way, I oblige her."

"You have done this for her before?"

Jack's eyes suddenly became secretive. "I'd rather not say."

"So my stepmother wanted Miss Maragon dead, and you were willing to oblige her?"

"Not for the money your mother . . . stepmother offered. If you want the girl done away with, it'll cost you more." Jack stroked his chin. "'Course, to my way of thinking, it'd be far better to kill the girl than to let her live in that hell pit."

Raile had to clench his hands to keep from thrashing the man. "So, instead of . . . killing Miss Maragon, you took her to Newgate. You must have someone inside who helped you."

"If you hire Jack Beale, he gets it done. But I can't be sure she's still there. You see, the guard who stowed her away in Newgate talked about selling her to a brothel. I can't be sure he did, though, 'cause he was found dead the next morning. Stabbed in the heart, he was."

Raile felt sick inside—he wanted to slam the man against the wall, but he had to remain calm so he could find out more.

"If I were to look for her, I would start my search in Newgate?"

"If you're thinking you need to make sure she's out of your way, I'd put my worry aside. She was of a delicate nature and wouldn't last long there. I'd say your troubles with Miss Maragon may already be over."

"Did you send a note to Miss Maragon's aunt, Lady Mary Rindhold?"

Jack shifted his eyes. "You can understand that I was angry because your mother, er, stepmother hadn't kept her bargain. I admit sending the letter was a mistake, and I should have come to you right away. But the aunt don't know where to find the girl, don't you worry none 'bout that." He glanced sideways at the duke. "Least not if I get my money."

"How much did my . . . stepmother offer you?"

"A hundred pounds. But when my brother went to collect, she claimed she didn't have the money just yet. You can see as how we got angry."

Raile looked at the man in disgust. "What made you conclude the woman was my stepmother? Surely she didn't tell you her name."

"Ole Jack ain't the buffoon some people might think. Even if she didn't give her name, I managed to follow her and find out who she was. And I'm glad I did, so I could come to you and get my money."

"I, too, am glad you came to me." Raile moved to his desk and unlocked the drawer and counted out a stack of gold coins.

Returning to the man, he held the money out to him. "I have included an extra fifty pounds, so that in the future, if my stepmother seeks you out, you will immediately come to me before doing her bidding."

Jack smiled. "That I will, Your Excellency. And may I say it's a real pleasure doing business with a gentleman like yourself."

Raile opened the door and spoke to Ambrose. "Escort this gentleman out the back way, and then attend me here. I will require my carriage at once."

So this was Lavinia's way of keeping Hugh from a marriage she didn't want. The irony in this was that Kassidy Maragon was the wrong girl.

14

When the daily gruel was pushed through the hatch, Kassidy barely had the strength to lift it to her mouth. As she gulped it down, it ran down her chin and onto the floor. Determined to get all the nourishment she could, Kassidy scooped it off the grimy floor and licked it off her fingers.

All thoughts of the civilized behavior were forgotten. She had become little more than an animal; her only concern was survival.

Suddenly, a key grated in the lock and the door swung open. Kassidy cowered against the wall as the light from a lantern blinded her. It took a moment for her eyes to focus on the two guards that stood over her. She trembled with relief when she saw neither of them was the man who had locked her in the cell and ravished her.

"Wonder what crime placed her in this hole?" one of the men asked. "Pathetic-looking creature, aren't she?"

Kassidy's hand went to her hair. She had always been considered pretty—this man had said she looked pathetic. When she had been abducted, she had been wearing her favorite green gown. Now it was so filthy and tattered, it was difficult to tell what color it was.

"It seems you are something of a trouble to us, girl. We don't know who you are, or who put you in solitary. We can't find any records that you even exist."

Raking her fingers through her tangled hair, Kassidy shook her head, too confused to talk.

"If Tom Brunson knew who you were, he took that knowledge with him to his grave. This whole matter seems odd to me."

Kassidy blinked her eyes. Was the man saying Brunson was dead? Was that why he never came back to torment her?

"Well, she's in a bad way and might die if we leave her here," the second guard observed. "I'm going to move her to the women's cells until we can find out about her."

Kassidy tried to concentrate on what the men were saying. Why did they think she might die? Was she that ill? She tried to stand, but her legs wouldn't hold her weight.

One of the men bent and unlocked her chains, and they fell to the floor with a clatter. Kassidy rubbed her raw wrists, with hope in her heart. Perhaps they were going to free her!

"What's your name, girl?" the guard demanded. "And it won't do you no good to lie."

"Kassidy Maragon," she managed to say, watching him write in a ledger. "I was incarcerated by mistake. I have done no wrong. Please let me out of here."

Both men laughed. "To hear them tell it, no one in here has done anything wrong. If any of you are to be believed, the criminals are on the streets, while the innocent are enjoying the hospitality of Newgate."

Kassidy knew she would get no help from either of these men. Their eyes were cold, and they looked through her rather than at her.

One of the guards took Kassidy's wrists and pulled her to her feet. She teetered until she leaned against the wall to get her balance.

"You better be able to walk if you want out of here," the man warned. "We don't intend to carry you." He motioned for her to follow him.

Clasping the iron bars for support, she inched her way out of the cell, fearing they would change their minds and leave her behind. She didn't breathe easy until she was out of the cell and the door was closed behind her.

She weakly plodded behind them, using the wall to help her stay erect. They passed through a damp, ill-lit maze, until they came to a stairway leading upward. Kassidy gripped the wooden rails—each step she took was agony.

Too weak to go on, Kassidy stumbled and fell, only to have the guard yank her up and forcefully slam her against the wall. There was cruelty in the man's eyes as he growled at her impatiently and shoved a wooden club into her ribs until she cried out in pain. He then brought the club down hard against her head, and she felt herself falling.

When he motioned for her to stand she quickly complied. At last they came to a large anteroom where women and children were wandering around aimlessly.

"Wait over there until we know what to do with you." The guard pointed to the corner with his club. "And stay away from the others."

Not wanting to be struck again, Kassidy pressed her body into the corner, sliding down the wall to sit on the cold floor. Her shoulders shook, and she bit her lips to keep her teeth from chattering.

When the prisoners in the room were herded back to their cells, no one paid the slightest attention to Kassidy. She looked at the door that stood open, knowing she was too weak to attempt to escape. Evidently, the guards had known that, too. She lowered her head, too weary to care.

A shadow fell across her face and she looked up to find a guard standing over her. "Come on, girl. You're still a mystery to us. But we'll find out about you."

Kassidy stood on wobbly legs and followed him as he unlocked the iron gate and led her down a long corridor to a large cell occupied by several women. Shoving her inside, he slammed and locked the door behind her.

Weakly, she moved to the corner and dropped down on one of the straw mats. She wanted to be left alone, to fall asleep and never awaken.

"Name's Elspeth O'Neill," one of the girls said, offering Kassidy a cup of water, which she gladly accepted. After a moment, she was able to catch her breath.

The Irish girl had light brown hair, and her face was covered with freckles. She was the first human being who had shown Kassidy kindness since she had come to this horrible place, and it brought tears to her eyes.

"I'm Kassidy Maragon," Kassidy said weakly.

"You don't look good to me," Elspeth said, placing her hand on Kassidy's forehead and finding it hot to the touch. "Here." She raised a cup to Kassidy's lips. "Have another drink of water. Tain't much, but it'll help some."

"Thank you," Kassidy said, drinking deeply.

"I can tell by the way you talk all fancy, that you be a lady born and fostered. What crime could you have done to be placed in this hell?"

Kassidy remembered her foolish attempt in trying to convince the guards of her innocence. She decided no one would believe the truth, but she would try to explain to Elspeth O'Neill. "I'm here," she said in a voice that trembled with emotion, "because I offended the wrong person."

"It matters not why you're here," Elspeth said philosophically. "They'd as soon hang you for the theft of a crust of bread as for stealing the crown jewels."

Kassidy felt cold inside, remembering what had happened to her at the hands of Tom Brunson. She would bury that deep within her mind. It was too painful to think about.

"It's imperative that I get out of here, Elspeth. There is something I must do."

"If you had wings you could fly, but seeing as you don't, you're doomed to serve out the sentence the court gave you."

Kassidy shook her head in misery. "I had no trial—no judge passed sentence on me." She looked into Elspeth's clear blue eyes. "I don't expect you to believe me, but it's the truth."

Elspeth spoke after a long silence. "I believe you." She lowered her voice. "How long you been here?"

"I . . . don't know. Would you know the date?"

Elspeth bit her lower lip in concentration. "I'd say it's right around July sixth, mayhaps the seventh. No later than that I don't 'spect."

"My God." Kassidy sobbed in despair, burying her face in her hands. "I was abducted on May twentieth. How long have you been here, Elspeth?"

"It's almost five years now. But it seems like I've always been here. My ma was widowed early and left with seven of us to feed. I had to help out by selling gingerbread in the streets. As soon as I was old enough, I was put to work as an apprentice to a jeweler. I didn't know the man was selling pilfered jewels. 'Course that didn't make no difference in the end. The magistrate said I was guilty all the same. I have only three months left to serve, and I'll be glad to be rid of this place."

"There's no hope for me, Elspeth. Most probably I'll die in here."

"Don't lose hope. If you do, you will die." Elspeth frowned when she saw the deep gash in Kassidy's head. "Who done that to you?"

"A guard."

Elspeth wet a rag and dabbed at the wound. "When I'm free, I'll go directly to your family and tell them you're here. They'll get you out."

Kassidy felt hope stir to life within her. "Oh, Elspeth, would you do that for me?"

"I'd do that and more. You put me in mind of my youngest sister, and being wrongly jailed myself, I know what you're feeling."

Kassidy tried to rise but fell back.

"You got what's called gaol distemper. I got it when I first come here. Took months to get well. Just when I thought I was well, it would return." Elspeth lifted a spoon of thin gruel to Kassidy's lips. "With only this slop to eat," she said in disgust, "it's hard to recover."

Every fourth day the inmates were ordered outside to walk in the courtyard. Once there, Kassidy drew in a breath of fresh air and gloried in feeling the sun on her upturned face. She listened to the hawkers in the street offering food to those who could pay. She watched the miserable press of humanity with their hands groping through the bars to passersby, begging for food.

How far she had fallen. She did not even have the price of a crust of bread. But she was too proud to beg for food—she would rather starve first. Her dignity had been sorely tested, but pride raged within her.

Hunger tightened the muscles of her stomach. With each indignity she suffered, Kassidy's resolve only became stronger to one day leave this place and confront the duke who had had her confined to this hell.

15

Accompanied by three outriders dressed in rich livery, the crested coach and six easily maneuvered through the narrow, bustling London streets.

When the coach stopped in front of Newgate, the two guards posted there watched with startled interest as a servant lowered the steps and held the door while a man descended. It was obvious from the man's manner of dress that he was someone of great importance. He looked neither to the left, nor to the right, as he entered the dreary halls of Newgate Prison.

With purposeful steps, Raile walked to the warden's office, Oliver one step behind.

When they entered the small dingy room, Raile approached the man at the desk. "I will speak to the warden at once," he said, removing his leather gloves and slapping them impatiently against his thigh.

"Are you expected, sir?" the man asked as he peered over a pile of legal-looking documents.

"Get the warden," Oliver intervened with a haughty manner. "And be so good as to inform him that the duke of Ravenworth wishes to talk to him in private. Be quick about it. His grace does not like to be kept waiting."

The little man scrambled to his feet, knocking over his chair in his haste to reach the inner office. "Yes, your grace," he called over his shoulder. "I'm certain Mr. Clarence will see you at once."

For two days Kassidy had not roused from her mattress. She could no longer tolerate the putrid gruel. She refused to eat when Elspeth tried to force it between her clenched teeth.

The other inmates had been taken for their daily exercise, but Elspeth had refused to leave Kassidy. Sadly, the Irish girl shook her head, knowing her charge would probably not last through the week.

When she heard a key grate in the lock and looked up to see the warden and two other men enter, Elspeth stared at them in bewilderment. It wasn't often that the warden himself visited the cells, and she wondered why he was there. As for the other men, one she dismissed as a servant, though a grand one, but the third man made her scramble to her feet. He was handsome and had about him an imperious air. His gaze swept past Elspeth to Kassidy, who was huddled on the mattress. Elspeth watched those dark eyes as they narrowed in anger, and then she saw them soften with pity.

Raile dropped down beside Kassidy, appalled at how thin and haggard she looked. Her blond hair was matted and filthy. He raised her limp hand and found that it was hot to the touch.

"She's ill," he said, looking accusingly at the warden. "I'm taking her out of here now."

"Yes, your grace. I don't know how this could have happened. I hope you don't blame me. If the plight had been called to my attention, I assure you——"

Raile silenced the man with a hard glance. "I suggest

you make certain such an atrocity does not happen in the future, Mr. Clarence. I am going to arrange for an investigation into certain criminal activities that are being conducted from here. As for Miss Maragon, I would be worried if I were you. If I told you the name of her uncle, you would tremble in fear, because he's an influential member of Parliament. If he so desires, he can cause you great trouble."

The warden's eyes filled with dread. "I want only to cooperate with you, your grace. I'll help in any way I can to make certain this doesn't happen again."

To Kassidy, everything was a blur. When she could focus, she saw the face of the man she hated most in the world.

"No," she moaned. "Not another nightmare. Don't touch me. I'm frightened of you. Go away—go away."

Elspeth tapped the duke on the shoulder. "Be you responsible for this?" She pointed a bony finger at Kassidy. "She's a good one and deserves better."

Raile scooped Kassidy up in his arms and peered down at the girl whose eyes bore into him. "She will come to no harm from me."

"She better not, or I'll find you when I'm out of here—and I get out soon."

The warden shoved Elspeth back against the bars.

"Here, now, don't you be bothering his grace. Get on out with the others and take your exercise."

Elspeth edged toward the door. "I'll go, but you best heed my warning. I know who you are, and I'll hunt you down if you hurt her." With a last look at Kassidy, she darted through the door and down the corridor.

Kassidy wasn't certain if she was dreaming. But if she was, she wanted to awaken. Fearfully, she reached out and touched Raile's face. This was no dream. He was real. What new torture had he in mind for her? she wondered in desperation.

She was too weak to fight him. Let him do what he would with her, she was just too weary to care.

Raile saw the fear in Kassidy's eyes and wished there was some way he could reassure her that he had come to help her.

"It's all right," he said soothingly. "I'm taking you out of here."

Her eyes blinked. She tried to move out of his arms, but he held her fast. When he enfolded her in his cloak, she wondered if he wanted to smother her.

"No, please don't hurt me anymore," she whispered through parched lips. "Just . . . let me die."

Raile felt his heart contract. "You are safe now, Miss Maragon. Please put your trust in me."

Closing her eyes, Kassidy went limp in his arms.

All through the long day Kassidy dwelled in a nightmarish world of pain and torment. She knew she was no longer in Newgate, but where was she? Wherever it was, she was being tortured.

Forceful voices urged her to roll over, and her gown was stripped over her head. Someone was bathing her in cool water, while she shivered with cold. She was then dressed in a fresh gown and forced to use energy she did not possess. She only wanted to be left alone to die.

Once, there was a man hovering over her, spooning foul-tasting liquid into her mouth. She was sure she was being poisoned, or they were drugging her once more.

At times she wished herself back in Newgate where she wouldn't be poked and prodded and no one would demand she awaken from her dreamworld.

Kassidy would have been much more frightened had she known that she had been brought to the duke of Ravenworth's town house.

Since Lady Mary was away from London searching

for her niece, Raile was trying to get word to her. In the meantime, he had assumed responsibility for Kassidy and installed her in his town house. He sent for Dr. Worthington.

Raile stood outside her bedroom, feeling helpless. In anger, he moved to the stairs, ready to confront Lavinia and Hugh.

He burst into the dining room, his face a mask of fury. "I asked you both here for a reason. Come to my study at once," he demanded.

Lavinia took a sip from her wineglass and studied his face. "What can be so important that we must interrupt our meal? Has it to do with Doctor Worthington being here?"

Hugh noticed the dangerous glint in Raile's eyes. "Perhaps we should do as he says, Mother."

"Unless you want the servants to know about family matters, I suggest you both come with me now," Raile ground out. Without another word, he spun on his heels and left the room. Lavinia placed her napkin on the table and slid her chair back. There was speculation in her eyes. "Come, Hugh, let us see what's plaguing Raile tonight." Her voice was laced with sarcasm. "I'm sure it won't be a pleasant encounter."

"Raile," she announced airily, settling herself in a leather chair in the study, "have you no better manners than to—"

"I have not called you here for a lesson in manners, madame." His voice was controlled, but his eyes showed his leashed anger.

"Then what do you want?" Hugh asked, picking up an antique snuffbox and examining it lazily.

Raile stood before his brother. "What would you say if I told you I have talked to Jack Beale?"

Hugh shrugged. "Then I would ask you, who the hell is Jack Beale?"

Raile was relieved. He believed his brother. Hugh had never been able to hide his feelings. It was obvious he knew nothing about his mother's dealings with Jack Beale.

Raile turned his attention to his stepmother, who was tightly gripping the arm of the chair, her face white, her eyes veiled. "And you, Lavinia." He moved to stand over her. "Would you say the same? Do you know Jack Beale?"

She shook her head. "I don't know what you're talking about, Raile. Is there something you are accusing me of?"

"I already know of your guilt, Lavinia. I have proof that you had Miss Maragon abducted and placed in Newgate."

Lavinia was shocked for a moment, but only because she hadn't known that the Maragon girl still lived.

She managed to answer Raile in an even voice and state quite honestly: "I know nothing about Miss Maragon being in Newgate."

"What's this?" Hugh asked in amazement. "Abigail's in Newgate?"

Lavinia came to her feet and walked to the desk, where she ran her fingers over the smooth surface. "I did not have anyone taken to Newgate, Raile," she repeated. "But make no mistake about this, my son will not be tied to that woman."

"Madame, I have learned about your little scheme to be rid of Miss Maragon." His words were clipped as if he were barely holding onto his temper. "You could have saved yourself so much trouble. You see, you had the wrong girl."

She stared at him with her mouth open—shock clearly written on her face. "What are you saying?"

"It's true, Lavinia." His eyes hardened like stones. "We all supposed the girl who came to Ravenworth

Castle was Abigail Maragon, when in truth, Abigail died in childbirth. The one I met was her sister, Kassidy Maragon."

Hugh's face whitened. "Abigail's dead?"

"Yes, Hugh, she's dead," Raile said, feeling revulsion for Hugh and his mother. "You left Abigail Maragon to bear your child alone and she died. I hope you realize that what you did to her was reprehensible."

Lavinia linked her arm through Hugh's. "He did nothing, Raile, and I won't allow you to blame him. It was the girl's frivolous actions that caused her death."

Hugh shook his mother's hand off his arm and walked to the window, where he stood staring out. "She died, and I never knew it. I loved Abigail," he murmured, knowing he meant it. There was an emptiness in his heart, and he wanted to be alone, to think about the peaceful days he had spent with his wife in the cottage beside the river.

"The time for lamenting has passed, Hugh," Raile said harshly. "You should have been there while she was alive."

For the first time in Hugh's life, he felt ashamed. "I never meant to leave her."

"As for you, madame," Raile said, turning back to Lavinia. "You had better pray that Kassidy Maragon doesn't die as a result of your actions. Make no mistake about it, if she does, I'll turn you over to the magistrate. And should she survive and wish to see you punished, I'll see that you are. In such case, the DeWinter name will not save you."

Lavinia saw the contempt in Raile's eyes and trembled with fear. He did not make idle threats. If he said he would turn her over to the magistrate, he would. "You can't prove I did anything wrong," she said defiantly.

"Oh, but I can, Lavinia. You and I are not the only ones who know about your part in all this."

"You go too far, Raile," Hugh exploded. "I know you hate my mother, but to suggest she would harm someone . . ."

Raile sneered. "Ask your mother about the midnight trip to the nursery where your daughter lay, and then tell me she wouldn't harm a total stranger."

Hugh looked uncertain. "I don't believe you," he said at last, but there was no conviction in his voice.

Raile smiled without humor. "I would believe anything of her, Hugh. You just haven't stood in her way when she wants something—and I pray you never do."

Lavinia's eyes narrowed. "I would fight you and the whole world to save my son, no matter what you say."

"But who, madame, will save your son from you?"

Lavinia's eyes blazed her hatred for Raile.

"Enough," he said, when she would have spoken. "I will hear no more of your lies. You and Hugh will vacate my home no later than tomorrow. I will no longer abide either of you living under my roof."

"Are you sending us back to the country?" Hugh asked, not wanting to leave London.

"Where you go, Hugh, and what you do, is no longer any concern of mine. But you will not occupy any of my houses."

Hugh looked confused. "Then where—"

Lavinia held up her hand to silence her son. "Surely you aren't going to turn us out without any means of support."

"Not at all. Hugh has his allowance and I have something for you." Raile moved to his desk, opened a drawer, and counted out several stacks of coins. He held them out to Lavinia, and when she wouldn't take them, dropped the money into her hand.

"One hundred pounds, madame. The amount you promised to pay Jack Beale." His eyes bore into her. "I would not try to enlist Mr. Beale's help again, Lavinia. You see, I bought his loyalty, and he will report only to me."

Lavinia was bravest when she was cornered. "Surely you don't expect me to live on this pittance," she scoffed. She flung the money down, and it scattered across the floor. "I don't need your charity, Raile."

Raile moved to the door before turning back to her. "You might not want to be so frivolous with the money, madame. You will get no more from me. I will allow you to take one of the coaches and the six grays, and your personal effects, but nothing more. Remember, I said I want you both gone from here by tomorrow."

After Raile departed, Hugh went down on his knees, gathering up the scattered coins. "I've never seen Raile so incensed."

"Oh, shut up. Are you so witless you don't understand the consequences of Raile's anger? I will have to move into the pitiful house your father left me. My existence will become a drudgery. My friends will pity me— I will become a nonentity. It will no longer be considered fashionable to invite me to parties. I'm ruined— ruined!"

Hugh dutifully handed the money to his mother. "Perhaps we should instruct the servants to pack our belongings. I think Raile meant what he said."

Lavinia's eyes gleamed with hatred. "He has won this skirmish, but I shall win the war."

Hugh glanced at his mother. "Did you do what Raile accused you of, Mother?"

Lavinia gritted her teeth. "Absurd boy, it's as you said. Raile hates me, and he would say anything to discredit me in your eyes."

16

Kassidy awoke in a gathering darkness. Storm clouds had blocked out the sun, and the sound of lightning ripped across the heavens in jagged splinters while thunder struck with a force that shook the house. She stared for a moment at the open window where lace curtains twisted in the wind.

She heard someone enter, and a middle-aged servant hurried to close the window.

"Who are you?" Kassidy asked in bewilderment. "And where is this place?"

"Well, bless you, miss," the woman said, lighting a candle. "You must have been frightened waking up in a strange room. I'm Mrs. Fitzwilliams, housekeeper for the duke of Ravenworth. And this is his town house."

At the sound of the dreaded name, Kassidy turned her face to the pillow, fear causing her slender body to quake. "So I am still a prisoner." Her eyes went to the door, as if she feared the duke would enter at any moment. "Why am I here?"

Mrs. Fitzwilliams shook her head as she straightened the covers. "Now, miss, you are certainly not a prisoner.

In fact, it was his grace who brought you here and engaged Doctor Worthington to attend you. You have been very ill. His grace had me come in from the country to look after you. He wants to do everything that will help you recover."

Kassidy moaned as weakness washed over her. "I don't understand why he's doing this."

"Now, now," the housekeeper said soothingly. "You are not to worry about anything. The doctor is very encouraged by your recovery. He just wants you to rest, eat well, and grow stronger."

Kassidy stared at the woman suspiciously. She looked grandmotherly, with white hair, rosy cheeks, and soft brown eyes. But how could she trust anyone who worked for that dreadful man? She voiced her doubts to the housekeeper.

"Why would the duke want to help me?"

"I'm sure his grace will explain it all to you in time. You just rest now."

"Are you from Ravenworth Castle?"

"Indeed I am. I have been in the DeWinters' service for over forty years," Mrs. Fitzwilliams said with pride.

Kassidy's eyes were so heavy she could hardly keep them open—the bed was soft, and snuggled beneath the downy coverlet, she was warm for the first time in weeks. She could hear the gentle rain pattering against the windowpane, and she yawned, giving the housekeeper an apologetic smile.

"If you are from Ravenworth Castle, perhaps you can tell me about my sister's baby."

"Indeed I can, miss. The child enjoys good health and is a darling little girl. We all love her, and I'm afraid we have spoiled her terribly. Sweetness is what she is, and it is what we call her."

Kassidy closed her eyes. Thank God, the child was well.

"Sweetness," she murmured sleepily. "If only I could see her."

"Soon, miss, soon. You must rest now."

Kassidy was asleep before Mrs. Fitzwilliams extinguished the candle. The housekeeper stood over her a long moment, thinking her color was better, but she still did not look well.

"Poor little girl," the housekeeper whispered compassionately. "Looks like life's been hard on you."

Lady Mary was shown into the salon, where Raile was waiting for her. It had been only three days since she had received word that her niece had been located.

Lady Mary looked anxiously at Raile. "Is my niece well? I want to see her at once."

"She has been very ill, but I am told she is recovering nicely." He looked uncomfortable. "You will understand about her illness when I tell you where I found her."

"Where was she?" Lady Mary was alarmed.

Raile had been dreading this moment. He drew in a deep breath as he prepared to recount what had befallen Miss Maragon. He did not spare Lavinia or Hugh, or for that matter, himself.

He watched the horror on Lady Mary's face turn to anger and indignation. When he finished, she rose to her feet, furiously pacing the floor.

"I will hold that woman and your brother both accountable for this atrocity. They have not yet paid for their crime."

"You have my pledge that I will deal with them. I thought you might want me to handle this matter delicately so your niece would not have to suffer public knowledge of her humiliation."

"It was a great deal more than humiliation, your

grace. I am not prepared to let that woman get away without punishment. What I don't understand is why she would have done such a thing to Kassidy."

Raile lowered his head, feeling the dishonor of his family weighing heavily on his heart. "We all mistakenly thought Kassidy was her sister, and when I insisted Hugh marry the girl he had wronged, Lavinia concocted this plan to be rid of her."

Lady Mary's eyes blazed with wrath. "But that's ridiculous. Your brother was already married to Abigail. I want to see your stepmother suffer the same degradation she forced Kassidy to endure. And my husband can make certain it happens."

"If that's what you want to do, then we shall. I am willing to help you in any way I can. Certainly Lavinia deserves to be punished for what she did. But that will not make up to Miss Maragon for what she has suffered. It might, in fact, make her suffer more."

Lady Mary dropped her head in her hands. "You are right. I must consider what this would do to Kassidy. I will not have her exposed to a public trial." She looked at Raile, seeing the pain in his eyes. He had been deeply affected by what had happened to Kassidy. "How will we punish them if not through the law?"

"I have already turned them both out of my home. And as for my stepmother, I am no longer answerable for her expenses. I have thought about sending Hugh out of the country to get him away from his mother's influence."

Lady Mary shook her head. "It's not enough."

"I agree. What would you have me do?"

"For now, nothing. I want to hear my husband's views on the matter." She reached out and touched Raile's hand. "I do not blame you in any of this, your grace. Without your help, we would never have found Kassidy."

"I don't excuse myself, Lady Mary. A young girl has suffered a great deal because of my family."

"I want to move my niece to my house as soon as possible. I intend to see that nothing like this will ever happen to her again."

"Before you go up to her, I wonder if you would allow me to speak to you about another matter." Raile watched the way the sunlight streaked across the oak floor. "I . . ." He paused as if trying to find the right words. "I would like to discuss Miss Maragon's future with you."

"I will take care of her future," Lady Mary said with assurance. "She will come and live with me."

Raile had never proposed marriage before, and he found the words stuck in his throat. "I would consider it an honor if you would allow me to ask your niece to become my wife."

Lady Mary stared at Raile as if he had lost his mind. "You cannot have said what I think you said. You don't even know Kassidy."

"Many marriages are arranged before the parties are well acquainted. I would make her an amiable husband."

"A marriage of convenience?" Lady Mary was astounded. "It wouldn't be a good match. Besides, I have always wanted Kassidy to marry for love. You would not be marrying her for that reason."

"That's true, Lady Mary. But I can give her all the advantages, and she will never want for anything."

"Kassidy has never been impressed with wealth." Lady Mary surveyed Raile. His dark good looks would make him popular with the ladies, even if he weren't wealthy and titled. He was the catch of the season—of the decade for that matter.

"What would be the advantage to you if you married my niece?"

He looked into her eyes, deciding to be truthful. "The prince has advised me to take a wife. I thought your niece might be willing to fill that role for me."

"I see that you have given this a great deal of thought. But why Kassidy?"

"My family has caused a great deal of harm to your niece. I want to make it up to her in any way I can." He dropped his gaze. "I feel I owe her that much."

"Surely you are far too noble," she said bitingly. "You want to marry my niece because of your guilt?"

"I prefer to say it's for honor, rather than guilt. And, as for being noble, I would say it's more selfish. Miss Maragon is from an old and respected family and would make a suitable duchess. She does not love me, so therefore would make no demands on me. And I would have a wife when I am ready for an heir. I like a well-ordered life."

Suddenly Lady Mary burst out laughing. "You don't know my niece if you believe life with her would be peaceful. Be warned that she has a way of making her presence known. You met her—you should know that."

"I admit she has intensity for one with so . . . modest an appearance."

"What?" Lady Mary said, straightening in her chair. "Kassidy? You think she's unattractive? Are we thinking of the same girl?"

Raile hoped he had not offended her. "I beg your pardon, Lady Mary. In my long association with the army, I have grown accustomed to plain speaking. Let me assure you that Miss Maragon's appearance is of no importance to me. Am I right in assuming she has no other prospects of marriage?"

"Why would you presume that?"

Raile looked uncomfortable. Surely Lady Mary knew that her niece was no beauty, and it was obvious that she was destitute. She did not seem to have much to offer a man. "Perhaps I was wrong." He decided to be gallant. "Is there a young man she would prefer to marry?"

"Kassidy has lived a secluded life. There is no gentleman in her life," Lady Mary admitted. "But, it's difficult for me to believe there is no lady you fancy. I'm sure you know you are considered to be a most desirable catch, your grace."

Raile smiled slightly. "Every man would like to think that's true about himself."

"It's not difficult to hear glowing comments about you. One has only to approach a group of unmarried ladies at a ball to hear them speculate how fortunate they would be to catch your eye, while the gentlemen speak of your daring exploits as a hero."

Raile had the strangest feeling Lady Mary was mocking him. "I have had little time to attend balls, and little liking of females who want only a title."

"Surely, your grace, you underestimate your other . . . attributes."

Raile's eyes gleamed with humor. "Can it be that you are trifling with me, Lady Mary?"

She caught her breath at the melting look in his dark eyes. She could only wonder how devastating he would be for a young and inexperienced girl like Kassidy.

"No, your grace. I was merely making a statement of fact. I am a wife who is content with my husband. We are very happy together."

"You don't think I'd make your niece happy, do you?" he observed shrewdly.

"On occasion someone will come along who is extraordinary in every way. Kassidy is just such a person. She has not known a great deal of happiness in her life—she needs to be cherished."

"I'm sure she is all you say," Raile agreed, thinking every aunt had a favorite. Kassidy obviously was hers.

The girl he had met had spirit, but he had seen nothing extraordinary about her.

"She is intelligent," Lady Mary continued, "and has probably already deduced that your family was involved in her abduction. She may see an offer of marriage from you as an affront." Lady Mary was certain her niece would never accept this arrogant man, who somehow felt it was his duty to make her his duchess as an atonement for his family's misdeeds. "I will release you from any feelings of guilt concerning my niece. And we shan't ever tell her about your proposal."

"I cannot wish my guilt away. I would consider it an honor to have her as my wife."

"Perhaps you should reconsider, your grace." Lady Mary could not suppress a smile. "If Kassidy were your wife, she would lead you a merry chase." She came to her feet in a whisper of silk. "I would like to see my niece at once. I have been most anxious about her well-being."

Raile gave a curt nod. "I'll have the housekeeper take you to her." Suddenly his eyes were probing. "You do not think your niece will look upon me with favor?"

"If you want my advice, abandon your plans to marry Kassidy. She is not the person you believe her to be."

"But you have no objections to my suit?"

She laughed with amusement. "None at all, your grace, but Kassidy will."

17

Kassidy was drifting in a dreamless sleep when she smelled the sweet fragrance of roses that reminded her of Aunt Mary. A cool cheek was pressed against hers, and she opened her eyes, afraid she was still dreaming.

"You have come," Kassidy whispered in a quivering voice. "Oh, Aunt Mary, you have found me."

"Yes, dearest. I have come to take you home with me."

The tears Kassidy had held back for so long now washed down her face. "I have been so frightened and alone. I cannot tell you the unspeakable things I have witnessed."

Lady Mary clutched her niece to her. "You need never be afraid again."

"Please take me away from this place," she pleaded. "Don't let that man near me."

Lady Mary held Kassidy back and looked at her inquiringly. "What man do you mean?"

"The duke. He's a monster!"

Her aunt motioned for several servants who had been waiting near the door to come forward. "Lift her and carry her gently," she ordered, placing a robe about Kassidy. "And take care on the steps."

Kassidy closed her eyes. At last she could sleep without fear.

Kassidy's long ordeal had ended. In her aunt's home, she felt safe from the long reach of the duke. She was propped against three fluffy pillows, and Aunt Mary sat beside her, noting how pale and ashen she was. Her once lustrous hair hung lankily, and her green eyes were dull, with no evidence of the spark of humor they had once held.

"My heart aches, dearest, for what you have had to endure." She placed a spoon to Kassidy's lips. "But you must put that behind you. Eat some of this broth," Lady Mary said coaxingly.

When Kassidy refused, Lady Mary gave her a warning glance and the girl took a small sip.

Kassidy sighed. "I don't want anything to eat, Aunt Mary."

"But you haven't eaten all day."

Again Kassidy took the spoon in her mouth to appease her aunt.

"Was it very awful for you in Newgate?" Aunt Mary asked, thinking it might help Kassidy to talk about her ordeal.

Kassidy shivered. "I don't want to think about it." Her voice rose hysterically. "I never want to remember what happened there."

"If it is your desire, we need never mention it again. But I feel something deeper is bothering you—can I be mistaken?"

Kassidy turned her head away as her aunt tried to put the spoon to her mouth again. How could she tell her aunt what that horrible guard had done to her—no, she would not think about it, and she would tell no one her terrible secret.

"Please take more of the broth," Aunt Mary coaxed. "How will you ever regain your strength if you don't eat?"

"I don't want to get well," Kassidy said in a rare show of self-pity. "Mother and Father are dead, and now Abigail is gone. I have no reason to live."

Lady Mary had never seen Kassidy so dejected. It was not like her to give up—she was a fighter, a survivor. It was apparent her spirit had been crushed, and she was only a shell of the beautiful young girl she had once been.

"Kassidy, you know Abigail would not have wanted you to grieve for her. She would want you to get well—to live a happy life." She took Kassidy's limp hand in hers. "You must fight this, Kassidy."

Tears glistened on the tip of Kassidy's eyelashes and then rolled down her cheek. She had no answer for her aunt, so she turned her head away.

Aunt Mary kissed Kassidy on the forehead. "You are wrong when you say you have no reason to get well. Have you forgotten Abigail's daughter? She will need you—I need you."

Kassidy began sobbing, and her aunt enfolded her in comforting arms.

"Oh, Aunt Mary, I have committed a grievous deed by placing Abigail's innocent baby in that monster's grasp. I suffer so, wondering at the fate of the child." Kassidy dabbed at her eyes with her sleeve. "I must get the baby back." Her eyes were frantic. "I will not rest until I hold her in my arms again."

Aunt Mary smoothed Kassidy's hair away from her face. "If we had the baby with us, would that make you happy?"

Kassidy nodded. "He . . . that monster—do you think he has harmed the child?"

"Kassidy, the duke is not the monster you suppose him to be. Don't fear that he will harm the baby. It was he who found you in Newgate and brought you to his house."

"Of course he found me, Aunt Mary," Kassidy said in desperation. "He knew where to look for me because he had me taken to Newgate."

Lady Mary shook her head. "We won't talk about this now, Kassidy. I just want to assure you that the duke is not the source of your troubles. He is a man of honor, and there is much goodness in him. He served with Wellington and was commended for his bravery at Waterloo. He even received the Order of the Garter."

There was a look of bewilderment on Kassidy's face. "He served at Waterloo?" She tried to clear her head. "He could not have seen the war through to its conclusion?"

"Yes, he did, Kassidy. He was desperately wounded at Waterloo and was in a hospital in Belgium for many months. So severe were his injuries that it was believed he would die. In fact," she added, "it seems I recall reading about his death in the *Times*."

Kassidy wished her head would stop pounding. "I don't understand. If the duke was with Wellington, how could he have been with Abigail? Perhaps he was home on furlough when he met her."

Mary squeezed her niece's hand and said in a kind voice, "Try to understand this, Kassidy. His grace never knew Abigail, and he was never her husband."

Kassidy's head was pounding, and she closed her eyes because the bright light in the room only made it ache unbearably. "If only I could think. Everything is mixed up in my head."

"There, there, dearest," Aunt Mary soothed. "You need not dwell on anything but getting well. When you have significantly recovered, we will talk on this again. All you need to remember now is that you have no reason to fear for Abigail's baby. I have seen her, and she is doing well."

"You saw her?"

"Indeed I did. She has the whole staff of servants at Ravenworth Castle as her slaves."

Kassidy's eyes were so heavy she couldn't open them. "I am weary, Aunt Mary. May I sleep now?"

"Of course you may. But I will expect you to eat when you awaken."

Aunt Mary removed two of the pillows from underneath Kassidy's head and pulled the bed covers to her chin.

"I will try, Aunt Mary," Kassidy murmured.

"There is something I want you to think about, dear. The duke has asked to see you. I believe he will be able to correct any misconceptions you may have about him."

Kassidy's eyes snapped open and widened with fear. "No! Never! Don't let him come near me. I don't ever want to see him again."

Aunt Mary's voice was soothing, "All right, dearest. Go to sleep now."

"I don't want to sleep." Kassidy shook her head until her limp hair swirled about her head. "Sometimes I have these . . . dreadful nightmares."

"Are you certain you wouldn't like to talk about your ordeal at Newgate? My father was fond of saying it was easy to talk one's troubles away with the right person. I have always found that to be true. I would like to be that person for you, Kassidy."

A deep sob racked Kassidy's body. "I cannot bear to think about that horrible place . . . and what happened to me there—I just can't."

"All right, dearest. Would you feel better if I sent for the baby?"

There was hope in Kassidy's eyes. "If only . . . if only I could hold Abigail's baby in my arms and know that she has come to no harm." Hope flamed in her eyes and then faded. "He would never allow me to have the child. He would withhold her from me as some new form of torture."

Aunt Mary felt Kassidy's forehead and realized she was feverish again. "Sleep now. I'll see what I can do about the baby."

A week passed, and with daily coaxing from her aunt, Kassidy began eating light meals.

One morning Kassidy awoke feeling stronger and was able to sit up in bed. The maid plaited her hair into a long braid to keep it from tangling. She then helped Kassidy bathe and dressed her in a powder-blue nightgown with pink ribbons at the throat and wrists.

Kassidy watched her aunt fluttering about the room, placing fresh flowers in bright-colored vases and tying back the curtains to let in the sunshine.

"Dearest Aunt Mary, how can I ever thank you for all you have done for me? I must have been a difficult patient at times. Surely I am a tiresome guest."

Aunt Mary planted a kiss on Kassidy's cheek. "Nonsense. And you aren't a guest. This is your home."

"Henry will never allow me to remain with you, Aunt Mary, though I wish he would," Kassidy said wistfully. I'm sure he will be here soon, insisting I return to the country with him."

"He has already indicated as much to me in a letter, Kassidy. I am determined to plead with him to let you live with me if it will help—but you know Henry."

Kassidy's eyes widened with dread. "Henry knows about me being in Newgate?"

"Yes, and being Henry, he believes it was your fault. I don't understand why he is always so harsh with you. He allowed Abigail much more freedom than he did you."

"I'm sure he is still angry that I ran away to be with Abigail."

Aunt Mary's face brightened. "We shall just have to keep telling him you are unfit for travel. I want to make the most of your time here. It's been so long since I've had a young girl in the house." She sighed. "I hardly see my daughter since she married and moved to Scotland."

Kassidy was very close to tears, but she would not cry. "I thank you for allowing me to stay with you. I'll try not to be a burden."

"Nonsense, don't even think it. Right now there is someone who has been waiting to see you."

Kassidy's hand went to her hair, and she knew she still looked frightfully ill. "I don't want to see anyone, Aunt Mary. Please don't make me."

"I believe you will want to see this person."

Lady Mary motioned to someone who was in the hallway, just out of Kassidy's sight.

Kassidy's hand went to her throat as Mrs. Fitzwilliams entered, carrying the baby. Kassidy held out her hands to the tiny girl, and the housekeeper placed the child in her arms.

Kassidy could hardly swallow past the lump in her throat as she stared down at the baby. She had Abigail's eyes and hair, as well as her delicate features. The chubby little hand curled about Kassidy's finger, and she smiled through her tears.

"She's beautiful." She lifted the baby to her and kissed the tiny lips. "Oh, she is so dear. I love her so much. How could I have given her away?"

Mrs. Fitzwilliams dabbed at her eyes. "She's a right hearty little baby. We at Ravenworth will miss her. But his grace believes she'll be better off with you, miss."

Kassidy's eyes took on a defiant look. "I'll not give her back to that man. He will never have her again," she said fiercely.

Lady Mary exchanged glances with the housekeeper and motioned for her to leave.

Kassidy glanced down at the infant. Aunt Mary was right. The baby needed her. And when the child was older, only Kassidy would be able to tell her how much her mother had loved her.

The baby suddenly smiled and Kassidy's heart swelled within her. She clasped the infant to her gently.

"Isn't she beautiful, Aunt Mary?"

"Indeed she is," Lady Mary agreed, dropping down on the bed and touching the child's smooth cheek. "But she doesn't yet have a name you know."

"That's right." Kassidy was thoughtful for a moment. "What do you think we should call her?"

"I believe Abigail would have wanted you to be the one to name her—don't you?"

Kassidy stroked the baby's soft blond hair. "I think Abigail would have liked me to name her after our mother."

She raised the baby over her head. "You are Arrian, little one."

Aunt Mary nodded approvingly. "It's a good name. My sister would have loved her namesake."

Suddenly Kassidy's eyes clouded. "Her full name is Arrian DeWinter."

Aunt Mary stood up and moved to the door. "Just love her—that's all she needs."

"Poor little baby is all alone in the world, Aunt Mary."

"She has you, Kassidy. I'll leave the two of you alone so you can become better acquainted."

Kassidy was so in awe of the tiny girl in her arms, she did not hear her aunt depart. All the love she had felt for her sister was now transferred to Abigail's daughter.

She examined her niece from head to toe and found her perfect and healthy.

"Well, little Arrian," she cooed. "It appears you were

well cared for, after all."

Kassidy curled up with the baby on her arm. "I am going to love you so much, you'll never miss not having a mother or father. You have my promise on that."

Later, when Aunt Mary returned with the wet nurse to collect the baby, they found Kassidy asleep, clutching the sleeping child in her arms.

A tear rolled down Lady Mary's cheek as she saw the half smile on Kassidy's face. This child would help Kassidy heal.

Over dinner that night Lady Mary said as much to her husband. "Now that the baby is with Kassidy, we will see her improve rapidly."

"My dear," said her practical husband, "think you that Henry will let Kassidy keep the baby?"

"Oh, George, he would not dare deny Kassidy's right to Abigail's baby."

"He'll try."

"I'll fight my pompous nephew in this. Kassidy must be allowed to keep the baby with her. George, just imagine what Kassidy's life will be like when she returns to the country with her brother. It's beyond thinking about. Have you noticed that Henry seems to have a strange obsession where Kassidy is concerned? I can't explain it, I only know it makes me uncomfortable and worries me."

"I have noticed, but I don't know what we can do about it, Mary."

"We must persuade Henry to let her stay with us. I know him—he's sadistic. He'll find some way to use the baby to hurt Kassidy."

"Don't forget, Henry is Kassidy's legal guardian," he reminded his wife.

18

On the days when Kassidy felt well enough, she kept Arrian in her bedroom, with the wet nurse nearby to help in case she was needed. Often when Lady Mary came to visit, she would hear Kassidy's laughter ring out, and smiled with satisfaction, knowing her niece was healing.

Today Kassidy had felt well enough to be carried downstairs and was lounging in the solarium, where she could look into the garden. Arrian's cradle was nearby so she could watch over her.

She was so distracted by the baby that she didn't see the maid who entered the solarium.

"Excuse me, Miss Maragon, but Lady Mary isn't home, and the duke of Ravenworth has asked if he might call on you. Shall I show him in, or ask him to return when her ladyship is home?"

Kassidy looked fearfully at the cradle, wondering if the duke had come for the baby. The thought of seeing him brought raging fear to her heart. She was about to tell the maid to send him away when she thought better of it. She would have to meet him one day, and what better place to face him than in the safety of her aunt's home.

"You may show him in," she said at last, pulling the coverlet across her lap and calling on all her courage for the encounter.

Raile paused in the doorway. The flickering rays of the sun caught the red in the young girl's hair and turned it the color of burnished gold. She looked small and insignificant in the oversized chair. Her face was pale and colorless, her green eyes filled with uncertainty. He approached her, his gaze moving to the cradle where his brother's baby slept.

"The child is well I trust?"

He was such a commanding presence that Kassidy's voice seemed trapped in her throat. All she could manage was a small nod. She wished her hands weren't trembling—she clasped them tightly in her lap, hoping he wouldn't notice. If only she weren't so weakened by her illness, perhaps she would have been better able to face him. It had been a mistake to see him alone.

"Miss Maragon," Raile said, "I'm pleased to learn that your health is much improved."

She wondered how he dared act as if he were concerned about her health. Her green eyes sparked with anger and her fear was forgotten.

"Do you think me so addle-brained that I do not know your true nature? Don't pretend you care about my feelings."

Raile moved to a chair, understanding her anger. "Do you mind if I am seated?"

"Do as you like," she said ungraciously, wishing she could send him away.

After Raile sat down he studied her for a long moment. "I admit you have reason to harbor animosity toward me, Miss Maragon, but let me assure you I have come here today to make amends."

"How can you make up for the weeks I spent in New-gate, or the nightmares that still plague my sleep? I want nothing from you except to be left alone."

He looked annoyed. "I see what I'm up against."

"I want you to leave now. I was mistaken in agreeing to see you."

He could tell that she was frightened of him—some-how he had expected the fearless young girl who had faced him at Ravenworth. He could only guess at what hell she must have lived through in prison.

"I ask only that you hear me out, Miss Maragon. Then if you like, I will leave. I have several matters I wish to discuss with you."

"Shall I call out for the butler? I have already asked you to leave."

Raile's chest expanded with the deep breath he inhaled. "After you hear what I have to say."

Kassidy stared at him as if he'd lost his mind. "My aunt explained to me that it was your brother who was responsible for my sister's death. To me you are one and the same." Suddenly she shook her head in bewilder-ment. "I cannot think why I was abducted and taken to that horrid place."

"I don't expect you to believe this, Miss Maragon, but I had nothing to do with your abduction. I can't tell you how sorry I am for what happened to you."

Unless he was a good actor, she thought she detected pity in his eyes. Pity was the one thing she didn't want from him.

And yet, somewhere in the dark recess of her mind Kassidy had a vague memory of the duke gently lifting her in his arms and carrying her out of the prison. He had taken her to his house where his housekeeper had cared for her. In the shadowed world of her feverish memory, she often confused truth with fiction.

"How do you explain away the fact that my abductors referred to your family by name?"

His eyes darkened with an expression she could not read. "I can explain that if you will only listen."

She pressed her hands over her eyes. "I . . . get events distorted sometimes. My dreams are so real, I sometimes mistake them for reality."

"You and I both made mistakes the day you left the baby with me, Miss Maragon—mine was in thinking you were the mother of the child—yours was in believing I was the father."

She leaned back against the pillow and closed her eyes. "I know that now," she admitted dully.

"Miss Maragon, whether you believe me or not, I want only to help you. I have your welfare uppermost in my mind."

He was handsome, she thought, and his dark eyes were hypnotic and mesmerizing. Most probably he was accustomed to having women give in to his slightest wish. What did he want from her? she wondered. "A villain may be handsome of face," she said at last, "but he is, nonetheless, a villain."

Raile's dark eyes danced with sudden humor. "So, you think me handsome?"

"Being handsome is no recommendation for a sterling character," Kassidy said flippantly.

"What would you say if I challenged you to reform me, Miss Maragon?"

"I would say, your grace, that challenge would be better left to those who would care whether or not you are reformed—I have no interest in you at all."

He found her quick wit refreshing. "Then I am to take it, it would be a futile effort if I asked you to become my wife?"

Kassidy stared at him in total bewilderment. "What did you say?" she asked, thinking she had surely misunderstood.

Raile stood. She had forgotten how tall he was, and how dark. She had to throw her head back to meet his eyes.

"I should not have blurted it out like that, but you see, I have matters that require my attention at my country estate and I have little time to spend on the gentility of courtship." He knew he was being imprudent, but it was too late to stop now. "What I ask, Miss Maragon, is if you would do me the honor of becoming my wife."

"Do you think me mad?" Kassidy gasped in disbelief. "How dare you insult me thus?"

The amusement was wiped off his face by a look of confusion. "I had meant it as a compliment, not an insult."

"Perhaps you suppose that by marrying me, you will keep me from informing the world about your brother's crimes?"

He sat in a chair near her. "I would be the first one to admit to the world that Hugh is a scoundrel."

She glared at him. "I would call him more than a scoundrel." She turned her face to the wall, striving to suppress the sob that was building deep inside. "You said you would leave if I wanted you to, and I do. Go away. I never want to see you again."

Raile felt such overwhelming pity for her. She was a pale, puny little creature, but she stirred to life within him a need to protect and care for her. He deeply felt blame for what had happened to her—after all it was his family who had brought her to this tragic state.

He reached out to her, only to let his hand drop to his side.

"I ask for only a moment more of your time to explain several matters to you."

She turned back to him, her eyes like ice. "You have nothing to say that I want to hear, and your proposal is unthinkable. How could you imagine I would marry the brother of the black-hearted brute who tricked my sister into marriage and then deserted her when she needed him most?"

Raile held her gaze by sheer force of will. He was quiet for a moment as he pondered her words. Was it possible that Hugh had married Abigail Maragon and kept it a secret from him and Lavinia? Lady Mary had thought so, and apparently Miss Maragon did also. "What exactly did your sister tell you?"

"When she was dying, Abigail asked me to take the baby to the duke of Ravenworth, who was her husband. Since you are the duke, you can see why I mistook you for her husband that day."

Raile felt anger build within him. So, Hugh had been up to his old tricks again, trying to woo a woman with the pretence of being titled. "If you believe nothing else, believe this—my family's honor is very important to me. I wish only to redeem the DeWinter integrity in your eyes."

There was something about him that made Kassidy believe in his sincerity. "Is it true that you fought at Waterloo?"

"Yes, I did, Miss Maragon. I have only recently returned after five years abroad."

"You cannot make up to me for the nights I lay on a straw mattress that was infested with lice. You cannot make up to me for the filthy gruel they served as food. You cannot make up to me for the loneliness and devastation I felt . . . and the unspeakable things that happened to me. No, your grace, you cannot compensate me for that by offering to marry me. I don't want to be associated with your family in any way."

There was a sick feeling in the pit of Raile's stomach as he gained more evidence of the poor girl's suffering. "I cannot make your pain go away any more than I can erase your memories," he said kindly. "But, Miss Maragon, you and I have a strong bond, whether you want to admit it or not."

"You are mistaken—I have no bond with you, your grace."

"But you have. The baby that came from your sister and my brother is that bond. Have you considered the child's future?"

Kassidy moved forward as if to stand, but fell back weakly. "Surely you aren't threatening me?"

"Of course not," he said in irritation. "I am merely suggesting that if we were married, we could give her a proper family."

"I don't want to marry you. Why should I? I am still not convinced you had nothing to do with my incarceration."

Raile was weary of defending himself to her. "I will be completely truthful with you, Miss Maragon. You were placed there by two men who were hired by my stepmother. She thought you were Abigail Maragon, and she thought she was protecting her son, Hugh, from an undesirable marriage."

"How could she do such a thing? You cannot imagine the unspeakable . . ."

"I'm sure we could never know the workings of Lavinia's mind," Raile said grimly. "But let me assure you that you need have no fear that she will ever harm you or the baby. She no longer has any interest in either of you."

"I would never marry you to ease your guilty conscience."

"I had hoped you might see it differently."

"I have higher expectations for my life, your grace. I have no desire to become involved in a loveless marriage." She blinked her eyes. "Furthermore, I, too, am proud. The Maragons might not be as wealthy and we may not be as powerful as the DeWinters, but we have an honored name."

"I know that. Do you think I would offer you my

name if I thought otherwise? Not even obligation would induce me to marry anyone unworthy of becoming the duchess of Ravenworth."

Kassidy's laughter was bitter. "I decline the honor."

"Consider well how your sister's child will benefit from such an arrangement. If you're of a mind to, with enough money, you can lift her so high, no one will dare look down on her."

Kassidy faced him proudly. "She doesn't need your money. I will take care of her."

"Then your final answer is no?"

Suddenly Kassidy shivered, remembering the filthy guard and what he had done to her while she had been unconscious. She would never feel clean again, and never be worthy of marrying any man, least of all this arrogant one before her.

"I would like you to leave now, your grace. We have nothing more to say to each other."

Raile stood up, looking deeply into her eyes. "Pity. I believe you and I would have dealt very well together, Miss Maragon."

She was too confused to answer.

"I take leave of you. But I shall not close the door on my proposal."

Kassidy could sense turmoil within him, but she also detected deep loneliness. She must be mistaken. Surely he was only trying to confuse her.

"Should you need me, I will be in my London house for the next two weeks, Miss Maragon, and then I return to Ravenworth."

Kassidy watched him walk away, wondering why she felt such a deep sense of loss.

19

Lady Mary came rushing into Kassidy's bedroom, her eyes filled with concern.

"Dearest, I heard that the duke of Ravenworth was here and you received him. I blame myself for not being with you. You should have sent him away."

"I was discourteous to him, Aunt Mary."

Lady Mary fluffed up Kassidy's pillow. "If you were rude to him or not, I'm sure it's not the end of the world. Don't worry about the incident."

"No," Kassidy whispered. "It's not that."

"You are obviously upset. Just don't think about the duke at all."

"Aunt Mary, you don't know what I've done."

Her aunt looked into Kassidy's eyes and saw fear there. "He said he wanted to ask you to marry him. Is that what he did that has upset you so?"

"You knew that man was contemplating such an absurd proposal, and you didn't warn me?"

"I tried to tell you on several occasions, Kassidy, but you forbade me to mention his name."

"I had no notion that was why he wanted to see me."

"He asked me for permission to speak to you of marriage. Although I didn't discourage him, I was sure you would decline his offer."

"I had to, Aunt Mary. But now I'm wondering if I made a grievous mistake."

"There, there, dearest. Don't fret. I don't want you to make yourself ill again."

A deep shudder shook Kassidy's body, and she handed a letter to Lady Mary. "I suppose this is what really has me upset. It's from Henry. He will be here tomorrow to take me home." She raised her hands in a hopeless gesture. "Perhaps I should marry the duke."

Lady Mary smiled encouragingly, trying to make light of the situation. "I won't have you marrying a man just to save you from Henry. When your brother arrives, I intend to convince him that you and Arrian will be better off with me."

Kassidy drew in a trembling breath. "Henry won't allow it."

"Just leave him to me. I believe with your Uncle George's help, we can get him to agree."

Kassidy was afraid to hope, but she couldn't help smiling at her aunt. "I would be so happy if only I could stay with you and Uncle George."

Lady Mary sat on the bed and took Kassidy's hand. "Let's not talk about Henry. Tell me more about the handsome duke, and how you tossed him out when every woman in the length and breadth of England would be glad to stand in your shoes."

"I found him to be not at all what I expected. He told me about his brother and stepmother. If he's all he appeared to be, he is a man of conviction, honor, and even compassion."

"And yet, feeling this way, you refused his suit."

"I also found him frightening."

Lady Mary looked deeply into Kassidy's eyes. "And intriguing also, I'll venture?"

"Yes, and that's the worst of it. I seem somehow drawn to him, and I don't know why. I felt this attraction the day I first saw him—I felt his presence even while I was in Newgate and if I were to close my eyes, I would feel his presence even now."

"Oh, dearest," Lady Mary said, brushing her cheek against Kassidy's, "you are only growing into a woman—with a woman's heart and a woman's yearnings. That is nothing to be distressed about. I can tell you that older and wiser women than you have lost their hearts to that handsome Raile DeWinter."

"So his name is Raile—I never knew." Kassidy traced the lacy pattern on her sleeve. "I am very confused about my feelings for him. But I can assure you I have not gone overnight from hate to love—but he is fascinating. Were you ever confused about your feelings for Uncle George?"

"Yes—in a way. But George is different from Raile DeWinter. George is like a quiet stream flowing in a steady direction with purpose and serenity. Raile DeWinter is like a storm-tossed sea, caught up in turmoil and excitement. He is troubled and seeking and needs someone to bring serenity to his life."

"Yes, I feel that, too. It's almost as if he's alone, with no one to care for him."

"Perhaps, Kassidy, you could be the one to bring him the peace he seeks."

"No, Aunt Mary," she said with regret, "it will not be I."

"Let's forget about Raile DeWinter for the moment and put our heads together so we can come up with a plan to thwart your brother."

Henry's voice was thick with fury as he faced his aunt. "I came for my sister, and I'll not leave without her. I insist you have her and the . . . child made ready to leave immediately."

"Be reasonable, Henry," Lady Mary pleaded, "Kassidy is still much too ill to travel. Allow her to remain here until she is stronger."

"To take her away now would be to court folly, Henry," George added his advice to his wife's. "Kassidy has been through a great deal."

"Yes, and had she stayed at home where she belonged, none of this would have happened to her."

Lady Mary glared at her nephew. "If I could lawfully keep Kassidy, I would do so."

Henry merely blinked. He knew his aunt did not hold him in high esteem, and he cared little for her opinion. "She will come home with me."

"What kind of life can she expect with you?" Lady Mary asked angrily. "Will she become your slave to clean and care for your children? And what about Abigail's daughter—will you allow her to remain with Kassidy? I demand to know the answers."

Henry rose to his feet. "I answer to no one where my sister is concerned. If you don't have her brought down at once, I'll go up and get her."

Kassidy stood in the doorway, using the doorknob for support. "There is no need for trouble, Aunt Mary. I'm prepared to leave with my brother."

Henry moved slowly to Kassidy, his eyes raking her face and then her body. "Have you no greeting for me, sister dear?"

"Hello, Henry," she said dully.

He turned to his aunt and uncle while he reached out and painfully gripped Kassidy's shoulder. "You see how it is," he said sarcastically, "my sister cannot wait to be back within the bosom of her family."

Lady Mary rushed forward and pulled Kassidy away from Henry. "We have failed, dearest. But have heart, I shall come for a visit as soon as possible." She turned her attention to Henry. "I shall expect you to take the greatest care of her health, and the baby."

Henry looked down his nose at his aunt. She was far too outspoken for a woman, and nothing like his sweet, gentle mother. "I know my responsibility and will discharge it as I see fit."

There was sorrow in Lady Mary's eyes as she hugged Kassidy. "Take heart. You are not alone."

Kassidy fought back her tears. "Yes, I know. I still have Abigail's daughter."

Kassidy sat beside Henry as the carriage left London and headed into open country. Thus far, Henry had been sullen, hardly speaking, and Kassidy found that worse than if he had raged at her—but the rage would come later—she knew it would.

She leaned back weakly against the headrest, and pulled the lap blanket around her.

The wet nurse that Henry had engaged was seated across from them, and Henry had refused to look at the baby.

At last Kassidy reached for Arrian and held her out for Henry's inspection. "Henry, I don't believe you have met your niece. I named her Arrian after our mother. Don't you think she would have been pleased?"

He glanced at the baby with blank eyes. "Give the child back to the nurse," he said gruffly. "It's not wise to get too attached to her."

Kassidy stared at him in trepidation. What could he mean by that? She dared not pursue the matter in front of the wet nurse; she would demand an explanation when they stopped for the night.

After an hour, the coach halted before a modest posting inn. Kassidy made certain that Arrian and the nurse were settled in comfortably for the night before she went to Henry's room. Her heart was beating with

dread as she knocked on his door. Henry was not a forgiving man, and she knew he still harbored anger
against her. She was sure he would vent that anger on
her tonight.

Henry wrenched open the door and indicated she
was to sit in the straight-backed chair. When she was
seated with her hands folded demurely in her lap, he
began pacing restlessly as if deep in thought.

At last he stopped in front of her, rocking back on
his heels. "Well, Kassidy, you managed to get yourself
in a fine mess. Had you and Abigail listened to me, she
would still be alive today, and you would not have dis-
graced us all with your antics."

She was too weary for an argument. She ached all
over, and was seized by moments of dizziness. "I'm sure
what you say is true, Henry," she concurred, hoping
that would appease him.

He looked at her suspiciously. It was unusual for
Kassidy to agree with him. "You must also admit that
you have been too long without benefit of a chaperon.
No gentleman will want to marry you."

Her spirit returned in the form of rage, and she had
no intention of telling him about the proposal from the
duke. "I do so sorely beg your pardon, Henry, if you feel
the proprieties have not been observed. Had I known I
was going to spend so much time in Newgate, I might
have arranged to have a chaperon with me while there."

"Just the kind of insolence I would expect from you,
Kassidy. I don't know why I bother with you at all, you
ungrateful baggage."

"I believe you are right about no man of good family
wanting to marry me if they knew about my unfortunate
experiences at Newgate."

He stared at her long and hard, his hands balled into
fists, the veins on his forehead bulging. "Just what did
happen to you in that place?"

She lowered her head, feeling for the first time the full impact of her shame. "I will not talk about it."

"You never want to talk to me. I should leave you to your own devices, and you would soon face the same tragic end as Abigail."

"I won't discuss Abigail with you, Henry."

"No, but you'll bring her brat to my home and expect me to raise it."

"I will take care of Arrian. She will be no trouble to you."

Henry poked his hands in his pockets and moved to the window, deep in thought. After a time, he turned back to Kassidy. "I believe Hugh DeWinter never married Abigail, no matter what Aunt Mary says."

Kassidy ached at his words. She had come to the same conclusion, herself, but she would not admit it to him. "Abigail thought they were married."

"If she had come to me and allowed me to guide her in this matter, she would not have—"

"How dare you say this, Henry? You are such a hypocrite. Don't you know you are to blame for much that happened to Abigail? She could not have come to you and asked your advice, because you would not have listened to her. You never allowed her to receive suitors, or to be with people her age. She lost her heart to the first man who showed her kindness."

"You could have stopped her from going away with him," Henry accused.

"Perhaps I could have, and in that I blame myself. At least Abigail had a few months of happiness, Henry, and that's more than she ever had while living in your house."

Henry glared at her. "You strumpet! How dare you talk to me like this?"

"I don't intend to talk to you about anything, Henry." She stood up. "I'm going to bed."

"Go to bed," he said sourly. "But think on this before you sleep. I have already made arrangements to place Arrian in a foundling home in Brighton."

Kassidy's head snapped up and her heart skipped a beat. "Oh, no, you aren't, Henry. I will never allow you to take the baby from me. How could you even consider doing such a monstrous act against one of your own flesh and blood?"

"Patricia and I discussed this before I left for London, and we both agree that we don't want our girls exposed to an illegitimate child, and certainly not in their own home."

"We don't know for sure that they weren't married. And I fail to see how an innocent baby could corrupt anyone."

"It took much convincing to get Patricia to allow you to return. She is certain you are an unsettling influence on our daughters."

"I'm not a fool, Henry. Patricia will be glad to have me take over the housekeeping again. How did you manage while I was away?" Kassidy asked with anger.

"I would expect you to show disrespect for the woman who gave you a home since Mother and Father died."

"If you had allowed me to remain with Aunt Mary, she would have been happy to give me and Arrian a home."

"It's settled, Kassidy. You will come with me, and the baby goes to Brighton."

Kassidy felt her legs tremble with weakness, and the floor started spinning around her. She must not become ill—not now. She had to be strong for the sake of the baby.

"I will not allow you to take Arrian away from me. I'll fight you on this, Henry."

He eyed her haughtily. "You have no say in the matter."

Kassidy saw the satisfied curl to his lips. Henry was enjoying torturing her. "Do you hate me so much, Henry, that you will take from me the one I love most in the world?"

"I find that I derive some satisfaction from disciplining you, Kassidy," he admitted. "You are headstrong and willful. I always said I would break you, and I shall."

Her green eyes sparkled like emeralds. "You will never do that, Henry. It would take a stronger man than you to bring me down."

His eyes suddenly lost their hardness, and he came to her. With a gentleness that surprised her, he touched her cheek. "It doesn't have to be this way between us, Kassidy."

She stared at him in puzzlement. He had never spoken to her in such a soft tone. Was that spirits she smelled on his breath? Henry never drank. Why was he acting so strangely?

His hand moved to her hair and tangled in a curly blond lock. "Whenever you have defied me, I have admired you for it, while wanting to punish you as well. While you were away, I searched for you for days. When I learned Abigail was dead and you were missing, I could not grieve for her, because of my distress for you."

She pushed his hand away and took a quick step back, still too stunned to speak.

He ran trembling hands through his hair while his eyes brightened with tears. "I'm obsessed with you, and I hate you for it. You are evil—a seductress."

Kassidy edged toward the door. "Dear God, you are mad, Henry. I'm your sister."

"Yes," he said, burying his head in his hands. "You have driven me to this state."

Kassidy felt sick inside. "I have done nothing to you. I don't even like you."

He looked at her with the old anger. "Get out, Kassidy—go to your room. But you will find that the baby is already on the way to Brighton with the wet nurse."

Kassidy turned quickly to the door and wrenched it open. She fled into the hallway, crying out Arrian's name. She rushed into the room where she had left Arrian and found it empty.

Frantically she ran to the stairs, where she could view the front of the inn through a high window. When she saw the nurse climbing into a carriage with the baby, she cried out in desperation, but no one heard her. Her head was spinning, and she had to clutch the bannister tightly as she made her way downstairs.

By the time she reached the road, the carriage had already pulled away, and Kassidy could only watch helplessly as it moved out of sight.

With a feeling of defeat, she moved to the side of the inn and leaned against the brick wall, staying in the shadows so Henry could not find her. She was too weary to move, and too heartsick to cry.

She stood there for a long time, not knowing what to do or where to go. She would never return to the inn because there was something twisted about Henry's attitude toward her. If only she never had to see him again.

Slowly reason returned, and Kassidy realized she had to take action. She looked across the cobblestone street where several men were loading a wagon with fresh vegetables. She heard one of the men mention he was going to London.

Feeling so weak she could hardly walk, Kassidy managed to cross the street and approach the man sitting in the drivers' seat.

"Please, kind sir," she said in a soft voice, "I have no money, but will you please take me to London with you?"

Seeing the desperation in the girl's eyes, the man nodded. "I'll let ya' ride along, miss, and glad for the company."

Gratefully she allowed him to assist her onto the wagon seat. She huddled beneath the blanket he tossed her. Kassidy did not feel safe from Henry until they pulled away from the village.

She could not return to Aunt Mary, because Henry would only find her there and force her to go with him.

Her eyes filled with hopeless tears. There was only one person who could help her now—only one person Henry would never dare defy.

Kassidy would seek the aid of Raile DeWinter.

20

The butler was ill and had retired to his bed hours ago; therefore, it was Oliver who answered the knock on the door with irritation at the late caller. His irritation turned to concern when he recognized Miss Maragon, who appeared to be terribly upset.

"I must see the duke at once," she said, taking a ragged breath. "It's most urgent."

"Come into the private study, Miss Maragon. I'll fetch his grace."

Wearily, Kassidy sat on the wide leather chair, leaned her head back, and closed her eyes. The duke would help her—she was sure of it.

Raile sat at the head of his table, his arm draped about the shoulder of Gabrielle Candeur, while the two of them presided over a party that was lasting well into the morning hours.

"To the handsomest couple in all London, our host and hostess," Lord Justin Callaret announced, raising his glass for a toast.

Gabrielle looked up lovingly at Raile, aching inside because there was only admiration in his eyes when he looked at her. She had contrived and schemed to become his mistress, and now that she was, she wanted more from him. But Raile would never give his heart to her, and perhaps not to any woman.

"And to the brightest star to grace the London stage in decades," Lord Justin continued, as he winked at Gabrielle. "Whose silver voice captured the most sought-after bachelor in town."

Raile placed his wineglass down, and when a servant would have refilled it, he waved him away. "Your glib tongue runs away with you tonight, Justin," Raile said, finding he was weary of this party. "Perhaps we should—"

He was interrupted when Oliver bent to whisper in his ear. Coming to his feet, Raile apologized to his guests, explaining that he must leave them for a moment. "Go on with the party."

There was a pout on Gabrielle's lips. "Do not stay away long."

When Raile entered the study, Kassidy came weakly to her feet. "Your grace," she said, "please help me."

Just as he reached her, Kassidy crumpled, and he lifted her into his arms. Placing her on the sofa, he motioned for Oliver to bring him a glass of sherry. When Kassidy tried to rise, he aided her.

"What has happened, Miss Maragon?"

"Please help me, your grace. My brother has taken Arrian away from me. You must get her back—you said you would always be interested in her welfare, so I came to you."

Oliver handed Raile a glass, which Raile raised to Kassidy's lips. "Drink this, and perhaps it will calm you.

Then you can tell me what has happened."

She took a sip and shoved it away, feeling its warmth spread inside her. "Henry has sent the baby away to a foundling home in Brighton. You must save her—she's your niece also."

"When did this happen?"

Kassidy looked at the clock on the mantel. "They will have had six hours' start."

Raile turned to Oliver. "Have the coach made ready, and you go to Brighton at once. Bring the baby back here."

Without hesitating, the valet nodded. "It will be as you say, your grace."

"And, Oliver, give my regrets to my guests and ask them to leave."

Kassidy came to her feet. "Oh, you are entertaining, your grace. It is I who should leave."

"You will do nothing of the kind." He nodded to Oliver, and the valet hurried from the room to do his bidding.

Kassidy's eyes shone with gratitude as she sank into the soft chair. "Will those in authority at the foundling home allow your man to take Arrian?"

"Let me assure you Oliver is most persuasive. He will bring her safely back to you."

Kassidy took his hand. "I will always be grateful to you, your grace. I don't know what I would do without Arrian."

Her hair was tangled about her face, her gown was wrinkled, and there was a black smudge on her cheek. He could only imagine what she had been through to bring her to such a state.

"I can't return to my brother." There was real terror in her eyes. "He will find me wherever I am."

"Why are you so afraid of your brother?"

"I . . . we do not always agree and Henry is a little

mad. I can never forgive him for taking Abigail's baby away from me."

"Then I believe your best solution is to marry me, Miss Maragon. Your brother cannot touch you as long as you are my wife."

She lowered her head. "I cannot marry any man, your grace."

He raised her chin. "Why is that?"

"There are reasons that are mine alone."

He saw a tear roll onto the tip of her long lash. "May I inquire what those reasons are?"

She met his eyes, deciding to be truthful with him. "I . . . am soiled." She turned her head away from him. "No man would want me for his wife."

Raile was silent for a moment. "You have been with a lover?"

She refused to meet his eyes, so great was her shame. "No, not a lover." Her voice faltered. "I . . . did not willingly . . . give myself to any man. It happened while I was at Newgate." She stopped to catch her breath. "One of the guards, the one who threatened to sell me to a brothel, he . . . I was unconscious at the time, and am grateful that I have no memory of the incident."

Raile closed his eyes, feeling her shame as if it were his own. He hated to ask, but he had to know: "Are you certain you are not with child?"

Shame stained her cheeks. Such a thought had never entered her mind. "Of course I am not."

"You don't need to say any more, Miss Maragon."

"I have told no one about this, not even Aunt Mary. I would not have told you, except you needed to know why I cannot marry you."

"Is this the only reason you refuse to be my wife?"

She looked into deep compassionate eyes, wishing she could rest her weary head against his broad shoulders. "It is surely reason enough, your grace."

"It does not deter me, Miss Maragon."

"How could you want me after—"

"Perhaps I should explain to you what I require in a wife. You see, the prince has virtually ordered me to marry."

At that moment the door was pushed open and Gabrielle entered. "Raile, would you send me away without a by-your-leave?"

Kassidy stared at the beautiful woman in a shimmering gold gown, wondering who she could be.

There was irritation in Raile's voice. "I'll call on you tomorrow, Gabrielle. As you can see, I am otherwise occupied at the moment."

Gabrielle glanced at the ragtag girl and mistook her for a servant. "If you find your domestic help more fascinating than me, then I shall allow Lord Justin to drive me home."

Gabrielle had hoped to make Raile jealous, but he merely took her elbow and guided her to the door, "Yes, you do that, Gabrielle."

When he had closed the door behind Gabrielle, he returned to Kassidy. "Forgive the interruption." He sat down, his eyes reflective. "Now where were we?"

"That woman was very beautiful."

"Gabrielle. Yes, I suppose she is."

"You must love her?"

"Miss Maragon, can you forget about her and allow us to go on with our conversation?" It was apparent he was losing patience with her. "I have asked you repeatedly to be my wife—and repeatedly you have refused."

"Then why do you keep asking when my answer is always the same?"

"Damned if I know," he said, his voice full of irritation. "I suppose it's because more than anything, I want a son. I'll make the offer to you only this one last time, and then I shall never ask you again."

"If you want only a son, there are any number of women you could marry. The one who just left here seemed genuinely fond of you."

In his aggravation, Raile forgot to be discreet. "Miss Maragon, one does not marry a woman like Gabrielle Candeur."

Kassidy's mouth flew open. "She is your . . . mistress!"

"Miss Maragon, let me say this to you so you will better understand. My mother's family was in trade. And while she brought enormous wealth to the DeWinter family, she was never accepted by the nobility. Each time she was hurt by them, I was hurt for her. I will not have a wife unworthy of being the duchess of Ravenworth."

"Oh."

"Also, I have no desire to have my life interfered with by a wife who would make demands on my time. Between us, there will be no illusions. I don't love you, and you don't love me. Ours could be an amiable union. My one goal is to restore Ravenworth Castle to its former glory. I believe that you would not demand attention and take me away from my work."

"What would be your demands on a wife?" Kassidy could not help but ask.

"I would require very little from you. I would allow you a free hand with money, so you would want for nothing. You can, if you like, live most of the year in my town house here in London—or if you like, with your aunt. I would, of course, eventually expect you to present me with an heir."

She couldn't keep from smiling. "What would happen, your grace, if your practical plans went awry and your wife should present you with a daughter instead of a son?"

"If such were the case, I would require her to bear

my children until she produced a son," he said seriously.

Her tone was mocking. "Quite a prize offering to become your brood mare."

For a moment, a look of disbelief crossed Raile's face. After all, was he not offering her a title, money, and freedom? "Don't be too hasty in turning down my offer." A slight smile twisted his lips. "You should know that my brood mares receive the very best of care from me."

"A great recommendation to a future bride," she said dryly.

"I should make it clear to you so there will be no mistake—I will never love you, Miss Maragon." His eyes bore into hers to drive home the truth. "But if you don't expect affection, you'll find me an admirable husband. After you have produced a male heir, I will not prevent you from seeking . . . affection . . . elsewhere, if you do it in a discreet manner."

Kassidy opened her mouth to speak, and her voice came out in a rush of amazement. "You would not mind a wife having an affair of the heart? Does this also mean that you would feel free to take a mistress after marriage?"

"Since we are speaking frankly, I would not like such an arrangement. I place no importance on love at all."

"I think, your grace, that you have the most amazing view of marriage."

"I believe in candor."

"But not decorum."

He smiled. "Your sharp tongue may make me reconsider my proposal."

"Perhaps you would want a dimwit for a wife," Kassidy said scornfully.

He studied her carefully. "I think not. I bore very easily."

Kassidy considered his proposal for a moment. If she became the duke's wife, Henry would no longer have any hold over her. After what had happened tonight, she was more frightened of her brother than ever. Also, she must consider Arrian. With the duke's help, she would be able to provide her niece with a good home.

"Before you reject my offer again, Miss Maragon, let me tell you of the arrangements I am prepared to make concerning the baby. Upon our marriage, I will settle on her the amount of one hundred thousand pounds. I would triple that amount to you the day you present me with an heir."

"It seems important to you that you have a son."

His eyes grew cold, and he seemed to look right through her. "Having a son means everything to me." A slight smile softened his features. "To make the offer more tempting to you, I will allow you to regain your strength for the period of one year before I would ask you to become a true wife to me."

"One year before you would . . ."

"Claim you for my wife," he finished for her.

A year was a long time, and many things could happen. To have the freedom of a married woman with none of the demands was all she desired at the moment. And yet, something stirred in her—something like excitement at the thought of giving this man his son.

"On considering all the aspects, your grace, my answer is yes. I am willing to play cards with the devil himself, if it will get me what I want."

He could not help but smile at her casting him in the role of the devil. "What is it you want, Miss Maragon?"

"I want to be able to raise my sister's daughter and live my life in relative comfort."

He nodded with assurance, as if he had known he could bend her to his will. "An admirable decision, for an admirable reason." As an afterthought, Raile took her hand and brushed it with his lips. "I will leave all the details to you and your aunt. I do request, however, that the ceremony be a small one and take place as soon as possible. I have been away from Ravenworth Castle far too long as it is." He stood up. "I will make arrangements to transport you to your aunt's residence at once." He smiled. "Kassidy."

"And you are Raile."

He took her hand and led her to the door. "There is a carriage standing by that will take you to Lady Mary. If you have no objections, I'll call on you tomorrow and we shall finalize our wedding plans."

The wedding would take place three days hence, and as the day grew near, Kassidy's apprehension intensified.

Each day gifts would arrive from her future husband, and she was touched by Raile's generosity. Her upstairs bedroom had been filled with flowers from his greenhouse, and when there was no more space in the bedroom, the bounty of flowers spilled over into other rooms in the house. The sweetest gift Kassidy received from her husband-to-be came on the eve before the wedding.

Kassidy's aunt and uncle had gone out and she had been alone in the sitting room when the butler announced Oliver Stewart. Oliver came in and placed the sleeping Arrian in Kassidy's arms. She cried and hugged the precious baby to her while she looked at the valet with gratitude.

"Oh, thank you, Oliver. I was so afraid I would never see her again."

"It wasn't any trouble," Oliver said, pleased that he had made her happy. "I have a message from his grace. I'm to tell you that he has instructed his solicitor to have several qualified wet nurses sent around for you to interview in the morning. He assures me that their credentials will be impeccable and you need not worry that this will ever happen again."

Kassidy nestled the sleeping child against her breast. "His grace has a way of making things happen, Oliver."

"Indeed he does, Miss Maragon. I have never seen him speak that others didn't listen. I was also to tell you his grace got your brother's consent to the marriage"

"Tell him . . . that he has my eternal gratitude," she said, flooded with relief.

Oliver moved to the door, his hat in hand. "I'll relay your message to him this very night, Miss Maragon."

The little man stopped at the door as if he had something else on his mind, so Kassidy looked at him expectantly.

"Miss Maragon, I just want to say how glad I am . . . we are that you are going to be our duchess."

Kassidy smiled at the valet as he nervously twisted his hat. "Thank you, Oliver."

She was filled with relief and happiness as she moved up the stairs with the sleeping child in her arms. No one would ever take Arrian away from her again, she vowed.

21

The sun rose brilliantly on Kassidy's wedding day. She climbed out of bed and moved to the window, watching the splash of dazzling colors reflecting against the eastern sky. How strange it felt to know her whole life would be changed forever today. There was neither elation nor sadness in her heart, merely a resigned conviction that she was doing the right thing.

She turned to the mirror, wondering if she would ever be pretty again. She looked too frail to be a bride. Her hair was so straight and strawlike, and there was no color to her face. She wished she could have been beautiful today.

When she was dressed, Kassidy admired the frothy white empire gown her aunt had given her. It hung in delicate folds to the floor and had a border of elaborate embroidery above the hem. Unfortunately, the color did little to brighten her already pale skin.

Blue forget-me-nots were woven through her hair that was simply arranged in a low coil at the back of her head, and short curls fringed across her forehead.

"Are you certain you want to do this?" Lady Mary

asked. "It's not too late to withdraw your consent."

"I will marry him."

"I think perhaps you are marrying the right man, for the wrong reasons. You want security for Arrian, while he wants a wife who will be as little trouble to him as possible."

"I don't intend to be any trouble to him. He'll remain at Ravenworth as he promised, and I'll be here in London."

Lady Mary smiled to herself. Knowing her niece's impassioned nature, she doubted their arrangement would last for one year.

"I look so dreadful," Kassidy observed, pinching her cheeks to bring more color to her face. Kassidy caught her aunt's eyes in the mirror. "I look plain, Aunt Mary." She added without conceit, "I always thought I was passingly pretty, but not any longer."

"It's the fever, dearest. When you are fully recovered from your illness, you will recover your beauty." Lady Mary smiled, thinking how surprised Raile would be when he learned he not only married a beauty, but he would have a wife who would never be docile. It wouldn't take Kassidy long to turn the duke's world upside down.

"It's time to go below, dearest," Lady Mary said, fastening a strand of pearls about Kassidy's neck. "The minister arrived some time ago, and your bridegroom has been here this past hour."

Suddenly Kassidy's eyes widened with panic. "I wish I hadn't agreed to this."

"Just remember who you are, Kassidy. And remember that when the ceremony is ended, his grace will go off to the country and you will remain with me."

Kassidy drew in a deep breath. "I'm ready."

"By the way, I had a letter from Henry."

Kassidy stopped in her tracks. "What did he say?"

"He was very impressed with the match and wishes you happiness. He even sent a wedding present." Lady Mary smiled. "I'm telling you this to lighten your mood."

"What is the gift?"

"A portrait of Henry, himself."

Kassidy and her aunt laughed until at last Lady Mary held up her hand. "Don't think about Henry anymore today."

"I shan't think of him ever again."

Leaning heavily on her aunt, Kassidy slowly descended the stairs. She faltered only once, and that was at the door where the ceremony would take place.

Upon entering the drawing room, she smiled warmly at her uncle and nodded to Reverend Wheatly. She then turned her attention to the man who was to be her husband.

He wore long blue trousers and a double-breasted waistcoat that fit snugly across his broad shoulders. The frilled shirt was enhanced by the cravat that formed a soft falling bow at the throat. There was about him an air of arrogance and mystery. He was indeed handsome, and she still wondered why he wanted to marry her.

Raile nodded at Kassidy briskly and moved forward to offer her his arm. "Shall we?"

The hand that she placed on his arm trembled. She walked beside him, feeling as if she was about to spend her life under this man's control. Sudden panic almost choked off her breathing and she had the strongest urge to run upstairs to the safety of her bedroom.

Raile glanced into tragic green eyes and wished there was something he could say that would reassure her that she would be safe with him. He dipped his head and whispered so only she could hear. "I give you leave to change your mind if you desire, but I would beseech you to have me."

Kassidy looked into eyes that danced with humor and felt the tension leave her. "I gave my word, and I'll not go back on it, your grace."

Raile motioned the minister forward. Reverend Wheatly was tall and stately and very aware of his duty. He recited with feeling, the age-old words that ultimately bound a man and woman together in a lifetime of devotion.

Raile replied to Reverend Wheatly in deep, even tones while Kassidy stumbled over the words *love, honor, until death do us part.*

She stood in stunned silence while Reverend Wheatly congratulated Raile and wished her happiness. "Dwell with God, your grace, and happiness will always find you," he said to Kassidy. "May you both have a long life together, and may your union be blessed with many children."

Sudden weakness washed over Kassidy, and she clutched at her new husband's arm. Seeing how pale Kassidy was, Raile lifted her in his arms.

"I believe my bride should be put to bed," he said, looking down at her in distress.

Her aunt led him quickly out of the room, while Lord George was left to deal with Reverend Wheatly.

"This way to her bedroom," Lady Mary said, hurriedly leading the way upstairs.

Raile glanced down at Kassidy, noticing the dark circles under her eyes and the shallowness of her breathing. He could feel the heat of her fever through his coat.

"Don't fret, little one," he told her, "I'll take care of you now. Put all of your troubles in my hands."

She pressed her cheek against the roughness of his coat, feeling as if he would bear all her troubles on his strong shoulders. With contentment, she closed her eyes, too weary to think.

Lady Mary rushed ahead of them and opened the

bedroom door. The bed had already been turned down, so Raile gently placed Kassidy among the soft covers before he turned to Lady Mary.

"She seems very weak. I will send my doctor around to examine her."

"The fever recurs. The doctor assures me it will soon pass."

"As you wish."

Lady Mary glanced down at Kassidy, who had closed her eyes. "I will leave you with her for a moment. But I would suggest you not remain too long." She quietly left the room so the newly married couple could be alone.

Raile gently raised Kassidy up and unfastened her gown. When she felt his hands on her back, her eyes opened and she struggled against him. "No—no," she moaned.

"Don't fret. All I'm doing is making you comfortable." He took her chin and forced her to look at him. "I have that right now, Kassidy. We are married."

The ordeal of the wedding seemed to have robbed her of her strength. Too weary to protest, she allowed him to undress her. With expert hands, he removed her gown. Impersonally, he reached for the nightgown at the foot of her bed and pulled it over her head. He then laid her back against the pillow and tied the satin bow at her throat.

Her eyes fluttered shut, but with great effort she managed to open them and look at him.

"You do that very well." She managed a smile. "Perhaps you've had practice."

There was a teasing light in his eyes. "If I say I had, would I sentence myself in your eyes?"

"No." She yawned. "You will merely confirm what I already thought to be true. A man such as you will have . . . known . . . many women."

He touched her lips with his finger. "Tonight I see

only one woman, and she is little more than a girl. Have I done wrong in marrying you?"

She somehow wanted to throw her arms around him, to have him hold her close. She wanted to be beautiful for him, and to have him say he loved her. "Only time will tell if our union was a mistake, your grace."

"Raile," he corrected her. "And my little duchess, you have the worst of a good bargain. But, as a husband, I shall try to be as little trial to you as possible." He stood up and tucked the covers about her neck. "You should sleep now."

"Will you stay here tonight?"

"No. Not for a year—have you forgotten?"

For the first time, he saw her eyes soften with laughter.

"I haven't forgotten."

Raile bent his head and brushed a kiss against her cheek. "Recover soon, my little duchess. One year will pass before you are aware of it, and then I shall come and claim what is mine."

"Will I see you before then?"

"Of course, every time I come to London."

She could no longer hold her eyes open. "Within a year you will forget all about me." She touched his hand. "I want to thank you for having Arrian brought back to me."

Raile smiled. "I'm glad to have her back, too." With a soft laugh, he moved out of the bedroom and down the hallway.

Kassidy drifted off to sleep with the vision of her dark, handsome husband moving through her dreams. For tonight she would have none of the nightmares that had plagued her. Instead, she would now dream of the man she had sworn before God, to love and honor.

* * *

Raile's coachman held the door for him. After he climbed aboard the carriage, it moved sprightly down the well-lit boulevard. He drew in a deep breath, thinking he had at last righted a great wrong. His family honor had been restored.

A light rain began to fall, and he restlessly watched how the wet streets glistened beneath the street lamps.

Raile considered having his coachman drive him to Action Street, where Gabrielle Candeur lived, but he quickly discarded that notion. He didn't relish a confrontation with Gabrielle tonight. Of late she had become clinging and demanding, two traits he did not admire in a woman. He would have to inform her of his marriage and break with her, but he would wait until his next visit to London. After all, he reasoned, it would be a year before he was a real husband.

Leaning back, he felt contented. Now that he had taken care of Kassidy's future, he decided he would leave London at first light.

With both his new wife and his mistress forgotten, Raile turned his thoughts to Ravenworth—his real love.

Gabrielle Candeur had a beautiful voice and had once been the rage in France. She was now enjoying great success on the London stage. But Gabrielle considered her greatest triumph to have been when she had caught the eye of the elusive duke of Ravenworth.

It had been no chance meeting that had thrown them together. Gabrielle had deliberately set out to entrap him. She had learned about his favorite foods, his passion for fine horseflesh, and what he liked in a woman.

It had not been an easy conquest. And it had been made even more difficult because he rarely left his country estate. She had bribed the downstairs maid at

Raile's town house to inform her whenever he would arrive in London.

Gabrielle's plans had gone even further than that. It had cost her a diamond necklace, her ruby ring, and a month's wages to buy the gray Arabian horse with an impeccable lineage.

On the day the duke's maid had informed Gabrielle that her employer was in London and that he would be spending the morning at Ascot, Gabrielle had been ecstatic. She had set her plans in motion. She had dressed with great care. Wearing a bright red riding habit and mounted on her Arabian, she prayed for success. How easy it had been to pay a startled stable boy to loosen her horse's shoe.

Once at Ascot, Gabrielle had dismounted where Raile had been talking with several other ladies and gentlemen. She had pretended distress when she had approached him, beseeching his help.

How admirably Raile had come to her rescue that day. His groom had tended to her horse, and Raile had given her a ride back to town in his phaeton. By the time they reached London, he had asked her to dine, and later he had attended her evening performance.

In no time at all, Gabrielle was installed in a house on Action Street. All her bills were sent to Raile, who had proven to be generous indeed.

She had been the mistress of an Italian count and of one of Napoleon's generals, but for the first time in her life, she was in love. When Raile was not with her, she was in the depths of despair. She was jealous of every hour he spent away from her and she feared he would one day tire of her and cast her aside.

Gabrielle first heard the rumor that Raile was married from one of the actors at Covent Garden, but she refused to believe him. Surely Raile wouldn't take a wife without first telling her.

When Gabrielle heard the knock on the front door, and her maid's voice as she greeted a visitor, she was annoyed because the caller was a woman. She had hoped it would be Raile. He hadn't been to see her in over four weeks. She tapped beautifully shaped fingernails in rhythmic motion against the top of her dressing table. She would tell Louise she wasn't receiving visitors today. She didn't want to face anyone who might come to gloat if the news of Raile's marriage was true.

The maid came bustling into the room. "Pardon, mademoiselle, but there is a Mrs. DeWinter calling. I thought you would want to see her."

Gabrielle looked at her maid in astonishment. "Did you say *Mrs.* DeWinter?"

"*Oui*, mademoiselle."

Gabrielle hurried to her sitting room, her thin pink robe flying out behind her. The only Mrs. DeWinter she knew of was Raile's stepmother. But what would the woman want with her?

"I was told you wanted to see me, Mrs. DeWinter?"

"Yes, Miss Candeur," Lavinia said. "I saw you perform once, and you were magnificent."

"You are too kind," Gabrielle said, noticing the woman was well dressed and had an air of superiority about her. She instantly took a dislike to her. "May I ask why you are here, Mrs. DeWinter? I have a performance tonight and must rest my throat if I am to be at my best."

Lavinia resented the woman's attitude. She was nothing but an actress, after all. "I came because I believe you and I have something in common."

"I can't think what that would be, madame."

"How about Raile?"

"I believe you would be his stepmother. I have heard it said you and Raile are not . . . shall we say . . . fond of one another."

"Did Raile tell you that?"

"No. Raile never discusses his family with me."

Lavinia's eyes turned catlike. "I suppose you heard he was married."

Gabrielle was well trained in masking her feelings, but this was too painful to hide. "I don't believe it!"

Lavinia smiled as the color drained from Gabrielle's face. In coming here today, she hoped to make Raile's life miserable. If she couldn't torture him through his new wife, she would torture him through his mistress.

"It's true, I can assure you. He is indeed married."

"Raile would have told me if he were going to marry. He owes me that much."

"My stepson does not always do the kind thing. It would seem he told neither you, nor his family."

Gabrielle pouted, her eyes flashing with jealousy. "Who is the woman he married?"

"I don't know her. She's from the country. I thought you might be able to tell me about her."

"I wonder why you thought that, madame? You and I are not confidantes."

Lavinia pulled on her white kid gloves and picked up her parasol. "As I said, we have something in common, Miss Candeur. Like you, I don't want to see Raile married. You, of course, have more to lose than I."

"What would you lose to his wife, madame? I have heard it said that he no longer speaks to you."

Lavinia moved to the door. "Mistresses are often forgotten when a man marries." She smiled sweetly. "You might want to remember that." She flung open the door. "Perhaps you have already been forgotten."

22

Anger and jealousy burned within Gabrielle's heart as she descended the steps of her private coach to sweep into Madame Estelle's establishment, with her footman trailing two steps behind her.

Since Madame Estelle and Gabrielle were both from France, they had formed an immediate friendship. At one time the dressmaker had designed gowns for Josephine, but it was not popular to disclose such a fact to the British. Madame Estelle now dressed many of the aristocracy, and she was always well-informed on the latest gossip.

Gabrielle knew this was the place she would learn the truth about Raile's wife.

Madame Estelle was trim and elegant in her black gown as she rushed forward to embrace Gabrielle. "Oh, my poor Gabby," madame cooed in heavily accented English. "It's no wonder we have not seen you in so long. I was sure you were devastated by the duke's marriage."

Before she answered, Gabrielle glanced around and was satisfied that they were alone, except for the two seamstresses who were on the other side of the room concentrating on their stitchery.

She removed her red leather gloves and dropped down on the pink settee, while her footman placed a stool under her extended feet.

"So it's true. Raile is married." She ached with fury, and her eyes flashed with burning jealousy. "Tell me everything you know about the woman."

Madame Estelle picked up a straw bonnet and busily poked blue flowers around the brim. "It is so strange, *chéri*. No one seems to know much about her. Nor have I met anyone who was invited to the wedding. When such an important man is married, you would expect no less than the Prince of Wales to attend the wedding, would you not?"

Seeing the stricken look on Gabrielle's face, the little woman paused at her task. "Of course, his grace having a wife has little to do with love, Gabby. Does the duke not continue to pay your expenses?" Without allowing Gabrielle time to answer, the dressmaker continued. "After he has tired of this woman, he will return to you more and more—you will see."

Gabrielle would not admit to her friend that Raile had not visited her in a month. She had always known he would one day take a wife, but he could have told her and not let her find out through others.

"He will never return to me, Estelle," she said dramatically. "I have always known that there was a part of Raile that I could never reach. He held himself apart from me, never allowing me to touch his inner mind, to really know him."

"He has always been generous with you," Madame Estelle reminded her. "That buys a lot of comfort—if not for him, certainly for you."

"Yes, but he never spoke of love. And he never discussed his personal life with me. I always wanted to be invited to Ravenworth Castle."

"*Chéri*, you know that will never happen. A man does not take his mistress to his family home."

Sudden anger boiled inside Gabrielle. "I will never allow him to push me aside for a mere wife. I'll make myself so necessary to him he will want to keep returning. What could a wife offer him that I cannot?"

"That's the way I like to hear you talk, Gabby," the dressmaker said with passion. "Fight for him!"

"Estelle, tell me all you have heard about this woman. What are people saying about her?"

Madame studied the straw bonnet before picking up a bright blue ribbon and tying it around the brim. "As I told you, I know very little of her. Of course, there is much speculation from my patrons, but oddly, no one seems to know her personally." She held out the bonnet and inspected her handiwork and nodded in satisfaction.

"They say," Estelle continued, "that she's straight from the country and has never had a London Season. I find it difficult to believe that a woman so unsophisticated could catch a man like your duke."

"She must be very beautiful, Estelle," Gabrielle speculated painfully.

"Not necessarily. You know how the nobles are— they marry among their own kind and think nothing about beauty or love." Her eyes brightened. "When a nobleman does love, it is usually his mistress, and not his wife."

Gabrielle wanted to believe Estelle, but still doubt nagged at her mind. "You cannot say for sure she is not beautiful because you have not seen Raile's wife."

Madame looked Gabrielle over carefully. Although she spent large amounts of money on clothing, her taste was rather garish and ornate. She was beautiful, but her lips were too severe, her gray eyes somehow without warmth. "No, I have not seen her yet—but she will be coming here to be measured for a new wardrobe. She and her aunt, Lady Mary Rindhold, have an appointment at noon tomorrow."

Gabrielle quickly came to her feet. "I will be here when they arrive so I can see her for myself. Raile will learn that he cannot treat Gabrielle Candeur without respect. I won't be put out by some little country mouse."

Madame Estelle had a dilemma. The duke of Ravenworth had been most generous in paying Gabrielle's bills. And if she remained his mistress, Estelle would still benefit by that relationship. But she could never allow Gabrielle to meet the duke's wife—no—it was unthinkable.

"*Cheri,* we are friends, and I would do anything for you—anything but allow you to be in my shop when the duchess of Ravenworth arrives. You must think of the scandal. Consider how angry his grace would be if he were to learn of such a meeting. I would be ruined."

"Estelle, Raile's wife will never suspect who I am. I just want to see her, and then I'll leave quietly. No one, not even Raile, will ever know that I was here."

Estelle was only too aware of Gabrielle's quick temper and doubted she could be trusted not to make a scene. But they were friends, so she agreed reluctantly. "It is not right that the duke did not tell you of his marriage. So, if you promise you will not speak directly to the duchess, I will allow you to be here when she arrives."

Gabrielle's gray eyes took on a secretive and cunning light. "You have my oath that I shall not exchange a single word with Raile's new duchess."

Kassidy glanced out the window of her aunt's town coach, noting the dark clouds that were gathering overhead. "It's sure to rain before we return home, Aunt Mary."

"Yes, I suspect it will, dear." Lady Mary studied her niece with a practiced eye. In the month since her marriage, Kassidy had made a miraculous recovery. Her once pale cheeks were rosy with health. Her green eyes shone with vitality. Her hair now curled and shimmered with golden highlights. Of course, she was still too thin, but in time, Lady Mary was certain that Kassidy would gain back the weight she had lost because of her illness.

"You look happy, dearest."

"I am, Aunt Mary. I'm with you and Uncle George. And I have Arrian. What more could I want?"

Lady Mary thought there should be much more to life for Kassidy than raising her sister's child. She needed to be with her husband and have children of her own. She had watched Kassidy's blossoming maturity, and in her, there was a beauty not only of face and body, but also a radiance that came from her soul. Sometimes, however, Lady Mary would catch a wistfulness in Kassidy's eyes and knew she was thinking about Raile DeWinter.

"Are you not excited at the prospect of buying a new wardrobe today, Kassidy? Lord knows you need one."

"Truth to tell, it feels most uncomfortable allowing Raile to pay for my clothing. I know I'm his wife, but I don't feel like a wife. I haven't heard from nor seen him since our wedding."

"Kassidy," Lady Mary said for at least the third time, "Raile is your husband, and it's his responsibility to make certain you are properly clothed. He told me before he left that I was to see that you had everything you required. You haven't been out because of your illness, but you are going to find that as the duchess of Ravenworth, your presence will be expected at many functions. Already I have turned down dozens of invitations on your behalf."

Kassidy glanced down at her yellow gown that had

been made over from one of her aunt's old ones. "I suppose I do need new clothes," she agreed.

"Yes, and just remember that as Raile's wife, you will want to be appropriately dressed so you can be a credit to your husband and to the title."

"I suppose there is truth in what you say. But it's difficult all the same."

Lady Mary smiled and patted Kassidy's hand. "We have arrived, dear. You will like the lovely gowns Madame Estelle creates. Even though it isn't popular to patronize a Frenchwoman, she is very much in vogue and has a devoted clientele."

Kassidy could only think of the cost. "She must be expensive."

"Indeed, yes. If she wasn't, I wouldn't bring you here."

Kassidy frowned. She had never had money to spend on clothing. She could not even imagine how much a gown would cost, and her aunt said she needed dozens.

The footman opened the door, and Lady Mary motioned for Kassidy to follow her. "This will be an adventure, dear. Just you wait and see."

From her vantage point on the pink settee, Gabrielle Candeur watched the two women approach the shop. She recognized Lady Mary Rindhold, a distinguished hostess. She could not see the other woman who walked on the opposite side of Lady Mary.

The bell tinkled merrily above the door and Gabrielle craned her neck so she could have a better view of Raile's wife. She stiffened in disbelief when she saw the beautiful creature who stood there. She was little more than a young girl.

Gabrielle clamped her teeth tightly together in anger. She had never been partial to blond hair on females, but on this girl, it was like a crown of shimmering gold. She envied the clear emerald-green eyes that were framed with sooty lashes. Every feature was delicate and beautiful. Her slender form was outlined by the thinness of the gown she wore. Raile had replaced her with a girl who was pure and innocent!

Malice ignited in Gabrielle's heart. The young duchess had everything she wanted: youth, beauty, and Raile DeWinter. Her anger burst forth into rage, and she wanted to hurt the perfect beauty who had taken Raile from her.

Estelle bustled forward to greet the new arrivals, pausing just long enough beside Gabrielle to whisper, "You must leave at once." She moved to her guests. "Lady Mary, what a pleasure it is to see you again."

"It's good to see you, madame," Lady Mary answered. "May I present you to my niece, her grace, the duchess of Ravenworth?"

Estelle looked at the young girl, knowing the anguish Gabrielle must be feeling because the duke's wife was breathtakingly beautiful. "It will be my pleasure to dress someone as lovely as your grace," she said, dipping into a curtsy.

Gabrielle rushed forward, pulling on her gloves, her eyes boring into the green eyes of the flawless creature who was the object of her jealousy.

"Madame Estelle," Gabrielle said in a honeyed voice, "be so kind as to have my purchase delivered to my address, and as usual, have the bill sent to the duke of Ravenworth. You know how generous he has always been." She extended her wrist, displaying a diamond bracelet, her spiteful eyes turned on Kassidy. "The latest trinket Raile gave me. Is it not extraordinary?"

Kassidy recognized the woman from the night she had gone to Raile to beseech him to help her find Arrian. She turned hurt eyes to her aunt.

Lady Mary pulled Kassidy to her as if to shield her from the actress who swept past them and out the door.

"What is the meaning of this, Madame Estelle?" Lady Mary demanded. "Who was that rude woman—and how dare she flaunt herself in front of my niece?"

Madame Estelle was wringing her hands. "I am very distressed this has happened in my establishment, Lady Mary. I had no notion Gabrielle would commit such a breech of etiquette. How can I make it up to you?"

Kassidy raised her hand to her burning cheek as understanding penetrated her consciousness. "Then that was . . . she is still Raile's . . ."

Lady Mary's face became a mask of fury. "If you and that woman meant this as a jest, be assured you won't be laughing for long. I hold you responsible for this atrocity, Madame Estelle."

"But, Lady Mary, your grace, Gabrielle only wanted to see—she gave me her word she would not—"

Furiously, Lady Mary took Kassidy's arm and steered her out of the shop. Kassidy climbed into the coach and waited for her aunt to join her, still bewildered by the scene she had just witnessed.

Lady Mary waved for the coachman to move along. "This is unforgivable," she declared. "It will not be tolerated. I think Madame Estelle's popularity with my friends will not last long."

Kassidy felt wounded in the deepest recesses of her heart. The night she had seen that woman at Raile's house, he had as much as admitted she was his mistress, but she had assumed he would end their liaison after they were married. "I want to go home now, Aunt Mary."

"Indeed, you will not go home," Lady Mary said stubbornly. "That is the worst reaction you could have. I will take you to another dressmaker, who will serve you just as well. You, my dearest niece, are no man's fool."

"That woman is Raile's . . . mistress," Kassidy said miserably.

"Don't think about her. I have decided that you are going to be gowned and coiffured to show off your beauty to the best advantage. I intend to introduce you to society with great pomp. You have the grace and beauty to break hearts. Every man who meets you will lay his heart at your feet." Lady Mary frowned. "I will also see that your husband hears of your many conquests."

Kassidy shook her head. "I do not want to conquer anyone, Aunt Mary. All I feel is humiliation."

Mary took Kassidy's chin, raised her face and said softly, "You did nothing to be humiliated about. You are no longer going to sit at home playing the docile little wife. You will never again be exposed to a tawdry display like the one you faced today. You are going to make Raile DeWinter so miserable and so jealous he'll want to take you to the country with him and hide you from all other men."

"I don't want to be with him," Kassidy said, some of her spirit returning. "I must never forget he married me out of obligation and pity."

"No, dearest. That's why he thought he married you. We have some surprises for your husband. With my help, you are going to bring him to his knees."

Kassidy leaned back and closed her eyes. "I want never to see him again."

Lady Mary nodded. "You are angry, and that's what I want you to feel, because your anger will give you the will to fight back. Just follow my guidance, and you will have more excitement in your life than you ever imagined."

"But how?"

"You are a married woman, and that gives you a freedom you never had as an unmarried girl. You can attend all the balls and parties and dance with whomever you choose, and no one will fault you." She laughed aloud. "You are going to have fun while you win that husband of yours."

"He will never love me, Aunt Mary. He told me that the day he asked me to marry him."

Lady Mary shook her head at Raile's folly. "Did he, indeed? We'll just see about that."

"I never expect to have his love, but I will have his respect," Kassidy said stubbornly.

"You'll have more than that. Raile DeWinter will fall so hard for you, you will have him begging for your favors."

Kassidy doubted Raile had ever begged a woman for anything. "I will do as you say, Aunt Mary. But all I want from Raile is that he beg my pardon for what happened at Madame Estelle's today," she said with determination.

23

Kassidy stared at the parcels that were stacked on her bed and on every available chair and spilled over onto the floor. There were gowns for every occasion, made of delicate imported silks, stiff satins, and soft muslin. Each one had been designed by a master hand. There were shoes, underclothes, bonnets, shawls and capes, and so many other items that Kassidy could not remember them all.

She was feeling guilty. "I cannot think what drove me to such extravagance, Aunt Mary. Surely no one could wear all these gowns in a year. There are too many."

"Nonsense," Lady Mary said, holding a yellow satin gown up to Kassidy and nodding approvingly. "These will only get you through this Season. You will need others for fall and still others for winter."

"Oh, I dare not purchase more. I am loath to think what Raile will say when he receives an accounting of this day's shopping."

"You need have no concern on that score. I happen to know that your husband has no worry about money.

His mother left him a great fortune, and when his mother's brother died childless, the remainder of the family wealth also went to Raile. What you spent on clothing will seem like a mere trifle to him. And, do not forget, he will want you to be a credit to him."

Kassidy remembered Raile's mistress flaunting the diamond bracelet Raile had given her and felt renewed indignity. "Sometimes I wish I had never heard of Raile DeWinter."

Lady Mary picked up a goblet and handed it to Kassidy. "Don't think about him now. You must drink this concoction that is my own creation. It's heavy cream with honey and crushed strawberries. If you drink one glass in the morning and one at bedtime, in no time at all, your complexion will glow with health."

Kassidy wrinkled her nose with distaste, but obediently lifted the drink to her lips, only to find it had a most pleasing taste.

"Tonight," Lady Mary said, lifting a shimmering white tulle ball gown that was adorned with white silk roses, "you will make your first appearance as the duchess of Ravenworth. I believe I'll have Betty weave fresh white roses in your hair, rather than jewels. Yes, with your pure beauty, you need no artificial adornment."

Kassidy touched a long lock of her hair and it curled about her finger. "I was ill for so long, and looked so sickly, and then I met that . . . woman, and she was so exquisite. I suppose I have lost my confidence."

"You are breathtakingly lovely, but you don't need me to tell you that. I fancy by the end of the evening you will have had dozens of gentlemen complimenting your beauty."

Kassidy threw off her gloom and smiled. "I have never been to a ball," she said with excitement. "Tell me what it will be like."

Lady Mary's eyes sparkled. "There will be music and

dancing, and of course food of every description—some you'll recognize and others you won't. There will be card games for those who fancy cards. Most of all, everyone will strut about, showing off their finery."

"I remember Mother and Father having parties, but I was too young to attend."

"You do know how to dance, don't you?" Aunt Mary said with a worried frown.

"Yes. Mother insisted we have a dancing master. Of course, that was a long time ago. Perhaps I will not know the latest dance steps."

"I fault your brother for this. He should have entertained for you and Abigail and not been so miserly. But let's not spoil the evening by thinking of Henry. Come, sit before the mirror." Lady Mary nodded to Betty, who was waiting to do Kassidy's hair. "I believe we'll arrange her hair in tiny curls to frame her face and let it fall naturally down her back. Here," she said, handing the maid three perfect white roses. "These will do nicely."

Kassidy leaned over the cradle and softly caressed Arrian's cheek while the child smiled at her and waved her arms in excitement.

"Isn't she extraordinary?" Kassidy asked, glancing up at her uncle George, who had just entered the nursery.

He moved to the cradle and nodded. "I'd say she is." He extended a finger and the baby clasped it. "It's been over twenty-seven years since there has been a baby in this nursery. I find myself coming in here more and more. I suppose I've missed having a child about."

Kassidy stood on her tiptoes and kissed him on the cheek. "I always thought Margaret was fortunate to have you for a father."

He looked pleased. "Now did you? I always thought of myself as a fortunate man that your Aunt Mary accepted me as her husband with all the other prospects she had to consider."

Kassidy linked her arm through his. "That's because Aunt Mary knew what a perfect husband you would be." Her eyes softened. "It's easy to see that the two of you were meant to be together."

"I suppose you are right—at least about me. I have never known an unhappy day with your aunt— each day with her is an adventure. She is everything one would want in a wife: beautiful, unpredictable." He cleared his throat and avoided Kassidy's eyes. "But there now, I'm running on, and I forgot the reason I came here. Your aunt says if we don't leave now, we'll be late for the festivities."

Kassidy twirled around in a circle. "Do you like my new gown?"

"Indeed I do. You remind me so much of your aunt at your age. She broke all the young men's hearts, and I suspect she still does."

"Yes, but she loves only you."

"Of that I have no doubt." He hugged Kassidy to him. "Your aunt and I both want to see you happy, Kassidy. And you will be. I speak from experience. I tell you with assurance that you will one day know great happiness in your marriage."

"But not all men are as wonderful as you, Uncle George," she replied, wishing Raile would look at her the way her uncle looked at her aunt. With a resigned sigh, she said, "We had better not keep Aunt Mary waiting."

She bent to kiss the baby, who had by now fallen asleep. Then she joined her uncle in the hall.

"Is it true that the prince will be at the gala tonight, Uncle George?"

"Indeed he will. You have never met him, have you, my dear?"

"No, I never imagined I would have an occasion to meet him."

George paused at the top of the stairs. "You should not be too impressed by him, Kassidy. You see, Prinny isn't brilliant, he merely manages, thank God, to surround himself with brilliant people. His limited interests are gambling, architecture, and women. I have known him to babble like a baby with tears rolling down his cheeks over a lost love, and he is most usually drunk. This is the man who will one day be our king."

Kassidy had never known her uncle to say an unkind word about anyone, and she was surprised by his assessment of the prince. "But he will be king, be he worthy or not."

"If he lives long enough, he certainly shall. I don't have to tell you that there are many of us in the House of Commons who wish it did not have to be so." He shook his head sadly. "But he is our burden, and we will bear him on our shoulders." He took her arm and accompanied her down the stairs, where his wife waited impatiently in the entryway.

"See how the fire plays in her eyes when she is perturbed about something," he whispered to Kassidy. "I'm a most fortunate man indeed."

The stiff-necked butler took the invitation from George Rindhold, and announced in a clear, distinct tone: "The duchess of Ravenworth, Lady Mary Rindhold, and Mr. Rindhold."

Curious heads turned in Kassidy's direction as she stood beside her aunt and uncle. She was unaware of the admiring glances that followed her as she gracefully descended the seven steps that brought her into the ballroom.

In no time at all they were surrounded by gentlemen

who insisted on being introduced to Kassidy. After a while, she lost her apprehension and began to enjoy herself. She felt young and carefree as she danced with one partner after another.

Later in the evening, Lady Mary tapped her husband on the shoulder and nodded at Kassidy, who was encircled by admiring gentlemen. "I knew she would be a sensation. Look how all the other women stare at her with envy. She is an incomparable."

George nodded. "She is the sensation of the evening, right enough, Mary, but take care you do not push too far."

"What do you mean?"

"Raile DeWinter is not a man to toy with, my dear."

"You disapprove of introducing Kassidy to our friends?" she inquired innocently.

He smiled, knowing the game she was playing. "Not at all, my dear. I just know you, and I would caution you to tread lightly."

Lady Mary was thoughtful. "It's just that I want Kassidy to be happy, and I believe that happiness lies with Raile DeWinter. But they cannot have a marriage from a distance. I'm merely going to get his attention."

Kassidy was unaccustomed to compliments, and felt uncomfortable at the flowery tributes that were so casually spoken in her ear. She supposed this was the way gentlemen behaved in London.

She managed to slip away unseen, hoping no one would follow her. Her feet hurt and she wanted a breath of cleansing air away from the smoke-filled ballroom. She leaned against a statue of some long dead English king, and glanced across the stone balcony at the flickering lights of London. How far away she was from her girlhood home. Was this what her life was going to be like from now on? she wondered.

A dark shadow fell across her face, and she looked

up to find a gentleman smiling down at her.

"We have not been introduced, but I have been watching you all evening, your grace."

Kassidy was in no mood for more speeches about her beauty. "How dull it must have been for you, sir."

She turned to walk away, but his laughter stopped her. "Pray allow me to introduce myself. I am Lord Justin Callaret. And perhaps I can redeem myself with you by first telling you that I'm an old friend of your husband's."

She paused. "You know Raile?"

"Quite well. We have been friends since boyhood and served together in Spain and finally at Waterloo."

While he was talking, Kassidy assessed him. He was blond and handsome, with a cleft in his chin, almost boyish in looks. If this man knew Raile, perhaps she could learn more about her husband from him.

"How long have you known my husband, my lord?"

"Since before his mother died. Raile was always the serious one. He studied in school and actually had the instructors' approval."

"And you, my lord?"

"I did not study and didn't have the instructors' approval."

Kassidy found Lord Justin amusing. They had begun to move down the wide steps leading to the garden below. She was unaware that he was leading her down a path brightly lit by Chinese lanterns.

"So you served under Wellington, as my husband did?" she asked with interest.

"Yes. But there again, Raile overshadowed me. He came home a hero, while I was sent home with a broken arm—not a battle wound, mind you, but broken when I fell from my horse while on parade."

Kassidy could not help but laugh. "Surely you are much too hard on yourself, Lord Justin."

"I can assure you I speak only the truth, your grace."

They paused beneath a swaying multicolored lantern. "What else do you and my husband not have in common?"

He looked down at her, and drew in his breath at her startling beauty. "We don't have you in common. Where did Raile find you?"

"You wouldn't believe me if I told you."

He reached out and caught her gloved hand, taking her by surprise. Slowly he raised her hand to his lips. "Would that I had seen you first."

She was young and inexperienced, and he was a most charming gentleman. "And what would you have done, Lord Justin, had you seen me first?" she dared to ask.

His arms slipped about her waist, and he pulled her toward him. She was stunned as he dipped his head to touch his lips to hers.

Kassidy jerked away. "Sir, your actions are reprehensible. No man, not even my husband, would dare take such liberties."

He stared at her in disbelief. "Are you saying that Raile has never kissed you? That cannot be the Raile I know."

Before she weighed the consequences, Kassidy blurted out: "Not like that. Raile and I hardly know one another."

A look of amusement was replaced by that of naked desire. Lord Justin moved closer to her, his hand trailing down her arm. "I wonder what it would be like to light a fire within you, little virgin duchess."

Kassidy spun away from him, her breasts heaving with indignation. "That's something you will never know." She turned around to leave, but was confused when she saw too many paths leading in different directions.

She looked at Lord Justin. "If you will be so kind as to direct me to the ballroom, I will be glad to be finished with your company, my lord."

"But of course, my little virgin duchess."

"Lord Justin," someone spoke up from the pathway, catching their attention. "No wonder you are hiding away from the rest of us. Who is this vision of loveliness you keep to yourself?"

Kassidy saw several people walking toward them. The man who had spoken was dressed in red satin, which looked grotesque on his bulky form.

"This, Your Highness, is Raile DeWinter's wife, the duchess of Ravenworth." Lord Justin spoke up, bowing slightly to the Prince of Wales.

When Kassidy realized it was the prince approaching, she quickly dipped into a curtsy.

Prinny walked around Kassidy, taking in every lovely detail and making her feel uncomfortable. "Lord Justin, did I just hear you refer to this charmer as 'the virgin duchess'?"

Lord Justin smiled devilishly. "That was not meant to be overheard, Your Highness."

"And where is your husband, madame? I have not seen him these last three months."

"He is in the country, Your Highness," Kassidy said, stepping back a pace because he was standing so near she could smell spirits on his breath.

"So," Prinny said, rocking back and forth on his heels, his eyes raking Kassidy. "Raile has married a beauty and left her to her own devices while he tinkers around in that drafty old castle of his." He exchanged a smirk with the woman at his side. "Until tonight I have never thought of Raile as a fool, but I have changed my opinion after seeing his neglected wife."

The prince gave a robust laugh, which was joined by the others. "England once had a virgin queen, now we have a virgin duchess. This is damned amusing." His eyes challenged Lord Justin. "Perhaps Raile should look to his pigeon before another robs his nest."

Prinny's laughter trailed after him as he moved on down the path, followed by his entourage. His laughter deepened and rose above the sound of music from the ballroom. "I must speak to Raile about neglecting his wife. He will give us all a bad name if it continues."

Kassidy realized her uncle had been right when he said the prince was not respectable. He had deliberately humiliated her, and no gentleman would have done that for his own amusement.

Lord Justin looked shamefaced. "I do so humbly apologize, your grace. I fear I have unwillingly left you open to ridicule, and that was not my intention."

"You said earlier that my husband is your friend. This was not the act of friendship."

"I can assure you Raile is my friend. If you were to ask him, he would agree."

Kassidy moved away from Lord Justin, heading in the direction of the music. "I would not consider you a friend of my husband's. But if you are, I would not think that friendship would survive this night."

Lord Justin rushed to catch up with Kassidy. "Do you intend to tell Raile about this evening?"

"No, I would not do that. But I believe he will hear about it all the same. It appears His Highness was amused by the situation and will delight in retelling it to others."

"You are right, of course." Lord Justin stepped into her path so she was forced to either stop or move around him. "I humbly beg your forgiveness for being the instrument of your embarrassment. If there were only some way I could make amends, I would do it."

"I can't think why you would need my goodwill when you obviously have the prince's."

"You have my word that I shall never by thought or deed, make you uncomfortable again. Please say you will forgive my bad manners."

He spoke with such sincerity she was inclined to believe him and her anger cooled. "I will forgive you," she said, wanting only to put distance between them. "But I'm not certain Raile will."

"I would like to be your friend, your grace. I would deem it an honor to serve you in any way I can." He raised his hand. "From this day forward, I'm a changed man. I swear it."

He was so charming and earnest she couldn't help but smile at him. "I wonder if it is so easy for a man to change. I fancy you will be up to your old ways the moment I am out of sight."

"If you will allow me to call on you tomorrow, I'll show you. You have my oath I will be nothing but a perfect gentleman."

She was thoughtful for a moment. "Yes, you may call if you like."

She moved around him and hurried down the path, leaving him to stare after her.

Lord Justin did indeed envy his friend, although he could not understand how Raile could leave his beautiful duchess alone and untouched, while he retired to the country.

"Prinny was right," he said aloud. "Raile is a fool."

24

Dear Raile,

    I'm writing you about a matter that has so distressed me that I thought you should be informed at once. It seems you have unwittingly become the object of a cruel jest. To put it delicately, Kassidy is being referred to as "The Virgin Duchess." The Prince, himself, is the author of the jest, so you can imagine what a popular topic you have become at every social gathering. As for Kassidy, you need have no concern for her. She is completely recovered from her illness and is the rage of London. She is never without adoring admirers who grant her slightest wish. It does you credit that she is so popular.

Lady Mary smiled to herself and signed her name. She glanced up at Kassidy, who had just entered the morning room.

"I believe, dearest, it will not be long until your husband will be arriving in London."

"Did he send word that he would come?" Kassidy

asked, feeling uneasy for fear Raile had heard the rumors the Prince of Wales had started about her.

Lady Mary sealed the letter, looking smugly confident. "I have not heard from him, as of yet, but I feel certain that your husband will arrive within the week."

Kassidy sat near the window, looking out at the park across the street rather than at the stack of invitations she clutched in her hand. "You were right when you said I would be the rage, Aunt Mary. I have so many invitations to balls and parties, I can't possibly attend them all."

"Here," her aunt said, holding out her hand, "I'll help you choose the proper ones." She looked Kassidy over carefully. "You are enjoying yourself are you not?"

"Very much so . . . but . . ."

"Yes?"

"It's so artificial. I'm from the country, Aunt Mary, I like to have purpose to my life. I find London boring."

"You shall soon be in the country," Lady Mary said with certainty. "I can assure you, Kassidy, that you will."

"Not for a year," Kassidy reminded her.

"Don't be too sure your husband won't become impatient and insist you accompany him to Ravenworth sooner than you expect."

Lady Mary's ball was a success. Kassidy's face was glowing from having danced four straight dances. She took a chair to catch her breath and was immediately surrounded by gentlemen.

She was not amused, nor did she feel comfortable with the attention she was receiving. So when she saw Lord Justin threading his way toward her, she felt relieved that he had come to rescue her.

Since the incident in the garden, the night they first

met, Lord Justin had proven to be her friend. He called on her every day, and true to his word, he had been the perfect gentleman. He took her riding in the park and was her escort at several teas. Kassidy now felt comfortable in his company.

When Lord Justin reached Kassidy's side, he pushed through the dozen gentlemen who surrounded her and took her offered hand. "You look ravishing tonight, your grace, and easily outshine every lady here."

Kassidy withdrew her hand. "I thought we agreed there would be no false compliments between us."

"My compliments to you are never false. Before becoming acquainted with you, I had never met a woman so opposed to praise. Surely you must know how beautiful you are?"

Kassidy's eyes gleamed with a warning. "I would rather be complimented about the knowledge I have acquired, rather than my appearance."

Lord Justin smiled. "It's difficult to think of your mind when it is wrapped in such a lovely package."

The other men agreed vocally, and Kassidy found herself lost in loud tributes to her mind and beauty.

Raile stood at the doorway, observing the dancers as they whirled by. His gaze moved over the crowd of faces, searching for a woman with blond hair. He was annoyed when he didn't see her right away. For a moment his gaze rested on the lovely vision in blue who was surrounded by admirers. Her face was upturned as she listened to one of the gentlemen, and Raile's eyes lingered on that beautiful face for a moment longer before he continued his quest for his wife.

After receiving Lady Mary's letter yesterday, he had lost no time in coming to London. He was perturbed to find the Rindholds were entertaining. And, it didn't help his mood that he could not locate his wife.

Lady Mary appeared at his side, smiling brightly.

"Raile, what a wonderful surprise! I had no notion you would be coming to London so soon."

He looked at her through lowered lashes. "Did you not, madame? After your informative letter, I would have thought you'd be expecting me."

Ignoring his innuendo, she tucked her hand into the crook of his arm. "Come and say hello to George."

"I am not dressed for the occasion. If you will just tell Kassidy I am here, I'll wait for her in your study."

Lady Mary was trying not to feel smug that her little plan was working so well. "Why don't you tell Kassidy, yourself." She pointed her fan. "She's there."

Raile stared for a long moment at the beautiful woman with golden hair who had caught his attention earlier. "Surely you jest, Lady Mary. I would know my own wife when I saw her."

Lady Mary smothered a laugh. "Why, your grace, apparently you don't know Kassidy—for that is indeed she." Lady Mary lowered her voice. "Pray don't let it get around that you didn't recognize her, your grace, or we'll never stop the rumors from flying."

Raile drew in an angry breath. "If you will excuse me, Lady Mary, I'll see to my wife."

Lord Justin raised Kassidy's gloved hand to his lips. "I admire your wit, as well as your intelligence. You are like a fresh breeze that has blown through London. You must know that many men have laid their hearts at your feet."

Raile stood behind Justin, his anger barely under control. The other gentlemen had already recognized the duke and had hastily departed.

Raile's voice was hard and cold. "I see you are making yourself charming again, Justin."

Kassidy spun around to her husband. Her eyes

were bright with welcome, and her heart was pounding at the sight of him. Raile, however, was looking at Lord Justin and not at her.

Lord Justin looked into eyes that were filled with turbulence, and his hand fell away from Kassidy's arm. "It's always good to see you, Raile." His eyes danced with humor. "But you could have stayed away longer—I have enjoyed keeping your charming wife company."

Raile spoke in a biting tone. "If you will excuse us, I would like to see my wife, alone."

"As you wish," Justin agreed, reluctantly moving away. He had known Raile would come to London, and that he would be angry. But he had sensed in Kassidy a loneliness and he was not sorry he had been her friend.

Kassidy noticed that Raile had avoided looking directly at her. "Don't you think you were rude to Lord Justin? After all, he is your friend."

At last Raile looked into the familiar green eyes. "Is he my friend, madame—or has he become your lapdog?"

Kassidy noticed that others were watching them with curiosity, so she lowered her voice. "Are you accusing me of something, Raile?"

He reached out and clamped her wrist. "I believe you have already made us the center of controversy. If we remain here much longer, it will only give the scandalmongers more to talk about."

He pulled her to her feet, leaving Kassidy no choice but to go with him. She caught her aunt's eye, hoping Lady Mary would intervene for her.

Lady Mary met them at the front door and handed Raile Kassidy's cloak. "There is a chill in the air. She may need this, I believe."

Apparently Kassidy would get no help from her aunt, for Lady Mary merely kissed her cheek and nodded her approval to Raile.

"Where are you taking me?" Kassidy asked, as Raile dropped the cloak about her shoulders, took her elbow, and guided her toward the front door.

"I'm taking you with me, where you belong, madame." He turned to Lady Mary. "You will have her things sent to the town house."

"I won't leave without Arrian," Kassidy said defiantly. "She needs me."

"I'll take care of the baby," Lady Mary assured her niece. "You go with your husband."

Kassidy would have protested, but Raile gave her no chance. With a curt nod to his hostess, he led his wife outside and helped her into his carriage. The coach lurched forward, and Kassidy settled in the corner, not knowing what to expect.

For a long moment there was silence.

"I don't understand why you acted so tyrannically tonight, Raile. Had you made known your intentions to me, I would readily have agreed to come with you. You didn't even let me know you were expected in London."

"Surely you knew I would come."

"How could I know? When you left, you assured me that I could have a year before you came for me. I trusted your word, and you have broken it."

Raile spoke with a biting tone. "Did you think you could make my family honor an object of ridicule and I would do nothing? You have put yourself beyond the pale, madame."

She wanted to lash out at him. "That's absurd. I can assure you I have done nothing to disgrace either your honor, or mine. If the truth be known, it was you who has shamed me, your grace."

As they passed a lamp light, Raile's face was outlined in the half light. She could feel his eyes boring into her. "In what way have I shamed you, madame?"

Kassidy pulled her cape tighter about her. "I'm talking about the actress, Miss Candeur—your mistress."

He was taken aback for a moment. "How could you know about her—from Justin, I suppose."

"Justin is a gentleman, he would never say anything to me about your . . . woman. It was Miss Candeur, herself, who made certain I knew about your relationship with her. Although I suspected it that night at your house, she publicly confirmed it."

Raile felt trapped. How did a husband explain a mistress to his wife? He took the coward's way out. "I will not discuss this with you," he said sourly.

"I am well aware that wives are not supposed to know about such things—and if they do find out, they are expected to look the other way. Well, we both know that I am not an ordinary wife, and I will not look the other way."

She was confusing him, and no woman had ever done that before. He was beginning to regret he had come to London at all.

"That's nonsense."

"I don't think so, Raile. I recall the conversation we had before we were married when you made it quite clear from the start that we did not owe fidelity to one another."

He was shocked that she was using his own words against him. How arrogant he had been that day he had so foolishly explained to Kassidy what he expected of their relationship. "I would not advise you to admit you had been unfaithful, Kassidy."

"Don't insult me, Raile. It is not *I* who flaunted a lover in *your* face."

"I would prefer we not speak of such things tonight. You should take a lesson from your aunt and display a more feminine nature."

"I love my aunt, but you cannot compare our marriage to hers and Uncle George's. Aunt Mary loves my uncle and clings to every word he says as if it were the golden truth. She is very intelligent, but sometimes when she is with my uncle, to make him feel superior, I have observed her acting as if she has no thought in her head that he hasn't put there. I could never be subservient to any man. The man I love must accept me as I am, and not be intimidated by me just because I can think for myself."

"I daresay it is because of that attitude that you were not married before now."

"I daresay you are right."

Raile raised a dark brow. "At last, something we agree upon."

She was angry with his high-handedness. "Pray God that does not happen too often."

He had not expected the sickly little girl he'd married would rip a man to shreds. He should have remembered their first meeting.

"I assume you are aware of the rumors concerning our marriage, Kassidy?"

"Yes, and it has not been pleasant for me to face the ridicule of being a neglected wife. The women laugh at me behind my back, and the gentlemen believe me to be fair game because I don't have a husband at my side to protect me."

"Was Justin one of the men who gave you protection?"

"He has become my friend, just as he is yours."

"I recall Justin always seemed to favor any woman with whom I had formed an attachment." Justin had even tried to take Gabrielle Candeur away from him, but Raile did not mention this to Kassidy.

"Justin kept me from being lonely," she said, angry that she had to defend herself.

"Oh, yes," he said sarcastically, "Justin was always helpful."

"I happen to know he likes you a great deal. He has only praised you to me, and I have come to know and respect him."

"What about me, do you also respect me?"

"I don't know you very well, your grace."

"You know my name—so use it," he demanded. "And, Kassidy, I can assure you that after tonight, you will know me very well."

She felt fear and excitement race through her body. "What do you mean?" she asked breathlessly.

The carriage came to a halt, and Raile jumped down and swung her to the ground. "I mean, madame, that I shall perform my husbandly duty toward you tonight, and quell any more rumors."

Kassidy pulled away from him, wishing she could run away. "You promised you would not—"

Raile took her arm and guided her up the steps of his town house, and lowered his voice so only she could hear. "The promise has been voided from necessity."

Without a word, she entered the house beside him. A butler rushed forward and took her cloak, and she almost looked to him for assistance, but realized no one could help her.

"Inform the servants that we are not to be disturbed," Raile told the butler.

"Yes, your grace."

As Raile steered Kassidy up the stairs, she felt trapped. She faced the unknown, and it was a frightening void. Kassidy felt his hand against her back as he guided her upward.

He swung open a door and indicated she should precede him inside the bedroom. She moved quickly to the window, hoping to put some distance between them. She was glad the window was open and she could take a big gulp of air to help diminish some of her uncertainty.

Raile watched Kassidy's slender form as she turned

to face him. But for the unusual green eyes, there was nothing about her that he recognized. Where her hair had once been dull in color, it now shimmered like a glimmering halo. She looked so lovely in the half light from the fire, all he could do was stare at her.

Wanting to put her at ease, he moved to the fireplace, where the fire danced in the grate. "We have a lot to learn about each other, Kassidy. Although we are married, we are virtual strangers."

"I'm not certain I want to know you, Raile," she admitted at last. "I believe I still fear you."

"I'm sorry if that's true. I would never harm you, Kassidy." His eyes became soft with understanding. "It's difficult for one person to measure the depth of another's fear. Or the bravery it takes to overcome that fear. Each man, or woman, has something they are afraid of."

She moved closer to him and the warmth of the fire. "I cannot imagine you being afraid of anything."

"But I am."

She moved even closer. "What could ever frighten a man such as you?"

He smiled slightly. "You do. You are a precocious woman-child, who I thought would fit into the order of my life—but I completely misjudged your character. I am not certain what I should do about you, Kassidy."

Now she had drawn even with him. "You could allow me to leave, your grace. Neither of us wanted this marriage. If you allow me to return to my aunt, you can feel free to return to your mistress."

"I can't do that, Kassidy." He reached out and touched a soft curl that lay against her cheek. "I'm sorry you had to find out about Miss Candeur, but you must believe me when I tell you that I have not seen her since our marriage."

"I have no reason to doubt your word." Her eyes

were challenging. "Except, you did promise to give me a year," she reminded him.

Suddenly his finger trailed across her cheek and down her throat. Kassidy felt as if her breathing had been cut off.

Raile's dark brooding eyes moved across her face, to rest at the swell of her breasts. His hand drifted through her hair, his fingers gently untangling the curls.

His voice vibrated a cord within her, and Kassidy felt as if a cleansing fire swept through her body.

"Perhaps you will want to release me from my promise, Kassidy. Perhaps you could pretend for this one night that we are a husband and wife who married for all the right reasons."

She looked up at him, feeling as if her body had no will of its own. "Why would I want to do that?" she asked in a whisper. She was trembling with emotions she could not understand. "We married for all the wrong reasons. You know we don't love each other."

Raile's smile was devastating. "We could pretend to be lovers, if it would make it easier for you."

"I have a feeling if a woman were to lose her heart to you, Raile, she would only raise your contempt, and you would no longer desire her."

"Not you, Kassidy," he whispered. When he touched his lips to hers, she could not move—could not think— she could only cling to him and press closer to the body that warmed her heart and her blood.

His kiss invoked a sweetness in her, and when he applied more pressure to her lips, his hands spanned her waist, pulling her against the hardness of his thighs, and the sweetness turned to raw desire.

Kassidy was as helpless against Raile's sensuous manipulation as a flower petal being hurled into a hurricane.

25

A moan of distress escaped Kassidy's lips as she moved away from the mouth that was draining all her will and at the same time, demanding more than she wanted to give.

In a desperate effort to save herself, she struck out at Raile, catching him a glazing blow across the cheek.

Raile grabbed her wrist and held it in a firm grip, while they stared at each other for endless moments. Kassidy saw her hand imprinted on his cheek, while he stared into green eyes that were filled with bewilderment.

"I did not mean to strike you," she said, appalled by her act of hostility. "I don't know why I did that. I have never struck another human being in my life."

Raile moved away from her to stand at the fireplace. His eyes focused on the dancing flame, but his mind was on the woman he had married. "This is a first for both of us. No woman has ever struck me." He took several deep breaths, hoping to bring the burning ache for her under control. The one thing he must not do was lose his head and frighten her.

Kassidy stood clutching her hands. "I ask your forgiveness, Raile. It's just that when you kissed me, I felt as if I were no longer in control. I don't know what's happening to me."

"I don't even know what's happening to me, Kassidy." He remembered her bad experience with the guard at Newgate and silently cursed himself for not being more understanding of her fear. He turned back to her with a smile. "Perhaps you would like a glass of wine?"

"No," she said shaking her head. "I want to be in possession of my reason."

When Raile reached out to her, she moved away from him.

Kassidy said in a confused voice: "I never wanted to like you, Raile. Then when I met Miss Candeur at the dressmaker, I became extremely angry with you. Many times I have reminded myself that your brother is responsible for my sister's death. I don't know if I trust even you."

"Yet you married me."

"It seemed the only thing to do at the time."

He reached for her hand and pulled her tightly against him. "You don't have to trust me—you can even hate me if you must, but do not deny me that which is mine by rights."

With a muffled cry, she buried her face against his shirtfront, absorbing the strong feel of him in every fiber of her being. For so long she had not allowed herself to think about Raile. But her dreams would betray her and she would awaken with a deep yearning for him that she neither understood nor welcomed.

His hands moved up her back, and he crushed her to him. "Come willingly to my bed, my little duchess." His mouth rested against her cheek.

Startled by the intensity she felt in him, Kassidy turned her head slightly and felt his lips touch hers. "We both know I am not—"

His hard lips sealed the words in her throat. Such

yearning burst forth within her that she pressed into him, wishing she could be part of his body.

He moved his lips just a bit and whispered, "Don't think about what happened at Newgate. I promise you, it makes no difference to me. I've never been with a virgin, anyway." His mouth covered hers, and for a moment, she couldn't breathe. She felt as if her body had no substance, no power of its own.

"Yes," he whispered against her mouth. "You will be willing enough when I take you."

His words didn't penetrate her consciousness. She wished he would go on forever kissing her. She was unaware when he unfastened her gown and slid if off her shoulders, allowing it to drop to the floor.

A sweet urgency shook Kassidy when his hungry, seeking mouth drifted across her shoulder, trailing downward, circling the swell of her breasts and brushing briefly the taut nipples that pressed against her silken chemise.

"No," she gasped, struggling against him. "This is wrong."

Raile smiled down at her in amusement. "How can it be wrong? We are husband and wife."

Raile watched the rise and fall of her breasts.

Kassidy became aware that her breasts were visible through the transparent chemise and crossed her arms over her chest. "I'm not ready for this."

He pulled her arms away from her body. "But you will be ready before this night is over," he whispered, his gaze moving over her perfect body. "Believe me when I tell you I will do nothing you don't want me to do, Kassidy."

Her tousled blond hair hung loosely about her face. Her creamy breasts shone like satin against the white silk undergarment.

A tremor shook Raile, and he clasped her shoulders. "Let us silence those wagging tongues that proclaim you the 'virgin duchess.'"

"But the guard—"

"Forget that man. He does not exist for you or me."

Before she could answer, his lips found hers in a kiss so drugging she could only hold onto him for fear of losing her balance. When Raile picked her up in his arms, she made no protest. Gone was the fear and uncertainty. In its place was a wild yearning so intense that she could hardly breathe.

Those magnificent dark eyes were mesmerizing as Kassidy's head drifted back against the pillow.

"Are you still frightened of me, Kassidy?" he asked, cupping her chin and forcing her to look at him.

"I don't think so. But I don't know what is expected of me."

"Are you willing to become my wife?"

"I . . . don't know. I don't know how."

He smiled slightly. "That is of no consequence." He lay beside her and raised up on his elbow to look down at her. He could feel her tense and wanted to put her at ease. Clasping her hand, he raised it to his lips—kissing each finger, one by one.

"Kassidy," he said softly, caressing her long hair, "you remind me of a wild bird—a nightingale—I once captured. It had mistakenly flown into my fishing net and became entangled. When I found it, it was badly injured and mistrustful."

She was trying to concentrate on his story, but his gaze had moved to her breasts, and she could feel a burning deep inside—a yearning—a wild sweetness stirring to life within her.

"What did you do?"

Raile slowly pulled her toward him until her head was resting against his shoulder. Suddenly, he felt her stiffen. "After untangling the poor creature," he continued, "I held it in my hand, ever so gently." His hand glided down her neck. "I could feel its heart beating rapidly." His hand moved lower, to rest against her heart. "Like your heart is beating now."

Kassidy felt dizzy with yearning. "D . . . id you let the bird go?"

She felt Raile's hand circle her breasts, and she bit her lip to keep from crying out. What was this aching need that made her tremble with yearning—why did she want to press her body against his and feel all of him?

"No, Kassidy. I didn't let the bird go at first because I had to tend its wounds, and I had to teach it to trust me."

His hands were hot against her skin as he pushed her chemise off her shoulders, all the while his hands worked magic: circling, caressing, gliding sensuously toward her now exposed breasts. "I stroked its feathers as gently as I could." To demonstrate, he stroked across one breast and then the other, sending a shiver of delight dancing across Kassidy's skin.

"Then what happened?" she managed to ask in an uneven voice, her eyes wide and dreamy.

His hand drifted across her stomach. "Like you, the nightingale feared me at first." He leaned forward and touched his lips to her ear, whispering and stirring her hair. "But I won the bird's trust after a while." His hands moved lower to lightly touch her thigh, making her moan softly.

"Eventually, that nightingale allowed me to open my hand, and it perched there, not wanting to fly away."

"It didn't try to fly away?" she asked, knowing she would never want to leave him.

"No, Kassidy. When the nightingale had healed, I had to force it to fly away by throwing it into the air." His lips moved along the curve of her face. "It circled above me, Kassidy, for a long time, before it finally flew away."

His hand slid between her legs, and he gently began to massage there. His voice was deep when he spoke again. "And I swear to you, Kassidy, that for that one whole summer, that very nightingale would sing outside my bedroom window every night."

His mouth was only inches away from hers. "Tonight, you will sing for me, little nightingale."

Raile didn't know why he had remembered the nightingale, because the incident had happened so long ago. He only knew that Kassidy had come to him like a bird with a broken wing, and it was his responsibility as her husband to help her heal.

Her skin was so smooth and soft, and her hair smelled of some exotic perfume. He was enchanted with her, and he had not expected to ever lose his head over a woman, but she was delighting him with her sweetness.

Raile found he wanted to possess all of her, not just her body, but her mind as well, and to hold on to her, so she wouldn't fly away like the nightingale.

He looked into green eyes that were so innocent and yet so alive. It was as if she were taunting him, pulling at him, and when he pressed his mouth to hers, he wanted to tear away the remaining barriers that came between him and her soft flesh.

Throwing off his clothing, he pulled her against him, while his body trembled and sank against her satin skin. He closed his eyes, relishing the feel of her.

"If you knew anything about nightingales, Raile," Kassidy whispered in a thick voice, "you would know it is only the male who sings."

"Then," he whispered, "you will make me sing tonight, little nightingale."

Kassidy gravitated toward the heat of his mouth. She had the feeling she was drowning in the essence of this overpowering, dominating male. But it did not matter, she only wanted to feel the thrill of his touch, to become one with him.

"I never knew it was like this between a man and a

woman," she said, gazing into the dark recesses of his eyes, forgetting that the guard at Newgate had defiled her body. "No one ever told me."

"It is much more than this," Raile said, as excitement throbbed through him. He would be the one to introduce Kassidy to a joy beyond belief. He tried not to think that he would not be the first man with her. He would be the only one she would remember.

Raile dared not examine his emotions for Kassidy too closely, for he felt more deeply about her than he had with any other woman. Perhaps it was because they were bound by marriage.

Suddenly Kassidy was afraid of what was happening to her. She gripped the sheet in her fists and tried to pull it over her. "Could we not wait until another time?" she asked in a hopeful voice.

"No, Kassidy," he told her, prying her fingers apart and placing her hands against his broad chest. "It must be tonight. You are as ready as you will ever be."

He slowly moved over her and poised above her. "Don't be frightened. I will be gentle with you."

As he lowered himself against her and pushed her thighs apart, she saw the swollen shaft, and her eyes rounded with fear. "Surely you aren't going to—"

His mouth covered hers, cutting off her protests. She felt herself surrendering to him once more. When she felt him glide between her legs, she opened to him, feeling the pressure and wanting to feel this pleasure he had promised her.

Their bodies were wet with perspiration, and he slid easily into her softness. He filled the empty cavity of her body with his throbbing shaft—filled her mind with new sensations—filled her heart to overflowing.

An aching need danced on Raile's nerve ends as he inched forward, taking care not to frighten her again.

"It won't hurt," he whispered. "It only hurts the first time."

"No," she gasped as he thrust forward, "I feel pain."

Her eyes were luminous and full of expectancy. She breathed in the manly scent of him, slid her fingers through his dark hair, opened her mouth to his probing tongue.

Suddenly Raile moved forward with a stabbing jab, and Kassidy could not keep from groaning at the beautiful lingering pain. She rolled her head back while his lips moved along her throat and across her shoulder.

He pulled back, a look of wonderment in his eyes. "Kassidy," he whispered, "look at me. No man has ever touched you. You were indeed 'the virgin duchess.' No man has been where I now rest inside you."

She searched his eyes, her heart racing with yearning and happiness. "You would not say that if it were not true?"

"I can assure you, Kassidy, I am the first man who has been intimate with you." He suddenly felt elated. "You see, your anguish all those months was for nothing."

Still, she was afraid to believe him. "Are you certain, Raile?"

He held her tightly to him. "On my mother's grave, Kassidy, I swear to you that I am the first man to enter you."

When he returned to her quivering lips, he kissed her with heightening urgency.

Kassidy thought nothing could rival this deepening feeling of pleasure and pain, but she was wrong. He drove deeper into her, and set a rhythmic motion that trapped her breath in her lungs.

Slowly and with care, Raile possessed her body. And when he had reached the height of satisfaction, he held her in his arms until his body ceased quaking.

For a long moment, Kassidy lay still, hardly daring to breathe. At last she understood what marriage was all about. It was being bound so tightly to another human being that only death could part you.

She somehow knew that there was still a deeper fulfillment, for she was strangely unsatisfied. She tilted her head up and found Raile watching her. Shyly, she glanced up at the gold brocade canopy, unable to look into his eyes.

He turned her face to him. She was so lovely, he could hardly speak. He ran his hand down her golden hair and stared into those amazing green eyes. "Never be shy with me, Kassidy. What happened between us was natural, and will happen many times again."

"Is this what love feels like?" she asked, wishing she dared lay her head on his shoulder and curl up against him and have him hold her forever.

Raile stiffened. "What you are feeling is not love, Kassidy. But does that matter? What happened between us is deeper than love." He smiled and twisted the knife in her heart. "Let us call it by its proper name—lust, desire, passion."

She tried not to show her hurt, but she spoke in confusion. "But can those things endure? Do they? Love is everlasting, isn't it?"

He lifted her chin and peered deeply into her eyes. "Desire will endure for a very long time if I planted my seed in you tonight and you give me the son I want."

She would not voice the hurt that surrounded her heart. Raile was reminding her that it was not love he wanted from her—merely a son. "You are right, of course. I hope the deed is done so I will no longer have to come to your bed."

He knew she spoke out of hurt, and was sorry that he could not say what she wanted to hear. "We won't be certain for some time. I will expect you to come to my bed until we know you are with child."

She lashed back at him. "You do remember you promised me my freedom once I deliver a son?"

Raile slid his arms around her and brought her rigid

body against him. "I have not forgotten." He lightly touched his lips to hers. "But it doesn't seem to matter at the moment. You don't expect to hold me to that, do you?"

She could not answer, because his lips burned into hers, cutting off her reply.

Against her will, Kassidy melted against him, unable to resist his practiced touch. She did not want to submit to him, but she knew she would. His kisses drained her of her strength, his touch made her tremble as he made her feel as if she were being wrapped in gossamer wings.

This time Raile's lovemaking reached a fevered pitch, and Kassidy clung to him breathlessly. Her body tingled and quaked, and finally erupted in a passionate burst of feelings.

She lay breathlessly in his arms, wondering how this could be anything but love. Surely when a man and woman had shared such a binding experience, it tied them together for all time.

"You have strange powers over me, Kassidy," he murmured in her ear. "I will have to guard against you."

She looked into his eyes, wishing she could be separated from her feelings. In this one night, she had gone from the depths of despair, to the soaring wings of passion, and again back to despair.

"We both made a bargain, and I shall keep mine, Raile. But the moment I give you a son, I will expect you to give me my freedom."

He arched a dark brow at her, and said with a teasing light in his eyes, "Hardly in my bed for two hours and already you tire of me."

She moved away and stood before him in all her naked glory. "You will find me willing to come to your bed until you have impregnated me. Then I shall never come again."

He stared at her, realizing how he had hurt her. But he had to be honest with her.

He rolled to his feet and quickly pulled on his clothing. He paused in the doorway, wanting desperately to take her back to his bed and caress that soft skin, to bury himself deep within her and once more experience the feeling of really being alive. "This bedroom is yours. I'll trouble you no more tonight."

Before she realized what she was doing she blurted out, "Are you going to that woman?" She wished she could call back the words.

He looked at her with a scowl on his face. "I, madame, am going to the bedroom next door, so I can get some sleep. I suggest you do the same. You journey tomorrow to Ravenworth, and it is a long ride."

"I won't leave without Arrian."

"I will keep my word. The child will follow with the servants."

"I'll want to say good-bye to Aunt Mary and Uncle George before I leave."

"I shall arrange it."

Without another word, he swept out of the room, leaving Kassidy feeling strangely lonely.

What would her life be like at Ravenworth Castle, where she would answer to the whims of this man? She smiled sadly. At least she would have Arrian with her, someone who belonged to her.

She was in a pensive mood. Raile had awakened emotions that frightened and, at the same time, fascinated her. She had experienced sensations she had not known she was capable of feeling. Her heart was heavy because she wanted something from Raile he would never give her. One day he would open his hand and expect her, like the nightingale he had tamed, to fly away.

26

Kassidy awoke when the maid drew the curtains, letting in the sunlight.

"I'm sorry, your grace." The maid dipped into a curtsy. "I'm Polly, and his grace has asked that I have you packed and ready to leave for Ravenworth by noon."

Kassidy reluctantly moved off the bed, looking about the room, where the night before, she had succumbed to Raile's seduction.

"Where is his grace?"

Polly pulled a trunk from behind a wide wardrobe. "He left early this morning after breakfast. He instructed me to tell you that all arrangements had been made for your journey so you will travel in comfort."

Kassidy was relieved she would not have to face Raile this morning. For all she knew, he might be with his mistress. Well, little she cared, she told herself.

She watched Polly lay out her blue traveling gown. "His grace sent for your belongings this morning, your grace," the maid answered Kassidy's inquiring glance. "He also said I was to tell you your aunt and uncle would be here later with your niece."

Kassidy swallowed her angry words, knowing the maid was only the messenger. It seemed Raile had thought of everything, she mused bitterly to herself.

The maid looked at Kassidy with uncertainty. "I dislike bringing this to your attention, your grace, but there is a person below of a doubtful nature. I would have sent her on her way without bothering your grace, but this person was most insistent that she knows you."

"What is her name?"

"She told me that her name is Elspeth O'Neill, your grace."

Kassidy stared at the maid for a moment. "She was quite right, we do know each other. Bring her to me at once."

Polly still looked doubtful that the duchess could know such an undignified person.

"You will have her come up at once," Kassidy stated more firmly. "And bring breakfast for two. Hurry, girl."

The maid scampered out of the room, and Kassidy moved to the pitcher of water and poured it into a bowl. Stepping out of her nightgown, she quickly washed and had just pulled on her gown when there was a knock on the door.

She called out for Polly to enter, but it was a shy Elspeth who poked her head around the corner.

"I wasn't sure you'd would want to see me, beings that you're a duchess now," Elspeth said, hesitantly. "But I promised I'd see to you when they let me out of that place, and I come to keep my word. I see that you be faring more than well, and I'll just leave now."

Kassidy smiled brightly. "Of course you won't leave, Elspeth. If it hadn't been for you, I would have died in that prison. I'll always be grateful to you."

The girl was aware of her shabby appearance and hovered near the door. "I don't want you to feel beholden to me. I just did what was right, and no more."

Kassidy moved forward, taking Elspeth's hand. "What do you know about being a ladies' maid?"

"Little or nothing," she answered with honesty.

"But you could learn, couldn't you, Elspeth?"

The Irish girl knew the most coveted position in a household was the one that served the lady of the house. All the other servants, even the butler and the housekeeper, looked up to the lady's personal maid.

Elspeth's eyes gleamed with hope. "Yes, your grace, I'm sure I could learn."

"Do you have plans to return to your family?"

"I don't expect they'd welcome me. My mother's dead, and the young ones are grown and married."

"Then you will come with me to Ravenworth Castle as my personal maid and as my friend."

Elspeth shook her head. "I'll serve you loyally till the day I die, but I can't be your friend. We come from different worlds, and what can't be, just can't be."

"We were friends in Newgate, Elspeth," Kassidy reminded her.

"You also befriended me."

"You believed me when no one else would. You cared for me as tenderly as a mother would have cared for her child. You will always be my friend, and I want everyone to know what you did for me."

Elspeth's face paled. "No, your grace, you must never tell anyone that. It can't do you no good if people find out you were in that place. Let me serve you. I'll even try to improve my rough manners to be worthy of you. But I'll not expect or want special privileges."

Kassidy realized Elspeth would feel uncomfortable in the role of her friend, and she would never want to do anything to make her feel awkward. "Then be my faithful maid, and always speak the truth to me."

Elspeth nodded happily. "I'll do that, your grace. No one will be more true to you than me."

At that moment, there was a light tap on the door and Elspeth moved to open it. When she saw the haughty maid who had so reluctantly shown her upstairs, she blocked her path. Seeing the maid was carrying a tray of food, Elspeth whisked it from her hands and looked down her nose at the girl.

"What is your name?" Elspeth inquired.

The maid looked as if she might not answer, but something in the Irish girl's eyes changed her mind. "I'm Polly."

"Well, Polly, from now on, her grace will be served only by me."

The maid looked taken aback and then questioningly at the duchess.

"Make it known to the other servants that Elspeth O'Neill is my personal maid," Kassidy said in a voice of authority.

Polly nodded. "Yes, your grace—I'll do that, your grace."

Kassidy smiled to herself, delighted that she was able to repay a debt, and at the same time, have a familiar face with her at Ravenworth Castle.

Raile stepped out of his coach, motioned for Oliver to remain inside, and climbed the steps of Gabrielle Candeur's house. He started to knock, but thought better of it, and inserted his key in the lock.

From the entryway, he could hear voices coming from the sitting room, so he moved in that direction.

Raile stood in the doorway, his gaze moving over the occupants of the room. Gabrielle was seated with her back to him, talking to Hugh. Apparently neither of them was aware of his presence.

"Dearest Hugh," Gabrielle was saying, "I would love to have you as my protector, but you see, you have no money, so therefore, it is impossible. Besides, it is said that Raile has not slept with his new bride, so therefore, he will surely come back to me."

"There are other things than money, Gabrielle," Hugh assured her. "I would be more attentive to you than Raile is, and I would never leave you alone for such a long time."

"My brother is correct," Raile said, startling them both. "There are more important things than money, such as the heart of a faithful woman, and the loyalty of a brother."

Gabrielle came to her feet and raced across the room to throw her arms around Raile. "Dearest, Raile. I knew you would come!"

He pushed her hands away and stood stiffly before her. There was no welcome in his eyes, only splintering coldness.

"I came, Gabrielle, only to inform you that I will no longer consider myself your protector. You are free to seek out whomever you choose, be it a gentleman with money, or my brother, who has little to offer."

Gabrielle's face fell. "Surely you cannot mean that." She reached out beseechingly to him, and placed her hand on his arm. "I want only to please you. If you are angry because Hugh is here, he came only as a friend."

"I care not who you entertain, Gabrielle. I just want you to know that I will continue to pay your expenses until you make other arrangements. However, I have taken steps to close your account with Madame Estelle's."

Her face paled. "You heard what happened. I suppose your wife told you."

Raile's eyes were cold. "Did you really think I would allow you to insult my wife in public?"

Tears brightened Gabrielle's eyes. "I love you, Raile, and was so desperately jealous." She grasped at his coat front. "Can you understand that? Your wife was so young and so sure of herself. I only wanted to . . ."

She fell silent when she saw his eyes harden. With a feeling of distaste, he pried her hands loose and turned to Hugh. "I make you a present of her, but you should understand she is an expensive toy."

Raile moved to the door while Gabrielle clung to the back of the chair, wanting to run after him and beseech him to forgive her and take her back. But pride stopped her. She knew Raile well enough to realize he would only despise her if she tried to hold him.

She fought back tears until he was out the door. She did not care that Hugh hurried after Raile, but collapsed into a heap on the floor, feeling as if her heart would break.

Hugh caught up with Raile before he climbed into the coach. "Well, brother, as usual, you leave broken hearts wherever you go."

Raile frowned. "I believe that is more your method than mine, Hugh."

Hugh grinned boyishly. "I was most taken aback when you married the Maragon girl. Did you feel obligated to once more save the family honor?" Hugh's eyes darkened. "God, you must think me a burden to carry."

"A burden I am no longer willing to carry." Raile curbed his impatience. "I have no wish to stand in the street and talk of family honor. Do you want a ride in my coach, or do you wish to return to your ladybird?"

With a shrug, Hugh swung into the coach, while Oliver quickly climbed on the top to ride beside the coachman.

"Poor Gabrielle," Hugh said. "She would have been better off if she had loved me rather than you. Your trouble is that you have no heart, Raile."

Raile moved into the coach and sat opposite his half brother. "You are hardly the one to talk to me about how to treat women, my brother. As I recall, the women

who are foolish enough to love you either have their
husbands fight a duel with you, or they end up dead
from bearing your bastard child," Raile said dryly.

"I don't like to think about Abigail," Hugh said sulki-
ly. "I believe I came as close to loving her as I am capable of. Pity she died."

"Have you given any thought of your daughter?"

"I can tell you in all honesty, I have not."

"Hugh, you are like a young boy playing at life. And
when you grow weary of one game, you move on to
another without any thought of the lives you have
destroyed along the way."

"What about poor Gabrielle? You left her with a broken heart. She was devastated, Raile."

"Gabrielle entered our relationship knowing what to
expect from me. It was she who stepped over those
bounds. I have little doubt she will have someone to
take my place before sunset—but it will not be you,
Hugh. Make no mistake about this, my brother,
Gabrielle is very shrewd. She will have only the men
who can afford to buy her pretty baubles. What I give
you to live on would hardly keep her in stockings."

Hugh did not like to be reminded that he lived on
Raile's charity. "I have heard strange stories about your
new wife, Raile. It is said that you have not bedded her at
all. How unlike you to overlook your husbandly duties."

Raile gave Hugh a warning glance. "Tell me where
you want to go, and I'll have my driver take you there
after he's delivered me to the club."

"Ah, so I touched a tender spot. Tell me, did you
marry for love, or because you felt honor bound?
What's Abigail's younger sister like? Abigail was a
beauty, but she always insisted her sister was the real
beauty of the family."

"I will not discuss my wife with you, but I'm willing
to talk of your daughter," Raile said in a cold voice. "I

doubt that you will be interested, but Kassidy is taking care of her. I have settled a substantial sum on the child, so her future is assured."

Hugh leaned back, his eyes filled with interest. "How much did you settle on my daughter?"

"That need not be your concern."

Hugh leaned forward. "I'm not as bad as you think I am—at least where Abigail was concerned. I never told you because my mother didn't want me to. But you see, I married Abigail. All the while you were insisting I marry her, she was already my wife."

Rage coiled like a snake in Raile's chest. "You dare say this to me now? We both know you cared nothing for the mother and you care even less for the child. You can never make me believe you married Abigail Maragon."

"It's true. I admit it was in a moment of madness. You see, she would not give herself to me unless it was legal. At that time, I burned for her." Hugh shrugged. "I can easily prove we were married. It's a public record."

Raile tapped on the coach, and the driver came to a halt. "Get out, Hugh. And don't let me see you again until you are more responsible."

Hugh laughed as he stepped down from the carriage. "Does this mean you will no longer pay my expenses?"

Raile glared at his brother. "I will continue to look after you until you settle in a profession where you can support yourself."

Hugh's voice dipped disagreeably. "I work? I will never do that, Raile. My mother would never permit it."

Raile signaled the driver to move on. This morning had not gone well at all. Perhaps Hugh had been right when he accused him of having no heart. Certainly it had not bothered him to end his association with Gabrielle.

Raile closed his eyes, remembering his green-eyed

wife. She was different from other women he had known—she had a proud, independent spirit—he had sensed it at their first meeting. Kassidy would be leaving for the country this morning. Should he go with her, or follow her later?

He knew very well how to treat a mistress, but damn it, how did one treat a wife? He could not buy Kassidy an expensive trinket and expect her to come willingly into his arms—not after last night.

Kassidy glanced out the window of the coach to see fields of primroses waving prettily in the breeze. She thought how different this journey was from the first time she had traveled to Ravenworth. At that time, her grief had been so new, she had paid little attention to the village. She had traveled in a public coach then. Now she was accompanied by a coachman, a footman, and four outriders, whose only purpose was to see to her comfort.

When they neared the village, the coach slowed. To Kassidy's surprise, the people rushed into the street, waving and smiling at her.

"Welcome, your grace," one woman called out. "Welcome home."

She glanced across at Elspeth. "How could they have known I would be passing through the village?"

"I'm sure they was told you was coming. They seem to be truly fond of you."

"They don't know me."

"No, but they know his grace, and it seems they hold him in high regard, or else they'd not welcome you with such gladness."

Kassidy shook her head, stunned by the outpouring of love she felt. "It's like coming home after a long journey."

She looked up at the magnificent castle that was

perched atop the chalk hills. She might feel welcome in the village, but at the castle she would feel like an imposter. She prayed that Raile had already planted his seed in her so she would not have to remain too long. She wondered if he would already be at the castle, and a strange excitement stirred within her. She gazed at the battlement, and saw there was no flag flying. Disappointment settled on her like a heavy hand—Raile was not in residence.

Elspeth watched her mistress with the protectiveness of a mother guarding her young. She saw sadness in Kassidy's eyes and wondered at it. Perhaps the marriage was not a happy one. She glanced up at the castle and could feel some of Kassidy's concern.

"It's a long road from Newgate to here, your grace," she observed, "but you made it in short time."

"Yes, it is, Elspeth. A very long road."

"Look how the wee ones run after the carriage, your grace. It's a tidy welcome, I'd say."

Kassidy smiled at the gleeful sounds of the children. But her gaze returned to the castle that seemed dark and ominous. What awaited her behind those impregnable walls?

27

The crested coach wound its way up the slope past open fields of grain and beautiful meadowlands. Suddenly the horses' hooves clattered on the cobblestone passageway that led through the high archway and continued into the courtyard of the castle itself. They came to a stop at the massive front steps, and a footman jumped down to hold the door for Kassidy.

As she looked up at the castle, she found the steps were lined with servants waiting to welcome her. Since Kassidy knew the housekeeper, she greeted her warmly. "I'm glad to see you again, Mrs. Fitzwilliams."

"We are delighted you are here, your grace." She had a special smile for the new duchess. "And may I say I'm so glad to see you well?"

"Thank you, Mrs. Fitzwilliams. I owe much of my recovery to your gentle ministrations." Kassidy turned to Elspeth, who stood just behind her. "This is my personal maid, Elspeth O'Neill. We left London in such a hurry that she has no uniform. I hope you will help her acquire whatever she needs."

The housekeeper smiled brightly at the Irish girl.

"We will be pleased to help, Miss O'Neill. Just tell me what you require, and it will be arranged."

Elspeth raised her head, feeling good about herself for the first time in many years. Her hair had been neatly covered with a white bonnet; she wore a new gray gown trimmed with white lace and new shoes pinched her feet. Pride ran through her as the servants of Ravenworth Castle welcomed her with respect.

Gratitude shone in her eyes as she looked at the young duchess. At last she had a home where she felt welcome and useful. She could forget about her dark past and look forward to a bright future.

"May I ask, your grace, if your little niece, Sweetness, will be arriving soon?" Mrs. Fitzwilliams asked eagerly.

Kassidy realized all the servants were waiting for her answer. "She will be here tomorrow, Mrs. Fitzwilliams. You might like to know her name is Arrian."

Mrs. Fitzwilliams had spent the morning showing Kassidy the castle. They had walked through the great gallery where family paintings hung. They examined several salons and state dining rooms with their fresco ceilings. Kassidy had climbed wide stairs with newly laid red carpet.

The castle had been built on five levels and was constructed of mason stone walls. There were arched windows and a red slate roof. Kassidy walked up the steps leading to the keep and marveled that the stones were worn smooth by centuries of use. She envisioned the first people to climb the steps had been knights in armor with their ladies wearing velvet slippers.

Kassidy learned that there were fifty-five acres of landscaped land and hunting parks attached to the castle. On the grounds, there was an old mill with a water-wheel which was still used to grind corn. The land, including the village of Ravenworth, consisted of three thousand acres, which had been granted to the DeWinter family in 1214, along with a sum of money to build the castle.

"Have you known my husband long, Mrs. Fitzwilliams?" Kassidy asked as they entered the huge hall.

"Oh, indeed. I've known his grace all his life."

"What is an ordinary day like at Ravenworth?" Kassidy asked with interest.

"As I'm sure you know, his grace is an early riser. His day usually starts at six in the morning. He will breakfast and then confer with his stewards and huntsmen. He will then instruct the workmen who are rebuilding the castle on their duties of the day."

Kassidy nodded. There was no reason to tell the housekeeper she knew so little about her husband's habits.

She watched as the massive chandeliers were being lowered and the candles lit. Her attention became focused on a beautiful silken tapestry of a lady and a unicorn. Moving to stand beneath it, she was saddened to discover that such a wonderful work of art had fallen to disrepair. Looking around the room, she saw there were twelve tapestries in all, each one sadly in need of mending.

Kassidy turned to the housekeeper. "Is there nothing that can be done to save these lovely old tapestries?"

"I'm afraid not, your grace. His grace had several experts come out from London, and they assured him they were beyond saving. But his grace refuses to take them down all the same. Only I am allowed to clean them, and I don't mind telling you it worries me."

As Kassidy looked at the wide stairs that led to her chamber, she was overcome with melancholy. How many DeWinter brides had walked where she had walked today? How many lonely duchesses had climbed these stairs, waiting for their husbands to return? How many had married for love; and how many never had the love of their husbands?

She wanted to ask Mrs. Fitzwilliams if she knew when Raile would be arriving, but pride sealed her lips.

Slowly she climbed the stairs feeling very lonely. When she reached her suite of rooms Elspeth had unpacked her trunks and had a hot bath waiting for her.

After her bath and a light meal, Kassidy crawled beneath silken covers to spend her first night alone at Ravenworth Castle.

During the night, Kassidy dreamed she was back in Newgate. She tossed feverishly on her bed, crying out in torment. With considerable effort, she pulled herself out of the nightmare's grip and sat up, her heart pounding with fear.

The room was dark, and she slid off the bed and padded to the window. Her heart slowed, and she could catch her breath when she saw there were no bars on the windows—she was not in Newgate. Pulling aside the heavy drapery, she watched a dark cloud block out the light of the moon.

"What am I doing here?" she asked aloud, comforted by the sound of her own voice. She moved back to bed, and lay awake, staring at the canopy overhead, fearing if she fell asleep the nightmare would return.

A thin mist hung over the valley as Kassidy reined in her horse. She turned to the groomsman, Atkins, who rode beside her. "It's wonderful to be mounted on so fine an animal," she said enthusiastically, patting the long neck of the gray Arabian.

"Indeed, Rounder here's a fine one, your grace. His sire won three times at Ascot, and sired two other champions besides Rounder."

Kassidy removed her brimmed hat and gazed across the valley. "It's lovely here. I can almost feel the presence of generations of DeWinters on this land, Atkins."

The old leather-faced groomsman smiled at the beautiful new duchess. She was already loved by those who served her, and Atkins was her willing slave. "I've been proud enough to serve three dukes of Ravenworth, your grace."

"That's wonderful, Atkins."

"His grace has a love for the land, just as his grandfather had. 'Course his uncle, the late duke, hadn't much devotion for the land. He spent his time in London, so we hardly saw him for the last twenty years."

"I suppose you knew my husband as a boy?"

"I did that, your grace. He was young when he came to live here. His mother had died, and he was sad for a long time." Atkins was quiet for a moment as if he were remembering. "Yes'er, his grace and Lord John grew up at my feet, riding and hunting. They both loved it here. But I believe young master Raile loved it more than Lord John."

"John was my husband's cousin?"

"Yes, your grace. He met with tragic circumstances."

"Yes, I had heard. 'Tis a pity."

Kassidy gazed up at the sky that had suddenly darkened.

"Looks like we're in for it, your grace. These storms come up without warning here, since we're so near the sea. We best ride hard, and even then, you'll likely get soaked before we reach the stable."

Kassidy laughingly agreed. With her blond hair flying in the wind, she urged Rounder into a full run. Over hills and down valleys they rode, heading for the castle that dominated the landscape.

As luck would have it, they reached the safety of the stables just as the first drops began to fall. Riding into the stable, Kassidy slid off the horse and proceeded to remove the bridle.

"So," a voice spoke up from behind her. "I find a wild-haired woman riding my horses while I'm away."

Kassidy spun around to find Raile smiling down at her.

"I can see you are a practiced horsewoman," he complimented her.

Her heart was beating against the wall of her chest. She felt a sudden lightening of her heart. "I have been taking advantage of your stables, Raile. You have fine horseflesh—for that matter, all of Ravenworth is magnificent."

Raile searched her eyes, looking for any sign that she welcomed him—he saw none. Her windblown hair was curling riotously about her face. She seemed to grow more beautiful every time they met. He had thought himself so noble in marrying her. Oh, yes, so noble in thinking he would be saving her from a life as a spinster.

A streak of lightning split the sky and landed so near that thunder rattled the stable. Kassidy moved to the wide doorway and watched the rain hammer against the earth. When Raile joined her there, she looked up at him and smiled. "I love the rain, don't you?"

"I confess to giving it little thought, except that with the repairs on the castle, it can sometimes be a hindrance."

She held out her cupped hand until it filled with rainwater. "My Scottish grandfather instilled in me a real love for the land and the rain that nourishes it. You have not truly been alive until you have stood on the moor, just after a rain. The air is so thick you feel you can almost touch it, and it smells so fresh and clean."

Raile smiled at Kassidy's enthusiasm. It had been a long time since he had felt passionate about anything. She spurred to life, that within him that he thought was dead.

"So you have a Scottish grandfather—that explains the blond hair."

Kassidy nodded. "I am not unlike my grandfather in many ways." She smiled up at him. "I'm told I have his temper."

"So I have him to thank for that," he said with a touch of humor.

"You would like my grandfather." She was thoughtful for a moment. "No, perhaps you wouldn't. Grandfather doesn't like the British and never misses an occasion to say so."

"But your mother married an Englishman, as did your Aunt Mary."

"Grandfather is an earl, but he would rather be referred to as Laird Gille MacIvors, as he is known to the clan. He never spoke to my father after he married my mother, and to this day has not uttered one word to Uncle George."

"Did your grandfather accept you children?"

"Oh, yes. You see, we were only half British, and that wasn't our fault. His devotion to family runs deep. Except," she added quickly, "for the British connection. Abigail and I spent wonderful summers riding down the rugged coastline with our Scottish cousins, exploring caves and pretending we were Viking raiders. Of course, Abigail had to be the fair princess who was captured and carried away by marauding armies."

Raile's dark gaze swept her face. "I'll bet you were the leader of the Vikings."

Her eyes danced with merriment. "Yes, always."

"How did your mother and father meet?"

"My father traveled to Scotland to buy horses. He met my mother there, they fell in love, and he brought her and the horses back to England with him."

"Is your grandfather still alive?"

Kassidy could not help but smile. "He is the most alive person I have ever known." She glanced up at Raile. "He would not speak to you, or approve of our marriage. I think he always hoped I would return to Scotland and marry a Scotsman."

"Did he also have a husband picked out for you?"

"Yes, indeed he did—Laird Fraser Robertson."

"You rejected the man's suit?"

"Of course. Fraser Robertson was three times my age and had already outlived two wives."

Raile lifted Kassidy onto a wooden barrel, and pulled one up for himself. He wanted to know more about her. "Was your childhood happy, Kassidy?"

Her eyes gleamed. "Oh, yes. My mother was so wonderful, always laughing and happy. My father adored her. Abigail and I had a wonderful childhood." Her eyes grew sad. "Then, my mother and father were gone, and my brother Henry and his wife moved into the house with their daughters. After that, there was little happiness for Abigail or myself."

"Why is that?"

"Henry and Patricia believe laughter is ungodly. You already know what happened to Abigail. You know about my being in Newgate. But what you don't know is that Henry always sought me out for punishment. I learned the night he took Arrian away from me that he had an unnatural attraction for me. I never want to see him again."

"Nor shall you." Raile reached out and picked a straw from her hair. "You never mentioned suitors. Surely you had many."

Kassidy heard the creak of leather and glanced to the back of the stable, where Atkins, out of earshot, was polishing a saddle. "Henry did not allow Abigail or me to attend parties—he thought they were frivolous. I believe if he had allowed Abigail the chance to meet young gentlemen, she would not have been so enchanted with your half brother."

Raile read the sadness and defiance in her eyes. He wanted to hear her laugh, to see her eyes dance with humor, then he wanted to see them soften with desire.

They both watched as Atkins dashed into the rain, making his way to his cottage. Now they were alone, but for the soft neighing of the horses and the sweet scent of hay, a smell heightened by the dampness.

Kassidy could feel Raile's gaze on her, and she stared out at the storm. By now it was raining so hard it was difficult to see as far as the castle.

"I hope you will feel that Ravenworth Castle is your home," Raile said, searching her face, and wondering why her answer was so important to him.

"Since Arrian arrived, I am content here." She turned her head away. "Except for . . ."

"Except for what?"

"It's nothing really. I hesitate to mention it."

"You will find me an attentive listener."

Feeling foolish, Kassidy avoided his eyes. "It's just that the nightmares have returned." She lowered her head. "I wouldn't mention it, but at night they seem so real and so terrifying. I dread to see the sunset."

As quickly as it had started, the rain stopped. But for the stomping of a horse in a nearby stall, the stable was strangely silent.

"No one can imagine the horror you have been through, Kassidy. I wish there was some way that I could erase it from your mind. Perhaps if you face that fear, it won't seem so bad."

"That's what Aunt Mary says, Raile. But how can I do that?"

He stood up and took her hand, pulling her to her feet. "I don't yet know. But when next you have one of the nightmares, you are to come to me. Nothing is as fearful if it can be battled by two people."

Her eyes rounded with wonder. "I would like that."

"Then that's what you will do."

Together they walked upon the wet cobblestone courtyard and Raile's chest seemed to swell with pride of ownership. For the first time in years, he was at peace.

His life had been in a turmoil when he returned to England and found both his uncle and cousin John dead. There had been times when he had felt like an imposter standing in his uncle's place—today, with Kassidy beside him, he knew he belonged.

He glanced up at the tall keep where his rain-wet flag flew, and unconsciously his arm slid around Kassidy's waist. All he needed now was a son. He glanced down at his wife, thinking a golden-haired daughter with green eyes wouldn't be so bad, either.

Lavinia's eyes gleamed with greed. "Hugh, are you certain Raile endowed a large settlement on the child?"

"That's what he said, Mother."

She tapped her foot in vexation. "We have to find a way to get that child." She leaned back against the satin pillow, her gaze riveting into her son's. "Did you tell Raile that you legally married Abigail Maragon?"

"I did make mention of the fact. That's when Raile ordered me out of his carriage. I don't think he believed me."

"If we could somehow get our hands on the money." Lavinia began to pace. "Let me think."

"We can't get the money, Mother, because Raile's new duchess feels maternal toward my daughter. And from what I understand, Raile will give his new wife anything she desires."

Lavinia tapped her fingers together. "Legally, we could take the baby. All we have to do is prove that you are the child's father. It is too cruel of Raile to keep my only grandchild from me."

"You may not mind raising Raile's ire, but I assure you I do, Mother. At the moment, I enjoy his limited bounty. But if I make him angry, he'll cut me off completely. Then where would we be? Besides, what would I do with the child."

"Fool! Imbecile! There is more here than the meager amount Raile doles out to you. You should be the duke, not Raile."

Hugh yawned. He had heard this all before and he was beginning to tire of the subject. "You forget my brother has a wife, and perhaps he has her with child by now."

"I have heard it said that he has not taken her to bed. Can this be true?"

Hugh picked up an apple from the fruit bowl and rubbed it against his sleeve. "If it was true, you can be sure Raile did something about it by now. I happen to know he rid himself of Gabrielle Candeur."

"Hummm," Lavinia said with a satisfied gleam in her eyes. "I didn't like that woman anyway."

"How do you know? You never met her, Mother."

She silenced him with a glance. "We both know this marriage of Raile's is not a match of passion. No doubt Raile felt it was his duty to marry the girl. We will just have to see if we can come between them. That shouldn't be too difficult."

Hugh paused with the apple halfway to his mouth. "It was rumored that Lord Justin Callaret was most attentive to Raile's wife while she was here in London. Perhaps there's something there."

"Will he be our ally?"

"Not he. He fancies himself Raile's friend. I suppose he is one of those men of principle." Hugh threw his head back and laughed. "Not a malady you and I are hampered with, is it, Mother? Why don't you forget about Raile, his wife, and my daughter. Your life is comfortable enough—be contented."

Lavinia gave him a scorching look.

"Don't forget, Mother, that Raile is quick to anger. And he has the power to punish. He is already angry with me. He expects me to settle down. I have little choice but to do what he wants."

"I will never allow him to tell you what to do. You are my son."

"You can't fight him, Mother. Learn to live with him. He's not as bad as you think."

"Try to remember how close you stand to the dukedom, my foolish son."

Hugh stared at the apple and took another bite. "And you try to remember how close you stand to disaster if you meddle in Raile's life."

Lavinia looked with disgust at her son. "You are as weak as your father was. I suppose I'll have to dispose of Raile and his wife with no help from you."

28

Arrian's nursery was two doors down from Kassidy's bedroom, and Kassidy spent much of her day tending to her niece, rather than leaving her care to the nurse.

In the gathering darkness, Kassidy had gone to Arrian, as was her habit each night, to rock her to sleep.

Arrian squealed with delight when she saw her aunt. She held her arms out to Kassidy, while her little face beamed with happiness. Kassidy dismissed the nurse with a nod and lifted the baby in her arms.

"Sweet, sweet, little girl," she said, placing a kiss on the top of Arrian's head. "Your mother would have loved you so dearly." Kassidy sat in the wooden rocker and began to sing an old Scottish lullaby her mother had sung to her as a child.

The baby curled up in Kassidy's arms and sleepily tugged on a blond curl.

"Little Arrian, Aunt Kassidy loves you most dearly. And I intend to see that your life is full of happiness."

Kassidy looked into blue eyes that reminded her so much of Abigail that she caught her breath. "Yes, sweet little one, you are very much loved." Tears brightened her eyes. "You have no last name, but the dishonor is not yours. And I'll see that you never suffer for the mistakes of others."

Raile stood in the shadow of the door and watched Kassidy with the baby. The candlelight fell on her face and her eyes glowed with love. For some unknown reason, he felt a dull ache surround his heart.

"Arrian may not have to suffer at all, Kassidy," he said, coming into the room and sitting on the edge of a trunk.

Kassidy had not known Raile was listening. "What do you mean?"

"I was going to tell you as soon as I could confirm it was true. Hugh told me that he and your sister had actually been married."

Kassidy stared at him in relief. "I knew in my heart that Abigail would never go away with a man without marriage. But you had almost convinced me otherwise."

"It will be easy enough to find out. I already have my solicitor looking into the matter. If Hugh was truthful, Arrian will have the DeWinter name."

Kassidy looked down at the baby who had fallen asleep in her arms. "If only it were true." Then a disturbing thought came to her. "I will never give Arrian to your brother, Raile. Be warned, that I'll fight you and your brother if you ever dare suggest such a thing."

"You should know by now that I wouldn't do anything to hurt you or Arrian."

Raile's eyes were dark and turbulent, and Kassidy was unable to read what he was thinking. "I want to believe you, Raile."

"Do you know me so little?"

"I don't know you at all."

He stood up and moved to the door, leaving her without a word.

Kassidy lay the child in the cradle and tiptoed out of the room. Why did she feel as if she had somehow disappointed Raile?

As she walked along the ancient hallway that had been trod by hundreds of feet before hers, Kassidy's thoughts were troubled. She was indebted to Raile for all he had done for her. And she must not forget he had rescued Arrian and had her brought back to her. They had struck a bargain. And if God was willing, she would give him the son he so desperately craved.

Raile lay awake, listening to the storm that was building over the valley. Lightning flashed across the sky, giving little illumination to his darkened bedroom.

He'd been on his own for so many years, it was difficult for him to consider a woman's feelings and needs, he thought. He had been in war and watched men die. He had come home to the treachery of his stepmother. He had married a woman out of duty and compassion. Today, in the stable with Kassidy, he'd felt a oneness with her. Tonight he had not the courage to go to her bed.

He heard a noise in the hall and thought it might be Oliver. Turning toward the door, Raile jerked his head up when he saw it was Kassidy.

She cupped her hand over the candle to keep it lit while it cut like a sword blade through the darkness ahead of her. Her long hair hung across her shoulders and rippled as she moved. Raile's eyes were drawn to her transparent gown that clung to her soft body.

"Raile," she said, her hand trembling so that she spilled tallow on the floor. "I had the nightmare again. You said I could come to you when I was frightened."

He saw how pale she was, and her eyes were wide with fright. He took the candle from her and blew it out. Grasping her hand, he eased her down beside him.

"You are trembling and cold," he said, pulling her against the warmth of his body.

She slid her arms around his neck and buried her head against his bare chest, needing to feel safe.

A sudden protectiveness came over Raile. He wanted to hold the night at bay for her and battle her nightmares.

"It was horrible. And so real. It was just like I was in Newgate again. I was, oh, so hungry and so cold. I was alone and no one knew where to find me. I cried out, but no one heard me, and no one came."

He brushed her tumbled hair from her face and felt tears on her cheeks. "Sweet Kassidy," he said, running his hand up and down her back, trying to still her quaking body. "Don't you know nothing can harm you while you are under my protection?"

"Yes," she murmured with a sob. "I came to you, knowing you would make the nightmares go away."

He lay his rough cheek against hers. "Kassidy, Kassidy, what can I do to make up for what you have suffered?"

"Talk to me to keep me from remembering. I want to hear about anything that will take my mind off the nightmares. Tell me about the French Campaign. What was Wellington's strategy at Waterloo?"

A streak of lightning illuminated the room and Raile looked into frightened green eyes. He tried not to notice the way her lips parted so enticingly. He knew she was clutching at anything to help push her nightmare out of her mind.

"Never ask a man about war unless you are prepared to hear about a subject that is unsuited for delicate ears," he said, thinking it would do Kassidy little good, in her state of mind, to hear about the horrors of war.

She moved away from him. "In other words, since I'm a woman, I am unfit to meddle in a male world? Does the fact that I wear a petticoat make me a mindless creature that is to be pampered and cannot be thought of past the bedroom?"

Raile was startled for a moment. How could she go from frightened child to Joan of Arc in so short a span of time?

He rolled to his side, shaking with laughter. "You come to me in fear, and you stay to berate me?"

He could not see her smile. "I did do that, didn't I? You must know that I have a frightful temper—I always have had. I warned you I was like Grandfather MacIvors."

"But prettier."

"Decidedly."

"God help me if I've married a Jacobite."

Again a flash of lightning lit the room, and Kassidy moved closer to Raile, her blond hair streaming down her shoulders, her eyes alive with fire.

"I am a Jacobite, your grace. And one who consumes Englishmen."

Raile was so captivated by her that he was losing his reasoning. His arms slid around her and he pulled her to him. "This Englishman voluntarily becomes your prisoner, little Jacobite." Primitive fires burned within Raile. He pushed her gown off her shoulder and buried his face against the softness of her breasts. He closed his eyes, feeling consumed by her.

Kassidy touched his face and trailed her hand down his chin. "It is you who consumes me, Raile." She could feel the strength of him as he pulled her tighter against him, and she gloried in that strength.

"I will have you," he whispered in her ear.

"Yes," she answered, melting against him.

The storm over the valley was losing its power, but the passion between Raile and Kassidy was intensifying. His hand trembled as he intimately touched her, while she willingly submitted to his burning kiss.

"I will fill you with sons," he murmured against her lips.

"Yes, Raile," she answered in a breathless voice.

"Strong sons like their father."

Their bodies merged, their minds entwined, and there was no one in the world but the two of them.

In the village of Ravenworth, hostile eyes looked up at the towering castle. A malignant mind was set on revenge.

Lavinia's face was distorted with hatred. She watched the clouds move away and saw that the castle was bathed in pristine moonlight. It looked almost ethereal and unobtainable—but she would have it! Her only regret was that she would not be a duchess—but her son would be the duke, of that she was certain.

She clamped her mouth together in a severe line, knowing she had already set in motion a scheme to separate forever Raile and his little bride.

Lavinia smiled maliciously. Soon her troubles would be over. Before long she would be situated in that castle with Hugh at her side.

Happy days passed for Kassidy. Each night she would go to Raile's bedroom and he would take her in his arms. There was no more fear and no more nightmares.

Last night Oliver had approached Kassidy with a message from Raile that he would be late and that she was to sleep in her room. She had been puzzled, but had thought little of it.

This morning she looked into the breakfast room to find it empty. When she inquired of Mrs. Fitzwilliams if Raile had come down, the housekeeper shook her head.

"Oliver informed me it is one of his grace's bad days. He was ill last night and will be laid up all day and maybe even tomorrow."

Kassidy wondered why Raile had not told her he was

ill. "What's the matter with my husband?"

"It's the head wound he got at Waterloo. Sometimes the headaches are so severe, the smallest light will make him cry out in pain. He just lies in a darkened room until it passes."

"I never knew. He never told me."

"His grace is a right proud man, your grace. And like most men, he doesn't like anyone to know he has bouts of sickness."

"I might be capable of helping him, Mrs. Fitzwilliams. Send Elspeth for my herb basket. I may also need herbs from the garden to make my brew."

"Your brew, your grace?" the housekeeper asked with curiosity.

"My mother was well versed in the ways of healing herbs, and she passed much of her knowledge on to me."

In no time at all there was a bubbling pot smelling strongly of camphor and wintergreen oil. Lastly, Kassidy added cider vinegar and poured the whole mixture into a bottle and packed it in ice.

"This should help," Kassidy said, moving out of the kitchen and leaving the housekeeper and Elspeth staring after her.

"His grace never sees anyone when he's like this. Oliver has orders to keep everyone away," Mrs. Fitzwilliams said.

"Oliver has never come up against her grace," Elspeth answered.

"True," Mrs. Fitzwilliams agreed. "Very true."

Kassidy didn't bother knocking on the door of her husband's room, but opened it as quietly as she could. It was dark inside, but she could make out the outline of Oliver standing by the window.

The valet came to her quickly and whispered in her ear.

"His grace is having one of his headaches today, your grace. He does not like anyone to see him this way."

"I'm here to help him, Oliver. Light a candle and put it at the foot of his bed so it won't give off too much light."

"Who is there?" Raile asked.

Kassidy approached him. "It's only me, Raile. I've come to help you."

"Go away," he moaned. "No one can help me."

"We'll never know until I try."

"Are you a witch?" he asked, clutching his head and turning away from the light of the candle Oliver had obediently lit.

"Some said my mother was, and perhaps they were right," Kassidy said lightly. "Show me where your head hurts."

"I could more easily tell you where it doesn't hurt," he groaned. "Just leave me in peace."

Kassidy saw she was going to get no help from Raile, so she turned to the valet. "Where was he wounded?"

Oliver stepped forward, unafraid of the angry look Raile cast at him. "Just here, your grace. You can see the scar if you part his hair."

"Yes, I see it. Was he wounded by shrapnel or a sword?"

"Shrapnel, your grace. The doctor who attended him said there was still a fragment left, but he dared not operate since it was close to the brain. That's what causes his headaches."

Raile sighed, knowing he would get no peace until Kassidy was satisfied. She touched his wound and motioned for Oliver to bring the light closer. "Dear God," she gasped. "I can feel a sharp point with my finger. I believe the fragment is working its way out."

"Nonsense," Raile growled. "Just go away."

Kassidy ignored him. "Oliver, bring me my sewing kit, and a kettle of boiling water. Also, I will want more light and Elspeth to assist me."

Raile raised up in bed. "Kassidy, this is none of your affair. If a medical man who treated hundreds of head wounds said I would have headaches for the rest of my life, I trust his judgment."

She gently pulled the pillow from under him so his head would lie flat. "I will want you to remain as still as possible. And have faith in me, Raile. I really do know what to do."

"Damn it, Kassidy, you are only a woman. How can you know more than the doctors?"

She merely smiled and placed a cool hand on his brow. "First, I want you to be as relaxed as possible." She massaged his forehead with some of the ice-cold mixture, as she had seen her mother do many times before when someone was ill. "That's right, Raile, already I feel your tension lessen."

By now Elspeth had appeared with the sewing basket and a steaming kettle of water.

Kassidy peered into her basket, indicating what she would need. "Take my needles and clamps and pour steaming water over them. Then I shall want you and Oliver to hold the candles steady at my husband's head so I can see."

"Damn it, Kassidy—"

"I feel you growing tense again, Raile," Kassidy warned. "You must relax."

He rolled his eyes at the ceiling, knowing he would have to endure her worst because he was too ill to make her go away, and it was certain she had made Oliver her ally.

The room was silent as Kassidy parted Raile's hair and found the jagged wound. She felt sadness at what he must have suffered, and was still suffering. Carefully running her finger over the scar, Kassidy located the sharp fragment. "Hand me the clamp," she told Elspeth.

Tense moments passed while Kassidy examined the wound. "I'll need a knife, and I shall also want it washed with boiling water."

Raile's eyes were so dulled with pain, it tore at Kassidy's heart to know she must cause him more agony. She had never seen him like this, and it made her angry that some doctor had left this fragment in his head.

Kassidy gripped the handle of the knife and nodded to Oliver to hold Raile's head still. As she cut into his scalp, Raile let out a soft moan. She threw down the knife and reached for the clamp. Her hand was steady as she removed the wide sliver object that was about an inch long. She dropped it into Oliver's hand while she washed away the blood and poured her healing herbs on the wound.

After this was accomplished, she wrapped Raile's head in clean bandages and gave him a glass in which she had mixed a sleeping potion. "I'm sorry if I hurt you," she said, clutching his hand.

"Give me the fragment you took from my head," he said in a bitter tone.

Oliver handed Raile the offending object, and his grace turned it over in his hand. "So this was the source of my pain for all these months."

Kassidy nodded. "I would assume it was pressing against a nerve. Your color is already better, but I suspect your head will be sore for a few days."

Raile stared at Kassidy. "Which are you, a witch or an angel?"

She gathered up her instruments and smiled at him. "I'll let you decide."

"The medical profession could benefit by your knowledge," Raile said dryly.

"I have other obligations. I belong to an arrogant young duke who is reluctant to accept help when it's offered."

Raile caught her hand. Already the potion was making him drowsy. "I suppose I should thank you."

"Go to sleep now. We'll see how you feel tomorrow."

Raile watched her walk to the door and close it

behind her.

Oliver spoke up in a voice of amazement: "Her grace is most remarkable, your grace."

"Yes," Raile said sleepily, "the pain is gone. She is my angel."

The next morning Raile awoke early. He sat up, waiting for the usual pain to hit him. He touched his head and found it a bit sore where Kassidy had removed the fragment. He stood up and moved to the window. For months he had lived with the headaches; sometimes they were mild, sometimes severe. Today there was no pain at all.

He was deep in thought. Kassidy was becoming too important to him—too much a part of his life. He had to put some distance between them so he could think clearly.

He instructed Oliver to pack his trunks.

"Will we be gone for a short time, or for an extended stay, your grace?" the valet inquired.

"We shall be away for at least a fortnight."

Kassidy placed Arrian in bed. She was amazed how quickly a baby could change. Already Arrian was crawling, and today for the first time, she had stood on her own. Kassidy moved down the hall. Dressed in her green riding habit, she found herself humming happily as she descended the stairs. She paused at the bottom, thinking how good life was.

Glancing at the closed door of Raile's study, Kassidy resisted the urge to knock. She was almost certain she was with child and was anxious to share the happy news with him. But, no, perhaps she should wait until she was positive.

She felt Raile was beginning to care for her. Perhaps he didn't love her yet, but he did desire her, and she knew he enjoyed her company. She hoped a baby might bind them together.

Her attention was drawn to the stairs where two servants carried trunks with Oliver issuing orders that they be placed in the traveling coach.

Kassidy's heart plummeted.

"Oliver, is his grace going away?"

The valet avoided her eyes. "He has already left for London, your grace. He asked that I tell you he will be gone for some time."

Kassidy turned her back so Oliver would not see the hurt in her eyes. With determined steps she moved back upstairs leaving the valet to stare sadly after her.

Dr. Worthington confirmed that Kassidy was indeed with child.

The news about the baby had awakened in Kassidy conflicting emotions. A new and wonderous awareness came over her. It was extraordinary to nourish and give birth to a new life. But sometimes at night she would be haunted by visions of Abigail as she writhed in pain giving birth to Arrian.

The weather had turned cold, and Kassidy was confined to the castle. Time lay heavily on her hands. There had been no word from Raile.

As days passed into weeks, Kassidy's waist disappeared, and it was obvious she was with child. She received kindness and consideration from the servants, but still there was no word from Raile.

29

Jack Beale was awakened from a deep sleep by the pounding on the door.

"See who's there," he called out to his brother in an angry voice. "And no matter who it is, send them away."

Grumbling about people calling too early in the morning, Gorden went to the door, swung it open, and wordlessly stared at two men who were dressed in double-breasted blue coats and trousers and the telltale scarlet waistcoat which earned them the name, Robin Redbreasts.

"Well, who is it?" Jack called out from the other room.

One of the men pushed past Gorden, making his way to Jack's bedroom, while the other subdued the startled Gorden.

Jack jumped to his feet as the man entered. "Bow Street Runner!" he exclaimed, looking to the door and seeing his only route of escape was blocked.

"Mr. Jack Beale, you and your brother, Gorden Beale, will be coming with us, and will be prosecuted for crimes against the king."

Jack could only stand helplessly as the Bow Street Runner clamped irons on his wrists. "Why are you taking us? Me and my brother ain't done nothing against the law."

"I have a message for you," the runner said, pushing Jack into the front room, where he was chained to his brother. "I was told by my superior to ask you, on behalf of the duke of Ravenworth, how you would like to spend the rest of your life in Newgate."

Gorden looked at his older brother with anger. "It was you that brought this down on us, Jack. You always saying how smart you was, and how you had a good friend who was titled. Well, look what that good friend with a title got you!"

For once Jack was speechless, but Gorden had found his voice after all these years.

"He'll have us put in Newgate, sure enough—he wants us to know what she felt like in there."

"Shut up, Gorden," Jack said, his eyes downcast. He knew Gorden was probably right.

Winter was encroaching upon the land, and gloom hung over London. Every day for the last week, a cold dreary rain had fallen.

Raile spent most of his days at his club, trying to pass the time, but he found he was no longer amused by playing cards and gaming, and had little in common with his friends there.

A weak sun had broken through the clouds. But Raile paid little attention as he entered his London house.

Oliver rushed forward, taking Raile's damp coat. "Lady Mary's here to see you, your grace. I informed her you might be late, but she insisted on waiting for you. I put her in the sitting room."

"Kassidy isn't ill, is she?"

"Her ladyship didn't say, your grace."

Raile hurried down the hall to find Lady Mary sitting in the window seat. As always, he was struck by the serenity and beauty of Kassidy's aunt.

"Have you word of Kassidy?" he blurted out.

"Not since last week. I received a letter telling me her waist has thickened and she can hardly fasten her gowns." She looked at Raile searchingly. "You must be so proud that you are to be a father. Although I admit it's difficult to think of you in that respect."

"Doctor Worthington only told me yesterday. I've waited a long time for a son."

"I would have thought you would want to share this time with Kassidy." There was a hint of reproach in Lady Mary's voice.

Raile unbuttoned his coat. "I have instructed Doctor Worthington to go to Ravenworth every weekend, and he will keep me informed of Kassidy's progress."

"An admirable arrangement, I'm sure." Lady Mary noticed Raile was in formal dress. "You must have been out all night."

He sat down wearily. "If you're asking, I was at the club all night. I won twenty-three hands straight and had nothing to drink. It was a dull night, and I saw no other women."

"It's none of my affair, I'm sure. I just came by to give you something that belongs to Kassidy."

He glanced at the carved wooden box she held in her lap. "Are they girlhood treasures?" he asked.

"In part. Actually, these are all of Kassidy's earthly possessions. Her brother, Henry, sent them to me, hoping I would take them to Kassidy. Of course, he wrote me that her clothing had all been passed down to her nieces."

"Why did you bring this to me?"

"You're her husband. Surely you wouldn't mind taking them to her . . . when you return to Ravenworth."

There was no rebuke in Lady Mary's tone now, but there was a light of concern in her blue eyes.

"I'll be glad to take them to . . . my wife . . . when I return to Ravenworth."

Lady Mary opened the box and withdrew a yellowed handkerchief and gently touched the initial that had been embroidered there. "I found something very astounding in this box that I would like to share with you." She handed him the handkerchief. "Have you seen this before?"

He recognized it. "Yes. It's mine. Oliver always has my handkerchiefs made by a seamstress in Dorchester." He looked at her curiously. "But how did it come to be with Kassidy's trinkets?"

"You may well ask. Kassidy has had this in her possession for a very long time. I remember the day you gave it to her. She was bursting with information about the handsome officer who rescued her in the park."

"You have me in the dark, Lady Mary. When did this happen?"

"It's very strange sometimes how life has its little twists and turns. Imagine you and Kassidy meeting each other so many years ago, and neither of you remembering the other."

"If you wanted to intrigue me, you have succeeded."

"The day you gave this to Kassidy was the very day she learned that her mother and father had drowned at sea."

"Pray explain, Lady Mary."

She smiled, knowing she had his complete attention. "Do you remember a little girl who had been pounced on by a chimney sweep, who threatened to throw her in the pond across from my house?"

He frowned as a vague memory tugged at his mind.

"Yes—yes, I do! As I recall, the boy soiled the child's dress and I"—he looked down at his handkerchief—"I cleaned the spot for her and gave her the handkerchief."

Raile shook his head in wonderment. "I often wondered what happened to that lovely little girl. She had the most expressive . . . my God, the green eyes—Kassidy!"

"You could not have known that day that Kassidy cried for her dead parents, using your handkerchief to dry her tears. Also, you could not know that she said a prayer for your safety every day of the war."

Raile felt a lump forming in his throat and he could hardly speak. "I . . . no."

Lady Mary smiled in satisfaction. "Oh, well, who can tell how life will turn out?"

Raile gently touched the handkerchief. "Do you think she remembers me as that officer—I believe she called me her champion that day?"

"I don't know if she does or not. Why don't you go home and ask her?"

"I see scorn in your eyes, Lady Mary."

"Not scorn, Raile. Concern perhaps."

"Do you judge me harshly?"

"I'm not doing that—at least I hope I'm not. Did you know that Kassidy is having nightmares again?"

Raile felt sick inside, remembering how terrifying those dreams were for her. "No. She didn't tell the doctor."

"Kassidy only told me because she was afraid it would harm the baby. You have been away for two months, Raile. Don't you think you should go home?"

His eyes were full of misery. "I think I have been punishing myself by staying away."

"I don't know what happened between the two of you. But go home, Raile. Kassidy needs you."

"Perhaps I shall. But first I need to settle several matters here in London. You might like to know I have had a man following Jack and Gorden Beale. He has gathered enough evidence on them so they will be imprisoned without us involving Kassidy in any way. Their crimes are so many they will be locked away for a long time."

"You're a shrewd man, Raile. I would hate to make an enemy of you. I knew you would find a way to punish those two, I just didn't think it would be so soon."

"The matter is closed as far as Kassidy is concerned. She will never have to fear those two again." Raile handed Lady Mary back the handkerchief, and watched as she placed it in the small chest.

"I wonder if she will ever connect you, Raile, with her champion in the park?"

"The man I was that day no longer exists."

"The little girl Kassidy was no longer exists, either. She is going to have your child—and she needs her champion."

He looked into warm, seeking eyes. "You need not fear that your niece will have my child alone. I am not my brother. I will be there when she gives birth."

Dr. Worthington had cautioned Kassidy against riding horseback, so she could no longer take her daily rides. Feeling restless, she had ordered the carriage with the intention of going into the village.

Elspeth settled Kassidy in the coach and spread a woolen lap blanket over her legs. "You'll want to keep warm, your grace. We can't have you taking a chill," the Irish girl cautioned.

As they rode along, Kassidy could see there had been a morning frost, and the meadowlands were still heavy with moisture. "I never liked winter, Elspeth. But I can imagine that this valley covered with snow would be beautiful."

"In Ireland, the snow comes early and stays late. Sometimes I'm lonely for my homeland, but I don't miss the winters."

"Perhaps you shall go home one day, Elspeth."

"It wouldn't be the same now. I doubt I'll ever return. Besides, I'll never leave you."

"Thank you for your loyalty, but still, I will want you to visit your family one day."

The coach had now reached the village. Today, as always, the people called out friendly greetings to her.

"There, Elspeth," Kassidy said, "the shop with the china displayed in the window. That's where I want to go."

Elspeth signaled for the coachman to stop, and Kassidy was helped to the ground.

When the shopkeeper saw the duchess approaching, she opened the door greeting her warmly. "Welcome, your grace. I'm Sally Mayhew. How can I be of service to you?"

Kassidy smiled at the woman and then glanced about her. The shop was bigger than it appeared from the front. It was neat and clean, and articles and crafts were displayed in shelves cut into the thick walls.

"Mrs. Mayhew, your shop is charming."

"We're pleased you think so. Would your grace care to have tea? It's a chilly day, and I have just made a nice pot." Mrs. Mayhew's eyes gleamed hopefully.

Kassidy picked up a delicate china teacup that had been hand-painted in a lacy pattern in blues and white—a pattern she had never before seen on china. "Not just yet, Mrs. Mayhew. Perhaps later. Who is responsible for the china painting?"

"This design's been in our village as far back as anyone can recall, your grace. The craft is always passed on from mother to daughter. No one knows who started it, but it's said Queen Elizabeth once ate off our plates."

"It's extraordinarily beautiful."

"If only others would share your views, your grace. We hardly make enough to keep this shop open."

"But the village is not far off the main London thoroughfare. You should get many patrons who travel that road."

"The village of Ravenworth's fallen on hard times, your grace. My sister's family had to move to London 'cause they couldn't put food on the table here. Our young people leave as soon as they are old enough. Of course, the reconstruction of the castle has brought work to many families, and we're grateful to his grace."

"I want to look around the village, and I'll be back to take tea with you later."

Mrs. Mayhew beamed. "I'll just have some nice little cakes for you, too, your grace."

Kassidy found the same friendliness in each shop she visited, and the same story of misfortune. And each shop displayed pieces of the unique china.

Kassidy wondered why Raile had done nothing about the poverty here in his own village. She could see the thinness of the children's faces and the hopelessness in their parents' eyes. Perhaps Raile had been too busy rebuilding the castle to notice what was happening to the villagers.

Kassidy's mind was racing. She was sure there was something that could be done to help the people who lived in the shadow of Ravenworth Castle.

She returned to Mrs. Mayhew's shop and was met at the door by the shopkeeper. "I have your tea laid out in my kitchen, your grace. I thought you would be more comfortable there. I'll just pour your tea and leave you alone."

"No," Kassidy said, "Please stay. I want to discuss something with you."

Mrs. Mayhew held the curtain aside so Kassidy and Elspeth could enter her quarters in the back. The room was small, but spotlessly clean, and smelled of lemon wax. A white cloth covered the kitchen table where tea and cakes awaited.

Kassidy's gaze went at once to the beautiful tapestry on the wall behind the table. "This reminds me of the tapestries at the castle," she said, touching it carefully. "But this has only been recently done, hasn't it?"

"Yes, your grace. My grandmother makes the tapestry, and my daughters help her."

"Could she also repair them? Even if they are in bad condition and very old and fragile?"

"Indeed yes, your grace. My grandmother has magic fingers." She poured the tea. "She's eighty-three, almost blind, and yet she still crafts beautiful creations."

"Join me, Mrs. Mayhew. I think I have an idea how to solve both our problems."

With curiosity, Lady Mary opened the box that had been delivered by a messenger from Ravenworth. She found Kassidy's letter on top and began to read:

Dearest Aunt Mary,
Enclosed you will find an extraordinarily beautiful twenty-place setting of china, which I'm sure you will agree is unique. It is a gift to you from the Ravenworth villagers. I ask only that you use the pieces at your next social, and emphasize where they were made. I have found the villagers here in need of revenue, and in this, I intend to help them. I would love to see my village in vogue, but most of all, I want to see it prosper. I could use your help in this.

Lady Mary smiled and handed the letter to George so he could read it. "That's our Kassidy. And Raile thought he would have an easy life with her."

George laughed. "I may have a few notions on how

to draw patrons to Ravenworth. I often thought if I had been born a tradesman, I would have done well."

"Surely you have a few pounds you can contribute to this worthy undertaking," Lady Mary said, catching her husband's exuberance.

Lady Mary held up a delicate plate. "Most extraordinary," she said. "It will be a welcome addition to my table."

She smiled, and her eyes became mischievous. "I believe I shall invite Lady Talmadge to tea. She has impeccable taste, and if I can interest her in this china, everyone in London will want a set."

Her husband became serious for a moment. "Kassidy is like you in many ways, my dear. You are both like a cat and will always land on your feet. I believe your niece just landed on hers."

"I land on my feet because I have you beside me, George. I'm not certain Kassidy has anyone."

30

Even though the weather had grown colder and the rain often turned to ice, Kassidy went each morning into the village and was welcomed with enthusiasm. She was now a familiar figure; the children would gather around her to vie for the chance to walk at her side.

She had located an empty barn outside Ravenworth, and with the help of the enthusiastic villagers, it had been transformed into a workshop. The men who were not employed at the castle worked tirelessly following Mrs. Mayhew's direction.

Twelve potter wheels had been assembled, and three heavy ovens stood against the back wall to bake the greenware. Tables were set up so Mrs. Mayhew and her daughters, and several other gifted craftsmen could paint the intricate details on the Ravenworth china.

Kassidy entered the factory and paused in the doorway, watching the activity around her. "This is marvelous, Elspeth," she said with satisfaction.

When Mrs. Mayhew saw the duchess, she set her work aside and came quickly to her. "Pardon the paint on my hands, your grace." She glanced about her with pride. "We have almost finished with five orders for Ravenworth china you brought last week."

Kassidy handed Mrs. Mayhew several letters. "Then," she said smiling, "you will be able to start on the twelve new orders I received today. Your fame is spreading. If this keeps up, Mrs. Mayhew, we'll have to build a larger shop."

"We owe it all to you, your grace."

"Nonsense. It's your talent and the other villagers' hard work that made it all possible. I merely helped you find a market for your lovely china."

Kassidy noticed that the other workers were gathering about her, all smiling.

"Your grace," Mrs. Mayhew said, "we would like to show you in a small way, how grateful we are for what you've done for us."

Everyone nodded in agreement.

"Would you follow me, your grace?"

Kassidy looked curiously from one smiling face to another as she walked beside Mrs. Mayhew. At the front door, the workers formed a circle about her and waited expectantly as Mrs. Mayhew began to speak. "For generations, we of the village of Ravenworth have dwelled in the shadows of the castle. Sometimes our ancestors have taken shelter there from our enemies, and sometimes we have shared food from the dukes' tables, but never have we had the lady of the manor come down to help us as you have, your grace."

Mrs. Mayhew called Kassidy's attention to the porcelain plaque which hung on the wall. It had the same intricate pattern as the china, and Kassidy read the words with tears in her eyes.

Dedicated gratefully to her grace, Kassidy DeWinter, the eighteenth duchess of Ravenworth, for her loving kindness to the village of Ravenworth.

Kassidy turned to the people and saw the anticipation on their faces, as if they expected her to respond.

"Thank you . . ." There was a catch in her throat, and she had to wait a moment before she could continue. "I can't tell you how much this gladdens my heart, and how I shall cherish your goodwill. The credit belongs to each of you. You were dedicated and worked hard. I will always be proud to have been a small part of all you have accomplished."

She looked at the sea of faces and read admiration in their eyes. This was where she belonged—this was where she wanted to remain to raise her child. She had come to know these people, to admire them, to care about them individually, and she knew they returned her affection.

Knowing if she remained longer she might cry, Kassidy gave a final wave of her hand and left abruptly. She was a fool to think Raile would allow her to live here after the baby was born. After all, she had a bargain to keep.

Kassidy stood at her bedroom window, staring into the courtyard below. It was the first snowfall of the season, and the flakes fell gently earthward. She watched as the cobblestones disappeared beneath a blanket of white.

She sighed and turned to Elspeth, who was sitting on a stool near the fireplace with a basket of mending beside her. "Each season here is more beautiful than the last, Elspeth."

"It'll be a hard winter, your grace. I'm right glad we're in the country and not in London."

"Yes, so am I. Except . . . it does get lonesome sometimes."

"And why not, I ask? You have only the servants to talk to, and the little one, of course. You need your husband with you at a time like this."

Kassidy touched her rounded stomach. "Sometimes I hope this is the boy Raile wants," she said, voicing her thoughts, "and sometimes I hope it's a girl."

Elspeth applied her needle into the material and took several stitches. "The baby'll be what it is, and nothing can change that." She laid her sewing aside and moved to her mistress.

"You mustn't be on your feet too much, your grace." She guided Kassidy to a chair, and when she was seated, placed a robe over her lap. "You don't want to take a chill, now do you?"

Kassidy gave in to Elspeth's pampering. She closed her eyes and listened to the peaceful crackling of the fire in the grate. It was tranquil here, and she loved Ravenworth Castle. It was as if carrying a child with DeWinter blood made her belong.

"I'll just go below and get you a nice cup of hot chocolate to fortify you against the cold, your grace," Elspeth said, hurrying out of the room.

Kassidy threw the blanket off and moved back to the window. By now, the ground was completely covered with snow, and the wind began blowing and swirling it around.

She felt an ache deep inside. Abigail had loved the snow so. Kassidy could envision her sister as she had run through the snow, her head turned upward, catching the snowflakes on her tongue.

If only she had Abigail with her now, to share this time with her. The baby inside of her moved, and it brought tears to her eyes.

The blinding snow tore at Raile's greatcoat as he dismounted and tossed the reins to Oliver. The valet led both horses toward the stables, wondering why his grace had insisted on riding all the way from London in such a fierce storm.

Raile raced up the steps and opened the door, sending a swirl of snow into the entryway. He tossed his coat at the butler. "Where is her grace?" he asked moving up the stairs.

"I believe she's in her room, your grace," the butler answered, undaunted by the duke's sudden appearance. "Her maid just went into the kitchen."

Raile moved through the hallway with an urgency. He couldn't explain the ache inside. He did admit to himself that for the first time in many years, he had missed another person. The thought of Kassidy had been with him day and night. Now that she was so near, he hastened his footsteps.

Kassidy was standing at the window with her back to him when he entered. Raile's eyes ran the length of her. She was dressed in a flowing green velvet robe, and her magnificent hair hung in long ringlets to her waist. He could see her beautiful face reflected in the window, although she had not yet noticed him. When he saw tears rolling down her cheeks, he felt a stab in his heart.

Suddenly she saw his reflection in the window and turned slowly to face him, saying in a calm voice: "I was not certain if it was you or an apparition, Raile."

He took two steps that brought him even with her. "You are crying, madame." He removed his handkerchief and gave it to her.

Kassidy wiped the tears from her face, ashamed that he had seen her in her weak moment. "It will pass."

She handed him back his handkerchief, but he closed his hand around hers. "You keep it, you never know when you might need it again."

Kassidy glanced down at the handkerchief, absently tracing the black embroidery, R. Suddenly her head snapped up and she stared at Raile, as a door in her mind opened. She remembered that scene in the park so many years ago when she had been rescued by a handsome officer who was going away to fight the French. How could she have forgotten about the handkerchief and the man who had given it to her?

"You, Raile—you were my champion?" she asked in disbelief. She tried to imagine the dashing officer who had passed so briefly through her life. "Was it you that day, Raile?"

He took her hand and pulled her tenderly into his arms. "You did not remember until now?" he asked, his whole being filled with the sweet smell of her hair.

She buried her face against his chest. "I never forgot the incident, but I could not recall your face." Kassidy closed her eyes, loving the feel of his arms about her. When he was holding her, there were no shadows in her world, no nightmares lurking in the recesses of her mind.

She raised her head. "How can it be that you and my champion are one and the same?"

Raile cupped her chin and looked into misty green eyes. "How can you be the lovely little girl who would probably have done the lad in, if I hadn't come along and rescued him?"

Kassidy loved the way his eyes shone when he smiled. "I thought of my champion so often and hoped he—you would come safely through the war." She shook her head. "I can't believe that we met for that brief moment, and then found one another again. If I had recognized you that day I came to the castle, I would have known you were not the man who had wronged Abigail."

He laughed, looking down at her. "Did I make such a lasting impression on you that day in the park?"

"Yes, you did," she said seriously. "Perhaps because that was the day I learned my mother and father had drowned, and thinking of you, and what you would have to face, helped me. As the years passed, I forgot your face, and remembered only the uniform, and"—she glanced into his eyes—"your wonderful dark eyes. I should have known you right away by your eyes, Raile."

He stroked her hair. "And I should have known those green eyes of yours." He lay his face against her smooth cheek. "Oh, Kassidy, I'm finding out that there are reflections in a woman's eyes that can melt a man's heart."

"Did I melt your heart, Raile?"

He held her at arm's length. "If you have not melted it, you have surely thawed it a bit."

For the first time, he noticed the roundness of her stomach. He wanted to crush her to him, but he dared not. Within her body, she carried his child—perhaps a son. For the first time, he thought of the child as a person, as a part of himself and Kassidy. Together, with God, they had created a new life.

"Are you feeling well?" he asked in concern.

She moved to the fireplace, still clutching his handkerchief and still reeling from the revelation that Raile was the man she had met so long ago. "My health is good," she answered.

"I was told that you are suffering from nightmares again."

Kassidy spun to face him. "You could only have heard that from my aunt."

"Why didn't you tell me? I would have come back sooner."

Now she averted her face, staring at the dancing flames. "I don't expect you to coddle me. Are you happy about the baby, Raile?"

He had expected her to accuse him of months of neglect but she had not. His eyes took on a tender light. "Extremely so. I don't intend to leave you until the baby is born."

She dropped down in a chair. "That won't be for

three months, Raile. Can we hold you here that long?"

He knelt before her and took her hands in his. "Kassidy, will you ever forgive me for leaving you alone for so long?"

She didn't hesitate. "Yes. I forgive you."

He stood up, his shadow falling across her face. "I hope I never again have reason to beg your forgiveness."

She smiled at him mischievously. "If I know you, there will be other times, Raile."

31

Meg Dower entered the room as quickly as her lame leg would allow. She slammed the door behind her and limped over to Lavinia, who was sitting with her elbows propped on the dressing table, staring into the mirror.

"Today's my birthday, Meg. I'm forty-seven. I'm getting old. Once I made men worship at my feet. Look," she said, moving the candle closer to the mirror, "there are wrinkles around my eyes and mouth."

Meg hiked up her skirt and backed up to the fireplace. "I'll not see the sunny side of sixty again. To me you're not old."

"I've always been beautiful, and I never thought about getting older until I saw that girl Raile married. Even in my youth, I was not as beautiful as she," Lavinia admitted grudgingly. "She has the kind of face that will only grow more beautiful with age."

"Why do you torture yourself thus?" Meg dreaded the thought of Lavinia working herself into a temper. "It's snowing hard out there," Meg said, trying to move on to a safer subject. "It ain't fit for a body to be out. I got splashed by a cabby, and I gave him what for."

Lavinia turned to the old woman. "Did you learn anything about my stepson?"

Meg squirmed, knowing she would have to tell Lavinia what she had discovered. "I talked to the street vendor who's sweet on one of his grace's maids."

"Well! well! Don't keep me waiting. What did the man say?"

"He said his grace has gone back to Ravenworth. Left yesterday morning."

Lavinia dipped her finger into her rouge pot and applied color to her cheeks. "Is that all you discovered?" She knew Meg was deliberately being vague.

Meg moved away from the fire to stand near the door, in the event she had to make a hasty retreat. "The man says the duchess is having a baby."

Lavinia jumped to her feet, her face a mask of rage. "I'll not have it! I've schemed too hard to have something go wrong now."

Meg stood halfway in the hall. "I always credited you with the insight to know when to quit. There's too much that stands between Mr. Hugh and what you want for him."

Lavinia picked up the rouge pot and threw it against the door, and watched as great globs plopped onto the floor, looking surprisingly like blood. "I'll not quit until my son stands in Raile's place."

Meg scrambled out the door and quickly down the hallway, her lame leg making a loud slapping sound against the polished, wood floor. She'd stay out of the way for a while and give her mistress time to gather her thoughts. The old servant shook her head. The mistress was getting meaner every day. Meg's sister had been asking her to come live with her; she might just consider doing that. If Mrs. DeWinter kept on like she was, the law would have her for sure. Raile DeWinter was no man to trifle with.

* * *

Raile had just settled behind his desk when Ambrose entered the study. "Mr. Mayhew's here from the village, asking to see her grace. I told him she's walking about the grounds. Mr. Mayhew asked if you could give him any orders that may have arrived."

Raile looked perplexed. "What orders are you referring to, Ambrose?"

"The orders that come in each week for the Ravenworth china, your grace."

"I haven't a notion what you are referring to, Ambrose. Show Mr. Mayhew in, and perhaps he can enlighten me."

Kassidy walked about the frozen ground, her white velvet cloak blending in with the snowy landscape. She was so lost in thought she didn't hear Raile come up behind her until he called out to her.

"Should you be out in this weather, Kassidy?"

She turned and smiled at him. "I can assure you I will not melt."

He watched her as she paced off the frozen rows where the kitchen garden would be planted in the spring. "May I ask what you are doing?"

"Raile, why are potatoes and vegetables only planted in kitchen gardens?"

"To feed the people of the castle, I would think."

"I have put a lot of consideration into an idea that I believe will bring more prosperity to the villagers."

He tucked a blond curl beneath her hood. "I'd be interested in hearing your thoughts. I learned today how you helped the villagers make and distribute their china."

"And they have done so well, Raile. I expect before long they will have to make the factory larger."

He watched a snowflake land on her eyelash and had

the strongest urge to remove it with his lips. "What is your new scheme?"

"It's my belief that if the villagers are to become even more self-sufficient, they should clear ground and plant fields of edible crops. Not for their own consumption, but to sell at the markets in London."

"A novel idea."

"Not at all, Raile. I've read extensively on this subject, and it's done quite successfully in America." Her eyes glowed with excitement. "There are many advantages for the villagers in this. They can sow clover to feed their own livestock."

"Assuming they have livestock."

"They can buy them with the earnings from the Ravenworth china."

"Of course, why didn't I think of that?" he mused.

"Raile, the villagers could even build a mill and man it with paid tenants so the grain can be sold to neighboring villages, where they are not nearly so ambitious. I have already encouraged the women who do not work at the china factory to set up a shop so their crafts can be sold. This will help them become less dependent on their husbands and give them pride."

"Are you asking me to become a tradesman?"

She smiled at the mock horror on his face. "Of course not, Raile. I'm merely asking you to encourage it in others."

She was quiet for a moment and then she asked, "Raile, are you still bothered by headaches?"

"No, my little physician, not since the night you operated on me."

"I'm glad. I was worried about that."

"Were you?"

"Yes, of course."

He drew her into his arms, wishing he could tell her how full his heart felt. She was bright, intelligent, and he adored her. "I will help the villagers in any way I can, if you will promise to come inside. It has begun to snow harder, and I don't want you losing your footing."

Raile scooped her up in his arms and walked toward the castle. He looked down at her, thinking she grew more beautiful every day and more necessary to him.

His gaze moved over her face that was framed by the green inner lining of her hood. "Are you cold?" he asked, wanting to tighten his arms about her and tell her of the many feelings that warred inside him.

"No. I love the snow, don't you?"

They had entered the house, and he set her on her feet and Ambrose appeared from out of nowhere and took their cloaks. Raile steered Kassidy toward the stairs before he answered her. "For a long time, Kassidy, I have hardly taken notice of the passing seasons."

"Is that true, Raile?"

"I can assure you it is."

She paused and placed her gloved hand on his arm. "What happened to you, Raile, that made you so cynical about life?"

"I wouldn't say I'm cynical, only mistrusting."

"Then what made you mistrusting?"

He drew in a long breath. "Let us just say, I know human nature and I allow for faults in others."

"But you don't allow for faults in yourself."

He took her arm and guided her up the stairs. "I have lost the thread of this conversation, Kassidy."

"Of that I have absolutely no doubt," she said, wishing she knew the real Raile, the one that he kept apart from her. "You don't like to talk about yourself, do you?"

They had reached her room, and he opened the door and guided her inside, seated her on a chair, and knelt to remove her boots. "I have always found talking about myself a bit tedious, Kassidy." He smiled up at her. "I'm certain you were taught at your mother's knee that it is proper to encourage a man to talk about himself, because we men are arrogant and filled with self-importance."

She laughed. "You know women well, don't you, Raile?"

"I thought I knew you, Kassidy. But I'm not sure that's true."

Mischief danced in her eyes. "I might allow a man to believe he understands me if he needed to feel superior."

He found himself shaking with laughter. "God help the man who thinks he understands you, my little hellion." He helped her into her slippers and then stood over her. "But I'm going to try."

He raised her legs and placed them on a hassock and pulled a blanket over her. "Would you like to have your dinner served here?"

She was touched by his gentleness, until she realized his solicitous manner was only because she carried his heir. "That would be nice. Will you join me?"

"Yes, if you don't mind. I'll have Oliver make the arrangements." He left her in search of his valet, but returned a short time later and sat down beside her. "You are certain you feel well?"

"My health has never been better," Kassidy assured him.

"I don't know much about childbirth, but I can only imagine it is cumbersome carrying a child within your body. You must tire easily."

Kassidy realized he was genuinely interested in how she was feeling. "No, it is not cumbersome—awkward, I suppose. I cannot tell you the joy that comes over me when I feel the baby move inside me. I feel a closeness with him."

"Him?"

"I think of the baby as him. I suppose it's because you want a son so badly." She looked into his eyes and saw a tenderness there. "It is my wish to give you a son, Raile."

"To put a finish to our bargain?"

She felt a tightness in her throat. "To put a finish to our bargain."

"You like children. I know how much you love Arrian, and she adores you."

"Yes, I find children to be honest. One always knows what they are thinking and feeling."

"That's not always the case with me, is it, Kassidy?"

She was thoughtful for a moment. He was a complex man, and if she lived with him forever, she would never truly know him. "You hide your true feelings very well, Raile."

He stood and moved to the door. "Have Elspeth come for me when you are ready to sup."

Before Kassidy could answer, he was gone.

A table had been set before the crackling fire. Kassidy was sure she didn't taste anything with Raile sitting across from her. When dessert was served, Elspeth and the maid withdrew, and she took a bite of the vanilla ice.

"I noticed you ate very little, Kassidy."

She pushed the bowl aside, wondering how she could swallow another spoonful with him watching her so closely. "Doctor Worthington assures me my diet is adequate."

Raile reached across the table and took her hand, studying the long fingers and the blue veins. "I suppose I'm beginning to sound like Elspeth."

"The two of you do tend to fuss, Raile. I am strong, and my health is good. I should give you a strong and healthy baby."

He dropped her hand. "I have never had a baby before, Kassidy." He smiled, and it made her catch her breath. "I will try not to fuss overmuch."

She leaned back in her chair and laced her fingers together. "I don't mind, Raile. I'm glad you are here."

"Are you?"

"Yes, I am." She stood and he came to his feet. "I do find that I tire easily. Would you mind if I excused myself and went to bed?"

"Do you want to sleep in my bed, or shall I sleep in yours?"

"I . . . it isn't necessary . . . I . . . am accustomed to sleeping alone now."

"But you are having the nightmares again."

"Yes."

He moved around the table and drew her into his arms. "I would like to lie beside you in the night so you can be assured that nothing real or imaginary can harm you."

She trembled with pent-up emotion as he pressed her head against his shoulder. "Oh, yes, Raile, please keep me from having the dreams." A shuddering sigh escaped her lips. "It's like living the terror over and over."

"I will take care of you, Kassidy," he said holding her tighter. "You need never fear the dreams again."

She wanted only to place herself in his care, to give herself over to the love she felt for him. But if she did, wouldn't she only be hurt in the end? Would she be able to walk away and leave him when the time came?

"Raile, even though it was you who asked me to marry you, you've never taken well to marriage, have you?"

"I have found it to be difficult at times," he admitted. "You do test a man's forbearance."

Kassidy stared into liquid brown eyes that made her heart flutter, and she pressed herself tightly against him. "I don't mean to be a trial to you, Raile."

He laughed and held her away from him. "Madame, you have no idea what you have put me through. Since the first day I met you, my life has been in turmoil."

32

Contentedly, Kassidy snuggled beneath a down-filled coverlet. Raile was working late in his study, but she knew he would come to her later, and she would sleep peacefully in his arms.

Her mind went back to the day, as a young girl, when she had gone to the park across from her aunt's house and the ruffian had tried to push her into the pond. She thought of her savior that day—the officer in his immaculate red uniform, his dark eyes so soft with kindness. Of course, it had been Raile—she could see him very clearly now. Why hadn't she recognized him as the champion of her girlhood?

Certain he had been younger then, but he had the same handsome features. At that time his eyes had been only sad, not brooding as they now were. Perhaps he had seen too much death in the war, and perhaps being near death himself had changed him.

She had the feeling that Raile had known very little tenderness in his life—there was something that haunted him and kept him from reaching out for happiness. Or . . . perhaps she was not the woman who could bring him happiness.

Kassidy touched her stomach, feeling overwhelmed with love for the baby nestled there. How fortunate she was to be having Raile's child. She could imagine a little boy with big brown eyes.

Somewhere, a clock chimed the tenth hour. Her eyes fluttered shut, and she drifted off to sleep with a smile on her lips.

When Kassidy awoke later, the fire had gone out, and she felt chilled, until she was pulled against a warm body, and she settled into Raile's arms.

She touched his hand, and turned her head to lay her lips against it. She was so filled with love for him she could hardly breathe. How could he have become so important to her in such a short time?

His breath tickled her ear. "Sorry if I disturbed you, Kassidy, but you were cold, and I wanted to warm you."

She turned over, pressing her face against his chest. "I'm warm now."

His hand moved down to lightly touch her stomach. He felt the roundness and drew his hand back. "Does it cause you discomfort when I touch you there?"

She smiled, taking his hand and placing it back on her stomach. "Of course it doesn't."

Gently his hand roamed around the swollen abdomen. He was awed by the thought that his child lay snugly within Kassidy's body. He felt something like a ripple against the palm of his hand, and his eyes widened with wonderment.

"Kassidy, did you feel that?" he asked, taking his hand quickly away.

"Yes, it was the baby."

"You mean I actually felt it move?"

"Of course." She raised her gown and placed his hand on her bare stomach. "There, you can feel it better now. He is becoming quite active at night."

Raile lightly placed his hand against her satiny skin, and again he felt the baby move. His heart was racing with excitement—to actually feel his child before it was born was something he had not expected to experience. It made the child seem more real, and his feelings ran so deep, it was almost like pain.

"So this is what it's like to feel immortal," he said, his hand gliding up to her swollen breasts.

Kassidy closed her eyes and bit her trembling lower lip. There was something different about Raile tonight. His caress was somehow loving without being passionate. He made her feel cherished and protected. Her heart was so full of love for him, but she could not speak of it.

He pulled her gown down and pressed her against him. "Are you warm?"

"Yes," she said, her eyes drooping.

The room was in total darkness as Raile's arms enveloped Kassidy so tightly she could feel his every intake of breath.

"Go to sleep, little mother," he whispered, his fingers lacing through hers.

Kassidy closed her eyes. Raile had reminded her that he was merely taking care of the mother of his child, but it did not matter. She would live on each touch, each word he spoke to her.

"It's snowing harder," Raile murmured against her ear. "We shall soon be snowbound if this continues."

She wouldn't mind being snowbound with him. "It's December tenth. Could we have a Yule log and celebrate like we did when I was a child?" she asked with sudden yearning.

He smiled against her hair. "Kassidy, you can have anything I can give you that will make you happy."

"I want to have a wonderful Christmas for Arrian."

"And so you shall," he promised.

* * *

A bright sun was shining as Raile helped Kassidy into the sleigh. Atkins climbed in the driver's seat and picked up the reins. Raile handed Arrian to Kassidy and then covered them both with soft fur robes. Elspeth placed a foot warmer at Kassidy's feet and instructed her not to take a chill. Raile leaped in beside them, and two white horses lurched forward with a jingle of bells.

Elspeth called out to Raile to have a care of Kassidy's health. "And don't let her slip down, your grace," she instructed in a loud voice. "She must remain in the sleigh while you get the Yule log."

Kassidy felt the cold wind against her cheek and smiled down at Arrian. "This will be a wonderful Christmas, Arrian. This was your mother's favorite time of the year."

Arrian looked so angelic in her fur hat and cape with only her lovely face visible. "Come and sit in my lap, dearest," Kassidy urged.

The tiny girl shook her head and held her arms out to Raile.

"I believe she wants you to hold her, Raile."

Awkwardly, he took Arrian upon his lap and was rewarded by a happy smile from the little charmer. She curled up in his arms, refusing to go back to Kassidy.

Kassidy smiled. "I believe she likes you, Uncle Raile."

Raile gently tugged at a golden curl peeping out from Arrian's white fur bonnet. "I have always had this trouble with women," Raile teased. "They can't leave me alone."

Arrian chose that moment to throw herself against him and kiss him soundly on the cheek.

Kassidy laughed at the startled look on Raile's face, but she could also tell he was pleased. "Does she look like your sister, Abigail?" Raile asked.

"Very much so. I wish you could have known Abigail. She was the sweet one of the family. She would never have disagreed with you. I cannot remember a time when Abigail was angry with anyone . . . except Henry, of course."

"Certainly she was nothing like you," Raile said dryly.

Kassidy arched her brow. "So long as you remember that."

He looked at Arrian. "Did you know that your Aunt Kassidy has a temper?"

The child smiled coyly, flirting with her handsome uncle and jabbering at him in her own language.

When they reached the meadow, Raile stepped onto the icy ground with Arrian in his arms. "Wave to Aunt Kassidy. She has to sit in the sleigh while we have all the fun."

Kassidy watched Raile perch Arrian on his shoulders and trudge through the snow. Atkins followed a few paces behind, carrying the axe. Kassidy opened the basket Elspeth had packed for her. She poured herself a steaming cup of chocolate and waited for Raile to return.

Just thinking about Raile made her giddy inside. She had tried not to love him—but she did—deeply and without reason. Life with him was an adventure. So many times he had come to her rescue. But when she tried to voice her gratitude to him, he merely changed the subject.

She felt the baby move inside her. The baby would be the greatest gift she could give him. She prayed it would be the son he so desperately wanted.

She thought of how good he had been with Arrian. A child would be fortunate, indeed, to have him for a father.

Christmas had come and gone, and the new year was in its second week.

Kassidy was in the sitting room and had just finished

reading a letter from her aunt when she heard a man's voice in the hallway.

"Never mind, Ambrose, I'll just announce myself," he said.

Kassidy had never seen the man who came walking briskly toward her with a broad smile on his face. He was blond and handsome, and his blue eyes danced with laughter.

"Ah, my dear sister-in-law. At last we meet."

Kassidy had never expected to meet Hugh DeWinter. She found her hands shaking and her heart racing with fear. She came quickly to her feet, scattering the pages of her letter on the floor.

When Hugh bent to retrieve them for her, she stood as if frozen. "I . . . my husband is not at home," she managed to say. What she really wanted to do was yell at him and to pound on his chest. She wanted to demand to know why he had deserted Abigail when she needed him most.

Hugh pressed the letters in her trembling hands, and she pulled away from him as if his was a viper's touch.

"Kassidy, I feel as if I know you."

Her eyes went to the door, and she wondered if she could make it to safety before he caught her. Should she yell out for Ambrose? Surely this man and his mother would not attempt to harm her or her unborn child with so many servants about. Kassidy knew she was not thinking rationally, but she couldn't ignore the fear that threatened to close off her breathing.

Hugh saw the apprehension in his sister-in-law's eyes and stepped back several paces. "I suppose . . . I should have waited to be introduced by Raile. I merely came to see my daughter—what's her name?—I don't even know."

Kassidy's voice came out in a trembling whisper. "No, I'll never allow you to see her. Please leave now, and if you must return, do so when Raile is at home."

Hugh saw her swaying on her feet and reached out to steady her, when she cried out, "No, don't touch me . . . don't ever touch me . . . I won't have you near Arrian or my unborn baby. After what you did to my sister, how can you think I would want to see you?"

Hugh was shocked. He had not expected such a violent reaction to his visit. "I can assure you—"

"Hugh, what in the hell are you doing here?" Raile said, rushing toward Kassidy. She turned into his arms, and he could feel her trembling. "You dare upset my wife, Hugh," Raile said in an angry voice. He led Kassidy toward the door so he could take her to her room.

Raile called over his shoulder to his brother. "Wait for me in the study. I want to talk to you."

Kassidy could not stop trembling, so Raile picked her up in his arms and carried her upstairs.

Elspeth was waiting for her in the bedroom, and she rushed forward when she saw Kassidy's white face.

"Stay with her," Raile said, laying Kassidy on the bed. "I'll return later."

Kassidy grabbed Raile's hand. "Don't let him take Arrian. Please don't let him have her."

Raile took her small hands in his. "I won't allow him near her if you don't want me to, and I certainly would never allow him to take her away from you."

"Why is he here? Did his mother come with him?"

Raile glanced up at Elspeth, who placed a coverlet on Kassidy that she had just warmed at the fireplace. "No, Kassidy, Lavinia would never dare to come here."

She turned her face into the pillow, her body racked with fear.

"See to her, Elspeth. Try to calm her," Raile said. "I will return in a few moments."

The maid nodded. "I take it your half brother's here, your grace?"

"I never thought his appearance would frighten Kassidy so much."

Elspeth stared into his eyes. "That's because you don't know how she suffered because of him."

Raile looked back to his wife. "Hugh will be gone within the hour, Kassidy. And I shall leave instructions with Ambrose that he is not to be admitted again. Will that make you feel better?"

"They will find me, Raile. No matter where I go, they will find me."

He touched her forehead and found it burning hot. "Elspeth, have Oliver send for Doctor Worthington," he said, in a worried voice. He left abruptly, making his way to his study where he knew he'd find Hugh waiting.

"Why in the hell are you here, Hugh? You know I have forbidden you to come to the castle."

"I swear to you, Raile, I never intended to frighten your wife. I never had a woman so afraid of me before and I can tell you, it isn't a pleasant experience."

"For once in your life, Hugh, think of others' feelings and not your own. I could thrash you for what you did to Kassidy."

Hugh looked deflated. "My mother did it to her, Raile—not me. I am guilty only in not stopping her when I could have." There was earnestness in his eyes. "The reason I am here now is to warn you that my mother is completely mad, Raile. Even faithful Meg has left her because she fears her."

Raile was skeptical. "How do I know this isn't just another of your schemes?"

"You don't. But I swear to you that I'm telling the truth, Raile. I need your help to stop her before she harms anyone else." Hugh's eyes snapped with fire. "She has to be stopped, Raile. My mother is insisting that she will destroy your child before it's born."

"Like hell, she will, Hugh. Do you think I'll let her near my wife?"

There was anguish in Hugh's eyes. "You can't stop her, Raile—no one can. She won't hesitate to crush anyone who stands in the way of what she wants. Your wife and baby stand in the way, Raile."

Raile looked into Hugh's eyes which had turned wild with fear. "Oh, God, you cannot imagine some of the things she's done."

"I'm listening, Hugh. Suppose you tell me."

"It's not pretty, Raile. She went out of her head when she learned your wife was with child and told me things. He shuddered. "If only I had known what she was capable of, perhaps I could have stopped her."

"Go on, Hugh," Raile said grimly.

"First of all, there's what she did to John. I would never have believed my mother was evil. I always thought her misguided and ambitious, but never capable of murder."

Raile listened, sickened by what Hugh was telling him. He was filled with rage when Hugh told him how Lavinia had hired the Beale brothers to kill their cousin.

"Where is Lavinia?" Raile asked. "It's time I put an end to her evil."

Hugh shook his head. "I don't know where to find her. But I feel she's nearby watching the castle for a chance to get to you and your wife. You should guard Kassidy day and night."

"How do you guard against a madwoman, Hugh? She could be anywhere."

"I don't know, Raile, but I had to warn you." He looked into his brother's eyes. "And I am most sincerely sorry I frightened your wife. I would like to have come to know her because Abigail loved her dearly. I would also like to become acquainted with my daughter."

"Neither will be possible at this time. I still don't know that I can trust you, Hugh."

"I deserve that. But if you don't believe anything I've

ever said, Raile, believe my mother is dangerous."

"You'd better leave. I promised Kassidy I would send you away."

"I'll go, but I will only be as far as the village. You watch for my mother here, and I'll watch for her there. Surely between us, we can find her."

Kassidy's fever had returned. Raile stayed at her side day and night, feeling powerless to help her, and worrying that this siege might harm his unborn child.

Around dawn on the third day, Kassidy's fever broke. As she began to recover, she felt ashamed of how emotionally she had received Raile's brother. But she was not sorry that Raile had sent Hugh away. She would never allow him near Arrian.

John Fielding, known as the Blind Magistrate of the Bow Street Runners, listened attentively to a letter from the duke of Ravenworth.

> *"And in conclusion, Mr. Fielding, I believe you will find evidence to bring the Beale brothers to trial for the murder of my cousin, the late Lord John DeWinter. I will have more information forthcoming when next I come to London,"* the secretary read.

John Fielding nodded. "I'll see those two hang," he said with feeling. "I always knew they were up to no good, but until the duke of Ravenworth became our ally, I could prove nothing on them."

"I wonder why he's so anxious to help?" his secretary asked.

"He helped us put them in Newgate. Now he helps us hang them. Never mind the reason, we got 'em now."

33

Cold March winds gave way to warmer April sunshine. Kassidy and Arrian often visited the stables or the kennel. Arrian would squeal with delight as the pups licked her face, jumped in her lap, and rolled her on the ground.

Kassidy began to suspect she was being watched—or guarded would be more likely. While she was in the castle, either Elspeth or Mrs. Fitzwilliams was always nearby. If she went out to the stables, Atkins or Oliver remained at her side.

She decided to face Raile and demand to know why her every movement was being monitored.

That night when Kassidy climbed into bed, Raile came in and draped his coat across the chair.

"Oliver has gone to London, and I find myself without a valet. I suspect I'll have to undress myself."

"That's the third time in as many weeks that Oliver has gone to London. I am not a child that I don't know something has occurred that you are all keeping from me. Why do Oliver and Atkins take turns going to London? And why does Elspeth sleep in my room when you are late?"

"You were very ill, you know, and you are going to have my baby," Raile said evasively.

"Your words are not convincing, Raile. I know you are keeping something from me, and I want to know what it is."

He feigned surprise. "Why do you think such a thing?"

"Don't condescend. I will not have this secrecy, where everyone knows what's happening, save myself."

He tried to lighten the mood. "Such malevolence. Only sweet words should come from those sweet lips."

Kassidy crawled under the covers and propped her head on a pillow. "I could easily be angry with you, Raile. Don't you know my imagination is worse than anything you could tell me?"

The bed swayed beneath his weight. He blew out the candle and the room was bathed in soft firelight. "It's true I have been keeping something from you, Kassidy. But it's only because I don't want you upset."

"Then tell me," she pleaded.

He hesitated for only a moment, trying to decide how much to say. "I'm sleepy, Kassidy. Could we not talk about this tomorrow?"

Kassidy's hair swirled about her as she turned to face him. "No. Tell me now."

"Are you becoming a fishwife?"

"Are you trying to distract me?"

He traced the outline of her lips with his finger. "Are you truly angry with me?"

"I . . . no . . . I'm not mad at you."

He raised up and glanced at her with mockery dancing in his eyes. "Now that I know that, perhaps you would allow me to sleep?"

"Indeed, I will not, Raile," Kassidy said demandingly. "I want to know why I am never left alone."

He let out an impatient breath. "Very well, Kassidy." He pulled her into his arms, hoping to keep her fear at bay. "Do you remember the day Hugh came to see me?"

"Yes. How could I forget?"

"He came to warn me about Lavinia. She is demented."

"There's more to it than that."

"Lavinia has aspirations that Hugh should be the duke, rather than me."

Kassidy shivered, knowing very well how evil Raile's stepmother was. "Do you trust Hugh?"

"Not entirely. But in this I believe he was being honest."

"All I see is that you are taking precautions to guard me, Raile, but what about yourself?"

"I am in no danger that I can't handle."

Her eyes rounded in horror, and her hand went to her stomach. "It's the baby she's after, isn't it? She wants to . . ." So horrible was her fear, that she could not continue.

Raile held her tightly in his arms. "I'll not let her harm you, Kassidy—I swear it. You do believe that, don't you?"

"Yes, Raile. I know I'm as safe as you can make me. I'm not frightened for myself, but for our baby."

She buried her face against his neck, refusing to give in to tears. She would be strong—she must. At last she raised her head and looked at him. "I will die before I let her harm our baby, Raile."

His arms tightened about her. "Everything is being done to find her, Kassidy." He raised her chin and made her look at him. "Promise me when you are outside the castle you will do nothing foolish. Never go anywhere without either Elspeth, Atkins, or Oliver."

"I promise, Raile."

He was unaware that he was gently stroking her hair. "She will have to go through me and the devil to get to you, Kassidy. And I swear to you, she could more easily deal with the devil than with me."

* * *

Lavinia had come once more to the village of Ravenworth in disguise. This time she wore a plain homespun gown. Her stockings were of thick cotton, and her shoes were heavy and uncomfortable like those worn by the village women. Her hair was tied back with a frayed scarf. No one suspected who she was, and she was able to walk among the villagers without anyone being suspicious of her.

She had chosen farmer Thomas Creag as a means of getting to Raile's wife. Thomas Creag was the farmer who delivered sweet cream and butter to Ravenworth Castle every Saturday. How easily she had convinced the unsuspecting man that she was a widow by the name of Betty Daniels, and in desperate need, and that she would work for him for the price of a bed at night and two meals a day.

Lavinia had no aversion to hard work if it got her what she wanted in the end. She did the washing and mending—she scrubbed the floors and cooked the meals. She watched after the farmer's five children and waited on his wife, who was about to deliver her sixth baby.

Lavinia's hands were chapped and bleeding, but it didn't matter. She would do anything to obtain her final goal. When she lived in the castle, she would have servants grovel at her feet. She would one day be mistress there, she swore.

She glanced out the thatched-roof cottage to the castle in the distance. Laughter escaped her throat. "You will never find me here, in the shadow of Ravenworth Castle, Raile," she said, her eyes dull with madness.

Gabrielle Candeur felt her heart racing as she stepped out of her coach and moved up the steps of Ravenworth

Castle. She had been so certain she would never see Raile again until the letter had arrived from him begging her to come to the castle at once, and in the letter he had proclaimed his love and devotion for her.

She had been too happy to question why Raile would invite her to his ancestral home, and she didn't care what had happened to his wife—she only knew he had asked her to come, and she was there.

The butler who answered her knock was polite but reserved. "I'm sorry, miss, but his grace did not mention to me that he was expecting anyone. If you will wait in here," he said, showing her into the formal sitting room, "I'll inform him you are here."

She glanced about the room that was decorated in sunny yellows. There was an aura of tradition here, of nobility, and of ancient ancestry.

Would Raile ask her to be a part of this world? Happiness burst within her breast. She was sure he would never let her go again. Perhaps he would want her to give up acting to be at his beck and call—and she would gladly do it for him.

Raile stared at Ambrose, thinking he must have misunderstood. "What name did the woman give you?"

The butler wondered why his grace seemed disturbed. "The lady said her name is Gabrielle Candeur."

Raile brushed past Ambrose, his anger simmering. "If this is someone's notion of a jest, I don't find it amusing."

When he entered the sitting room, Gabrielle rushed to him, throwing herself into his arms.

"Raile, I came as soon as I could." She looked into his face. "I am so happy you missed me as much as I missed you."

He gripped her shoulders and pushed her away from

him. "What nonsense is this, Gabrielle? Why are you here?"

Her bottom lip trembled, and her large eyes filled with tears. "But the letter you sent . . . I thought . . ."

Raile turned away from her. "I sent you no letter."

Gabrielle picked up her muff and moved with jerky steps toward the door. "Obviously, I made a mistake." She brushed the tears from her eyes. "I won't trouble you further, Raile."

He reached for her hand, feeling sorry that she had obviously been a victim of Lavinia's cruelty. "Don't go just yet, Gabrielle. Tell me about the letter, and I'll try to explain to you what I think happened."

She shook her head, feeling foolish and humiliated. "I realize by your reaction that you did not send for me. But who would do such a thing to me?"

He pulled her near the fireplace and took her muff, laying it on a chair. "It was sent by a demented mind that used you to hurt me."

"Your stepmother?" Gabrielle said without hesitation.

"Why would you guess it was she?"

"Because Mrs. DeWinter came to see me just after . . . your marriage. It was apparent she hated you, and I had a feeling she wanted to enlist my help to hurt you in some way."

"But you didn't help her?"

"Of course not, Raile. I would never do that. Although at the time I wanted to hurt you."

He felt responsible for the humiliation she was suffering. "Are you faring well, Gabrielle?"

She raised tear-bright eyes to him. "Not very, Raile." She smiled slightly, not wanting him to know how she had suffered without him. "For a time now, I have been unable to work. I vacated the house and have been living in a smaller place outside of London. I have been thinking about returning to France."

Guilt lay heavily on Raile's shoulders. He had to help her. Obviously she had no money, and now she had been shamefully manipulated by Lavinia.

On her way back from the stables, Kassidy saw the carriage, and wondered who had come to call. With Elspeth beside her, she pushed open the door and handed her cape to Ambrose.

"Do we have guests, Ambrose?" she asked.

"Yes, your grace," Ambrose informed her, not knowing he was about to make a mistake. "It's a Miss Gabrielle Candeur. She is in the formal sitting room with his grace."

Angrily, Kassidy moved in that direction. How dare Raile have his mistress come to Ravenworth Castle!

Kassidy stood in the open doorway, watching Raile embrace the actress. Her heart felt bruised when she heard him speak to the woman tenderly.

"I will make arrangements for you to move back into the house on Action Street. In fact, I'll have it deeded to you to do with as you will. Have your bills sent to me, and I'll see that they are paid."

"Oh, Raile," Gabrielle said. "You are so good to me."

Kassidy stayed to hear no more. She turned away to be met by the sympathetic glance of Elspeth. Without a word, the maid helped Kassidy up the stairs.

"Don't tell my husband that I saw him with that woman," Kassidy said.

"Who is she?" Elspeth asked, not really understanding.

Kassidy entered her bedroom and sat on the edge of the bed. "That is the actress, Gabrielle Candeur. She's Raile's mistress. I'd thought he'd given her up some time ago. Apparently I was wrong."

Elspeth knew the duke well enough to be sure he'd never bring a mistress into his home when he was so worried about Kassidy's health. No, something wasn't right. "I have come to respect his grace, and he isn't a man who would have a mistress under the same roof as his wife who is expecting his baby. There must be some explanation, your grace."

Kassidy lay back on the bed, staring at the overhead canopy. She felt wounded and betrayed. Even though Raile did not love her, she had thought he respected her. His actions today were not those of a man who put honor above all else. "You cannot deny you saw her in his arms."

Elspeth nodded, feeling her mistress's hurt in her own heart. "No, your grace. I can't deny that."

"You heard him offer her a house and to pay her bills?"

"I did that."

"There is no more to say."

"You should talk to his grace about it. I'm sure he has a reason for having that woman here. Perhaps he didn't know she was coming."

Kassidy sat up and stared at Elspeth. "Can you think of a reason why she would be in his arms?"

"Only one, your grace," the maid answered with honesty as she always had.

"There you have it then," Kassidy said, feeling pain in the very depths of her heart.

It was dark in the bedroom when Raile entered. He thought Kassidy was asleep, so he quietly moved toward her bed. He had expected to find her in his bed, but had been informed by Elspeth that Kassidy would be sleeping in her own room. He had not had dinner with her, because she had sent word to him that she was going to bed early.

"Raile," Kassidy said, hearing him near the bed. "I

have not slept well for the last week, and I'm so restless I will only keep you awake. I have decided that I will sleep in my room." She was glad it was dark so he could not see the tears in her eyes.

He was reluctant to leave her. "What about your nightmares?"

"I have willed myself to no longer have nightmares. I have put all such foolishness behind me."

Raile heard a coldness in her voice, and he thought he knew what was bothering her. "You saw Gabrielle today, didn't you, Kassidy?"

She was quiet for a moment. "Yes. I saw you and her together."

He sat down on the bed, feeling for her hand, but she pulled it out of his grip. "It wasn't what you thought, Kassidy. I know it looked like we were—"

"I don't care what you and your mistress do, Raile." She brushed tears off her cheek. "My only request is that you have your rendezvous with her elsewhere in the future. I found it very humiliating."

He stood up, feeling helpless. "Damn it, Kassidy, it wasn't like that."

She turned her back on him and her voice trembled. "Please leave me alone, Raile. I'm very tired."

He wanted to take her and shake her, until she listened to reason. But he dared not distress her more. Tomorrow he would explain about the letter when she was thinking more clearly. "I'll just leave the connecting door open so I can hear you during the night, should you need me."

When she did not answer, he went to his own bedroom, which felt cold and empty without her. He removed his shirt and breeches and lay on the bed. He had grown accustomed to having Kassidy beside him. He reached out for her pillow and tucked it beneath his head, smelling the sweet aroma that still clung to it.

He couldn't help but smile. Kassidy was so much a part of his life, he couldn't imagine being without her. She had made him into a husband—the kind he had always despised in the past—the kind who wanted only to please their wives.

He remembered telling her he would never love her—but he did, with a deep lasting love that consumed him day and night.

His desire to have a son was now overshadowed by his need to have Kassidy with him—he would have loved her even if she had been barren and could not give him a son.

Yes, he thought with confidence, tomorrow he would make her understand about Gabrielle.

34

Raile was awakened in the middle of the night by an agitated Oliver. "Atkins has asked that you come to the stable at once, your grace."

Raile sat up and shook his head to clear it. He knew Oliver would never wake him unless it was for a good reason.

"Did he say what it was about?"

"Atkins is in an outraged state. It has to do with one of the horses, your grace."

Raile quickly dressed and moved down the candlelit hallway, with Oliver leading the way. When they reached the stable, Atkins met them at the door.

"It's the new prized Arabian, your grace. The one that was to foal any day."

"What's happened to her?"

Atkins looked shamefaced. "I consider it my fault, your grace. I never thought this would happen. I should have been more watchful."

"Tell me what happened, Atkins!" Raile demanded.

"Her throat's been cut, your grace, and the foal's been cut right out of her belly, and its throat's cut, too."

Atkins gulped, his eyes flashing with fury. "I heard the mare carrying on something awful. By the time I dressed and got here, she was thrashing about in her own blood."

The groomsman closed his eyes for a moment as if he were trying to forget the sight. "Who could have done this, your grace?"

Raile ran back to the stall, while Atkins held a torch for him. The grim spectacle that met Raile's eyes made him sick inside. How could anyone destroy such a beautiful animal, and one that was about to give birth?

Raile's eyes narrowed with anger. "By God, someone will pay for this. I'll find out who did it, and when I do, they'll regret this night's work."

Atkins handed Raile a note that was splattered with blood. "I believe this will explain it, your grace. It was pinned to the stall door with the same knife that was used to kill the mare and foal."

Raile read the pitiful, blood-splattered scrawling. He knew before he finished reading who had done the deed.

> *This is how easily I can get your wife and child. You can't stop me—no one can.*

Raile crushed the note in his fists. "Atkins, did you see anyone suspicious hanging about?"

"No, your grace—no one."

"I want you to employ ten men from the village whom you can trust. Have them patrol the castle and grounds day and night. No one is allowed inside the walls unless they are personally known. Is that clear?"

"Do you believe Mrs. DeWinters is responsible for this, your grace?" Atkins asked.

"I know she is. She is dangerous and is trying to get to the duchess."

"You can count on me, your grace," Atkins said with conviction.

Raile nodded toward the stall. "I will expect you to see that this doesn't happen again."

Atkins ducked his head in shame. "It won't, your grace."

"At sunup I shall require the carriage. I will be going into London. I don't want to leave her grace at this time, but I must make the authorities aware of my step-mother's actions." His eyes hardened in the torch light. "I also want to make arrangements for my wife and child's future should anything happen to me."

Oliver and Atkins exchanged glances but said nothing.

"No one is to speak of what happened here tonight, is that understood?" Raile said.

Both Oliver and Atkins quickly agreed.

Kassidy sensed something strange in the air when she came downstairs the next morning. It wasn't what any-one said, it was more the watchful glances and hushed whispers behind her back.

When she learned that Raile had gone into London without first telling her, she assumed it had something to do with Gabrielle Candeur, and she also assumed everyone was feeling pity for her.

Kassidy returned to her room, wondering how she would live through the weeks until the baby was born. Her only happiness came from being with Arrian, so she spent most of her days in a child's world—it was too painful to dwell in her own.

Two days passed and then three, but Raile did not return. When he did come, it took Kassidy by surprise.

She was sitting in the window seat in the nursery, reading to Arrian, when he appeared at the door.

"How are my two favorite girls?" he asked.

Arrian climbed off Kassidy's lap and ran into Raile's open arms, giggling and kissing his cheek.

Kassidy set the book aside. "You come and go so quickly, your grace, one wonders how poor Oliver keeps up with you."

Raile received a sympathetic glance from Elspeth. "I regret the business that took me to London, but it could not be avoided."

Kassidy walked past him and into the hallway. He handed Arrian to her nurse and followed his wife.

"I know, Raile," Kassidy said when they were out of hearing distance of the others, "what business took you to London. I'd be a fool not to."

"Damn it, Kassidy, will you condemn me without a hearing?"

She turned on him, her eyes flashing like green fire. "You condemn yourself, Raile. Do as you will, only leave me in peace."

Raile could only stare after her. When she went into her bedroom and closed the door behind her, he resisted the urge to go to her. He knew she had been humiliated by Gabrielle's visit, and he could see how she would draw the wrong conclusion. Perhaps he should tell her about Lavinia's latest threat, but he feared it would only upset her more. He was new at being a husband, and it wasn't always easy to do the right thing.

Raile made his way to the stable, saddled his horse, and rode into the village. Since Kassidy was heavy with child and could no longer go into Ravenworth, it fell to him to help the villagers with their china factory. The Ravenworth china was in demand and the village was flourishing.

Raile thrust the heel of his boot into the horse's flank and rode through the brown meadow grass. He was realizing more and more that Kassidy was the most important person in his life. She had altered his conviction and tempered his ambitions. Most of all, being with her had given him the family he had always craved.

But he was afraid for Kassidy because there was a madwoman who wanted her dead and would stop at nothing to carry out her threat.

Lavinia was now a familiar sight in the village of Ravenworth. She often brought the farmer's cheese to town so it could in turn be transported to London.

She was sick of hearing the villagers rave about the virtues of their precious duchess and how she had brought prosperity to the village. Lavinia would grind her teeth when she heard the women discussing the baby the duchess carried. But most of all, Lavinia hated any mention of Raile.

She had thought long and hard on how to bring him the most pain. And she had come up with the perfect plan. She could tear his heart out and make him a broken man if she destroyed his wife and unborn child.

That was her goal—that was what she would do.

She had to make her move soon—before the baby was born. She was causing Raile a great deal of concern, she knew that. How easily she had outsmarted him when she slipped past the men he had posted at the arched entryway of the castle and slain his prize mare and her foal. After the deed had been accomplished, she had slipped away without detection and returned to the village without anyone being the wiser.

Lavinia suddenly saw a familiar figure riding down the street, and she turned her face aside as though pretending to look into a shop window. Raile DeWinter rode right past her, never looking in her direction.

A sinister smile curved Lavinia's lips. She had waited patiently for this day. At last she had convinced Thomas

Creag to allow her to accompany him when he delivered sweet cream and butter to Ravenworth Castle.

She now trudged along beside the ox-drawn cart with her head down when they entered the arched gate that led to the inner courtyard of the castle. The guard at the gatehouse merely waved them inside, paying little heed to Farmer Creag or the old woman in peasant dress, who carried a block of cheese on her stooped shoulders.

The rickety cart groaned over the cobblestones on its way to the kitchen door.

Lavinia smothered a gleeful laugh as the cart stopped and the head cook stood with the back door open, beckoning her inside.

"Come on, old woman, don't take all day. Bring in the cheese, I need it now."

Lavinia kept her head bowed as she moved up the steep kitchen steps. Her eyes gleamed with triumph—she was inside the castle!

Kassidy sat at the dining-room table, toying with her food while Raile watched her impatiently.

"Is it such a chore for you to dine with me, Kassidy?"

"Of course not, Raile. I'm not very hungry." She raised her eyes to him. "There is no cause for worry. It's just that I feel clumsy and tire easily."

He thought her face looked pale, but the doctor had assured him Kassidy was in good health. He never saw her smile anymore, and she was most often in her room or in the nursery with Arrian.

"Kassidy, you are nice to my servants, you are nice to the people in the village. Why do you never show me the slightest consideration?"

She didn't know how to answer him. Surely he knew she was still angry with him. "I have never been unkind to you, Raile."

"No," he admitted, "not unkind exactly."

"What do you expect of me?" she asked.

He pushed his plate back and took a long look at her. "I expect you to deliver a healthy baby," he said at last. "And nothing more."

Her eyes narrowed. "I will do my best, your grace."

"I don't know what to do about you, Kassidy. Perhaps after the baby is born we can—"

She stood up, cutting him off in midsentence. "When the baby is born, I will have fulfilled my part of our bargain, and I will be free to go." Pain stabbed through her heart at the thought of leaving her unborn baby. But she would not cry—she would not give Raile that satisfaction.

"Kassidy—"

She moved hurriedly out of the room.

Kassidy walked into the garden, too heartsick to notice that the tulips had burst into scarlet blooms. There she remained until the sun on her face calmed her spirit.

Why should she care if Raile didn't love her? she reasoned. Would she be able to deliver this baby and return to London? Repressing a sob, she realized she would be contented to live out her life at Ravenworth Castle and glean some small happiness in being near Raile.

With a heavy sigh, she went inside and slowly climbed the steps to her bedroom, using the banisters for support. Her back had been aching since she awoke this morning, and the pain had now spread to her abdomen. It was too soon for the baby to be born, so she thought if she lay down, the pain would subside.

When she reached the second floor, the pain had ceased, and she stopped a moment to catch her breath.

"Your grace," a servant said, coming out of the shadows. "His grace has asked if you will come to him in the tower room. There is something he wants to show you there."

Kassidy turned to the woman. "I have not seen you before. You must be new."

"Name's Betty Daniels. I work in the kitchen, your grace. Cook told me to take lunch to the workmen in the tower room, and his grace was there and he sent me to fetch you."

"I didn't realize they were working in the tower today," Kassidy said, dreading the thought of climbing the steep stairs. She nodded at the woman. "Thank you, Betty. You may return to the kitchen now. I can find my way up the tower."

"If it please you, your grace, the duke asked that I accompany you. Says he don't want you being alone."

"As you wish." Kassidy sighed. "I'm not feeling well, perhaps you will allow me to lean on you."

Lavinia could hardly contain her elation. How easily this foolish girl had fallen into her trap. "Yes, your grace," she said, smiling, "lean on me." Her voice trembled with expectation. "I'll help you right enough."

Kassidy had never been to the tower room. Raile had forbidden anyone to go there until the repairs were completed because he insisted it was too dangerous.

As Kassidy climbed past the third floor, she had to stop and catch her breath. "Perhaps it isn't wise for me to go to the tower today."

"Just a bit farther, your grace," Lavinia encouraged.

They came to the winding staircase that was only wide enough for one person at a time. "You go ahead of me, your grace, and I'll just come up behind."

Kassidy realized her mistake when she was halfway up the winding stairs and another pain hit her with such a force she felt as if it were cutting her in half. She stopped, leaning against the wall, trying to catch her breath. The pain was becoming more forceful, and she clung desperately to the railing. Beads of perspiration stood out on her brow, and she felt lightheaded.

"Just a few steps more, your grace."

Kassidy climbed slowly upward until she came to the top. Stepping onto a wide board, she saw the whole side of the tower had been ripped away so new stones could replace the old ones. She glanced through the gaping hole where she could see only the sky.

In fear she braced her back against the wall. "I never realized it was so high. I'm not feeling very well." She looked for Raile, but there was no one there but her and the servant, Betty.

"Where is my husband?"

"I'm certain he will return soon." Lavinia moved ahead of Kassidy and stood on the edge of the scaffold that projected outward. "Look, your grace, have you seen the view from here? You can see the whole countryside."

Kassidy shook her head. "Thank you, no. I will just wait here for my husband. Perhaps you should find him and have him come to me at once. I am not at all well."

Lavinia looked at Kassidy's white face. "Is it the baby?"

"Yes, I believe so. Please hurry."

Lavinia took Kassidy's hand and pulled her forward. "I'll just help you sit down. Come a little farther. That's good. Lean on me."

"No," Kassidy said, trying to pull her hand free of the woman's strong grasp. "I won't go near the edge. I'll just remain here until my husband returns."

Lavinia's eyes glistened with madness. "I'm afraid that won't do, dearie. You see, Raile isn't coming. No one will come to help you."

Kassidy struggled as the servant pulled her toward the edge of the scaffold. "What are you doing!" she cried in fear.

Lavinia smiled maliciously, her evil laughter reverberating around the tower room. "You should know who I am. Search your mind, your grace. Can't you guess why I brought you here?"

Kassidy swallowed a lump of fear. This had to be Raile's stepmother—the woman who had imprisoned her in Newgate.

"You must be Lavinia DeWinter—but I don't know why you are doing this."

"I've been waiting and planning for this day for a long time. Pity Raile isn't here to witness your death."

"No, don't, please. Think of my baby!" Kassidy cried, her hand going to her abdomen. Pain ripped through her body, and she knew Raile's child was about to be born.

She held a pleading hand out to the woman. "Mrs. DeWinter, please think about my baby. You cannot want to kill an innocent child."

"But that's exactly what I want. Raile will not have an heir to put my son out of his rightful place."

Lavinia grabbed both of Kassidy's wrists and seemed to have inhuman strength as she pulled her toward the gaping hole.

Kassidy tugged and twisted to escape her, but it was useless. Lavinia was pulling her nearer the scaffold that projected out the arched window.

There was no escape.

"Was all this worth the passion you found in Raile's bed?" Lavinia taunted. "Raile, always so arrogant, always so sure of himself. Women love him, and he cruelly pushes them aside. I could have loved him, but he never looked at me."

Her laughter sent chills down Kassidy's spine. Lavinia gave her a hard shove, and Kassidy went flying to the edge of the scaffold. She closed her eyes to keep from looking down.

"My fondest hope was that I might witness Raile's torment when that which he wants most in his life, lies crushed on the stones below."

Kassidy almost lost her balance, but she grabbed a slim rope and held on tightly.

"I just wanted you to know I have nothing against you." Lavinia seemed to take pleasure in torturing Kassidy. "Pity you just happened to get in the way of what I wanted. You have to die, you know."

Kassidy raised her head and looked at the woman who had already caused her so much pain. "You are mad."

"Perhaps. But that isn't your worry, is it?" Lavinia moved closer to Kassidy. "It will be over in a moment. Don't think of the pain."

35

Thomas Creag had unloaded the cart and looked in irritation for Betty Daniels. "You seen the woman that came with me?" he asked the cook. "She surely wasn't much help with the unloading."

Cook looked at Mr. Creag with indifference. "Now, what would I be doing keeping up with your duties? You'd best find her though, and leave at once. His grace don't want anyone not from the castle staying around these days."

"I seen the guard at the gates. What's the trouble?"

"Can't say for certain. The haughty personal servants know what's happened, but they don't inform us about nothing. The best we can tell is that some woman's causing mischief for the duchess, and we're told to watch out for any strange women hanging about."

The cook's face whitened. "You said your servant was missing?"

"She wouldn't be the one you're looking for. She's been working for me for a fortnight."

"That don't mean you know her well," the cook declared, wiping her hands on her apron. "You best find her at once."

"I tell you, this woman wouldn't harm no one. She even looks after my little ones."

Cook pushed Thomas Creag toward the door. "You look for her in the courtyard, and I'll get help searching for her inside."

Before the cook could enlist help from the servants, Thomas Creag came rushing back inside, his eyes wild with anxiety. "Get the duke at once—the tower, quickly!"

Kassidy felt the scaffold dip under her weight as Lavinia forced her farther from the safety of the tower. She stared straight ahead, too terrified to look down at the courtyard below.

Lavinia's frenzied laughter froze Kassidy's blood. "It seems I have been discovered. It won't be long until your husband comes charging to your rescue." She toyed with several ropes that secured the scaffold in place. "I'll just wait till he gets here to cut these ropes."

"Please don't do this," Kassidy pleaded. "You have a son, so you know how much I love my unborn baby."

Lavinia whipped out a knife from the folds of her gown and slashed through two of the seven ropes that secured the scaffold. The board swayed dangerously while Kassidy tightened her grip and held on tightly to keep from falling.

"Such small threads that holds your life, don't you think, your grace? When I cut these others, you'll fall to your death."

Kassidy bit her lip to keep from crying out. She would not give the woman the satisfaction she seemed to derive from torturing her. "Go ahead—do it if you must."

For a moment, there was a grudging respect in Lavinia's eyes. "You should have been my son's wife instead of Raile's. You would have been worthy of him."

They heard rushing footsteps on the stairs—they both knew it would be Raile.

"My wish is about to come true." Lavinia's laughter was uncontrollable. "Raile will witness you falling to your death."

Raile reached the tower room crying out for Kassidy to hold on. When he would have rushed forward, Lavinia grabbed hold of the only remaining ropes, her eyes gleaming with triumph as she applied the knife.

"Don't come too near, Raile. If you do, I'll slice these ropes, and your wife will fall to her death."

Raile watched Kassidy struggle to keep her footing. He knew if he rushed Lavinia, she would do what she threatened and cut the ropes. When Kassidy lost her footing and fell forward, he held his breath as she grabbed hold of the board, saving herself at the last moment.

Kassidy's feet dangled over the sides, and she held on with all her strength.

"Kassidy!" Raile cried out, enraged that he could do nothing to help her. "Hold on, my love. Don't let go."

A new pain ripped through Kassidy's body and her grip on the ropes slipped. "Raile, I'm sorry. I can't hold on—I can't. The baby . . . is coming!"

He took a step toward her, but when Lavinia sliced through several ropes, Raile stopped, hardly daring to breathe, watching as the scaffold dipped and swayed. "Don't do this, Lavinia. My wife has done nothing to you. It's me you want. Let her go."

"Are you hurting so bad you feel as if your guts are being ripped apart, Raile?" Lavinia asked in a hard voice, searching his face for evidence of his suffering.

"Yes, damn you. I am hurting like hell, if that's what you want."

Lavinia's eyes danced eagerly across Raile's face. "Is it more than you can bear to watch the woman you love struggle for her own life even as she is in pain to deliver your baby? Which will come first, Raile," Lavinia taunted, "the fall or the baby? How long do you suppose she can hold on? See how her life's blood drips onto the cobblestones below?"

"Allow me to change places with her, Lavinia. Then you can do with me what you will." Raile realized he was pleading, but he would do what he must to save Kassidy."

Lavinia's eyes hardened. "Do you think me a fool? I don't want you to die, Raile—not yet. I want you to live in torment, to cry out in the night because you saw the mangled body of the woman you love crushed beyond recognition."

Kassidy looked at Raile, and she wanted to cry out at the agony she saw in his eyes. He was such a proud man, how it must pain him to be at Lavinia's mercy. She wanted to tell him many things, but her strength was ebbing and it was all she could do to hold on.

Raile had not heard his brother come up behind him until Hugh spoke. "Let me take care of this, Raile," Hugh said hurriedly. "Move aside."

Raile couldn't be sure if Hugh had come to help his mother or if it was his brother's intention to help Kassidy, so he barred his way. "I'll deal with your mother, Hugh."

"Don't be a fool, Raile. She's gone beyond reason. Only I can handle her now."

Hugh saw Raile's agonizing indecision. "No matter what you may think of me, brother, I could never hurt you or anyone you love."

Raile stepped aside with desperation in his voice. "I have to trust you, Hugh. I don't know how much longer Kassidy can hold on—make it quick."

The brothers exchanged glances, and in that moment, they both knew what had to be done. There was hope in Raile's eyes and sorrow in Hugh's. "I'll not let her harm your wife, Raile."

Lavinia saw Hugh, and she smiled at him. "You are just in time to witness our triumph, my son. Come, stand beside me."

Out of the corner of his eye, Hugh saw Kassidy struggling—she could not hold on much longer.

"You knew I'd come, Mother," he said soothingly. "I have searched for you everywhere, but couldn't find you." He talked to her as if she were a child, each step he took bringing him closer to her. "Then, when the cart pulled into the courtyard today, I didn't recognize you at once."

"I'm doing this for you, Hugh. I had John killed for you." She looked at Raile. "You'll have to admit it was clever of me to have the actress come to Ravenworth Castle. Bet that caused you trouble, Raile."

Hugh moved closer to Lavinia. "Give me the knife, Mother."

"Yes, you can cut the rope." Her eyes hardened, and she pulled the knife back. "I don't know that I can trust you. You never wanted to take Raile's place. You always had an admiration for him that I couldn't rid you of, no matter how I tried."

"Come, Mother, give me the knife and I'll take you away with me."

"No." Lavinia whirled around and slashed out at the remaining ropes. The scaffold teetered, and Kassidy slipped farther to the edge.

Hugh leaped forward, his body slamming against his mother's. The force of his thrust took them both through the gaping hole, and a loud scream pierced the air, as they fell downward into the courtyard below.

Kassidy cried aloud as she heard their bodies thud against the cobblestones. Her grip slipped, just as Raile caught her hand and pulled her into his arms. He held her tightly against him, kissing her eyelids, her cheek, her mouth. "Dearest," he whispered, "it's all over. You're safe now—thank God, you're safe."

Kassidy laid her head against his shoulder as her body was shaken with tremors. "The baby, Raile."

He lifted her gently into his arms and carried her down the winding stairs where they were met by anxious servants.

Oliver and Elspeth ran ahead of Raile to open doors. When he reached Kassidy's bedroom, Raile placed her on the bed and dropped down beside her. "Elspeth, help her," Raile said, glancing at the maid for guidance. "The baby is coming."

Elspeth nodded before rushing to the stairs calling out for hot water and bandages.

Raile spoke hurriedly to Oliver: "Go by the fastest means and bring the doctor. Send someone to the village to fetch the midwife to help until the doctor arrives."

Kassidy's body twisted with pain. She bit her lower lip to keep from crying out. "Too late . . . for . . . doctor, Raile." Her eyes were soft with acceptance. "Will I die giving birth as my sister did, Raile?"

"Kassidy, don't talk nonsense. Hold on to my hand and draw on my strength. I will help you through this."

Her grip on his hand tightened. "You have to make me a promise, Raile." She smiled sadly, now knowing what Abigail had felt in her last moments.

"Anything, Kassidy."

"If . . . I don't make it, Raile, please allow my baby and Arrian to spend time with Aunt Mary. I want them to know her and love her as I do."

"Nothing is going to happen to you. I won't let it."

For all his assuring words, she saw the uncertainty in his dark eyes. "Don't be distressed, Raile." Suddenly she was hit by another pain, and she twisted her body.

All Raile could do was hold her hand, wishing it was him suffering and not her.

"The baby . . . it's too soon, Raile." Her eyes fluttered, and she lost consciousness.

Raile dropped to his knees, holding her tightly against him. "I don't care about the baby, Kassidy," he cried, "I only care about you."

Kassidy did not hear Raile's declaration of love, nor did she feel the next pain that ripped through her body. She was in the shadowy world between life and death.

Elspeth returned and she drew in her breath at the tears she saw in the duke's eyes. "I can't lose her now, Elspeth—I just can't."

"Here now, your grace," she said, wanting to reassure him but fearing herself that Kassidy might die. "I have had some experience with birth. She's exhausted from fear and pain."

"Help her," Raile said, raising Kassidy's limp hand to his lips. He brushed a golden curl from Kassidy's face. She looked so pale and defenseless. "I haven't taken good care of her, have I, Elspeth?"

The maid tapped him on the shoulder. "You'll have to give way for me to work on her, your grace."

Reluctantly Raile released Kassidy's hand and stood up. "Pray God she lives."

"I'll do that, your grace. But she's got spirit, and it'll take more than this to get her."

A heaviness fell over Ravenworth Castle. The bodies of Hugh and Lavinia had been removed from the courtyard. Hugh was laid out in the castle church, where he would lie in state, while Lavinia was taken without ceremony to the village for a quick burial.

The atmosphere in the castle was oppressed as the whole household waited to hear news of the young duchess. Servants talked in whispers as they went about their work.

When word reached the village of what had happened to the duchess, men, women, and children arrived to stand in the courtyard below. They would remain there throughout the night. Many prayers went up for the young woman they had come to love.

Dr. Worthington had arrived an hour ago, and still the baby had not been born. Raile stood at the foot of the bed his eyes on Kassidy's pale face. "It's been too long. Surely she can bear no more pain."

"She's been through a frightful experience. But she's strong," he assured Raile.

"What about the baby?" Raile wanted to know.

"This baby will be born within the next few hours."

Lady Mary hovered near Kassidy. "Her sister died after a long childbirth."

Dr. Worthington raised Kassidy's eyelids and then pressed his hand against her stomach. "It's taking a long time, but that happens sometimes. I'll do all I can."

Raile stood at the window of his bedroom, watching the night sky. He went to the connecting doors that led to Kassidy's room many times and stood there waiting.

Oliver brought his dinner, but Raile refused to eat. How could he when Kassidy lay so near death? He pushed his window open to breathe in the fresh air. There, perched in the branches of the oak tree, was a nightingale. But its song was silent, and when Raile reached out to the bird, it took wing and disappeared among the clouds.

"She's going to die, Oliver. I know it."

The valet had never seen Raile like this, not even when he lay wounded after the battle of Waterloo.

"God would surely not take her from you, your grace . . . from any of us."

Raile turned to look at Oliver. "You're fond of her, aren't you?"

"I don't know anyone who isn't, your grace. If you'll recall, I told you from the first that she was exceptional."

Raile leaned against the window, thinking back to the first time Kassidy had come to Ravenworth Castle. "I didn't see her worth at first, or even later, not fully. I do now, when it may be too late."

"I'm going to think she'll be all right, your grace." Oliver poured a pan of water and held a towel out to Raile. "Before long, you will be a father."

At that moment, they both heard a cry—the cry was strong and lusty, and it drowned out the song of the nightingale that had returned to perch on a branch of the oak tree.

36

Raile drew in a deep breath of fresh air. He didn't need to be told he had a son. Like Kassidy, he had always felt the baby she carried was a boy.

At the moment, there was no elation in his heart. He was overcome with unleashed grief—Kassidy was dead, he knew it. How could he live without her?

Unmindful of the duke's agony, Oliver was beaming. "Congratulations, your grace."

Raile walked to the connecting doors and opened them. He could see the doctor bending over Kassidy, and blood—so much blood on the bed—on the doctor's hands—on Kassidy!

Lady Mary came to Raile with the baby in her arms. "You have a son, Raile. He's healthy and strong, and has the look of you about him."

Raile gazed down at the tiny red face, thinking the child could not possibly resemble anyone. For the son he had craved, there were no feelings at all. He could only stare at Kassidy, who lay so pale, so still.

"She's very weak, Raile," Lady Mary told him. "Why don't you come with me, and I'll sit with you while the doctor does what he can for her. Perhaps you would like to hold your son?"

"Not now," he said, brushing past her and standing over Kassidy. She was almost as white as the sheet she lay upon, and he felt his heart wrench inside him.

"Will she live, Doctor?"

"I will do everything I can, your grace."

Raile left the room and walked down the long corridor. He climbed up the stairs until he came to the winding steps that took him to the tower room. He stood at the arched window where the life-and-death struggle had taken place earlier in the day. He relived every agonizing moment in his mind. Could he have done more to save Kassidy?

Lavinia was dead, and for that he was not sorry. Hugh had proven to have a strength of character that Raile had never imagined. His brother might not have lived a useful life, but he had died bravely. He had purposely given his life to save Kassidy and the baby, an act of sacrifice Raile had not expected. Raile felt remorse that he had not taken an interest in Hugh early on. If he had, perhaps he could have saved him from Lavinia.

Raile bowed his head, a whispered prayer on his lips. "God, could you have given Kassidy to me only to take her away from me when I need her the most?"

He watched as tiny splinters of light streaked through the eastern sky. With the rising of the sun came the chiming of the church bells, proclaiming that the duke and duchess of Ravenworth had a son.

The master of the castle and of the lands as far as the eye could see, stood silently at the top of his world, in the depths of despair.

Kassidy awoke to sunlight pouring into her bedroom. She felt so weak and seemed to ache all over when she tried to move.

"Kassidy," Aunt Mary said, taking her hand, "you have been asleep for hours."

Kassidy's lips quivered. "I lost the baby, didn't I?"

"Indeed you did not. You have a wonderful son. Shall I bring him to you?"

Kassidy felt intense joy and tried to sit up, but her aunt placed a restraining hand on her arm. "You must be very still. I'll get your son."

Kassidy closed her eyes and said a quick prayer of thanks that her baby had survived the awful ordeal. She tried not to think about Lavinia and Hugh—not yet—when she was stronger perhaps she would say a prayer for them both.

When Lady Mary returned with the baby, she held him out for Kassidy's inspection. "Doctor Worthington says you are not to hold him yet. He is handsome, is he not?"

Kassidy touched her son's small hand in awe. He had black hair and dark eyes. "He looks like Raile," she said, touching the small mouth with a kiss. "Oh, he is so dear, Aunt Mary."

"Indeed he is. Now this young fellow needs to eat, and you need nourishment as well. You must build back your strength."

"Has Raile seen the baby?"

Lady Mary's eyes clouded. "He is suffering a great deal, Kassidy. He blames himself for so much of what happened yesterday."

"But none of it was his fault."

"Give him time." Lady Mary moved to the door. "After the doctor assured Raile that you and the baby were fine, he left for London. He said I was to tell you he would return as soon as he had settled some matters. He also asked if you would consider naming the baby Michael Donovan DeWinter after his father. He will be home for the christening. He said to remind you that the baby has inherited one of the DeWinters' lesser titles and is an earl."

Kassidy felt a dull ache inside. "I don't suppose Raile felt it necessary to tell me about the name himself."

"Sometimes men are difficult to understand, Kassidy. But I find when they are the most troubled, they pull more into themselves."

Kassidy wondered if perhaps Raile needed the comfort only Gabrielle Candeur could give him, but she didn't say this to her aunt.

Each day Kassidy grew stronger and was contented to spend her waking hours with her new son and Arrian. Arrian, of course, believed that little Michael belonged to her. She was protective and possessive of him, and Kassidy was delighted with them both.

The sadness of Hugh's death ebbed as sunny days blessed the land around Ravenworth. The fields were green, promising an abundant harvest. But days passed, and then weeks, and still the master of Ravenworth Castle did not return.

Kassidy was instructing the workmen who were hanging the silken tapestries in the great hall. They had been repaired and cleaned by the women of the village, and presented to their duke and duchess as a gift of gratitude.

Kassidy moved forward to examine the lady and the unicorn, which was her particular favorite.

"Elspeth, I cannot tell where it has been repaired. They did wonderful work. I was told by Mrs. Mayhew that it had been a labor of love. Isn't that a dear thing for her to say?"

"I'm certain she spoke the truth. For they all love you, Kassidy," said a deep, familiar voice.

Kassidy spun around to find Raile behind her. Her heart was throbbing with excitement that quickly turned to anger. "So, your grace, you have come home."

He feasted his eyes on her, thinking she had never looked lovelier. "Yes," he said at last. "I have come home."

"And did you find Miss Candeur to be in good spirits?" She was sorry as soon as the words left her lips.

His pupils dilated. "I did see Gabrielle, Kassidy. I'm telling you this only because you have questions about her, and I don't want there ever to be any misunderstanding between us."

Kassidy thought perhaps it would not hurt so much if he were a little less honest. There was ice in her voice. "Do you like the tapestries, Raile?"

"Indeed. I was told you had sent them to a woman in the village, but I had little hope they would come back looking so fine. I'm glad they were restored." He gripped her shoulders and turned her to face him. "You have put my house in order, taken care of my villagers, and my servants adore you."

Her eyes were burning. "You forgot to add that I have given you the son and heir you craved."

"Yes, you have done that also."

"I don't understand you, Raile. You seemed to want a son desperately. Then when he was born, you left for London and ignored him completely."

Mockery played in his dark eyes. "Are you chastising me, madame, for being neglectful of my duty?"

She was embarrassed and lowered her gaze. "I would not like to think so, Raile. But perhaps I have turned into a shrewish wife."

His lips twitched in a smile. "If it is my fate to have a shrewish wife, then so be it."

She turned away from him and walked to the second tapestry with the pretense of examining it, when in truth all she could think of was him. Her whole body came alive when he was near.

"I had dinner with your Aunt Mary and Uncle George last night. They send their love."

"I ate alone last night," she said, feeling the anger building inside her.

He took her arm and steered her down the hallway. "I have something to say to you, Kassidy. I believe the time has come for the two of us to talk about our future."

So, she thought, the time had come at last. He had his son, now he wanted her to leave so he could have his freedom. The ache inside was deeper than anything she had thus far experienced.

Would he expect her to leave Michael? That had been their bargain, but she hadn't thought about the baby at the time, or known how much she was going to love him. To leave her husband and her son would tear her heart out.

Raile seated her in the oversized chair, while he perched on the edge of his desk. She looked up at him expectantly. "Today is the day of reckoning, Raile. I already know what you want to talk about."

"Do you, Kassidy? Then perhaps you can tell me how to say what I want to say to you."

"You might want to start with the London house. I know you said I could live there, but I would prefer not to. I believe I shall travel abroad for a time."

He stood up, and she followed him with her eyes. Raile was everything a woman could desire. He was generous, compassionate, and handsome. He could charm her with a smile, or send her heart racing with a glance. She saw him as her champion who had helped her as a girl, she saw him as the father of her son, and the husband who had held her in the night to keep her from having bad dreams. But he had never belonged to her, and she must let him go.

Raile poured two glasses of brandy and handed one to Kassidy, but she shook her head. He tossed his down his throat and turned back to her.

"I needed that to get through the next few moments."

"There is nothing that should cause you concern, Raile. I remember well the pact we made before our marriage. I'm willing to stand by our agreement."

He looked into her eyes as if searching for something. "Are you saying you can leave our baby?"

She would not cry, she would not show weakness, but oh, yes, it would be so painful to leave her son.

"I am prepared to stand by our agreement, Raile."

He inhaled slowly as the pain of loss cut through his heart. "I had hoped if I stayed away long enough, you would become attached to the baby and would be unwilling to leave him."

Kassidy twisted her hands in her lap. "Do you say this to torture me, Raile?"

He moved away from her and sat down at his desk. "I can tell you something about torment, Kassidy."

"I know you can, Raile. I can imagine what it feels like to be married to someone while loving another."

He looked taken aback, but quickly recovered. "Are you speaking of me?"

"I know how you feel about Miss Candeur."

He pressed his hands together and braced them on his desk. "I doubt that you do, Kassidy. When I said I had seen Gabrielle, I didn't tell you why. Perhaps I should."

"There is no need, Raile. I have always known how you feel about her."

"Kassidy, did you hear Lavinia when she taunted me about having Gabrielle come here?"

"I didn't hear her say that."

"You were otherwise occupied. But to get back to Gabrielle. When she came to Ravenworth, she thought I had sent for her. She had received a letter which she thought was signed by me."

"Oh."

"Exactly. Lavinia was the author of the letter."

"Poor woman. She was so demented."

"Back to Gabrielle, Kassidy," Raile continued. "That day pity was all I felt for her because she had been ill-used by Lavinia. I suppose I also felt guilty because I ended my association with Gabrielle after you and I were married, in a very cowardly way. I allowed her to learn from others that I had married you. I'm not proud of that."

"You ended your affair with her after we were married?" She looked at him in surprise. "I thought you loved her."

"No. I never loved her, Kassidy. But so there will be no misunderstanding, I want you to know that I am paying her bills and making arrangements for her return to France. It is out of compassion, Kassidy, and nothing more."

"Yes, I have known you to be a very compassionate man."

He smiled, and then laughed aloud. "In my arrogance, I offered you compassion. I thought in marrying you, I had saved you from a solitary life, when in truth you could have any man you wanted. Can you ever forgive a fool?"

She stared at him, not in the least amused. "It appears you have done your duty by everyone, Raile. You saved me from a life of loneliness, you saved Miss Candeur from humiliation, you even saved Arrian from an orphanage. Sainthood appears to be your lot in life."

Raile realized he wasn't doing well in explaining his intentions. "You might like to know I've confirmed that Hugh married Abigail, and Arrian can rightfully take the DeWinter name."

"Well, Raile, it seems you have your well-ordered life, after all."

"Not entirely, Kassidy," he said ruefully. "Not where you're concerned."

"I'm your wife. All you have to do is tell me what you require of me, your grace, and I'll do your bidding."

He rolled his eyes upward. "Would that it were true."

"No man will ever control me, Raile. You should know that by now."

He was reminded of the day she had brought Arrian to him and had faced him in defiance. "In this room, we first met, Kassidy. Had I known what was in store for me, I wonder if I would have fled from you."

"You would have been wise to, Raile. But to say we first met in this room is not altogether true, is it? We met in the park when I was only a child."

"So we did. The pity was in forgetting that. But you were so young that day."

"And you were so sad."

"I still am, Kassidy."

She glared at him. "Except for our son, it would have been better for us both if we had never married."

There was pain in Raile's eyes, and he was quiet for a moment as he walked over to her and pulled her to her feet. "As you know, Kassidy, in the beginning, I put little importance on marriage."

"You made that very clear to me. I married you, knowing we would not always live together."

"Please, just listen to what I have to say."

She looked at him, her heart breaking, wishing he did not feel bound to utter the words that would tear her heart out. "Very well, I'm listening."

"I have come to believe, Kassidy, that if a man has a wife who just happens to have the greenest eyes he has ever seen . . ." He reached out to gather a handful of silken hair that felt alive in his hands. "And if her golden hair rivals the setting sun on a summer's evening . . ." He laced his hands through her hair and brought her face closer to his. "Add to that she is loyal, generous, and loving. And if she has a temper that rises like a live volcano and a forgiving nature that can calm a man like a tranquil sea at low tide. If she's stubborn and always speaks her mind . . ." His eyes closed for a moment before he continued, "then a man can count himself fortunate indeed."

His chest expanded with unbearable pain, fearing she would not have him. "I ask you, Kassidy, would a man toss away such a rare and precious jewel?"

She stared into his eyes, hoping she had heard him right. "Are you saying you like being married to me?"

He pulled her head to rest against his shoulder, wanting to hold her like that forever. "I have been in torment while I was away from you. I have grown accustomed to seeing you every day. I have never missed anyone since my mother died, Kassidy—but I hungered for the sight of your face, the sound of your laughter, the feel of your hand in mine."

Her eyes rounded with hope and wonder. "Raile, I—"

"Please forgive me, Kassidy," he interrupted her, afraid if he didn't finish what he had to say, he would be unable to continue. "You see, I have never loved a woman before you, and I don't know how to act with you. I know I did everything wrong."

She stepped back, her heart beating with hope. "You love me, Raile?"

He smiled down at her. "I am most irreversibly in love with you, my little wife."

"But you said you would never—"

He placed his finger over her mouth. "I said many foolish things, Kassidy. I hope you will be generous and not remind me of them too often."

She touched his cheek softly, as doubt filled the green eyes that were swimming with tears. "Oh, Raile, I cannot believe you could love me. I have been nothing but trouble to you."

His lip curved into a smile. "I won't deny that. Since the moment I've known you, you have turned my world upside down." Then he became serious, his eyes searching hers. "Kassidy, I wonder if you would allow me to break another promise to you?"

Happiness was bursting forth within her. She wanted to press her body against his and allow his nearness to fill her whole being.

"Which promise, Raile?" she asked softly.

"The one where I promised you your freedom if you gave me a son."

Her green eyes took on the glow of a siren. "Just you try to send me away, Raile. Everywhere you go, I will be one step behind you."

"I have not always treated you well."

"That is not so, Raile. Each time I have been in trouble, it has been you who stood beside me and made everything right again."

There was triumph in his eyes and he picked her up in his arms and carried her to the French doors and out into the garden. "You are fixed to me now, Kassidy. I'll never let you go."

Were the ghosts of past DeWinter wives glancing down at her from the high turrets of the castle and shaking their heads in satisfaction—she felt as if they were. Kassidy pressed her cheek to his while happiness filled her mind. "Oh, Raile, my love, my love, why would I want to leave paradise?"

He bent his dark head and lightly touched his mouth to hers. She melted against him and thus they stood locked in each other's arms until at last he pulled away.

He laid his rough cheek against hers. "You have allowed me to live again, and to believe that things such as love and honor still exist."

At that moment, a bird took flight from a nearby thicket, and Kassidy followed it with her eyes, her heart soaring as if it had also taken wing. She looked up to find Raile smiling at her, for he, too, had seen the nightingale.

"Look." Raile pointed to the tall oak that shaded the far end of the garden. "The male waits for her just there on the highest branch—do you see him?"

"Yes, I see him," Kassidy said, as Raile enfolded her in his arms, crushing her against him.

"Listen, my love," Raile whispered against her ear, "do you hear him singing to his mate?"

"Yes, Raile, I very definitely hear the nightingale sing to his lady love."

He turned her to face him, his dark eyes warm and soft with intense longing. "The nightingale sings for us also, Kassidy."

She pressed her head against his chest, hearing the thundering of his heart. "I know that, too, my dearest."

Kassidy could say no more, because the sweet song of the nightingale echoed in her ears as her husband's lips pressed against hers. And soon, even the nightingale's song was drowned out by the beating of the lovers' hearts.

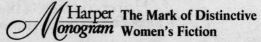

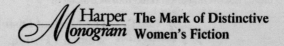